They were too pleased to keep up the mystery any longer.

The greeting between the old friends was quite affecting, and Mr. Mole was as pleased to see Lena as Jack.

A long explanation followed.

Jack told the story of his wanderings after Lena, and Mr. Mole, in his turn, informed him of what had taken place at Singapore.

After Hunston's death, during the earthquake, Harkaway recovered from his faint, and found that the storm was over.

Harkaway returned to Singapore, where he fitted out the ship for Jack's help.

Mr. Mole and Monday started for the Isle of Palms with an efficient crew.

Their lucky meeting with Jack and Lena cut the voyage short, and changing the ship's course, they returned to Singapore without accident.

*   *   *   *   *

Harkaway was delighted to meet his son safe and sound, and the entire party returned to America.

The third prediction of the fortune-teller of Karnack was verified.

In six months, Jack married Lena, and started in business on his own account.

Harkaway, Viola, Harvey, and Hilda live in the same house in the country.

Mr. Mole reopened his school and is doing well.

Monday lives with young Jack at his New York house, and Lena is happy with the husband of her choice.

THE END.

On Wednesday next, July 12,

WILL BE PUBLISHED

Nos. 1 and 2 of

STINGBOYS SCHOOL

And Its Many Mysteries.

Beautifully Illustrated.   16 Large Pages Weekly.

No. 2 and a Coloured Picture

WILL BE

Given Away with No. 1.

THE WHOLE IN AN ILLUMINATED WRAPPER, PRICE 1d.

Orders should be given at once to your Bookseller.

NOTICE!—Other Coloured Pictures will be Given Away for Binding with the Work.

JACK HARKAWAY
in the Transvaal

· EDWIN · J · BRETT · LIMITED ·
· HARKAWAY · HOUSE · 6 · WEST · HARDING · ST ·
· LONDON · E · C ·

JACK HARKAWAY

IN THE

TRANSVAAL;

OR, FIGHTING FOR THE FLAG.

BEAUTIFULLY ILLUSTRATED.

COMPLETE.

LONDON:
HARKAWAY HOUSE, 6, WEST HARDING STREET, FETTER LANE,
FLEET STREET, E.C., AND ALL BOOKSELLERS.

Jack Harkaway in the Transvaal;

Or, FIGHTING FOR THE FLAG.

"A KAFFIR, ARMED WITH A SPEAR, RAN AT JACK, INTENDING TO STAB HIM IN THE BACK."

No. 1.

JACK HARKAWAY IN THE TRANSVAAL;

or, FIGHTING FOR THE FLAG.

By the Author of "JACK HARKAWAY'S SCHOOLDAYS," &c.

CHAPTER I.

GUNFIRE AT MAFEKING—HARKAWAY MEETS HIS FRIEND, FRED DAWSON—A SCENE TAKES PLACE IN THE TOWN—ENGLISH AGAINST BOER AND KAFFIR.

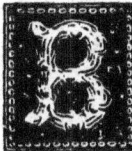OOM !

It was the sound of gunfire at Mafeking, on a beautiful night, with stars brightly shining, and a cool breeze blowing from the west.

"Halt ! Who goes there ? " cried a sentry.

"Friend," was the rejoinder.

"Pass, friend, and all is well."

The person who had been challenged by the sentry was young Jack Harkaway, who, at the age of sixteen. had been gazetted subaltern in the 7th Hussars, a few weeks after being sent with his famous regiment to South Africa to fight the Boers.

The regiment remained at Ladysmith under the command of Sir George White ; and young Jack Harkaway—who, in a short time, had gained the reputation of being a smart officer—was sent to Mafeking with despatches for Colonel Baden-Powell, and remained with him on the staff.

President Kruger had defied the British Government, and declared war ; consequently an attack in force on our principal towns in Natal was hourly expected.

Colonel Powell had little more than two thousand men, chiefly Colonials.

Mafeking was the nearest British garrison to Pretoria, and it was known that the Boers were massing and ready to cross the border-line.

Entrenchments had been made and earthworks thrown up.

The troops were under canvas outside the town.

Jack was leaving the camp to go into Mafeking on a visit to a young man about his own age, named Fred Dawson.

They had been at school together in England.

Dawson's father was a settler in Mafeking, where he had a large corn and forage business.

Fred Dawson, animated by the war fever, which was strong within every man who had a drop of English blood in his veins, had volunteered for active service, and, as he knew the country well, was engaged as a scout by the Imperial Intelligence Department.

Going a little way up the road, the lights of the town being visible in the distance, Jack Harkaway, who was in full hussar uniform, with his sword clanking by his side, was overtaken by a young man on a bicycle ; the latter got off his wheel, and waving his hand, hailed Jack.

"You are just the fellow I wanted to see ! " he exclaimed. "I suppose you were coming up to my diggings ? "

It was Fred Dawson, the scout, who had been out all day on the veldt, to find out all he could about the enemy on the other side of the border.

"Quite correct, Fred," replied Jack. "We do not hear much in camp, and I thought I might get some news from you. This suspense is becoming tedious ; and all the men are dying to have a cut at the Boers. What do you know ? "

"Small parties of the enemy are lurking about, but I could not discover where the main body is. I was fired at twice, by some men hiding behind a rock, not more than a dozen miles out. They had a fire burning, and seemed to have taken up their quarters there. I think their object is to draw us out ; but the colonel is not likely to make any advance. There are traitors in this town, living right in our midst ; and I am sure they are in communication with the outside Boers."

"That is my opinion also. Who do you suspect to be the leader of them ? I have a reason for asking, as I am told the Military Police have orders to turn all suspected characters out of the town ; and if we could put a name or two on the list, we might be doing good service to the authorities."

"I should say that the arch-traitor in correspondence with the foe is that tall, brawny, brutal ruffian, Krause, who keeps the billiard saloon in Main Street," replied Fred Dawson. "He never loses a chance of insulting an Englishman; and only this morning I saw his lanky nigger, Dunko, the Kaffir, close to the very spot where I was shot at; and the conclusion I came to is that Dunko was taking a message from his master, Krause, to some commander, who, with a small force, is ahead of the rest."

As they walked along, Dawson pushing his machine, they had to pass by the police barracks.

Jack Harkaway, going in, had a chat with the officer in charge, informing him of their suspicions with regard to Krause, whose sympathy with the Boers was well known.

"I am going to make a raid to-night on a few places," said the officer, "and, acting on your suggestion, I will take in the billiard saloon you mention, and drive Krause, as well as any loafers I find, out of the town, right away. If you like to drop in you will see the fun, and may expect me and my men to be there at any time between this and twelve."

They continued their journey, and Dawson, who had been several times insulted by Krause, looked highly pleased at what they had done.

"That's what I call making it hot for the Dutchman," he remarked. "I have no liking for the man; he is always chaffing us in his coarse way. You are a comparative stranger here, and don't know him as I do. A friend of his, named Webb, is just as bad; his father has several shares in a mine, and he does nothing to speak of except look at his father's books occasionally, which he pretends to keep. He has always got a cue in his hand and a cigar in his mouth. He calls himself an Outlander, but he was born in Pretoria, and is quite a young dandy in his dress and manner. He would be no loss to the town, but I do not know that I could accuse him of anything."

Dawson left his bicycle at his house, and Harkaway borrowed a light coat, which he threw over his uniform, after which they made their way to the billiard-room, which was a centre of attraction in the evening to several of the townsfolk; and since the war broke out the latest rumours were discussed there.

A writing-table was provided, telegrams were posted on a board, and all the papers— English and African—could be found, drink being plentiful, which made it resemble an open club.

When the young men entered, the click of the balls was heard.

Not many men were there.

Dunko was acting as waiter, Krause was reading a paper, and Dawson was greeted by two friends, to whom he introduced young Harkaway.

One was Bill Brick, the son of a storekeeper, a great talker, who knew everybody's business, good-natured, and loyal to the backbone.

The other was Mr. Fish, War Corre-

spondent of the *Capetown Slasher*, a very bellicose sheet, and Mr. Fish thought himself quite an up-to-date gleaner and transmitter of news.

He had just dropped into Krause's to pick up some items for copy if he could.

Note-book in hand, he tackled Dawson.

"Is it true that General Viljohn and five thousand men in his commando are within half-a-day's march of us, with twelve field guns and two thousand horses? I heard that Rhodes was captured, an armoured train destroyed, and Newcastle taken."

"Very probably," replied Fred, "but I can't authenticate it, though there are Boers within a dozen miles of us, for I was shot at a few hours ago. The colour of a khaki suit throws a man off his aim, and I put my escape down to that."

"Good," said Fish, wielding his pencil. "I shall wire my people presently that the items I mentioned require confirmation, but Boers firing at scouts and threatening town."

"Here is something for you," continued Dawson. "Out on the veldt is a flat-faced rock that looks like a tombstone, and the Boers have had the cheek to get some black paint and write 'The Buried Flag! In memory of the British Flag in the Transvaal, which departed this life August 2nd, 1881, aged four years. Never to rise again!' For cool impudence I think that's lovely. This is the land of rivers without water, women without beauty, flowers without smell, but the Boers make up for that with brag."

Krause, who was close by, and had been listening to Dawson's remarks, threw down his paper, and with an insolent glare observed "Dot vas nodings. An English soldier does not know the colour of his own flag."

"Does that speech refer to me?" demanded Jack Harkaway, throwing open his coat, and revealing his cavalry uniform.

"You can take it if you like. The officers are as bad as the Tommies. I was speaking of all soldiers of your old Queen."

"Perhaps you will be good enough to explain your meaning."

"Your flag is white; that is its colour," answered the Dutchman, with arrogance. "I have seen it three times, once at Brunkerspruit, again at Laing's Nek, and finally at a little place called Majuba; but I won't say final, because we are sure to see it again before long. You will be glad to ask General Joubert for another truce, when your men are shot down at their guns, like a lot of birds on a tree."

"Those words tell me that you are a traitor," continued Jack. "You are living under the protection of our flag now, and ought to be ashamed of yourself. If I were in command, I would hang you before breakfast to-morrow. Now listen. Pay attention. The colours on our flag are red, white, and blue. Presently you and your friends will see a big patch of red, represented by your blood; and, in a blue funk, you will hold out the white flag as a token of surrender."

"Ha, ha! Some little boys like to hear themselves talk. Because they have a bit of gold lace on their tunics, they think they are men. Bah! You cannot fight. What is the use of sending a boy to do a man's work?"

Brick had ordered a bottle of hock, which Dunko, the Kaffir, had poured into four glasses.

He was carrying them on a silver salver, and, deliberately pushing against Harkaway, upset the wine over his shoulder.

"You clumsy hound!" cried Jack, "why don't you look out, and see where you are going?"

"Englishman no good; Boer heap good," replied the Kaffir," with a contemptuous sneer.

Without wasting any further words on him, young Harkaway struck out from the shoulder, and knocked him down.

The Kaffir scrambled to his feet, and, snatching up an assegai which was concealed under a seat, stood at bay near the entrance-door.

"How dare you strike my nigger?" asked Krause, his dark brow lowering, and his sallow face reddening. "He is my servant, and the faithful fellow could not help what he did. Is your uniform so sacred that you can't bear to have a drop of white wine spilled on it? If you English think you have come here to lord it over us you are mistaken, Oom Paul Kruger will drive you into the sea, and the banner of the Republic will wave over the land."

Harkaway turned his back on the blustering Dutchman, and began to converse with Fred Dawson and Brick, while Fish, the War Correspondent of the *Capetown Slasher*, made an entry in his note-book to the following effect:

"English cavalry officer openly insulted by Dutchmen and Kaffirs in a public reading and billiard saloon. Striking display of racial hatred."

Terribly annoyed at being so conspicuously ignored, and severely left alone, Krause lost his temper completely.

There was a large dachshund lying on a rug in front of the fireplace.

Krause whistled to him.

"Hi! Wilhelm, fetch him down," he shouted. "It has come to a pretty pass if I am not goot enough to be talked to. Make that young officer run oot as if there was a Boer behind him."

Getting up, the dog snarled and barked, baring his gums and showing his teeth.

With a spring he flew at Harkaway, who, standing with his back to the animal, did not notice the aggressive movement.

"Look out, Jack," cried Fred Dawson, "the Dutchman has set the dog on you."

Alarmed at this intimation, Jack had just time to turn round and draw his sword, in the use of which he was proficient.

As the dachshund, which was a magnificent creature, was about to jump at his throat, his eyes red as fire, and his mouth flecked with foam, Jack made a circle in the air with his sword, and, bringing it down with tremendous force, severed the dog's head from its body, just as if, at a military tournament, he had been cutting a dead sheep in half.

It was a splendid feat, which Fred Dawson and Brick highly applauded, clapping their hands.

Half-a-dozen evil-looking loafers, who seemed to have been recruited from the scum of the earth, incited by the cries of the Kaffir,

swooped from the bar outside into the room, brandishing various weapons.

They looked very fierce and grotesque in their border attire.

Some having knives stuck in their belts, Harkaway stood in front of his companions, sword in hand, and defied the uncouth mob to come on.

He did not desire to be engaged in a brawl which was not of his own seeking, but he had to defend himself.

In fact, he would not have been in the place at all if Fred Dawson's remarks about Krause had not induced him to consider it part of his duty to look after and expose traitors.

Seeing his determined attitude, the loafers stood still, hesitating how to act.

They were awed by one man.

"Down with him!" cried Krause. "What are you afraid off? A snipe like that can't eat you. Outspan him, and make him treck."

The men set up a loud shout, and were about to precipitate themselves upon Harkaway, when Dawson and Brick drew their revolvers, making them halt again.

The war correspondent Fish, who was always on the safe side, had sought refuge under a table, where he knelt, book in hand, hastily jotting down notes:

"Mafeking, latest. Sanguinary affray. British officer assailed by hounds and loafers. Dutch traitors inciting to crime. Afrikander Bond suspected to be at the bottom of the riot."

Suddenly the heavy tramp of armed men was heard, and a dozen policemen, headed by a captain, made their appearance.

A fight ensued between them and the loafers, who were speedily driven into the street.

Krause was curtly informed that he must leave the town within half-an-hour, and that his house would be closed by the police, as he was considered to be a suspected person.

Jack put his sword back in the scabbard, and taking Dawson's arm, was leaving the room, with a smile, when the Dutchman called after him.

"Hi! young man, hear me before you go; Hans Krause is talking. This is all your doing. You shall pay dearly for the loss of my business and the life of my dog. The worst thing you ever did was to offend me. I will fight you in the dark, and you shall not know where the hand is that strikes you. Bitterly will you rue this night, for nothing but your death will satisfy me. I have said it, and I am Hans Krause, who never told a lie."

"This Kaffir echoes all that," said Dunko. "I have taken his measurement, and shall know how to dig his grave."

Mr. Fish was busy with his pencil again, and scribbled: "Awful threats uttered by Boers and Kaffirs against English cavalry officer."

These threats only caused young Jack Harkaway to laugh carelessly, which so enraged the Dutchman that he stooped down over the dead dog, which was lying on the floor, dipped one of the fingers of his right hand in a pool of blood, and, before Jack could divine his intention, sprang forward and made a red cross on his forehead.

"The death mark! Behold it!" he cried, wildly, and, with his face distorted by passion until it assumed a look of fiendish hideousness, pushed by the police, who did not attempt to stop him, and stalked from the room, closely followed by his Kaffir.

The spectators of this extraordinary scene were stricken with horror; even Fred Dawson trembled.

Harkaway alone was calm and unconcerned.

As Jack had a pass, he could return to his quarters when he liked. He invited his friend Dawson to have supper with him at an hotel.

Owing to the confusion caused by the war, delicacies were out of the question. They were obliged to put up with homely fare.

"Krause is fairly ruined, as far as his trade goes here," remarked Dawson, "but I daresay he has sent his money on to one of the banks in Pretoria. He is awfully savage with you. I am sorry I took you to his place to-night, for he will seek to destroy you. Dunko is a bad Kaffir, worse than the usual run, and his mind is poisoned against you. Though you rubbed that mark with your handkerchief, I can see the cross yet. He meant it as a sentence of death. But let us talk of something more cheerful. I shall be off on the veldt again at sunrise. There are plenty of bok about, if you like to come with me and have some sport."

"If I can get leave, I will. I won't promise to start as early as you, but I'll meet you at any spot you like to appoint."

"My orders are to scout in the neighbourhood of Ottoshoop, near Maimain Gold Fields," replied Fred Dawson. "I shall take my grub with me, and break the journey near the place where I was attacked to-day. It is only ten or twelve miles down the road, and with a good horse you ought to do the distance in a couple of hours easy. Look out for hidden foes, as the Boers will drop any stray Roonek, as they call us."

"I'll be on the watch," said Harkaway. "I will ride out to-morrow, and shall hope to meet you."

With this understanding they parted, and, lighting a cigar, young Jack Harkaway, under a brightly shining moon, walked back to the camp.

CHAPTER II.

DEPARTURE OF THE ARMOURED TRAIN— MALACHI THE JEW—THE SECRET MINE— THE AMBUSCADE—AN ADVENTURE ON THE VELDT—HARKAWAY IS HARD PRESSED.

CONSIDERABLE excitement prevailed in the early morning at Mafeking Railroad Station.

There was a glorious burst of sunshine, and the sky was azure blue.

An armoured train, with steam up, was standing by the platform, ready to depart.

Soldiers, with their quick-firing guns, were in the strange-looking trucks.

Captain Nisbitt was in command, having orders to explore the line in the direction of Vryburg, and, if attacked, give a good account of the enemy.

It was a perilous expedition, but Nisbitt was a Victoria Cross man, and loved danger for its own sake.

The station was crowded, and, among others, young Harkaway had come to give him a send-off.

Little Brick was there, as a matter of of course.

He could not be left out of anything that was going on.

The war correspondent, Fish, came out of the telegraph office and joined him.

"Rather a dearth of news this morning; but I have sent on a description of this queer-looking train."

"I see nothing odd about it," replied Brick. "If we have an iron-clad ship, why not a train of the same description? It is an event in warfare. I don't think we shall see it again, because it can be easily derailed. There will be fighting here directly. When Powell left England he said he hoped they would give him a hot corner, and, by Jove! he has got one. So have we, as far as that goes. Hallo! There's that Kaffir Dunko. I should not have thought he would have shown his face after what happened last night. There is more mischief brewing. He is talking in a confidential manner to Webb, who is an intimate friend of Krause, and as big a traitor as there is in the town. It is a pity the police don't send him further, but I suppose his father's position protects him."

"I'll make a note of that," remarked Fish. "Traitors in high places would sound well as a head-line."

Webb, who was a well-dressed, good-looking young fellow, with a cunning expression and sarcastic smile, saw Brick looking at him and Dunko, and came up to him with his hands in his pockets, exclaiming, "Perhaps you will know me again when you see me, Mr. Busybody. Why don't you carry a Kodak and take snapshots of people?"

"That is not a bad idea," said Brick. "I should like to have your portrait to put in the rogues' gallery along with a few other spies in the pay of the Boers, whose money you have got in your pocket now. Dunko, how much did you bring him from Krause?"

This was a random shot, but it completely threw the ignorant Kaffir off his guard.

"Only five hundred pounds this time, boss," he answered, while Brick and Fish roared with laughter at the Kaffir allowing himself to be so easily drawn, and the evident confusion of Webb, who, seizing the Kaffir's arm, led him into the crowd, where they were lost to sight.

"Confound you," hissed Webb, who was white with rage, "what made you give me away like that? I don't want all to know that I am a paid spy of the Boers. Don't do it again, or you will get me into serious trouble. Even now I may have the police down on me, through that chattering monkey Brick. However, I won't say any more this time, but I'll knock your mutton-head off if you do it again."

Dunko expressed his sorrow, and began to mutter excuses; but Webb, from whose eyes the fiery rage had died away, cut him short.

"Listen here," he continued. "As soon as the armoured train goes out the cars from Kimberley, which are now in the siding, will come up, and I have a job for you. A Jew, named Moses Malachi, bent with age, and grey, having a long beard coming to his waist, is on board this train. He is rich, having friends and important interests in this town ; and, from private information I have received, he carries in one of his pockets a scroll of parchment. In some way you must get this from him. Take it at once to Krause, on the veldt, and ask him to keep it for me. At the same time let the Boers know that the armoured train has started for Vryburg. Give the number of men and guns they have with them.

"If I find I am in danger, from what you let fall just now, tell them that I shall not be long in throwing off the mask and joining them, though I can be of more service to the cause of the Republic by staying here. Leave me and look out for the Jew, Malachi. We must not be seen together any more than we can help."

The Kaffir nodded and glided away like an eel.

Presently the train started, amidst loud cheers, and the platform was soon cleared, only a few people remaining who expected friends by the Kimberley cars.

Dunko hid himself in the waiting-room until the passengers alighted.

He had no difficulty in perceiving a Hebrew resembling Webb's description.

He had a travelling-bag in his hand, and looked up and down the platform as if to find someone to answer his questions.

This was the Kaffir's opportunity, and he promptly advanced, saying—

"Carry your bag, boss? I'm not above earning half-a-dollar. Where do you want to go?"

"Do you know Jacobi, who has the large canned provision warehouse?" was the rejoinder. "If so, conduct me to him, for I am a stranger in the gates."

Dunko responded in the affirmative, took possession of the bag, and told the Jew to follow him, but, instead of taking him to the town, led him down the road which went into the open country.

There was no one about ; anything more desolate and lonely could not be imagined.

The Jew grew alarmed and suddenly stopped.

Seeing that he was beginning to doubt his honesty, Dunko turned sharply round, striking him on the head with his assegai, which caused the old man to fall down, stunned and covered with blood.

Rapidly the Kaffir rifled his victim's pockets, finding the parchment which Webb coveted, and two leather bags, one containing gold, and the other diamonds.

With this booty he ran away with the speed for which the Bechuana natives are famous.

Nearly an hour the Jew remained like one dead.

At length he tried to rise, but staggering, sat down.

His strength was quickly waning owing to the loss of blood.

He was roused by the sound of a horse's hoofs clattering along the hard road, and in a couple of minutes an English officer pulled up by his side.

It was Jack Harkaway, who had changed his hussar uniform for khaki.

Dismounting, Jack gave him a little brandy out of a flask, and tied up his head with his handkerchief.

"Too late, my friend," said the Jew, in a shaky voice. "The days of Moses Malachi are numbered. I have fallen among thieves ; but I thank thee all the same. A cowardly Kaffir struck me down."

"That must have been Dunko ; I saw you talking to him at the station," remarked Jack.

"I know him not, neither can I fathom his motive. For your kindly attempt at succour I will give you the means of becoming rich beyond the dreams of avarice. I am dying, my arms are useless, but in my pocket you will find a parchment ; it contains a plan of a secret mine in Rhodesia, that land of wonders. It was partly worked in past ages. I meant to have reopened it, but the war stopped everything. Take it for your own. I could tell more if my breath did not fail me."

Harkaway did not scruple to search the Jew for this rich prize, but to his disappointment all the pockets were empty.

"By Heaven," gasped the Jew. "I have been robbed. May the curse of Naaman fall upon that vile Kaffir."

A spasm of the heart convulsed him, and he fell back dead.

Remounting his horse, Jack Harkaway pursued his way, and after a brisk ride of a few miles arrived at the spot assigned by Dawson for a meeting place.

There was no one there, however, and he did not know whether to ride further or remain where he was.

In front of him was a long, low rock behind which a man could stand and be protected breast high.

He fancied he saw something move in that direction.

The next moment a bullet flew over his head, and Harkaway saw that, through some means, an ambuscade had been prepared for him.

Adopting the tactics of a mounted rifleman, and having a trained steed, he jumped to the ground and ordered his horse to lie down on its side, which it did with automatic precision and celerity.

His short magazine rifle was in his hand.

He saw three or four heads behind the rock.

There was no time to count his foes.

He fired several shots in quick succession ; there was a cry of agony, and the heads which were clearly those of cowardly, ambushed Boers, vanished.

Thinking it advisable to retreat and risk running the gauntlet, Harkaway was about to order the horse to rise, when a fresh danger threatened him in the rear.

A Kaffir, who had been concealed behind one of the small boulders scattered over the plain, made his appearance, and ran at Jack with a short spear, intending to stab him in the back.

His death would have been certain had not a young man come up with the speed of a deer, panting for breath, and with his revolver fired a shot at the native, who rolled over, frantically clawing the sandy soil with his long fingers.

At the same time five men, who had quitted the shelter of the rock, were seen running across the veldt in the direction of Ottoshoop.

Jack gave them the benefit of half-a-dozen shots from his rifle, and managed to drop two of them, the others escaping without attempting to return his fire.

Then he was able to look round and see who his preserver was.

"Fred, my boy!" exclaimed Jack, heartily, as he recognised Dawson, "you came up just in the nick. That rock was a hot shop for a minute or two. Who is this nigger you've shot?"

"Dunko," replied Fred Dawson. "You were caught between two fires. The Boers were behind the rock, under the lead of Krause; I saw his face. There is no mistake, we have foiled him this time. Dunko was placed behind the boulder to make sure of spitting you while your attention was engaged in front. A couple of miles off I saw a score of mounted Boers, and made my wheel spin along the road to this place, and seeing your peril, got off, and came up. You know the rest."

They had no time to ascertain if Dunko was actually dead, though it was certain he was hard hit, for Harkaway's quick eye discerned some horsemen careering over the plain towards them.

"Up," he said to his horse. "We shall be attacked in a minute. Get on your bike, Fred, and follow me. If we lose any time, we are lost!"

Dawson nodded, and, raising his machine, was soon astride.

Jack mounted his horse, and they went at speed up the road.

But Harkaway had not exaggerated the danger, for hoarse cries rang in their ears, and shots were fired after them.

Harkaway had often had a hard ride in the old country.

He had been in at the death when out fox-hunting, and on one occasion his charger had run away with him in the Long Valley at Aldershot; but he had never had a ride for dear life before.

It is no exaggeration to say that when he heard the crack of the Boers' rifles, and the ping of the bullets, he felt uncomfortable.

Being well mounted, he was quickly out of range, and Fred Dawson wheeled along by his side.

It would take a good hour to reach the English lines, yet he began to feel safe, until his serenity was disturbed by a fresh alarm.

Gaining the summit of a small koppey, or hill, he saw a mounted Boer, whom he presumed to be the advanced guard of a body coming in the same direction.

He was hemmed in.

The Boer and he raised their rifles at the same time, and each took a flying shot.

One of his shoulder straps was knocked off, and the Boer's saddle was emptied of its rider, the horse galloping on as if nothing had happened.

Jack reined up, and caught hold of the bridle, stopping it.

"Drop your wheel, Fred," he cried, "and get on this horse. We must cut across country, or we are done for. The enemy have us in front and rear. We shall have to cross the line near Kraai Pan. It's deucid awkward, but it can't be helped."

Fred Dawson was glad of the chance.

He abandoned his bicycle, and springing on the horse, which had so fortunately come in his way, he galloped over the plain with Jack.

Their enemies were not near enough to see the direction they took, and they did not come to a halt until it was really necessary to breathe their horses.

The country was very wild, but here and there grew gooseberries, and red plums were to be seen.

Some water flowed from a rock, which they found cool and refreshing.

Jack judged his way by a pocket compass, and starting again, they made a detour, which brought them to the railroad, where they were astonished to find the wreck of the armoured train, which had started so gaily in the morning.

The engines and some of the trucks were thrown on their sides, as if a mine had been sprung beneath them.

They counted the dead bodies of seventeen Boers, who had been killed, but they could find no trace of the English, which made them think that Captain Nisbitt and his men had been captured after a brave resistance.

They were about to cross the line when they perceived a party of mounted Boers on the Natal side, which compelled them to hurry back into the enemies' territory for a few miles.

It seemed as if they would have no chance of getting home that night, and they began to look out for a farmhouse where they could obtain rest and refreshment, as they had now reached a cultivated district where corn grew, and sheep and oxen were reared.

In front of them was a roughly-built barn, by the side of which were a few ricks of hay and corn, shadowed by a dozen or more trees, and they felt sure that the farmer's house could not be very far off.

A wailing sound reached their ears, and riding up, they perceived a woman, holding by the hand a boy of fourteen.

She appeared to be in great distress, and was so weak that she was scarcely able to stand.

"Heaven help us, and save us from those beasts in human form!" she moaned, in an hysterical voice.

"Help is at hand," Jack cried. "I am an Englishman, and it is my mission to take vengeance on these cowards."

Dashing up to her side, Harkaway enquired the cause of her grief, and was surprised to perceive that she was bleeding from cuts on the neck and shoulders, which seemed to have been inflicted by the thong of a whip.

The lad was also cut about the head and face; but he was too plucky to join in his mother's tears.

"I can see, sir, by your uniform, that you are a British officer," replied the woman. "Thank Heaven you have come to our aid. Look at yonder cottage, from which the smoke is rising. The smouldering embers represent our home, or, I should say, all that remains of it. I am Jenny Pearson; this is my son, Andy. My husband was manager to Mr. Welland, the old Boer farmer near by. His three sons have gone to the war. An hour ago some Boers came, commanded by a man wearing a helmet with a black eagle's plume in it."

"That must be Krause," said Dawson. "That was his headgear when I saw him behind the rock just now."

"I know not his name, sir," replied Mrs. Pearson ; "but we are Outlanders, and, worst of all, English. This man of whom I speak set fire to our cottage, lashed me and my child with his whip, and made us get out of the Vaal as quickly as possible."

"What has become of your husband?" asked Harkaway, who was rather puzzled at his absence from the wife's side in such an emergency.

The woman's tears flowed afresh, and, averting her gaze, she pointed to a tree.

The young men followed her action with their eyes, and to their horror beheld a man with a rope round his neck hanging to a tree, his feet just touching the ground.

"Good Heavens!" cried Jack. "This is atrocious. The brutal Boers have hanged him for no crime at all."

Clapping spurs to his horse's sides, he dashed forward, and with his sword cut the rope in half, causing the man Pearson to fall on his back.

In a moment Fred and he were by the man's side, one chafing his hands and the other pouring brandy down his throat.

They had arrived in time to save the man's life, for the Boers had not many minutes departed before they came up.

The woman's gratitude was boundless.

Andy shook Jack by the hand, declaring that he would never forget him, and Harkaway knew that he had made a friend, if it was only a little one.

The Pearsons said they had some acquaintances living a few miles off, with whom they would take refuge until they could get to Mafeking.

The day was declining ; the horses ridden by Jack and Fred were thoroughly worn out, so they tethered them near the rocks, while they walked on to the farmhouse occupied by Welland, in the front window of which they perceived a light burning.

"I am famished," remarked Jack, "and I know you must be as hungry as a bear, Fred ; while I am tired enough to sleep on a doormat, without any covering. We shall have to quarter ourselves on the enemy to-night, whether they like it or not."

"Before we rap at the door it may be advisable to look in at the window, as I notice the blind is only partially drawn down, and there is no curtain," replied Fred Dawson, who had all the instincts of the spy about him. "We don't want to poke our heads into a hornet's nest ; it would be better to camp out at the foot of the hayrick and go hungry."

Assenting to this, Harkaway walked up the stoop, and proceeded cautiously along the verandah until the window was reached, when he bent one knee and looked into the room, which was a small one, plainly furnished, and having a sanded floor.

The fireplace was old-fashioned, burning logs of wood on a brick hearth.

On one side sat an old man smoking a pipe with a big bowl ; this was Welland, the Dutch farmer.

Opposite him was a woman, grey and wrinkled, almost as old as himself, who was his vrow, or wife.

Jack expected to see this, from what Mrs. Pearson had told him, but he was astonished to notice at a table on the left the traitor Krause and the young dandy of Mafeking, Webb.

Some papers were stretched out on a table before them, and they were talking earnestly together.

Both were smoking, and applied themselves now and then to a bottle of Hollands.

Each had a revolver by his side, and some rifles were piled in a corner, which showed that they were prepared for any emergency which might arise.

Krause had his right hand placed on a square piece of parchment, to which he was drawing the attention of his companion, and, like a flash of lightning, the dying words of Moses Malachi came across Jack's memory.

CHAPTER III.

A FIGHT SURPRISE— SURRENDER IN THE QUEEN'S NAME—KRAUSE AND THE SPY WEBB ARE CAPTURED—A REVERSE OF FORTUNE—HARKAWAY IN DISTRESS.

RISING from his recumbent position, Harkaway retired along the verandah, until he came to front door, which he was not surprised to find open, as the owner of the house had sent his three sons to the front, and had nothing to fear from the Boers.

Probably he expected more visitors, who could enter without the ceremony of knocking.

"I can see the whole plot now," whispered Jack to his friend. "The dandy, Webb, who is a double-dyed traitor, and spy of the Boers, was notified of the old Jew's coming to Mafeking. He hired Dunko to kill, and rob him. The map of the secret mine in Rhodesia, which really belongs to me, since it was the dying gift of Malachi, was handed by the Kaffir to Krause. This is what they are studying. It is no war map. The traitors have given the plans of our defences long ago to General Kronje, who is in command here."

"Dunko will speak no more. What do you propose to do? There is no shelter for us in this place," replied Dawson.

"Don't be so sure about that. I have a bold plan in my head, which I will submit for your approval. Let us go into the passage, and listen at the door of the room, to what those two vile conspirators are talking of. When we have gleaned all we can, I suggest that we rush in, revolvers in hand, make them prisoners, and when day breaks, drag them with ropes attached to our saddles, into the town ; when, if I am not greatly mistaken, Colonel Baden-Powell will order them to be shot, as a warning to others."

"That is a capital idea, and I vote that we proceed to put it into execution at once. There is no time like the present, and we cannot stand here all night."

With their hearts beating quicker than usual, they entered the passage, and, guided by a light which came through the chinks in the door, stopped to listen, and heard Krause exclaim ·

"The site of the secret mine is not more than thirty miles from Bulawayo. From something scribbled on the back, I see that this plan, which is quite ancient, was dug up in a gold casket by a miner. It was possibly worked as far back as the days of Solomon, and is supposed to be filled with diamonds. Near by is a fertile spot hemmed in by rocks. There is a waterfall which gives life to grass, trees, and shrubs. It was called Jarkin, which in the Hebrew means an ear of corn and falling water. The miners sold the gold box to Malachi, and inside the Jew found the plan which I am describing to you."

"Good luck to us," cried Webb, in delight. "It is a fortune ; we will be partners in the concern and divide it."

"Will you," thought Jack. "Not if I know it."

"And now with regard to the war," continued Webb. "The moon will be up directly. I shall ride back to-night, for I always do my work in the dark when people think I am in bed and asleep. When shall you see General Kronje?"

"In a few hours," answered Krause. "His camp is not more than six miles from here, and he has a force of three thousand men under his command. The Boers are elated at destroying the armoured train. They have captured Captain Nesbitt, who is wounded, and fifteen other Britishers."

"Tell him from me," said Webb, "that Colonel Powell will to-morrow night send Captain Hore to attack him, with three hundred men ; if he is on the alert, he can easily repulse them, and in that event I should advise an immediate advance on Mafeking."

"Good!" murmured Krause, smiling, "Kronje is very slim (cunning). He means to settle all the Roosbaatjes (red-coats), and your news will make him baas op (boss up). He will have the stad (town) and every winkel (store) in it. Joubert and Kronje will soon bring the oortog (war) to an end."

The words had scarcely left his lips, when the door was thrown violently open.

Young Harkaway and Dawson stepped forward, holding their revolvers in their hands, carefully covering the two dastards.

The farmer Welland and his vrow (wife) turned their faces to the intruders, startled and aghast, seeming transfixed to their chairs with fright.

Krause and Webb appeared to shrink into themselves, and become smaller.

Their countenances were livid, for they imagined that Webb had been followed, and that Jack had a troop of horse outside, which was not an unnatural inference to draw.

"Do not move," shouted Harkaway, "or you are both dead men. I call upon you to surrender in the Queen's name."

Webb maintained a sullen silence, but Krause asked in a hoarse, trembling voice :

"What have we done ! Are we not on the soil of the South African Republic ?"

"You have been living under the British Protectorate in Natal. I denounce you as disloyal, and by virtue of the recent proclamation issued at Capetown I place you under arrest."

"This is rather a high-handed proceeding," observed Webb at length, recovering himself. "I am a British subject, and I protest against it. I do not come within the scope of the proclamation, and there is no martial law by which you can arrest me."

"Scoundrel and spy, why are you here," vociferated Jack. "I have been listening for the last quarter of an hour to your conversation with this Dutchman, and have heard enough to hang half-a-dozen men."

In a corner were a couple of halters, such as are used for horses.

Taking these, while Fred Dawson cornered the two men with his pistol, he bound them hand and foot to the chairs on which they were sitting.

They submitted with an ill-grace, and if looks could have killed him, Harkaway would not have lived long.

They were now masters of the situation.

They looked round for the old farmer, but could see nothing of him.

He had mysteriously left the apartment without being perceived.

"Where has the old man gone, mother?" asked Harkaway.

"He has gone oot," replied the woman, with stolid Dutch composure. "Maybe he was tired ; we all get so at night. It is his time to go oop to bed."

"Bustle yourself, and get us some supper. Bread and cheese will do, if you have nothing else."

"Dot was goot enough for a Rooinek (Redneck)," muttered the old woman, as she went to a cupboard to supply the wants of the intruders, who helped themselves to a draught of Hollands.

Without any ceremony, Harkaway searched Krause, and took possession of the plan of the Jarkin Mine.

"Ah," said Krause, with sarcastic emphasis. "I see you are a thief as well as a military policeman, my fine officer ! You think you have done a brave thing, but you have my red cross, which is the death-mark, on your forehead still. It is all bad business for you."

"At any rate your hand is powerless. I can afford to laugh at a played-out traitor.

Saying this, Jack sat down to supper with Dawson.

They did ample justice to what was spread before them, as they had been a long time without food.

"There is something suspicious," remarked Fred, "about the old Boer farmer vanishing as he did. I don't half like it. I fancy he has gone to bring the enemy down on us."

"The moon is shining," replied Harkaway, "rising and going to the window. "I am not at all easy in my mind, and if there is anything in your suggestion, it will be best to start for camp at once, as I have not a wink of sleep in me."

He drew up the blind and looked out.

A breeze had sprung up, and dark clouds were drifting across the skyline.

There had been no rain for months, and a change in the weather was daily expected.

The air had been dry, and sand-storms frequent, with the temperature between ninety and a hundred.

There wasn't a vlei (pool of water) to be seen on the veldt.

The wind had fanned the smouldering embers of the Englishman's, Pearson's, cottage, to which the Boers had set fire when they drove him, his wife, and son with blows and curses, helpless and friendless, from their home, Krause adding to the brutal act by trying to hang the man whom Jack saved at the last moment.

These embers emitted a bright light, and Harkaway fancied he saw dim figures in the distance, like weird spectres, on horseback, looking eerie and uncanny; but between the fire and the moonlight he was dazzled, and could not be sure that his imagination was not mocking him.

All at once the moon became obscured, and, strange to say, at precisely the same time the lamp in the room, from some cause or another, went out; so that darkness, only lightened by the stars and the rapidly declining fire in the room, with an occasional flash from the ruins of the cottage, prevailed.

Annoyed at this sudden change, Jack made a half-turn to see to the lamp, as light was an absolute necessity.

Welland's vrow, who was a thorough Boer sympathiser, and an artful one in the bargain, as her keen face proved, might seize the chance to liberate the captives, which would mean a free fight in the dark, with no prospect of the best man winning.

His movement was arrested by the sound of a boyish voice on the verandah, a shrill treble, which said, in a terribly earnest tone:

"Hush! Look out, boss, there's rocks ahead! I came back to tell you, but I can't stop."

It was so dark that Harkaway could see no one, though he thought that he had heard the voice before, but could not tell where, and, in a tone of anxiety, he asked:

"Who are you?"

"Little Andy Pearson, sir, who swore to be your pal through life, for saving father when he was at his last gasp. That time when the Boers burnt us out of house and home, and half-killed mother and me with their sjamboks (whips). Father and mother are at Kraai Pau, lying down under the krautz (cliff) close to the fontein (spring). There are a lot of Boers on the boschveld (an open plain covered with bush), and being a good runner, I thought I'd come and tell you to look out. If anything happens, I shan't be far off. Welland has gone to tell the Boers where you are. I met him coming along. Don't trust his wife; she is as sly as an old cat, and as vicious as they make them."

Andy Pearson did not stay to say anything more.

He was nervous and excited.

Thinking he had done his duty by warning Harkaway, to whom he had taken a strong liking at first sight, he quitted the verandah, and the young hussar was left in a very puzzled condition of mind, for there was no doubt that Welland had gone to bring the foe down upon him.

It was of the utmost importance that he should get back to Mafeking at once, and tell the colonel that Webb, the spy, had betrayed his plans as far as he knew.

It would only have been justice if he had shot the two traitors, Webb and Krause; but he could not bring himself to kill them in cold blood.

Having noticed a quantity of chump wood in a corner, Jack seized an armful and threw it on the fire, causing the sparks to fly right and left, and a blaze to spring up which irradiated the room.

The woman had resumed her seat in the chair; her face was buried in her hands, and she pretended to be asleep.

The prisoners, sullen and defiant, were as he had left them.

Dawson was smoking a cigar a few paces off, pistol in hand, keeping watch, and ready for any contingency which might occur.

"Wake up, mother," said Jack, shaking the vrow gently by the arm. "What's the matter with the lamp? This isn't blind man's holiday. We want a light."

"You won't want it long," replied the old woman, rousing herself. "Darkness always comes before dawn, but the sun will never rise for you again. The die is cast. Your life hangs by a single thread, and Fate will cut it. Why do you and yours come across the sea to disturb us? We want you not; leave us in peace. We were the voortrekkers" (pioneers) "and would be happy were it not for the Britishers' greed for gold."

Turning away, as he did not think it worth while to argue with the old crone, Harkaway went to the table, and, finding that the lamp —which was nearly full of oil—had been purposely extinguished, as part of a deep design, he relighted it with a match.

"There is some game on foot!" exclaimed Dawson. "The lamp didn't go out of its own accord; and the vrow's remarks, to say the least of it, are not complimentary. Who was that I heard you talking to on the verandah?"

"That little chap, Andy, whose father I saved to-day," replied Jack. "He seems to have taken a liking to me, for he came back here to warn us that Welland, the farmer, had gone to bring the Boers down on us; so we must evacuate the position at once, though I fear we are too late. It's an awful hole to be in. We can never drag our prisoners to Mafeking to-night."

"Give them the benefit of a bullet," replied Dawson, who had not the high sense of honour and humanity which animated Jack. "Mercy is thrown away on such wretches as these. Why do you hesitate? Don't act like a fool. Their lives are justly forfeited. By killing them we shall only anticipate a few hours the sentence which our commander will pass upon them. By Heaven, Jack, if you don't shoot, I will do it myself!"

Dawson raised his arm and pointed his revolver at Webb and Krause, who sat still, motionless, helpless, with the pallor of death on their faces, like condemned murderers listening to the knell of doom.

"No, no!" cried Jack, catching hold of his arm. "It would be wicked, a sin, a crime. I cannot consent."

The old woman, seeing their preoccupation, had risen from her chair, and taking a lighted lantern from a cupboard, was standing at the window, waving it to and fro in the air, evidently giving a signal to someone without.

In a few seconds, by a couple of flashes coming quickly out of the darkness, resembling those of a heliograph, she was answered; and apparently satisfied, the aged vrow resumed her seat by the fireplace,. crooning to herself as if she was muttering a prayer.

"Have your own way," said Dawson, impatiently, looking vexed and worried as he lowered his revolver. "You will be sorry for this mistaken clemency before long. You are so generous that I don't believe you would kill a viper if you saw it crawling in your path. People can carry a virtue too far, my boy, and that's what you're doing. The only thing for us to do now, is, as the boys say, to bunk out of this place as quick as possible."

"All right," answered Jack; "our nags are not far off, and have had time to get rested. As for the Dutchman and Mr. Webb——"

"Don't mention their names, unless you want to irritate me," interrupted Dawson. "You have acted foolishly, and are wasting time now. Come on."

They advanced to the door, and were confronted by three Boers, with their rifles at their shoulders, and bayonets fixed.

"We are betrayed!" cried Dawson. "To the window, quick!"

They turned in that direction, and to their infinite dismay the same alarming spectacle met their gaze.

A double row of armed burghers were on the verandah.

What to do they knew not.

Pale and disconcerted, they stood in the centre of the room.

Harkaway drew his sword, as if determined to cut his way out; but a moment's reflection showed him that, if he endeavoured to attack his foes, he would be mercilessly shot down.

To give in or to fight was the question.

In either case death seemed certain.

There was very little hope, for either Dawson or him, if Krause had any influence in the councils of the Boers.

"Buck up, Jack," said Dawson, in a voice which he intended to be cheery, while a sad expression stole over his youthful face. "We will die fighting, although it would be no disgrace to submit to such overwhelming odds."

"You are right, Fred," replied Jack. "I would rather fall, sword in hand, than be calmly butchered by these ruffians. Follow me, and let's make a dash for it. Hold your fire until I strike the first blow, and then let them have it red-hot."

Fred Dawson set his teeth together, and they advanced with a quick step to the door, where they seemed to have more chance than at the window.

CHAPTER IV.

A FORLORN HOPE—SUDDEN APPEARANCE OF GENERAL KRONJE—PRISONERS OF WAR—THE BROKEN SWORD—AN ASSASSIN—THE BOY FRIEND — ANDY PROVES HIMSELF USEFUL.

No order was given to fire.

The Boers at the door looked calmly at the young men, as if awaiting their attack before they took action.

Harkaway could not understand their cool attitude, and raising his sword to run a man through, was astonished at seeing the soldiers fall back and allow a tall, powerfully built man pass by them.

This personage stood on the threshold, with his hand upon his sword.

On his head was a brass helmet, surmounted by a red plume.

His body was protected by a cuirass.

His face, though fat and ungainly, was not devoid of intelligence.

There was blood on his spurs, which showed that he had been riding hard and had not spared his horse.

"Your sword, if you please," he exclaimed, addressing Jack. "I understand you are a British officer, kept out of your lines by our men, and came here, hoping to find shelter till the morning. I presume you will consider it no humiliation to surrender to General Kronje—I am he. You will be treated as a prisoner of war, and be interned at Pretoria until the war is happily over. I beg of you not to act rashly, and speak for your own sake, as I have fifty troopers in and outside this farmhouse, who, at one word from me, would consign you to eternity."

Disheartening as it was, Harkaway could not refuse this invitation.

He was obliged to admit to himself that General Kronje was polite, and acting as an European commander would have done.

But before he gave up his sword he snapped it in half over his knee, and threw the broken pieces on the floor.

With equal petulance Dawson tossed his revolver into a corner, where it harmlessly exploded.

The general's lip curled with a half smile at this youthful display of temper; but he made no remark, for he saw that Harkaway's heart was fully broken, as his sword; and as a soldier himself he could make allowance for his feelings.

A long inglorious confinement awaited him and his warlike aspirations were nipped in the bud.

General Kronje gave some orders to two of his men, who marched the prisoners across the passage into a sort of lumber room, where the farmer kept all sorts of odds and ends.

It had one window, which opened on to the verandah.

There was no necessity for a light, as the moon had shone out again from behind a cloud which had hidden it for a time.

The soldiers made them sit down with their backs to the wall, confining their hands and feet with stout cord, as it was easy enough to get through the window.

This done, one man remained as a sentry. He lighted his pipe and walked up and down for a quarter-of-an-hour, when he tired of his monotonous duty, and went outside to hold converse with some of his comrades who were drinking on the stoop.

In fact, these armed burghers had little idea of discipline, especially when on the march or making a raid.

Neither Harkaway nor Dawson spoke to one another. They were cast down and gloomy.

General Kronje had promised to treat them as prisoners of war; but when his back was turned he could not be responsible for the acts of those under his command, or that of some other officer.

The prospect before them was not cheering.

They were not asleep. Dawson had closed his eyes, but Harkaway's were open. He saw something come in at the doorway like a wild beast. It drew nearer.

Soon he saw that it was a man on his hands and knees with a head of shaggy hair. Between his teeth was a long knife. Nearer it came by slow degrees.

"Heaven help us!" muttered Jack. "It is Krause!"

At this very critical moment in Harkaway's career, he bethought himself of the peculiar gift he possessed.

He was an excellent ventriloquist, being able to imitate any sound or voice, and place his words in any direction he chose.

Determined to startle the assassin, he exclaimed, gruffly, making his tones appear to come from behind some sacks in a corner of the lumber-room:

"Pas op (look out)! We won't allow the prisoners to be murdered. Fire low, and make sure of your aim. The general will not blame us if we kill the villain."

Krause naturally thought that a Boer was talking to another; and was so alarmed at being detected when he thought himself secure, that he sprang to his feet, and ran to the door.

"Ha, ha!" said the same voice, with a contemptuous laugh. "I thought the fellow was a coward; all nocturnal assassins are. If I could see the rascal's face, I would report him to Kronje. Put up your gun, and save your bullet. I suppose he thought the captain had some valuable stuff about him. The rogue is a sneak thief, and hasn't the pluck to be a robber."

Gnashing his teeth with rage, Krause retired into the darkness of the passage, where Webb was waiting for him.

"How did you get on?" asked Webb. "Have you secured the plan of the secret mine?"

"Voetsak (get out)," replied Krause, in an irritable tone. "I am that mad, I could eat my head! Just as I was going to stab this young man, Harkaway, and had measured the distance of my knife from his heart, a Boer sentry disturbed me, threatening to give me the contents of his Mauser. It is bad business. I will some more Schnapps take, and in half-an-hour make another try. That plan we must have! I'll watch it. I feel as mean as if someone had been doing a shot (swindling) on me! Pshaw! I'm not fit to ride for sour apples!"

"It is very galling," replied Webb. "I'm afraid you've missed your chance. We shall have the daylight here directly."

"I wish the war was over already," continued Krause, despondently. "I feel inclined to say hinstoe (let's go home), look after the mealie-crops, and see the vrow en kinders (wife and children) once more."

"I don't; that's where you and I differ," remarked Webb, with a sly chuckle. "I never liked work, and want to get rich in a hurry. I hope the war will last long over Christmas, so that I can put plenty of old Kruger's money in my pocket for playing the spy on the English. I am under orders to go to Dundee and Ladysmith, where Generals Symons and White are. Big fighting is expected there before long. Your dashing General Koch and the veteran Joubert, with twelve thousand men in their commandos, will make the Red-necks sit up."

"Ah, well, that is so," said Krause, complacently. "Of course we shall drive the British into the sea. They never could stand up against us. Majuba, for instance, showed what we can do. Their soldiers cannot compare with ours."

Boasting in this manner, Krause and his companion re-entered the sitting-room.

The general and his men had thrown themselves down on the floor, wrapped in their overcoats, taking anything they could find for a pillow.

As soon as he sat down, Webb began to doze off; but Krause, muttering curses and imprecations to himself, applied his lips frequently to the spirit-bottle and savagely sharpened his knife on the hearth.

Meanwhile Harkaway breathed more freely.

He had escaped a great danger, but his mind was far from being at rest.

Krause had shown to what lengths he was ready to go, and there was no telling at what time he might repeat his deadly purpose.

All at once the window was pushed up from the outside very gently, and a youthful form crept lightly in.

Fred Dawson was still fast asleep.

The stranger advanced towards Jack.

"Hush!" he whispered. "Do not be alarmed; it is I, Andy Pearson. I promised to be your boy, and have come here to set you free. Those verdómde Boers are wrapped in slumber."

"How about the sentry?" enquired Jack.

"He had a glass of squareface (Dutch gin), and I put some sleep-herbs in it. He won't trouble us, for he is as harmless as if he were down amongst the dead men. Wake your friend, and tell him to keep quiet while I cut you both loose. Mind you don't fall over anyone as you are going out, for the ground is covered with sleeping Boers."

Jack expressed his gratitude with his eyes but did not say anything more.

Andy severed the cords that bound them, and Fred, being wakened and cautioned, the three made their way out of the farmhouse, and contrived to reach the spot where the horses had been picketed without rousing their sleeping foes.

"Hurrah! we are free once more!" cried Jack, springing into the saddle, an example which was followed by Fred Dawson.

Both were overjoyed at having escaped a long captivity, for they might have been sent to Pretoria, where they must have languished for weeks in some squalid gaol until Sir Redvers Buller routed the enemy and hoisted the Union Jack in the Boer capital.

"What are you going to do, Andy?" enquired Harkaway.

"I shan't be long after you in Mafeking, sir," replied the lad. "I'm a slim kerel (smart chap), and can baas op as well as anyone. Leave me to take care of myself. If you want to do anything for me, ask Colonel Powell to make me a bugler. I can blow a horn, and will soon pick up the calls."

"You may depend on me for that," answered Jack. "Consider yourself already appointed to the high position you covet."

Waving his hand, Harkaway spurred his horse, he and Fred cantering off in the direction of the town.

The country they traversed was flat, covered in places with low mimosa bush, hardly more than two feet high.

When they got within a distance of two miles of the town the ground gradually rose, while five miles off, to the west, a few small hills were visible.

It was now daylight, and they had a good view of Mafeking, which is merely a collection of galvanized iron buildings with a few brick and stone stores and offices.

Before the war it only possessed five hundred inhabitants, who enjoy a decent club and several drinking-bars.

It is high above the sea level, and has a good supply of water from the River Molopo, which flows a quarter-of-a-mile from the town.

The young men were glad enough to draw rein at the entrance to the camp, and at once sought an interview with the colonel, who commended them highly for what they had done.

Learning that Kronje was so close, the colonel resolved to draw and engage him, if he could, a few miles down the line, and ordered an armoured train to be got ready, each truck to contain thirty men, with Hotchkis and Maxim guns.

The men selected for this service were a section of British South Africa Police, while two squadrons of the Protectorate Regiment were to ride on in front.

Harkaway and Dawson asked permission, tired though they were, to go with the force, which was granted.

"I must check these Boers and teach them to keep at a distance," said Colonel Powell. "I don't want to waste ammunition, because we have not too much. Food is plentiful; we do not expect to live on prairie chicken and antelope, but Wiel's store contains enough provisions to last us a year. I only wish Colonel Plumer would come to our aid from Rhodesia."

The colonel knew that he had a tough job in hand, but he knew that his men would rather die a hundred times than surrender.

"Talking of ammunition," said Jack, "reminds me that there are two large trucks of dynamite in the station. They are only a source of danger in the event of a Boer bullet coming that way."

"I have thought of that, but do not know what to do with them."

"If my reckoning is correct, I fancy I know where the Boers will be in an hour's time," added Harkaway. "I can drive an engine as well as anyone, and if you will let me take those two trucks of dynamite on the line, I'll show you some fun with the Krugerites."

"Capital," said Colonel Powell, laughing. "I understand your plan without any further explanation. Go to the station-master for an engine, take care what you are about, and don't hoist yourself instead of the enemy."

"Not I," replied Jack. "Thank you, sir, for your kind permission. I shan't be long

over the job, and will be back with the engine before you want to send the armoured train out; but allow me to ask you one question before I go."

"Certainly. "What is it?"

"Do you intend to order the police to look out for Webb, the spy? He has probably ridden back to town by this time, and is in bed recruiting himself."

"Of course, I shall have him arrested as quickly as possible. Martial law reigns here. There is no occasion for an ordinary trial; the wretch will be convicted on your evidence, and that of Mr. Dawson, alone. You have only to repeat what you heard him say to Krause in Welland's farmhouse, and I'll have him shot in an hour. Do you know where he lives?"

"He has a bedroom in the club house, I think. Wait until I come back, and I will unearth him for you."

This ended the interview with the colonel, Jack and Fred proceeding to the mess tent of the Protectorate regiment, where they were sure of getting some breakfast.

"I'm as hungry as a bear," exclaimed Dawson. "A fellow can't live on air, you know. I say, shan't we corner Webb nicely?"

"That is doubtful," said Harkaway. "If he ventures to come back here, it will be more than daring; I shall call it a piece of magnificent cheek. Everyone around Kronje must know by this time that we have escaped, and that we shall be down upon him. No, he will try to do what he mentioned. That is, get over to Ladysmith or Dundee, which he could do with a good horse in a fortnight. However, if he does turn up, we'll nab him as sure as there are snakes in Africa."

Jack had hardly spoken before a long, ugly-looking black snake wriggled itself out of a hole in the ground, and darting its forked tongue to and fro, hissed at him spitefully.

"Down you go, you beast," cried Dawson, giving the reptile a blow with his riding-whip. "What the deuce did you come out of your hole to interview us for?"

The whip cut the reptile in half; the upper portion falling writhing on the ground, while the lower vanished into the earth.

This was a common occurrence in that country.

It was not unusual in the camp for a soldier to wake up in the night and see a snake circling up his tent-pole.

Just outside the mess marquee they encountered Andy Pearson, who had arrived and was making inquiries for them.

"Here I am, boss," cried Andy, cheerily. "Give me a bugle and a revolver; I'm ready to start fighting at once. There's a lot of Boers four miles down the line."

"All right, my boy. Wait a few minutes, and you shall be attended to," replied Jack; adding: "What is that you have got in your arms?"

"Only a little murcat," answered Andy, holding up an impudent-looking, lithe, dun-coloured animal, something between a ferret and a weasel, with short, silver-tipped fur, a knowing snout, and bright, beady eyes. "I thought I would make you a present of it. It's been my pet for ever so long. He'll make himself entirely at home in your tent, squat on your blanket, and make faces at you."

"Keep it for me," said Jack, touched at the lad's effort to please him.

He had nothing else to give, so he was willing to part with his pet murcat, which made a quaint, whirring sound in its throat, and flapped its little fore-paws in a funny sort of way.

Entering the mess tent, Jack and Fred saw some friends.

Fish, the war correspondent, was talking to Lieutenant Bentinck, of the Lancers ; and Brick, the gossip, was button-holing Lieutenant Brady, one of the Protectorate officers.

"Welcome, Harkaway, and you, too, Dawson," exclaimed Bentinck ; while Fish, from force of habit, took out his notebook and got his pencil ready. "We thought you were lost."

"I have been in the thick of it ; so has Dawson," responded Jack. "We've been fighting Boers, got taken prisoners, and we were nearly murdered in the night. But, of your charity, dear old chappie, give us something to eat."

"Would you like what the Boers offer an Englishman, when he claims their hospitality ? "

"I don't think I should turn up my nose at anything, not even a bit of roast rhinoceros ; but what are you alluding to ? "

"Potatoes, and point, my boy," replied Lieutenant Bentinck ; "it's a standing dish for the tramping Britisher. The Boer offers you a plate of cold potatoes and points to a piece of stale, unwholesome, evil-smelling, uneatable steak, hanging by a string to a beam in the roof. You get the smell of the steak to go with the sodden, measly potatoes. That's potatoes and point ; but if you like to sit down, you will find plenty of canned stuff on the table, and I think there is a drop of coffee left in the pot. Breakfast has been over an hour or more, you know."

"Have you seen the chief, Harkaway ? " enquired Lieutenant Brady. "Is he going to make any move. I'm getting positively mouldy for want of a fight, as the Irishman said."

"You will get your orders directly, both of you," replied Jack, "but you will have to wait until I come back from a sortie I am going to make. The Boers are tricky, but if I don't go them one better at their own game you are at liberty to call me a fool. By the way, have either of you fellows been up to the club this morning. If so, did you see anything of Webb ? "

"I strolled up after parade," answered Bentinck, " and I recollect now that I did see Mr. Webb. He was asleep in an arm-chair in the billiard-room. He looked awfully fagged, as if he had been up all night."

"It will be his last sleep in this world."

"How is that ? " demanded his listeners, earnestly.

"Dawson and I can prove him to be a spy and a traitor. He was in the Boer lines last night with General Cronje, and the colonel has just assured me that he intends to have him shot, though I think he deserves hanging."

"Serve him right," said Brady, "I've no sympathy for him ; but you might tell us what's up, Harkaway ? "You know all the secrets, and we poor beggars don't hear a word."

"Well, if you must have it, listen. I am going to take the dynamite up the line. When I see the Boers, I shall uncouple the engine and run back, leaving the trucks for them to fire at. There will be some scattered remnants of humanity flying about, you bet. After that an armoured train is going out : so you will have a battle before dinner to-day."

Having gratified their curiosity, Jack sat down to the table and began to eat.

He mentioned Andy Pearson, whom Brady said he would take care of ; while Fish scribbled in his book : " Daring adventure of Sub-lieutenant Harkaway. He penetrates Boer camp. Made prisoner and escapes. Dynamite for Cronje.* Impending battle."

CHAPTER V.

A STRANGE BALLOON IS SEEN—JACK TRICKS THE BOERS—THE DYNAMITE EXPLOSION— A LIVELY BATTLE—WEBB GETS OFF— ALARM AT THE CLUB.

YOUNG JACK HARKAWAY was one of those smart fellows who can put a hand to anything.

It was not that his skill and aptitude came naturally to him ; he worked hard to learn, and was never idle.

Being acquainted with the working of a locomotive, he did not require any assistance.

The station master always kept steam up on one engine night and day, in case a part of his rolling-stock should be wanted in an emergency.

As Jack walked through the camp to the station, he heard the bugle sounding the assembly, and the men of the Protectorate regiment were to be seen quickly falling in, with their Martini-Henry rifles.

To his surprise, he noticed that the bugler was no other than Andy, whom Lieutenant Brady had quickly taken in hand, dressing him in a suit of uniform a size too large for him ; but that did not matter.

He was as proud as a peacock, and blew the bugle pretty well for a beginner.

When the station master heard what Jack required, he was soon accommodated.

The engine was placed behind the trucks, so that it could be easily detached for the run home, and there would not be any danger of sparks falling on the explosive.

"Shall I go with you, Mr. Harkaway ? " asked the master.

"No thank you," replied Jack, "I am going to do this on my own. The gentle Boers made it hot for me last night, and I am going to warm them up to-day. I am obliged to you, all the same. I know Cronje is rather thick, and to get the best of him will take a bit of doing. I intend to run this engine, and if I fail, and you can find a few fragments of what you now see before you, namely myself, you can bury them with military honours."

"Jolly good luck to you, Mr. Harkaway. You are always bright and cheerful, making the best of things, but I shouldn't like to stand in your shoes. and that's a fact. A

*This general's name has been spelt in the press both as Cronje and Kronge. Cronje appears to be correct.—ED.

bullet will soon go through one of those trucks, and then 'up goes the donkey,' as the saying is."

"Thank you for the compliment. I didn't know I belonged to the assinine family," said Jack, with a laugh; " my ears must have sprouted during the night."

" I didn't mean that," protested the station master, " you've nothing of the moke about you. A smarter, or more intelligent officer never handled a sword, or wore the Queen's uniform."

" That's better, there's nothing like laying it on with a heavy hand, while you are about it. If you want to borrow something, I'm sorry I have no money with me, but I'll promise to open a bottle the next time you come into camp," replied Jack, springing into the cab of the engine.

"Hold hard one minute," cried the station master; " when you were on the veldt yesterday, did you see anything peculiar in the sky?"

" That I did not," answered Harkaway, wondering why the question was put to him: " there was scarcely a cloud. What are you driving at?"

" I could swear that I saw a large balloon. It struck me that our officers had brought a war balloon with them, and were prospecting in our neighbourhood; or else the Boers have had one made in Germany, as most things are nowadays, though I don't think our foes find the Mauser cartridges much to their liking."

"Are you sure you were not mistaken? Which way did the balloon go?"

"It hovered about for a little while, and then went due east. Ha! by the living jingo, there it is again. Look! it is coming towards us."

"You are right, by Jove," answered Harkaway; "but I can't stop now to discuss the matter. We are going to attack the enemy directly, and time is precious. Get a glass, scan it closely, and tell me all about it when I come back—if I do."

It certainly did look like a balloon, but its altitude was such as to make it a mere speck.

There was scarcely any wind, and it was moving slowly; but still it did move, nobody could deny that.

It was not a cloud, and it was impossible to regard it as a bird.

Bestowing no further attention upon it, Jack set the engine in motion, and proceeded up the line, which is a single track, with convenient sidings.

In ten minutes he had travelled four miles, and, judging that he had reached the spot where he supposed the Boers to be collecting for an attack on the town, he slackened speed. He was not mistaken.

Little more than a mile off he saw scores of them galloping about, and keeping his field glass to his eyes, distinctly made out a number of Boers on foot in full marching order.

It was also evident that they had perceived him, and were greatly excited by the spectacle of the smoke coming from the engine.

The commanding officers waved their swords, and a number of men began to fire as they rushed headlong towards the line.

Without losing a moment, Harkaway un-

coupled the engine, and fell back upon Mafeking as fast as possible.

After placing a good distance between himself and the dynamite trucks, he slacked up again to watch what took place.

In their eagerness to capture what they supposed to be trucks containing stores, about seventy Boers outdistanced the rest of their comrades, keeping up a dropping fire on the waggons, which they imagined were guarded by soldiers who had been deserted in a cowardly manner by the engine-driver.

At last a bullet exploded the dynamite, with which was several barrels of cordite. The force was terrific, the concussion making the ground shake.

Deep holes were rent in the soil. Half-a-dozen thunderstorms added to the discharge of a park of artillery could not have equalled it.

Everyone of the Boers in advance were killed, their bodies being frightfully mangled and mutilated.

Gratified with the success of his trick, Jack returned to the station, passing as he did so, a detachment of British troops, who were marching to assist those in the armoured train, which was in readiness to depart, the driver only waiting for Jack's return to clear the line.

The colonel's plan was for the advance party to draw the Boers' fire, and bring them into action, when the armoured train would rush up and mow the enemy down with machine guns and rifles.

Lieutenant Brady and little Andy, now the bugler, were seen by Jack with those in front.

All cheered him loudly, as he stood proudly on the engine, and he was again applauded as he ran into the station.

The driver of the armoured train blew his whistle, and the trucks began to move. Fearing he would be left behind, Harkaway made a clean spring from his engine into one of the trucks, and was caught in the arms of Lieutenant Bentinck and another officer named Fitzclarence, who let him down gently on his legs as the cars were rattling out of the station.

He had stopped his own engine, so that no harm was done, there being a double track through the station, which allowed two trains to be in at once.

"No you don't, boys!" cried Harkaway. "You tried to steal a march on me, but it didn't come off. Fight the Boers, if you like, but not without me. I like to see some fun, as well as the rest of you."

The men, of whom there were about thirty in the truck, laughed heartily at this sally, for Jack was a great favourite with all of them, as they could not help admiring his dash and pluck; and there was a peculiar kind of easy good-nature about him which attracted both rank and file.

The train went along slowly, halting occasionally to give Bentinck's men time to attract the attention of the Boers.

It was now nearing mid-day, and the rays of the sun were almost dazzling.

In spite of the check the Boers had received through the dynamite, they seemed to be more savage than ever, for they no sooner perceived Bentinck's force than they

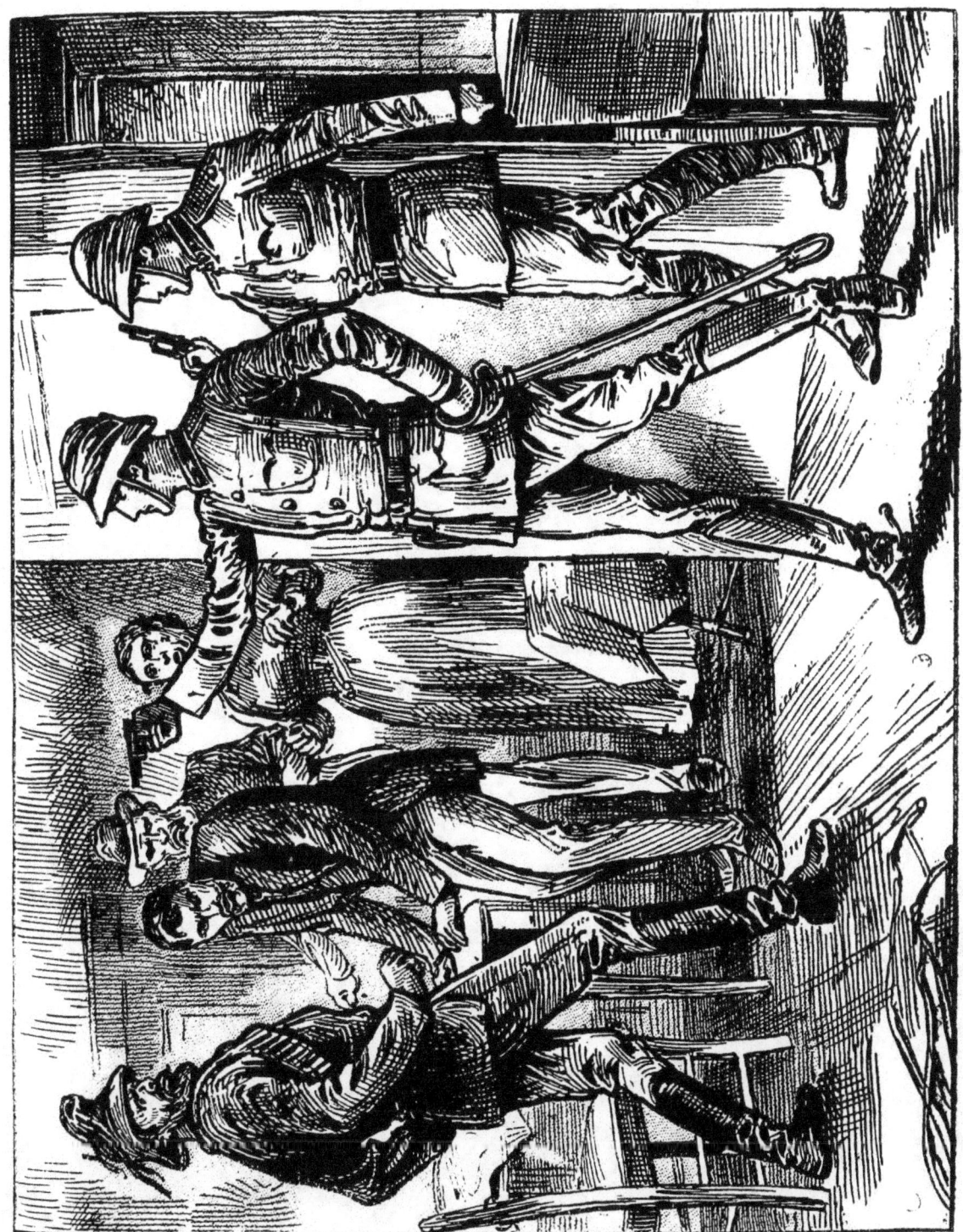

"'DO NOT MOVE,' SHOUTED HARKAWAY, 'OR YOU ARE BOTH DEAD MEN. I CALL UPON YOU TO SURRENDER.'"

No. 2.

flew at them like a lot of hornets, and a fierce conflict ensued, many falling on either side.

Above the din of the firing, and the cries of the wounded, could be heard the shrill blast of Andy's bugle.

The boy perceived Lieutenant Brady, sword in hand, engaged with, and hemmed in by, half-a-dozen Boers.

The lieutenant disposed of two, whom he ran through the body, and Andy bravely shot three with his revolver, the sixth being bayoneted by a corporal of the Protectorate regiment just as he had put a bullet into Brady's leg.

The latter fell, but, bravely sitting up, made a tourniquet with his handkerchief, which Andy, who knew something about giving first aid to the wounded, helped him to tie round his leg.

He then coolly filled his pipe, and amused himself by popping at the enemy with his revolver.

The Boers were pressing us heavily, swarming in large numbers, as it was intended they should do.

When the armoured train came to a standstill, the wounded were carried off, and the British beat a retreat ; whereupon the South Africa Police in the trucks poured a deadly hail into the Boers, who were fairly staggered.

Our men fired through loopholes, being invisible to the enemy ; and, leaving a quantity of their number on the field, the latter were glad enough to seek shelter where they could.

They did not come up for their wounded until the train was out of sight.

It stopped when Brady's party were overtaken, and the men congratulated one another on their splendid victory.

One truck was cleared for the use of the wounded, of whom fifteen were badly hurt.

The ambulance men, conspicuous by the Geneva Cross and a white flag, were slightly in the rear.

Dawson, who had fought with Brady, eagerly shook Jack by the hand when he got out of the train.

"It was pretty sharp while it lasted," observed Harkaway. "Where is the lieutenant ? "

"He insisted upon being picked up last," replied Fred.

"Just like him ; a more self-sacrificing fellow never lived. I saw him fall. Is he hard hit ? "

"Shot in the leg. I wish the bearers would hurry up. They are close to some rocks, and we know what the Boers can do when they have got cover. Let us go back and see if we can help the hospital men."

They did as Dawson suggested, and when near the rocks alluded to, were surprised to hear firing.

The guard were only three in number : one fell, and four Boers left their shelter to attack the others at close quarters, firing as they came.

Another guard was hit, and it seemed as if Brady was actually in danger.

With the fleetness of a deer, Harkaway ran forward, closely followed by Fred.

He emptied his revolver, killing one man.

Bullets whizzed past him, but he was untouched.

Arriving on the scene, he cut down two more, when his foot slipped ; he fell heavily, and was at the mercy of the foe, who pointed his Mauser at his head.

Before he could draw the trigger, the cowardly violator of the sacredness of the hospital flag threw up his arms and rolled over as a ball discharged by Dawson crashed through his skull.

Free from danger, Jack jumped up and slapped Fred on the shoulder, exclaiming :

"This is the second time you have saved my life. If you keep on doing this sort of thing, I shall never be able to pay the debt of gratitude I owe you."

"As far as I am concerned, I shall never ask you," replied Fred, "unless I am placed in the same fix I have found you. The war isn't over yet by a long chalk, and it may be my turn next."

"I think the Boers might have respected the Hospital Service Corps," remarked Jack ; "but by the look of these fellows I am inclined to regard them as what they term tramp Boers, and not regular burghers. So we must make allowance for the enemy, who cannot be held responsible for all their campfollowers. How are you, Brady ? " he added, addressing the lieutenant. "I suppose you were in a state of funk just now ? "

"That is a mental condition to which I am never reduced, my dear boy," answered the wounded man. "I must die some day, and when a man becomes a soldier he has to take all kinds of chances. War makes me a philosopher."

The men went on again, Jack and Fred bringing up the rear.

It had been a brilliant sortie, and the colonel was quite satisfied with what had been done.

When he got into camp, Harkaway was accosted by a sergeant, who said :

"I have been waiting for you, sir, by Colonel Powell's orders."

"They concern a civilian named Webb, do they not ? " replied Jack. "If so, I am ready to march into the town with you without a moment's delay, as I fear we shall lose our man if we don't look sharp. If he should offer any resistance, shoot him down, as you would a mad dog."

"Shall we take a file of the guard with us ? "

"It is not necessary. You and I are a match for him, sergeant. Put yourself by my side, and look to your revolver."

After his exertions that day, Jack would have been glad enough to throw himself upon his camp bedstead, but when there was duty to perform, he was willing to keep on until he dropped.

As they passed the hospital tent they peeped in, and saw that the surgeons and their assistants were very busy.

The pluck of our men was shown in a marked manner.

Several of those who were slightly injured, and had had their wounds dressed, were clamouring to be allowed to go out and have another shot at the enemy.

Of course this could not have been permitted if the battle had still been going on, and it was with difficulty that they were pacified.

Looking back in the direction of the scene of conflict, Jack noticed a flock of vultures, which abound in the Transvaal, hovering over and pouncing down upon the slain.

These birds are known as aasvogels, and act as scavengers on the veldt.

Thousands of oxen are used in transport and trekking service.

Many of them die from exhaustion, want of water, eating poisonous food, or cruelty from their Boer masters.

The dead ox is their prey.

Within a few minutes the aasvogels, in a grisly horde, swoop down upon the still warm beast, and commence their ghoulish feast.

In looking upward Jack was in reality searching the sky for the mysterious balloon mentioned by the station-master, but he could see nothing of it, and was inclined to consider it an optical delusion on the part of his friend.

As the sergeant and Jack neared the club they noticed a horse, saddled and bridled, waiting outside.

It was held by a small boy, who was apparently watching for somebody to come out.

"Hurry up," cried Jack. "I feel confident that horse is for Webb's use, and if we don't watch it we shall lose him."

"Let us advance at the double," replied the serjeant.

They were about a hundred yards distant from the club, and commenced to run up the street, which was empty, as most of the people had gone down to the camp to glean all the particulars they could of the fight.

Scarcely had they accomplished a third of the distance when they saw a man rush out of the club, take one hurried look at them, and spring on the horse like lightning.

It was Webb, who seemed to be ghastly pale and terribly alarmed.

Without pausing, Harkaway and the sergeant opened fire at him with their revolvers, whereupon Webb, who was not touched, unslung a short rifle from his shoulder, and aimed at his pursuers.

The crack of the rifle was heard, and almost at the same time the sergeant fell against Jack, crying in an hoarse voice:

"By Heaven, I am hit!"

"I'll see to you in a minute," replied Jack, letting him sink gently to the ground, while he ran up the street firing wildly at Webb.

The latter set spurs to his horse, and galloped off like the wind, his mocking laughter ringing painfully in Harkaway's ears.

In a few minutes Jack was out-distanced and gave up the unequal chase in despair, returning to the sergeant, who had received an ugly lacerated wound in the neck, which was bleeding profusely.

A woman came out of a house and brought him some linen, with which he stopped the flow as well as he could, and a messenger was despatched for an ambulance. He waited till this arrived, and was glad to see Fred Dawson come with it.

"What has happened?" asked Fred. "I hope you haven't lost your man."

"That is just what it amounts to," answered Jack. "Webb has given us the slip, and put the sergeant on the casualty list, though I have little doubt the bullet was intended for me. Hang it! I am annoyed. If I was not so dead beat, I would mount my horse and be after him like a shot, but I haven't the strength to lift a fiddle."

"Never mind," said Dawson, consolingly; "he is gone, but perhaps it is all for the best."

Their attention was attracted by the proprietor of the club—a respectable man named Fremlin, who was throwing up his hands and beckoning to them with frantic gestures.

"Help!" he shouted, in wild and despairing tones. "There has been an attempt at murder here! Quick! it is life or death! Do not delay! Help! Help! Don't you hear! Come, for the love of Heaven!"

CHAPTER VI.

THE ATTACK ON THE AIDE-DE-CAMP— WEBB IS HOTLY PURSUED—JACK AND FRED LOST ON THE VELDT—THE BALLOON AGAIN—UP IN THE AIR— BAFFLED BOERS.

IT was clear that Fremlin was in a great state of agitation and alarm, which it would take an extraordinary occurrence to account for, as he was a stolid Free Stater, and one of the coolest men in the town.

"Something's up!" said Jack. "It seems as if our adventures will never be over. Webb's at the bottom of this, I'll lay a sovereign, or he wouldn't have been off in such a mighty big hurry."

"Come on! or Fremlin will have a fit," replied Dawson.

They ran up to the club, and were excitedly addressed by the proprietor, who explained that ten minutes previously he left Mr. Webb and Captain Sartoris in the billiard-room.

Webb had dined in the restaurant, and was anxious to play a game with someone.

The captain consented to do so, and Fremlin went to his private-room to read a paper.

He was roused by the noise of a pistol shot coming from the billiard saloon, and again by the firing in the street.

Going out, he was horrified to find the captain lying on his back, with a bullet wound in the chest.

What made the case more important was that Sartoris was the colonel's aide-de-camp, and had with him a small despatch-box containing valuable documents belonging to the Intelligence Department, which box had been abstracted.

"Come into the club, gentlemen, and do what you can for the captain while I hasten for a surgeon."

"Was there no one with him but Webb? If not, that rascally spy must be the thief, and the crime was committed to obtain the papers, which will, no doubt, be of great use to the enemy. It is really a case for the mounted police."

"That is also my opinion," rejoined Fremlin. "I have always had my suspicions about Webb, and when I saw the tin box sticking out of the captain's pocket, I said to him, with a significant look 'Pas op foor zackenrollers (Look out for pickpockets), but he only smiled, and——"

"That will do," interrupted Jack. "These particulars will keep. The thief must not be allowed to escape, nor must Sartoris bleed to death."

"Why do you not go and chase him?" continued Fremlin, excitedly. "You are everything, Mr. Harkaway—officer, scout, engine-driver, and Boer killer extraordinary. Why not, I say, chase this Webb?"

"By Jove! I wouldn't hesitate a moment if I only had my horse here," responded Jack.

"There are two horses in my stable now ready to mount; their riders are in the restaurant. Take them; I will explain. You have your cartridge-belts, and there are rifles in the hall. Ach! yes, everyone has a rifle in these hard times. Who is that I see? Thank goodness it is the town doctor running up to us. He and I will attend to Captain Sartoris."

"Good!" ejaculated Harkaway. "Let the colonel know where Mr. Dawson and I have gone, or he will wonder at our absence, and we shall get a wigging in the orderly tent for being absent without leave. Anyhow, you may expect us back before morning."

Little did Jack think, as he was speaking, that his journey was destined to be a long one, and that neither he or Dawson would see Mafeking again for some time to come.

The first thing he and Fred did was to take possession of two rifles.

They had their full water-bottles slung over their shoulders, and had a few hard army biscuits in their pockets.

It was rather an off-hand act to take the travellers' horses without permission, but it was war time, when great licence prevails, and they did not hesitate to do so.

The steeds had been given time to rest, and were tolerably serviceable cattle, capable of enduring fatigue, though not very fleet on their legs.

Mounting, they rode after Webb along a thoroughfare which was known as the old Coach Road.

This led to the large town of Lichtenburg, there branching off to Johannesburg and Pretoria.

It was now growing late, and darkness would soon overtake them.

They might expect to encounter Boers at any moment, and after riding a couple of hours without seeing anything of the man they were pursuing, they came to a halt, looking blankly at one another.

"I'm dog-tired, Fred, and fear we are on a wild goose chase. If I ride another mile I shall go to sleep in the saddle, and that's the simple truth," said young Harkaway.

"Shall we inspan, as the Boers call it, and laager ourselves behind some rock until morning?" suggested Dawson.

"I can think of nothing better. In me behold exhausted human nature. Endurance has its limits, and I suppose the strongest man gets dead beat sometimes; especially when he has had no grub to speak of all day. There is a likely looking kopje a quarter-of-a-mile off on the left; let us requisition that. I don't propose going back, because we may come across Webb to-morrow, but sleep I must."

"Agreed," said Fred. "Never give up the flag. Webb will take it easy; he is not likely to make forced marches. What he wants is to get to General Joubert, who, with several large commandoes, is supposed to be near Ladysmith and Dundee, where Generals White and Symons are with a good force of English regulars. To do this, he must cross the Orange Free State and get to the borders of Natal."

"You see," replied Jack, "the Boers have cut the railroad and the telegraph wires, so that we don't know what is going on in the outside world."

"I heard that a runner, as they call a special messenger, had come to us with despatches from Durban sent by Sir Redvers Buller."

"That accounts for the cowardly attack upon Captain Sartoris. If they contain details of Buller's plan of campaign, they will be of great use to Joubert."

"All the more reason why we should overtake Webb and get them away," answered Dawson.

They turned their horses' heads towards the kopje, picketed there when they reached it, selected a warm, dry nook for sleeping, and, after having some biscuit and water, fell into a profound slumber just as the darkness of night enveloped them, and did not wake until the sun was high in the heavens.

To their consternation they found that their horses were in a dying condition, and the filthy aasvogel was hovering over them.

They had been eating a poisonous bulbous plant called tulp.

A few of the vultures had the assurance to perch on the rock, flapping their wings, and croaking dismally.

"Confound the luck!" exclaimed Jack, munching a biscuit. "What are we to do now? If we go back for fresh horses, Webb will be miles away before we can make another start."

"It is sickening," replied Dawson, gnawing his lip. "I am getting thoroughly disheartened. War I can understand and appreciate, but spy-hunting is a soul-deadening kind of business."

"Especially when we have such a cunning fellow as Webb to deal with," put in Harkaway.

"You are right. He has the artfulness and wickedness of Old Nick. Hark!—what is that I hear in the distance?"

As he spoke Dawson put his hand to his ear and listened.

Borne upon the wind came the dull, reverberating sound of heavy guns being fired in the neighbourhood of Mafeking.

"Cronje has brought up his artillery at last," said Jack. "Our small force will have a hard time of it. Do you know your way back? I am quite lost out here."

"So am I," answered Fred, dubiously. "The worst of this country is, it is so much alike wherever you go—an arid waste. Rocks, some hills, mimosa scent, and nothing else to relieve the monotony. However, I will try and steer straight, as soon as I've had some biscuit and water."

Presently they commenced the attempt to regain their camp, and after wandering about for a couple of miles, Fred was obliged to confess that he was hopelessly out of his reckoning.

Every moment they were in danger of coming in contact with prowling Boers, who would be only too glad to give them the benefit of a bullet.

They were surrounded by small hills, which prevented them getting a view of the plain.

Rounding one of these, which was higher than the rest, they uttered an exclamation of surprise in chorus.

This was not to be wondered at, for right in front of them they saw a balloon, the car of which was securely moored by an anchor-like grapnel to a projecting piece of rock.

The balloon was made of drab-coloured silk, on which was written in red letters the name "Fiery Star."

A rope ladder, depending from the car, touched the ground, but there was no sign of anyone within.

"This is curious," cried Harkaway. "Our station master was right when he said he saw a balloon; but I didn't believe him. Who the deuce does it belong to?"

"There does not appear to be anyone at home," answered Dawson; "yet if there is, I will try to make him hear. Hullo, up above! What cheer?"

He received no answer, and the young men were fairly puzzled at the fact of finding a balloon moored on the veldt, entirely deserted.

They came to the conclusion that it must be a war balloon, belonging either to the Transvaal forces or to the Imperial Intelligence Department, as they knew that several military aeronauts had been ordered to leave Aldershot for the Cape.

"The occupants must have got out for some purpose," remarked Jack, "or an accident has happened. Suppose two men are travelling together; one may have been taken ill in the car, and the other has gone in search of assistance."

"Is there any harm in climbing up to see?" asked Dawson.

"None at all," replied Harkaway. "We can tell in a moment if it belongs to the Boers, in which case I should make it the spoil of war, and take it into our lines."

"It would be jolly useful," answered Fred. "We could take up some shrapnel shells, and drop them down on a Boer commando. By Jove! I fancy I see the Dutchmen running."

"Up we go; follow me," said Jack.

He climbed up the rope with the readiness of a sailor.

It was not the first time he had been in a car; he understood how to navigate a balloon as well as anybody, and had crossed the English Channel twice with a professional scientist.

The car they found roomy, besides being concave, and four-feet-and-a-half high.

There were several lockers for stores, blankets, a water keg, some rifles, and other things.

"It is comfortable enough," observed Dawson, "and I should have no objection at all to a cruise in high latitudes. There must be a supreme pleasure in soaring among the clouds. Set her going, Jack; she doesn't appear to belong to anybody."

"Hold on," replied Harkaway, who had picked up a diary, and was reading its contents.

"What have you got there? A book of fairy tales, or the map of another secret mine like Jarkin?"

"It sounds like, or I should say, reads like a romance," exclaimed Jack, who was deeply interested. "Listen. It begins with 'The Diary of Cyrus Vanderbilt, Citizen of the United States of America. Left Boston August 1st, arrived in Europe, Norway, on the 16th. Visited Russia and Spain, crossed Mediterranean, near Gibraltar, September 10th; stayed in Morocco, and had some lion shooting. Reached Durban October 5th; surveyed Transvaal. Preparations for war everywhere. Killed some giraffes, but have not seen any ostriches yet.'

"What do you think of that?" asked Jack, when he had finished reading.

"It is plain enough to me that the Fiery Star is private property, owned by a rich, enterprising, adventurous American gentleman, a thorough sportsman, who, tired of shooting bears and buffaloes, has extended his sphere of operations to South Africa," replied Dawson.

"I should be glad to make his acquaintance, if we stay here, though he might resent it as a liberty. Shall we risk it?"

"I'm willing to do so if you are. I should think Mr. Vanderbilt is a man worth knowing."

Scarcely had the sound of his words died away, when they were startled by the crack of a rifle, and, looking over the side of the car, they beheld a short, thin young man, in khaki dress, running at the top of his speed towards the balloon.

A rifle, with the smoke still hanging round the muzzle, was in his hand.

Looking behind him they saw a body of Boers, nearly a score in number, who were giving chase to the fugitive.

The latter, as soon as he gained the rope-ladder, went up hand over hand, agile as a monkey, and leaped into the car, where he stood dumbfounded at seeing two strangers.

His first impulse was to draw his revolver, as he took them for enemies, but Harkaway's Hussar uniform made him hesitate, and looking steadfastly at Fred, he demanded—

"Who are you, and what are you doing here?"

"Friends," replied Dawson.

Meanwhile Jack, who now saw how pressing the danger was, took upon himself to unfasten the grapnel, letting the rope drop to the ground, and, hastily throwing out a bag of ballast to allow the balloon to rise in the air, looked again at the pursuers, who were firing at the car as they ran.

CHAPTER VII.

A NEW FRIEND — OSTRICH HUNTING — A STRANGE TRICK—KRAUSE IS SEIZED—A LONG JOURNEY—IN TIME FOR THE BATTLE —HARKAWAY'S PERIL.

So rapid was the ascent of the balloon, that when the Boers got underneath, it was out of range, and they left off firing, seeing that it was a mere waste of ammunition.

Their gestures, however, showed that they were wildly excited at the strange apparition which had so suddenly come into their midst; giving the idea that they had never seen such a thing as a balloon before, unless it were in a picture.

The wind was blowing in a southerly direction, and the balloon travelled fast, Mr. Vanderbilt, the owner, fixing the altitude at a mile from the earth's surface.

He had now time to turn his attention to his new and unsought for companions, selecting Harkaway as the one to talk to.

Jack was still looking over the side of the car with much interest, for he fancied that he recognised his deadly enemy Krause among the Boers below.

If so, it was certain that Webb was not far off, as these two always acted in concert, and it was probable that he and Fred Dawson had narrowly escaped falling into their hands; but they were left far behind, and he could well afford to forget them.

"I think you owe me an explanation," said the balloonist. "You stormed my air castle, as I may term it, and to express the matter tersely, you're travelling without a ticket."

"We are willing to pay all expenses," replied Jack; "but, perhaps, first of all it will be best to exchange cards, as is usual among gentlemen."

They did so, and an explanation followed.

Cyrus Vanderbilt said that he was travelling alone, for sport and pleasure, his objective just then being ostriches.

He had descended where they found the balloon, thinking that he saw some of these creatures among the hills, but on closer investigation they turned out to be Boers.

Jack's tale was quickly told, and they soon understood one another.

"I cannot undertake to restore you to your friends at Mafeking, because the wind is blowing us away from that place, and it will not be safe to drop you either in the Transvaal or the Orange Free State, both being hostile territory, so I fear you will have to put up with life in a balloon car, such as it is, until I can land you in Natal. How would you like to go to Ladysmith, where you have a strong British garrison?"

"Nothing would suit me better," replied Jack. "My regiment, the Seventh Hussars, ought to be there, if Sir George White has not moved it to Dundee to help General Symons."

"Then consider it settled, Mr. Harkaway," rejoined Cyrus Vanderbilt. "You and your friend, Mr. Dawson, will be my guests for the next thousand miles or so in the car of the Fiery Star, and all I can add is, I hope you will enjoy the voyage."

They both thanked him for his kindness, and he prepared dinner, which did not take long, as he only had to open a can or two, and draw the cork from a bottle of wine.

While they refreshed themselves, he amused them with stories of his travels, during which he had gone through some remarkable adventures.

"I am perfectly neutral in this war," he remarked, "and would no more injure a Boer than I would a Britisher. When I was in Pretoria a little while ago I lunched with the President, and found Mr. Kruger a very decent fellow. He is not the bogey people take him for, and I suppose has a right to his opinions. He gave me a safe permit, which allows me to visit any town, though I am afraid it would be different with you, who would be looked on as spies. He named me the Ostrich-hunter. There was something about me in the papers, for the Fiery Star and I made quite a sensation. I only had one quarrel in Pretoria, which was not of my seeking."

"Who was that with?" inquired Jack.

"A fellow named Krause; perhaps you know him. He came from Mafeking on some business, and had with him a chap called Webb."

"To my sorrow, I do," said Harkaway. "He is a bloodthirsty, vindictive wretch, and Webb is a paid spy of Kruger's. He is on his way now to Ladysmith to betray us."

"I think Krause is a bag of wind more than anything else; that is how I size him up," continued Cyrus Vanderbilt.

"You are mistaken. He is as full of venom as a poisonous snake."

"I could not help laughing at the threat he made. He said: 'I'll follow you and your wonderful balloon, Mr. Ostrich-hunter, and I swear I'll let the daylight into your carcase. I hate you, because you are an American, and, since the Spanish War, the Yanks are hand in glove with the accursed Britishers.'"

"What was your reply?"

"I told him I was willing to meet him at any time, for I hadn't shot a blackguard lately, and it might do me good; and I further informed him that I could kill a fly on a wall at a thousand yards."

"Bravo!" exclaimed Fred Dawson. "That is the way to talk. Hatred is only born of contempt. Show a man that you are firm and brave, and he will respect you. But I say, Mr. Vanderbilt! weren't you talking ostrich just now?"

"If you mean that I want to hunt some you are right."

"I know something about this country, and below us is a pool of water; by the look of the ground I should say ostriches are not far off. Will you descend and try your luck?"

"By all means," replied the American, who pulled the valve, letting out some gas, and went down to the earth in a few minutes, when he threw out another anchor and made the Fiery Star fast.

Fred Dawson went out among the rocks, and was only gone ten minutes, when he came running back with the information that he had discovered a group of ten or a dozen ostriches basking in the sun, and warned Jack and Vanderbilt to be very careful how they approached, as the birds soon took the alarm.

"I should advise you also to look out for Krause," added Fred, laughing.

"Truly I feel safer in cloudland," replied Vanderbilt. "Krause means to have the ostrich-man if he can catch him, but I always keep my eyes peeled."

The three now advanced to the spot where Fred had seen the ostriches, and the American raised his rifle.

"Put a feather in your cap—go in and win!" cried Harkaway. "You shall have the first chance of scoring."

Vanderbilt smiled, and, pulling the trigger, fired, with a result which astonished him.

With the exception of one, which remained struggling on the ground, as if badly hurt, the others jumped up, and a dozen rifles gleamed in the sunshine.

The supposed ostriches were in reality Boers disguised in the skins of those birds, the feathers of which descended to their waists.

The long necks and heads were held up on pieces of broken telegraph wire, and when they were sitting down in the grass they could easily be mistaken for the feathered bipeds they pretended to represent.

The foremost among them was Krause, whose face wore an expression of demoniac glee at the success of his plan to attract the balloon and its occupants.

"Back, for your lives!" cried Fred Dawson. "It is a Boer trick, and I have been fooled by it."

They all retreated, firing as they went.

Bullets flew around them, but by a miracle they escaped unhurt until the car was reached, when Fred cried out that he was shot in the arm.

"Keep on firing, Harkaway," said the American, in a hard voice. "I'll soon settle these fellows. Keep them at bay. It's the balloon I'm afraid of."

He was up the ladder in a moment, and taking a small but deadly shell from a basket, hurled it with all his force into the midst of the Boers.

It exploded with an appalling result.

Every man was struck down, some being terribly mutilated.

"That has done the business," remarked Vanderbilt coolly, as he descended again. "I am always prepared for the worst; and they have brought their fate upon themselves. It was a clever dodge, but I never thought I should be sucked in by an ostrich."

Dawson was in great pain, and groaning heavily.

It was with some difficulty that they got him into the car and laid him on a blanket.

The American produced a box of surgical instruments; he probed for the bullet, and, with no little skill, extracted it.

The wound was sponged, a bandage fastened round it, and the sufferer became more easy.

"I'm grateful we got off as well as we did!" exclaimed Harkaway. "I thought we were in queer street when I saw the rifles and the gaitered legs of the Boers. I shall never see an ostrich feather in a lady's hat without thinking of this day. Shall we go up again now?"

"Bide a wee, as the Scotch say," replied Vanderbilt. "Give me half a mo to see if my friend Krause is alive or dead."

He went down again, and seeing that Fred was all right, Harkaway followed him.

A sickening sight presented itself when they came up to the scene of carnage.

Only three Boers remained alive, and one of these was Krause, whose forehead had been grazed by a splinter, the effect being a stunning sensation, from which he recovered as his foes approached.

The skin was cut, and his face covered with blood, which made him look hideous and repulsive.

Seeing Harkaway and Vanderbilt, the two men he hated most in the world, he picked up his rifle, which he had dropped as he fell, and, staggering to his feet, was about to fire, when Jack knocked it out of his grasp, crying: "No you don't, my boy; you are our prisoner. Where is Webb?"

"Where you won't find him," replied Krause, with a scowl. "He has passed through Lichtenburg by this time."

"I shall keep a sharp look out for him. It is a pity you should have parted, as you are such close friends; and, to tell the truth, I should like to see both of you hanging to the same tree."

"What can you do to me? I am a Boer soldier, fighting for his country and his rights."

"Liar!" retorted Jack, "you are a paid spy, and were driven out of Mafeking as a suspect. Half-a-dozen words from me would hang you any day."

"Nevertheless, it is not for you to harm me. I demand to be taken before one of your generals. Prove your case first, and afterwards talk of hanging. We are a good way from a court-martial now, and you had best say 'good-bye.'"

Cyrus Vanderbilt looked at him contemptuously, and said: "You mean specimen of white trash. Your assumed wish to go into the British lines can easily be gratified, as I can find room for you in the bottom of my car. Harkaway, shall we take him along to Dundee?"

"You can't touch pitch without being defiled; but I should like to see his neck stretched, all the same," answered Jack.

"That settles it," exclaimed Vanderbilt. "Come on, you sir. We will use you as ballast, and if you don't behave yourself I'll fire you overboard like a sky-rocket."

"This is infringing the liberty of a subject," protested Krause. "I am a free citizen, and when General Joubert is in Cape Town he will hold you responsible for this outrage. Have a care, Mr. Ostrich-man. You are going too far."

Vanderbilt's only reply was to push him along and point a revolver at his shaggy head, which had been ignorant of the tonsorial art for some long period.

Finding that there was no help for him, Krause submitted with a bad grace, and was conducted to the car, in which he was forced to take a seat.

Ballast was thrown out to equalise his weight, and the balloon once more ascended.

He was given to thoroughly understand that as long as he behaved himself he would be well treated, but at the slightest sign of mutiny, he would be shot dead.

The journey in the air was continued without any further incident.

Krause was docile.

It was Dawson's left arm that was hurt; he was unable to use it, and wore it in a sling.

The wind continued in a favourable direction, and after travelling for two days and nights they heard the sound of firing, and presently saw a British force preparing to attack an army of Boers, who were sheltered behind three successive ridges, on hilly and broken ground.

An artillery duel was proceeding, and it

was at once a terrible and splendid sight to behold the shells bursting in quick continuation.

The powder used was smokeless, and therefore the view was not obscured.

Harkaway's heart gave a big thump; like a war-horse, he sniffed the battle afar off.

The sound of the guns and the bursting of the shells was as music in his ears, and longing to be in the thick of the fight, he begged Vanderbilt to descend.

"You've got a lovely view here, and are out of danger. What more do you want?" asked the balloonist.

"Death or glory!" replied Jack. "Poor Dawson will be out of this, owing to his wound, and he can enjoy the drama from the gallery, but I must have a front seat."

"Me too," chimed in Krause. "I want to fight, with my own people."

"Not much, my fine fellow," said Vanderbilt, shaking his head. "You are to be tried as a spy, and I shall hold you until the morning. But Mr. Harkaway's desire shall be gratified, though I am loath to part with him."

The next minute the Fiery Star began to sink, and the objects below became more distinct.

As they anchored, an officer on horseback came dashing by; but he had not gone more than twenty yards, before a stray bullet, coming from the nearest ridge, struck his horse, which fell, throwing its rider to the ground.

"That is Willoughby, of ours!" exclaimed Jack, springing out of the car, at the risk of breaking his neck, and running forward to the fallen officer.

"Is that you, Harkaway? I thought you were hundreds of miles away," said Lieutenant Willoughby, a smart Hussar officer, looking in bewilderment at the balloon, which was swiftly rising in the air. "I was carrying a message from General White to French, who is in command of the Light Horse."

"Where am I, and what is going on?" asked Jack.

"This place is called Elands Laagte, and we are attacking the Boers, who are under their famous Generals, Viljoen and Koch, with Joubert somewhere in the rear. We won a battle two days ago at Glencoe, where Symons was mortally wounded."

"Glorious news," replied Jack, "but our fellows could never carry those heights."

"They've got to do it. In the front are four companies of the Devonshire Regiment, then come the Manchesters, and after them the Gordon Highlanders. In the road you can see the 21st Field Battery, the 5th Lancers, and the Natal Volunteers. As I can't get on with my message, we will, if you like, join the Gordons, and charge with them."

"Certainly," answered Harkaway. "We shall have just time to reach them without getting in the line of fire."

As they started to run, Jack heard a peal of mocking laughter not far off, and turning round, beheld, to his extreme disgust, the hated form of Krause; who, by some means had contrived to slip out of the car, as the balloon went up.

"Ha! Redneck, you have not seen the last of me. That red mark is on your forehead yet," shouted the spy in triumph, while a malignant glare flashed from his eyes.

There was no time to make any retort, and dashing forward, the two cavalry officers joined the Gordons, who were full of fire.

A part of their regiment had been at Majuba Hill, and the Boers, in derision, called them "Kaffirs in kilts," and "Majubas," which was an insult they meant to wipe out.

There was no time to salute the two volunteer officers, who, sword in hand, took the first place they could find.

The position taken by the Boers suited them admirably; as ridge after ridge had to be crossed, and small, stony boulders offered excellent cover to them.

By the railway line could be seen the long dull drab cavalry columns of the 5th Dragoon Guards and the 42nd Field Battery.

The Gordons advanced in magnificent order, and were promptly met with a heavy fire, which told from the first, as Lieutenant-Colonel Cunyngham was almost the soonest to be hit, but his gallant men pressed on.

Man after man now dropped.

Still our shooting proceeded briskly. The men darting from one cover to another, bravely led, and never lagging for a moment.

As the kilted heroes fell, rear-rank men reinforced the firing line, but alas! when the final ridge was neared, almost every officer was down.

The bugles were sounding, bag-pipes shrieking, rifles cracking, shells bursting, and the men yelling like demons.

Gordons, Manchesters, Devons, and dismounted Light Horse were all mixed.

Now ensued a hand-to-hand fight.

The Boers had fought gallantly, and fired remarkably well, as they always do, but they could not stand the onslaught of cold steel, and fled before the bayonets of the brawny Highlanders, who literally forked them out of their shelters.

Harkaway and Willoughby performed prodigies of valour, fighting side by side, and were lucky enough to escape the storm of bullets which had been raining around them.

"What price Majuba?" cried Harkaway, cutting down a brawny Boer, over six feet in height.

Down the hill rushed those of the enemy who had survived the charge, and dozens of them fell before our fire.

The Gordons had suffered heavily, and so had the Devons, but those who came out of the action alive had the proud consciousness of knowing that they had contributed largely to the brilliant victory gained by our arms.

"We have done all we can here, and thank heaven we got out with a whole skin!" exclaimed Lieutenant Willoughby. "It was the hottest work I have ever heard of. What a lot of officers are killed. I can see a troop of the 18th Hussars in the road, forming, as if they were going to pursue the foe; and I can also perceive some riderless Boer horses."

"What good are they to us?" asked Harkaway.

"Let us capture a couple and join the 18th. I have not had half enough fun yet."

Jack laughed, but consented to do as Willoughby suggested.

Picking their way through dead and dying, they caught two horses, and mounting, rode after the Hussars, but before they could overtake them night came on, accompanied by heavy rain. Not knowing where they were, they halted. All was still as the grave.

Firing had ceased, for the battle of Elands Laagte had been fought and won.

The position of Harkaway and his brother officer was critical in the extreme.

CHAPTER VIII.

THE LIGHT IN THE CAVE—A DYING SOLDIER —THE NIGHT WATCH—SURPRISED BY THE ENEMY—KRAUSE'S REVENGE—JACK IS TO BE SHOT AS A SPY.

THE night was very dark: not a star was visible.

Harkaway and Lieutenant Willoughby were enveloped as if with a pall, for inky blackness had suddenly descended upon them.

The rain came down in driving sheets of water, aided by gusts of wind, and the two were soon soaked to the skin.

This night on the veldt was anything but a pleasant experience, and they wished sincerely that they were back in the British camp.

They could neither advance or retreat, for they were hopelessly lost.

If they groped their way in the darkness, they might rush into the arms of the Boers.

What had become of the detachment of the 18th Hussars they could not imagine, though it was more than likely they had gone too far, and been captured.

They knew that the ground in front of them was dangerous to travel over at night.

It was full of dongas (a deep ditch).

There were also spruits (a small river or stream), and ponds or small lakes, all of which are extremely awkward for horses.

"Dismount," said Jack, gloomily. "We can't ride any further. To do so will be to risk a broken neck or limb ; and unpleasant though it may be, we shall have to pitch on the ground. We are birds without a nest."

"I feel a very damp, miserable kind of bird, and don't you forget it," replied Willoughby. "I haven't a dry rag on me ; but I am an old campaigner, and have seen worse nights than this. We have won a victory, and must live on glory until something turns up."

"It isn't very filling," answered Harkaway. "I'd rather have a tin of beef. But, I say, if I am not dreaming, I can see a light in front of me. It seems as if it came from a kopje ; this valley is full of them. We will advance cautiously."

"Take care," said Willoughby, warningly. "It may be a Boer fire."

"Not likely. The rain would soon put any camp-fire out ; besides, there is no wood about here to light one with. Follow me ; I'll show you the way."

They got off their horses, not caring if they wandered away, as they had no further use for them.

Gradually approaching the light, keeping their hands in touch with their revolvers, they at length found themselves at the entrance to a small cave, in which they perceived a trooper of the Hussars stretched upon the sandy floor.

Bending over him, and trying to staunch the blood which flowed from a wound in the breast, was a corporal of the Army Service, formerly known as the Hospital Corps.

On a ledge of rock stood a lantern, by the side of which was a water-bottle and some provisions.

"Halt ! who goes there ? " cried the corporal, roused by the sound of footsteps, and springing up, his eyes dilating and his lips quivering.

"British officers lost in the rain," replied Jack.

The Army Service man came to attention at once, and saluted.

He explained that he had gone out with an ambulance to pick up the wounded.

A party of Boers, paying no respect to the flag, fired upon them.

He was separated from his comrades, and, seeking his way home, he came across the wounded Hussar.

Night fell all at once, and not knowing what to do, he was attracted by a light in the cave, which he presumed was a Boer hiding-place.

Being desperate, he determined to run all risks, and dragged the wounded soldier into the shelter, which he was glad to find untenanted, though he knew it had been recently used, or the lamp would not have been left burning, nor would the bread, water, and biltong (strips of dried meat) have been left on the shelf.

"My name is Simpson, sir, and I've been four years in the service," continued the corporal ; "but though I've seen fighting in Chitral, this is the tightest fix I've been in yet. I'm a Guildford man, and if some of my mates could see me now they'd open their eyes a bit. Still, where there is life there is hope, though I can't see much for this poor fellow. He is bleeding internally, with one of those ugly Lee-Metford bullets inside of him."

He pointed to the Hussar, who was gasping and catching his breath, his lips being stained with blood.

His jacket was open, and the little red wound was distinctly visible.

Hanging round his neck by a piece of faded blue ribbon was a small silver Maltese Cross.

He contrived to raise his hand and touch it with his finger, and looked pleadingly with his lack-lustre eyes at Harkaway.

"Do you wish to speak to me, my lad ? " asked Jack, addressing the young soldier, who was not more than twenty.

"Yes, sir," replied the Hussar, faintly. "This trinket was the gift of the girl I left behind me, and I should like her to know that Harry Marner—that's me, Number 13,011—thought of her when he was dying. I should like the cross buried with me. I die for my country, but the cross comes before the flag."

He paused a moment to gain breath, and a tear rolled down his cheek.

"Her name's Rosie, sir," he went on, " Rose Barns. She lives at Maidstone, that's where I come from. Tell her I loved her to the last, and have been always true. I—I can't say any more; but you—you know what I mean, sir. It won't hurt you to say a word over me. How dark it is getting!"

A film was coming over the eyes of the dying man.

His voice was so inarticulate as to be scarcely audible.

Jack, Willoughby, and the corporal uncovered their heads, which they bowed in the presence of that strange power which levels all, while their lips moved.

It was an affecting scene.

They were all young, and far from home and friends; neither of them could tell when his turn would come.

The Hussar did not last long, and when the breath had left his body, they carried him reverently to a corner, and closed his eyes.

The dried meat and the water-bottle next engaged their attention, for they were nearly famished, and so engrossed were they with the danger of their situation that they soon forgot a comrade had passed away from them.

Such is war, with all its attendant horrors.

"I shall fight if we are attacked," exclaimed Jack, biting a piece of the hard, tough biltong. "We can hold this cave against a dozen."

"I hope it won't come to that," replied Lieutenant Willoughby. "With the first streak of dawn we can make a bold dash for our camp."

Harkaway agreed with this, and only hoped they would have the opportunity.

They arranged for a two-hours' watch, Corporal Simpson taking the first turn, Willoughby to be the next, and Jack the last.

It was about two in the morning when the latter was roused.

Leaning against the rock Jack looked outside, but could distinguish nothing, the darkness being made more intense by the light within.

As the time went by the vigil seemed long and weary.

He was more nervous and excited than he had been in the rush and din of battle.

It was a relief to his anxiety when the eastern sky was streaked with grey, and the sun rose in a bright, yellow blaze.

The rain had ceased falling, and the big guns were silent.

Both sides were taking a rest after the hard fighting of yesterday.

It was the hush before the storm.

Each army had lost heavily; but quietude could not last long, as Joubert had to exert himself to the utmost to crush the small British force before Sir Redvers Buller sent up fresh men.

"Wake up," cried Jack; "it is time to be stirring."

The lieutenant and Corporal Simpson were soon on their feet.

"Is the coast clear?" enquired Willoughby, rubbing his eyes.

"There is such a mist hanging over the Boers' position that I can't see plainly, though the wind is driving it rapidly to the west, and I think we may chance a run."

"Hold on! What's that?" cried Lieutenant Willoughby.

Half-a-dozen dull, grey-looking forms appeared from behind a boulder, and, seeing the three Englishmen, they raised their rifles; but before they could discharge them Harkaway shouted "Fire!"

The Army Service man had no weapon, but Jack and Willoughby each dropped their man.

Bullets were quickly returned, and the two officers beat a retreat into the cave.

Corporal Simpson was hit in the leg, and fell down outside.

The next moment they saw the muzzle of a machine gun, which had been dragged up within a few yards of the cave's entrance, and a loud voice exclaimed:

"Surrender, or you will be riddled with shot."

"It's a case of throwing up the sponge," said Harkaway. "We can't fight Maxims."

"Confound it," replied Willoughby, biting his lip with vexation. "Hang the luck, I say. They will send us to Pretoria, and we shall be out of the game. No more fun; no more honour. Simply stagnation."

It was, indeed, a reverse of fortune.

Reluctantly they walked outside, where they saw a force of at least a hundred Boers, led by a tall, stout man on horseback, and by his side was Jack's old enemy, Krause, whom Harkaway devoutly wished was back in Mafeking.

"I am General Van Nort," exclaimed the commander, "and you have done well for yourselves to come forth at my bidding. Your wounded companion shall be attended to, and you will be taken to the rear to be sent in a few hours by train to Pretoria with other prisoners. I see by your dress that belong to the cavalry, and you will no doubt be surprised to hear that we have captured a troop of your famous Hussars, who rode into our lines last night by mistake."

"It is the fortune of war, general," replied Harkaway, assuming an air of indifference which he was far from feeling.

"When an officer makes a blunder, we call it a military crime, for which there is no excuse," answered Van Nort, bluntly. "War is a perilous game, and a soldier cannot afford to make a mistake. However, you will be treated with all the respect your position deserves."

Three soldiers placed themselves on each side of the prisoners to form a guard.

They were ready to fire at a moment's notice.

"One moment, general, if you please," said Krause, whose eyes scintillated with gratified malice.

"What is it now?" inquired Van Nort, bending his shaggy eyebrows and looking keenly at the burgher.

"The man you have been addressing is the notorious spy, Harkaway. He knows me as well as I do him," explained Krause. "We were at Mafeking together. Cronje was going to shoot him, but he escaped. Sometimes he is in a balloon, spying out our movements. He has all sorts of disguises, and it is difficult to tell what he is; but I'll swear he's not a British officer. Yesterday he was got up like one of ourselves, and I saw him on the hill tampering with the breech of one of our sixteen-inch guns. Perceiving me, he fled. Shoot him, by all means, or you will regret your clemency. And I should treat his companion the same, as he is sure to be one of the same kidney."

"Is it true that your name is Harkaway?" enquired Van Nort.

"Yes, general," replied Jack. "I am a lieutenant in the 7th Hussars; and it is also true that I was at Mafeking, on the staff of Colonel Baden-Powell. I have only just arrived at Ladysmith, and have not had time to report myself at headquarters."

"Can you refer me to your general, Sir George White?"

"He thinks I am miles away; but you can trust to my honour, as an officer and a gentleman, when I tell you that I am no spy, as this villain alleges."

"At least, sir, you can tell me what you are doing here."

"I and my friend here, Lieutenant Willoughby, charged the heights yesterday with the Gordon Highlanders, and got lost in the darkness."

"I am not at all satisfied with the account you give of yourself," said Van Nort, sternly. "Krause I know to be a true Boer to the backbone, and would rather take his word than yours. He has fought and bled for the Vierkleur (the four-coloured Transvaal flag). I convict you on his statement, and it is my painful duty to order you to be shot."

"Good Heaven!" cried Harkaway, astounded, "do you call this civilised warfare?"

"We have to be smart with you rednecks, or we should soon be crushed. Our experience has proved that there is nothing too mean or contemptible for a Britisher to do."

"But, my good fellow, this won't do at all," protested Harkaway.

"I have pronounced sentence," interrupted Van Nort. "It is useless for you to say any more."

The doom was so sudden that Jack and Willoughby thought they must be dreaming, until they were forced on their knees by the soldiers, their arms being bound behind them and their eyes blindfolded with bandages of coarse linen.

They had not even time to say farewell to one another.

Krause saw to the pinioning and the blindfolding.

"Ah!" he whispered, in Harkaway's ear, with a harsh, grating sound, "my threat has come true sooner than you expected. I put the red mark on you."

"I care not," replied Harkaway. "Your lies and hatred will come home to you."

"I can save you even now," added Krause. "Tell me where I can find the plan of the Jarkin Mine, which was given you by the Jew Malachi."

Jack had the map in his pocket, for it had never been out of his possession, and he determined to baffle the Boer if he could.

"It is where you will never find it," he said. "If after the war is over I cannot enjoy the wealth it contains, I am sure you shan't."

"Die, dog!" hissed Krause, his cadaverous face assuming a fiendish look.

A firing-party had been told off, and, hearing the click of their rifles, Krause retired to witness a tragedy which would be nothing short of a murder.

Harkaway and Lieutenant Willoughby resigned themselves to their fate.

CHAPTER IX.

GENERAL JOUBERT'S CLEMENCY — HARKAWAY CONCEIVES A BOLD IDEA—A RACE BETWEEN TWO LOCOMOTIVES—A CLEVER DEVICE—THE COLLISION—A NEW DANGER.

IT was an awful moment for the condemned men, and the silence of the pathless veldt was so intense that Harkaway could hear his heart beat.

"Good-bye, Willoughby, old fellow," he murmured. "I can't see you, but I know you're not far off."

"God bless you, Harkaway," replied the lieutenant. "We are going to take the long journey. Hurrah for the old flag!"

"Make ready!" cried General Van Nort in a stentorian voice.

The soldiers raised their rifles to their shoulders and deliberately sighted their victims, intending to aim for the head and heart.

Before the general could give the order to fire, an officer, who had been riding over the plain at full speed, dashed up.

He wore a spiked helmet, and was evidently one high in command; in fact it was General Joubert, the chief of the Boer Army.

"Hold!" he thundered, at the top of his voice. "What are you doing here, Van Nort, when you should be with your command on Kop Hill?"

"I was only looking out for stragglers, general," replied Van Nort, "and having caught two English spies, I ordered them to be executed."

"How do you know they are spies?" demanded Joubert, sharply.

"On the authority of our excellent friend, Krause, who knew them well in Mafeking. They have come from Powell to White; but, if it is your pleasure, they shall be released."

General Joubert nodded his head, and the prisoners were at once set free, being overwhelmed with joy at such an unlooked for event.

Harkaway lost no time in giving an account of himself and his friend Willoughby.

"Do you know any of the officers of the 18th Hussars who will vouch for your good faith and the rank you claim in the British Army?" asked Joubert.

"I am acquainted with all of them," replied Jack, "having frequently dined at their mess. My regiment has been brigaded with them more than once."

"That is enough. I can see that Krause is labouring under a mistake. We were lucky last night in capturing a squadron of your Horse. You can go to the rear and be sent with them to Pretoria at once, so your troubles will cease until the war is over. If we go on as well as we are beginning, you will have plenty of companions in misfortune, for I fully expect to capture Ladysmith and its defenders before long."

"Don't make too sure of that, general. We have an Army Corps on the sea."

"Bah! what is the use of that?" said General Joubert, contemptuously. "I shall be in Cape Town before they arrive, and our good friends, the Russians and French, will step in and put a stop to the war. South Africa is for the Boers, not for the English. Your General Buller will have to take his men home again, and you Britishers will have to pay the bill for all the expense and inconvenience you have put us to."

"I am glad that you are of so sanguine a turn of mind," remarked Jack, quietly; "but I don't mind betting you a new hat, general, that Buller hoists the English flag in Pretoria before Christmas."

"I shall consider that a bet, young gentleman, and will not fail to remind you of it," answered Joubert, with a good-natured smile. "But you must excuse me; I cannot waste time. It is necessary that I should speak to General Van Nort."

Jack bowed politely, and, as a soldier ordered him to fall in by his side, he heard Joubert exclaim:

"Since we lost the German officer Schiel, at Elands Laagte, you are our best artilleryman. We want a good gunner to serve our forty-pounder, which the enemy call Long Tom. My plan is to bombard Ladysmith, until White makes a desperate sortie or surrenders. But a serious difficulty has arisen."

"What is that?" queried Van Nort, curiously.

"A spy has just come in with news that a Naval Brigade has arrived from Durban, with long-distance guns, superior to our own."

"You should have torn up the railway and cut the telegraph wire."

"That has been done this morning. Ladysmith is isolated, and I have a force closing in on Colenso. There will be hot work before many days are over."

Jack could hear no more, as he and Willoughby were hurried away.

As they walked along they saw many bodies, both Boer and British.

The wounded had been removed, but there had been no time to collect or bury the dead, who were lying stark, cold, and drenched with the rain, on the dreary ground.

A march of a few miles brought them to a siding, on the line of railway going to Pretoria.

There were a few wooden sheds, and a long train, with two engines, was in waiting.

Here they found a number of officers and troopers of the 18th Hussars lounging about, chatting and smoking, preparatory to starting for their long internment.

The officers shook hands cordially and sympathisingly with Harkaway and Willoughby, whom they knew well.

Krause had disappeared. His malicious intent had failed; but Jack knew that he had not by any means got rid of him, and might expect another attack at any moment.

"This is a bad job, Harkaway," said Captain Wilson, who was in command of the squadron.

"How did it happen," inquired Jack. "Did you fellows go to sleep in the saddle?"

"We were wide awake enough," answered the captain, "but we could not see our way, and rode deliberately into the enemies' lines. There was nothing for it but to throw down our arms."

"That was just the case with me," replied Harkaway. "Doesn't it make a man savage

to think of it. I could bite the hilt off my sword."

"It's a crying shame that we, who are a mere handful of men, should be left to defend the Natal frontier against an overwhelming army of truculent Boers, who hate us like poison for nothing at all, and have declared war against us before the home government was ready," continued Captain Wilson, bitterly.

"Of course we shall lick them in the end," replied Harkaway, "but the odds against us are terrible at present."

"It was always thus with our War Office; always Red Tape, my boy, and the Circumlocution Office. I am an old stager, and not a beardless boy like some of you chaps. I can go back to the Crimean War and the Indian Mutiny."

"Don't growl!" said Jack. "It wasn't the fault of the War Office that you lost your way and got caught in a trap. I only blame myself for the fix I'm in, and what's more, I don't mean to stick it."

"What are you going to do?" asked the captain, elevating his eyebrows in surprise.

"Wait a little while and you'll see," answered Jack. "I must go and talk to Willoughby. We are both in the same boat, and I think he'll sink or swim with me."

The lieutenant was sitting on an empty packing-case, close to one of the sheds we have mentioned.

He was pensively smoking a cigar.

The guards were not taking much notice of the prisoners of war, for their arms had been taken away from them, and they could not break out into any revolt.

There were two engine-drivers and two stokers for each locomotive.

Steam was up, and these men were eating their dinner in a shady spot.

"A penny for your thoughts!" exclaimed Jack, touching the lieutenant on the shoulder.

"You shall have them for nothing," replied Willoughby. "I was wondering how the deuce we could get out of this hole."

"I can enlighten your darkness if you have the pluck to follow me; but I needn't ask that, for courage is a quality you were never deficient in."

"Thank you for the compliment. Our amily are known as the fighting Willoughbys. You will always find some of us in the Army or Navy. What is the idea, my young and intelligent friend?"

"Simply this," answered Jack; "there are two engines attached to this train, which is intended to convey us to Pretoria or some other sweet place of retirement, where we shall be caged up like a lot of monkeys, to be stared at by the populace, free, gratis, for nothing. If we were on show at a shilling a head it would be more flattering, but to be grinned at without any charge is more than I can stand."

"That is exactly what sticks in my throat. Fancy an English Hussar being on a fool's parade all day! It has taken me down a peg or two, I can tell you."

"Our guards are not watching us," whispered Harkaway, eagerly. "I propose that we uncouple the foremost engine, get on board, and make a dash for freedom."

"By Jove! that is capital," cried Willoughby in admiration. "But how far do you intend to run the machine?"

"Oh, twenty or thirty miles up the line; then we can jump off and tramp back to Ladysmith. Will you do it?"

"Like a bird," rejoined the lieutenant. "Of course we run the risk of being shot, but the cab of the engine will protect us to some extent, and once we have got a lead I shan't care."

"All right. Stay where you are, and watch my movements. When you see me hold up my hand, it will be a signal for you to come on board the engine. Don't hurry; show no sign of being in a fluster. Act as coolly as if you were trooping the colours at the Horse Guards on the Queen's birthday."

With these words, Harkaway walked carelessly along the line, until he came to the first locomotive.

Getting behind the tender, he uncoupled it without making any noise.

No sooner had he accomplished this task than he stepped on the engine and waved his hand to Willoughby, who at once responded by coming forward and joining him.

In the tender was a quantity of coal, over which some rough mats had been thrown for some purpose or another by the engineer.

No one seemed to pay any attention to them.

The heat of the sun was excessive, and the guards looked as indolent as their prisoners.

"Now, then," said Jack, in a low tone, "we will shoot Niagara, or suppose we are going to the Cape to Cairo; but that we can't do, as the line isn't made yet; and only exists in the fertile imagination of Mr. Rhodes."

"I don't care if we drive to Jericho, as long as we get out of this, and get the laugh on General Joubert," replied Willoughby.

Harkaway laid his hand on the lever and started the engine slowly.

Just at that critical moment, two or three of the mats in the tender to which we have alluded were moved, and the head of a red-faced, burly Boer popped up.

"What was you doing there, my friends?" he inquired, raising himself on his elbow and blinking like an owl in the sunshine, without noticing that the engine was gliding away.

"Just having a look round, that's all," replied Willoughby, who was the nearest to him, with praiseworthy presence of mind.

"You two has got to get off that engine, so I tell you," continued the man; "you will have enough of it before you get to Johnisburg. Ha, ha!"

"Shake hands, old fellow. I should like to know you better before we part. This is a fine engine. Was it made in Germany?"

"Mind your own business, or I will talk to you in the jaal (the Low-Dutch language spoken by the Boers) in a way you won't like, my young springbok."

Willoughby by this time had got close to the Boer, and taking up a lump of coal, struck him on the head.

The man fell back, but he had strength enough left to raise a tremendous outcry.

"Help! Murder!" he yelled.

"Oh, you want a little bit more of it, do you?" said Willoughby, who hit him the second time, and silenced him effectually, rendering him senseless and covered with blood.

"Forge ahead, Jack, old man," he exclaimed. "Look out for bullets. We shall have the beggars down on us in a minute."

His prediction was correct.

The Boers had heard the cry of their companion, and instantly sprang to their arms, hurrying down to the line in confusion to find out what had happened; but the sight of the swiftly receding engine and the two fugitives upon the stand opened their eyes in a remarkably short space of time.

They raised their rifles, and began to fire.

Harkaway had opened the throttle valve, and the engine was fairly jumping over the rails.

"Lie low," said Jack, "we shall soon be out of range."

They both crouched down, and the bullets flew harmlessly over them, or flattened themselves against the ironwork.

It was truly a desperate ride for life.

It was a clear course, however, for there was nothing ahead.

The fugitives could not return the fire directed upon them, for their weapons had been taken away.

The Boers were furious; they seemed to be like a set of madmen.

It takes a great deal to ruffle the serenity of a Transvaaler, but on this occasion they were fairly put out, and did not try to conceal their vexation and annoyance.

They waved their arms, and shouted themselves hoarse.

At length four of them rushed frantically to the remaining engine, which they boarded.

Others uncoupled it, and soon the second engine was pursuing the first.

Jack could see the English prisoners clapping their hands to show their delight at the clever stratagem devised by Harkaway on the spur of the moment; and he fancied he heard them wishing him good speed.

The race between the two engines was very exciting.

Jack certainly had an excellent start, which, in sporting parlance, may be termed a time allowance of ten minutes; but it was clear that the Boers possessed a more powerful locomotive than the other.

It was a level grade, with the rails as straight as a bee-line, and before the chase had continued a mile, Jack saw that they were slowly, but surely, being overhauled.

He piled on more coals, and put on a full head of steam, but it was of no avail.

The Boers crept up inch by inch, and the result could not be doubtful.

After this daring attempt at escape, if captured, Harkaway and Willoughby could expect no mercy.

The Boers would certainly shoot them with as little compunction as they would a couple of buzzards; and Jack had to puzzle his brain once more, or his dream of freedom would have a rude awakening.

"What are we going to do now?" asked Willoughby. "These villains are after us in hot haste, and in another minute or two we shall hear the crack of their rifles. We are no sooner out of one pitfall than we get into another."

"That's the worst of it," replied Harkaway. "I shouldn't care if we could only give them as good as they sent. If we don't look out there will be a flying, runaway engine, with a couple of corpses on board, labelled respectively Harkaway and Willoughby, without a funeral note, neither a volley or the sound of a drum. We shall be alone in our glory; but I think I can baffle them yet."

"How in the name of all that's wonderful are you going to do that? If we could fly they would shoot us on the wing. I will admit that you are a modern magician, and have the wand of the necromancer, but——"

He paused abruptly, and looked enquiringly at his friend, who replied:

"This is a time for deeds, not words."

The line passed through a series of hills, which, as far as Jack could judge, extended for several miles, affording excellent cover.

"If I slacken speed," he said, slowly and thoughtfully, "can you jump off with safety to yourself, by accommodating your movement to that of the engine?"

"I have got off a horse at full gallop without being hurt, if that will do," replied Willoughby.

"Very well. When I give the word, down you go, and get behind a kopje as quickly as possible. Not another word now, I want to keep a clear head, and judge my distance."

Onward flew the engine, like a thing of life, and it made Jack feel how much of the man there was in him.

He looked back, and saw two Boers with their rifles at the present, ready to fire as soon as they got near enough.

Jack opened the furnace-door and raked the burning coals together, sending a shower of sparks through the funnel. The engine jumped and rocked to such an extent that it was with difficulty they maintained their footing. It was fitted with a patent brake of great strength and immediate action. This he examined carefully.

"Isn't she a beauty?" observed Jack. "She travels like a streak of lightning. You can feel her leap."

"Bravo!" said Willoughby. "The trouble is we have another of the same sort behind us, and a trifle better. You have got her racing speed up."

"Of course, I have, and she's doing her best, pretty dear," replied Jack with a laugh. "But look out, dear old chappie, I am going to stop her in a minute."

The line now went round a curve, and it seemed ten to one that the engine would go off, but it did not.

The corner was turned safely and the pursuers were out of sight; yet there was no time to be lost, as they would quickly come up.

Shutting off steam, Harkaway applied the brake, and put it hard down, jamming it tightly. Speed began to lessen sensibly, and and it was evident that in a brief space the engine would come to a standstill.

"Jump for your life!" cried Jack, whose voice was scarcely to be heard amidst the hiss of the escaping steam and the jarring, grating sound of the huge iron wheels under the brakes.

Willoughby was the first to get down, which he did without stumbling, and Harkaway was not a second in following him.

Quitting the line they ran behind a hill. The engine stopped within a distance of a hundred-and-fifty yards, and the panting machine looked like a stationary automobile.

The Boers, wholly unaware of the trick which had been played upon them, dashed round the corner in splendid style.

When, to their amazement, they beheld the motionless locomotive, they tried to stop their own; but for some reason the brake refused to work at the first endeavour, and when it did move it was too late.

The pace they were going at was so great that to jump off would be to court certain death.

Swearing and cursing, they were carried on to their doom.

The inevitable collision came with tremendous force, and the crash of the two engines could be heard a mile off.

The first was knocked clean off the track, and the second, rearing up, fell smashed and splintered on its side, its four occupants being killed outright, lying mangled on the ground in a cloud of steam.

As soon as the vapour cleared off, Jack and Willoughby approached the fatal spot, and picked up a couple of the dead Boers' rifles.

They also took from them their cartridge-belts, which made them feel to some extent independent.

"We scored that time," exclaimed Harkaway. "I may say I made a very good drive for four off my own bat, and have done some damage to the rolling stock, and now I suppose we must get across this arid plain, and see if we can't regain our cantonments."

"It will be a dangerous journey," answered Willoughby. "Let us climb up this hill and have a look round us. I should not like to run right into the arms of a party of Boer foragers or scouts."

Jack made no objection.

They walked on, with their heads in the air, not looking at the ground, and Willoughby pitched into an ant-hill four feet high, while Jack, trying to save him, fell down on another.

The lively little insects got into their clothes, and for hours afterwards they felt as if they were plagued with prickly heat.

Gaining the summit of the hill, they were much concerned to see coming towards them a troop of mounted Boers, about a score in number.

They crouched down to conceal themselves, but loud shouts indicated that they had been seen, and the next moment the Boers, setting spurs to their horses, galloped towards the hill, firing as they came.

CHAPTER X.

DEATH OF WILLOUGHBY — THE LYDDITE SHELL — JACK IS SAVED — PIGEON POST — THE GENERAL'S CONFIDENCE — A NEW MISSION — THE DANGEROUS JOURNEY.

THE mounted Boers seen by Harkaway and Lieutenant Willoughby advanced towards the hill with alarming rapidity, urging their horses to the top of their speed. Their sight was very keen, and they had not failed to distinguish the uniform worn by the British officers.

Sheltering themselves as well as they were able, the young men fired at the advancing foe, and had the satisfaction of seeing two Boers fall from their saddles; but the others pressed on, undismayed by the fate of their companions.

They did not ride in a solid body, but were separated by several yards of ground.

At times they made their horses swerve and curvet, so that it was extremely difficult to hit them, and the defenders of the hill wasted many of their bullets.

"They intend to take us in the rear. I am afraid; if so it is all up with us, for we haven't got eyes in the back of our heads," exclaimed Harkaway.

"Keep on firing, we are not dead yet," replied Willoughby. "We must fight to the end, whatever that may be. Down goes another. That was a good shot of yours, now I will see what I can do."

He was lying on his side, and his rifle rested on a slight rocky projection.

In order to get a better view of the enemy he raised himself up on his elbow, exposing himself more than was prudent.

Scarcely had he done so than a ball struck him on the forehead, killing him instantly.

"Good Heaven!" cried Jack, horrified; "this is war with a vengeance. Little do our people at home know what we are going through out here."

An awful feeling of loneliness crept over Harkaway as he gazed sadly upon the face of his dead friend and gallant partner in danger.

The features were not distorted, but wore a frightened, startled look, as if he had seen something unutterably dreadful, which had convulsed his mind.

The sensation experienced by Jack was that of the abomination of desolation.

It was not fear, or anything akin to it; but he felt as if he had not a friend in the world, and did not care whether he lived or died.

"Poor Willoughby!" he groaned. "Well, he died like a soldier."

Still, Jack went on firing like a machine, slipping the cartridges into the breech as calmly as if he had been shelling peas.

The Boers had now reached the base of the hill, having lost only five of their number.

They dismounted, and were preparing to scale the eminence.

The sides were irregular, and afforded them excellent shelter, and unless he stood up, Jack had no chance whatever of hitting them.

To show himself would have been fatal, so he grasped his rifle firmly and awaited the onset.

He knew that his foes were every minute drawing closer to him, but he could not see them.

He was in as much danger as if fifteen venomous serpents were gliding up the hills in sinuous folds.

All at once it seemed as if a shadow came between Harkaway and the sun.

Looking up to ascertain the cause of this phenomenon, he was astonished, but at the same time delighted to perceive a balloon which, from its colour and shape of the car, he recognised to be the Fiery Star, belong-

ing to Mr. Vanderbilt, the American millionaire.

The Boers also saw it, and fired some shots at the car, but it was too high up in the air for them to do any injury.

Someone in the car was waving a small flag.

In answer to this display, or signal, as Jack took it to be, he placed his cap on the muzzle of his gun, and elevated it by way of answer.

When he took it down, he found that three Boer bullets had gone through it, which showed what would have happened if his head had been inside.

At the same moment a dark substance, which resembled a ball, was dropped from the balloon.

It descended with remarkable velocity, and struck that portion of the hill up which the Boers were climbing.

As it did so, it exploded with a loud noise, the fragments flying in all directions.

It emitted a noxious vapour, which was so deadly that all those within a hundred-and-fifty yards who inhaled it were suffocated by the fumes.

This was what is known as a lyddite shell, and the vapour was that of picric acid.

Needless to say, it is the most formidable weapon of modern warfare.

It instantly destroyed all the Boers but two, who stood dazed and bewildered, with upturned faces, looking at the sky, wondering what the havoc-working thing was, and whence it came.

Quick as a dart, Harkaway sent a couple of bullets at them, ending their career, after which he waved his cap, and, to relieve his pent-up feelings, gave vent to a mighty shout, which was echoed from the clouds.

"Hurrah! Hurrah!"

The Fiery Star now began to descend with great rapidity.

Watching it, Jack saw Cyrus Vanderbilt and Fred Dawson, who were waving their hands, while by their side was a boy, whose head just reached over the side of the car.

"By jove," muttered Jack, "that looks like my little bugler, Andy Pearson, who I left in Mafeking! This is most extraordinary! Anyhow, they arrived just in the nick of time to save me, for I thought it was a case of being up an apple tree, with the farmer and his bulldog at the foot."

He was so overjoyed that he burst out laughing; then he sat down, for the reaction made him feel faint.

Soon the grapnel caught the ground, the rope ladder was lowered, and he contrived to ascend into the car, where he was quickly shaking hands cordially with his friends.

The American caused the balloon to rise again, and she was soon sailing along towards Ladysmith, the positions occupied by the Boer forces being distinctly visible as they passed over them.

"We did not hope to see you so soon," exclaimed Vanderbilt, "but fancied we should meet you in Ladysmith if you got out of the battle all right. We have been over the veldt since we left you, and had some sport among the ostriches, which you know is my hobby. Our great regret was that Krause managed to escape."

"I fired a couple of shots at him, but the

"JACK FELL HEAVILY, AND WAS AT THE MERCY OF HIS FOE, WHO PRESENTED HIS MAUSER AT HIS HEAD."

No. 3.

beggar seems to bear a charmed life," said Fred Dawson.

"How is it that I find my little friend Andy here?" asked Jack.

"The faithful fellow followed you on to the veldt, and toiled on for days, hoping to find you. We picked him up, exhausted with fatigue and hunger, but I guess he will forget all his troubles now he is once more with his master."

Jack patted him on the back, thanking him for his devotion, and related his late perilous adventures.

Fred made a neat sketch of the Boers' camps, which were more than one in number, as they were day by day surrounding Ladysmith.

This he intended for General White.

While they were talking they became interested in the movements of a pigeon, which was flying feebly against the wind.

It seemed to have lost its way, and looked very tired.

As the balloon approached, the bird, which was of the carrier species, alighted on the edge of the car, and was easily captured by Fred Dawson, who had recovered from the wound in his arm.

He did not intend to hurt it, and was about to lay it down on a rug so that it might recover its strength, when Harkaway noticed a piece of paper tied to one of its legs, by means of some silk.

"Hold it tight, Fred," he cried. "This is a pigeon post, and may prove a lucky capture, and has been sent by some spy in Ladysmith, probably to a friend in Pretoria, who would at once communicate with General Joubert. This is how our plans are betrayed to the enemy."

"I should not have thought of that," remarked Vanderbilt. "I guess you are a mighty cute fellow, Harkaway."

Jack smiled at the compliment, and gently unfastening the silk, took the paper from the bird's leg, allowing the latter to flutter to the bottom of the car, where it rested peacefully.

The writing was very small, but Vanderbilt lent him a magnifying glass, by the aid of which he read the contents without difficulty.

They ran as follows:

From Mrs. Steyner's house, 16, Fairmount Street, Ladysmith.

"I have arrived in this town, pretending to be an Outlander refugee, and have found shelter with our kind and loyal friend, Mrs. Steyner, who is also the hostess of Skiller, the German, who is only waiting for a chance to assassinate General White. I have found out that the English are expecting a Naval Brigade from Durban, which is only one-hundred-and-fifty miles distant, with new guns firing lyddite shells. The sailors are coming from Her Majesty's ships 'Powerful' and 'Terrible.' Wire this to Joubert at once, as they ought to be stopped on the way, and never be allowed to reach Ladysmith, which would be disastrous to our cause. I will write again, as soon as anything transpires. Believe me, now, as ever, your faithful spy, in heart and soul, Webb.

"For President Kruger, immediate and confidential."

"It is very fortunate indeed that you have intercepted this despatch," exclaimed Fred Dawson, "but I think I can claim half the honour, as I caught the bird. By George! The general will receive us with open arms, for his life is in danger, and we, under Providence, may be the means of saving it."

"Not only that," replied Harkaway, "we can put the rope round the neck of that villain Webb, whose downfall I am very anxious to see."

They both felt that they had met with a piece of luck, and were extremely anxious to visit the general at headquarters.

He was a man in whom the troops had every confidence, having fought his way inch by inch, until he gained distinction and became commander of our forces in India.

The arrival of the Fiery Star at Ladysmith caused great excitement.

Vanderbilt displayed the British and American flags, and descended just outside the English lines.

It was nearly dinner-time, and a number of soldiers crowded round the aeronauts when they alighted from the balloon.

Harkaway shook hands with the officers whom he knew.

He was highly complimented for his bravery on the preceding day, and general regret was expressed for the untimely fate of poor Willoughby.

As he and Fred walked to the general's quarters they passed through the camp of the Gordon Highlanders.

The men were singing, and seemed to be in high spirits.

Their ditties were the most recent war-songs, and Jack caught the following words:

The men were bred in England, in England:
  The yeomen, the bowmen, the lads of dale and fell;
Here's to you, and to you—to the hearts that are true,
And the land where the true hearts dwell.
Here's to you, and to you—to the hearts that are true,
And the land where the true hearts dwell.

This was thoroughly up-to-date, and so were several others which followed.

At least a dozen men rushed up to Harkaway as soon as they saw him, and grasped his hand in a most friendly manner.

"You fought like a brick, yesterday, sir, when you joined us, and saved my life when I had three of the enemy on me," exclaimed one. "There is no danger of British soldiers not following where you lead. We're proud of you."

"That's all right," replied Jack, "and so am I of you, my fine fellow."

A rousing cheer went after him, and he proceeded.

The Absent-minded Beggars, as Kipling calls them, seemed to revel in the excitement of war.

The general received the young men directly, and was deeply interested at all they had to tell him.

"I am very pleased with you both," he said. "The pigeon-post has put me on my guard about the guns, and I mean to entrust you with a mission."

"I am ready to go anywhere and do anything, sir," answered Harkaway.

"No better spirit could animate a young soldier. The Naval contingent ought to have arrived here by this time. I cannot account for the delay, as I know that the 'Powerful' has been a couple of days at Durban."

"Perhaps there is a difficulty in getting the guns into the trucks," suggested Harkaway.

"You must take an engine and run down to Durban at once. Tell Captain Scott that he alone can save us with his artillery; and don't come back here without the guns. You and Mr. Dawson must be very careful, as you may expect the railway track to be torn up at any point. This is a very solemn duty, and in selecting you I show my confidence."

"Do not forget the house where the spies are," said Harkaway.

"The police shall go up at once and arrest the woman and the two men. I know I am surrounded by spies, and it will have a good effect to make an example of some," replied General White.

As they were departing an orderly came in with the news that the Boers were massing to the south of Ladysmith.

At the same time they opened fire with their artillery and bombarded the town. Our guns returned the compliment, and a duel between the two sets of batteries took place.

"I shall engage them in front, and endeavour to outflank them," said the general.

"That's the way to do it," said Jack, whose high spirits sometimes carried him beyond the bounds of strict decorum. "Silence their artillery, charge them with infantry, and cut them up with the cavalry. Smite them hip and thigh, sir; for, after all, there isn't much difference between a Boer and a pig."

The general pretended not to hear this remark, and went on talking to the orderly and some members of his staff who dropped in.

The young men now walked towards the railroad station to make arrangements for their journey to the coast, and were surprised to meet their old friend Mr. Fish, the war correspondent.

"Ah! Harkaway, dear boy," he exclaimed, "so glad to meet you, don't you know. There's rather more fun here than at Mafeking."

"How did you get to this place?" asked Jack. "You haven't the wings of a bird, and are not provided with seven-league boots."

"Don't ask questions," said Fish. "The motto of a correspondent is 'Everywhere.' We are here to-day and gone to-morrow; for our paper must have news, or beware of editorial wrath. By the way, can you tell me anything about the balloon I saw just now? The owner is rather shy, and wouldn't talk to me. I want something fresh for the *Capetown Slasher*."

"As you are an old friend you shall have it, my dear Fish," replied Jack. "The balloon has been presented to us by the Americans. In the car are four Fenians, practised in the use of dynamite. The balloon floats over the veldt, and when they see a commando camped beneath them, or on the march, the dynamite fiends ruthlessly destroy them."

Out came the note-book, and down went the news.

"Anything else?" queried Mr. Fish, eagerly.

"Half-a-dozen hospital balloons are coming over from Australia, fitted with beds, and provided with trained nurses."

"Good idea that. Rattling. Can't be beat. Got any more war items?"

"The friendly Zulus and Basutos are preparing animal corps to assist us."

"What in thunder are those?"

"First of all comes the trained elephant corps, consisting of one thousand pachyderms; next five hundred rhinosceri, whose horns have been sharpened to a fine point; thirdly, the ostrich corps, three thousand strong, to whose bills are attached small sword-bayonets, double edged, and very deadly. There is some talk of getting up a reptile brigade, composed of trained poisonous snakes, but I don't know if it will come to anything."

"Wonderful," ejaculated Fish. "That will be a blood-curdler for my readers."

"I suppose you will be knocking about our camp, and if I hear anything more I will let you know."

Leaving the correspondent they gained the station and had an interview with the master.

"When do you want to start?" enquired the latter, after they had told him their business. "I can give you an engine, and an armoured truck with a couple of Maxims in it for use on each side if you are stopped, but the difficulty is to get a driver and stoker, for all my hands have volunteered, and I shall have to call them in from the camp."

Little Andy, who had followed his master, overheard this remark.

"There are two chaps lounging about the yard," he said; "they spoke to me, asking for a job. One is a clean-shaven, German-looking fellow; the other has a long dark beard, like a Polish Jew."

"I'll take them on," replied the station master, "they can light the fire and get up steam while you gentlemen take a rest in the truck."

"That is good enough," answered Jack, "I would drive the engine myself if I was not so tired. We shall be eight or ten hours going to Durban, and I really must have rest."

"I should think so," remarked Fred Dawson. "You have gone through enough lately to shake up any man's nerves."

They walked with the station master to a siding where the engine and truck were standing.

To do so, they had to cross the yard, and saw the two men alluded to by Andy.

The master spoke to them, and it seemed to Jack that the one with the beard purposely turned his back, as if he could not look him in the face.

Entering the truck, they satisfied themselves that the guns were in working order; the station master supplied them with some old cushions, and also gave them food and water.

"You will let me go with you, won't you?" enquired Andy, anxiously.

"If you like, my little cock-sparrow," replied Jack, "but I am going to have a doss, and I reckon Dawson is of the same mind. Keep a sharp look-out, watch the driver and stoker, and if you see anything wrong, rouse me."

Andy nodded and disappeared.

He hid himself behind a pile of empty boxes, and kept his eye fixed upon the two newly-engaged men, but saw nothing to excite his suspicions.

"If I drop off," observed Dawson, "the least unusual sound is sure to wake me. I am not a fighting man, but a trained scout, and am always on the look-out. You cannot catch me napping."

"Yes," replied Jack ; "I have noticed that. You are always looking at something else when I am talking to you, alert, and wide-awake, with a never-say-die feeling."

"That's what we call ' jump' and 'push.' We never give in, and risk our lives all day long. I can find my way by day and night, in a strange country, by compass, sun, or stars, and my ears and eyes are wonderfully quick. Perhaps you didn't notice that the man with the beard wouldn't look at you, or allow you to size him up ?"

"That fact dawned upon me faintly, but I did not attach much importance to it."

"He is a wrong.'un, and I don't half like riding with him, though, if he ditches the train, he will endanger his own life as well as ours ; but——"

He paused a moment, and looked intently at his companion.

"Go on," said Jack. "If you want to spoil my forty winks I can't help it."

"Suppose he is a Boer spy."

"What did you say ?" asked Jack, with a yawn, as he sank back on the cushions in the truck and fell asleep through sheer exhaustion.

Fred uttered an exclamation of impatience, and lighted his pipe.

It was not long before he also slept, the sound of the cannon-firing not disturbing him in the least.

When he saw steam up, and the train beginning to move, Andy jumped on board, and the journey commenced.

The boy kept awake, and climbing up one side of the truck, looked at the engine.

He was surprised to see a large flag of the Transvaal fastened to the funnel.

The driver and stoker were smoking, and occasionally drinking out of a stone bottle.

Now and then small parties of Boers were passed, but they made no attempt to fire at the passing train.

Gradually the sun went down, and night came on.

CHAPTER XI.

STOPPED ON THE LINE — ATTACKED BY FREE STATERS—ON TO DURBAN—NAVAL BRIGADE TO THE FRONT — DUNKO RE-APPEARS—THE DEN OF SPIES.

HARKAWAY and Dawson slept on soundly, and little Andy sank into a doze.

All at once Fred was awakened by a perceptible decrease in the motion of the train, and, starting to his feet, looked around him.

Overhead the Southern Cross was shining in the sky, and the Milky Way had myriads of tiny scintillating constellations.

The train now came to an absolute standstill, and, opening the door carefully, he got out to see what was the matter.

The South African night was solemnly impressive ; the air was fresh and cool, and the silence was only broken by busy hummings of insects.

The veldt rolled out in great waves of stubble, interrupted by sugar-loafed shaped ant-heaps, and a sparse vegetation of dwarf mimosa, called zuikerbosch.

The shrill, high, vibrating note of the cicada was heard, with the monotony of a tightly-strung tom-tom.

Walking to the engine, he found that the driver and stoker had deserted their posts.

The fire had gone out, and there was no wood to light another one with.

Looking at his watch, he found that it was nearly ten o'clock, so that they had travelled some distance since they left Ladysmith, and it was not the Boers so much as the Free Staters that they would have to fear.

"Hi ! Jack, wake up !" he cried. "We are betrayed."

"What is the matter now ?" asked Jack, springing out of the truck, followed by Andy.

"We are the victims of a trick. The engine fire is out, and the two men have bolted ; add to which there is not a bit of wood to be found. So here we are, stuck, halfway between Ladysmith and Durban. It's deuced awkward, when time is of the utmost importance."

"I believe that man with the beard was Webb in disguise," observed Jack, thoughtfully.

"If you had said that before, I would have put a bullet through him, and chanced it. It's no use talking ; we are done, and I fear we have got to look out for something else."

His words were followed by a shot.

The bullet passed within an inch of him, and, without waiting to return it, or ascertain from whence it came, he ran back to the truck, and jumped in, Jack and Andy following quickly.

The door was closed, and then a perfect fusilade was opened upon them, the balls rattling like peas against the armour-plates.

They looked through the sight-holes, and perceived a large body of men on either side of them, which distinctly proved that they had been led into an ambush by the men who had been driving the engine.

"It is fortunate I woke up when I did," said Fred. "The idea evidently was that we should be asleep when the train stopped, and fall easily into the hands of the enemy."

"It didn't come off," replied Jack, "and now I think we had better give them a hot reception. Set your Maxim going, and I will work my gun."

"Look out, sir !" shouted Andy, discharging a revolver over his head.

Harkaway did so, and saw some Boers who had climbed up the side of the truck, and were about to level their rifles at them.

It was a clever move to carry the truck by assault, but, thanks to the boy's watchfulness, it was frustrated.

The adventurous foes were quickly disposed of, and their friends, deterred by their fate, did not attempt to repeat the experiment.

Then could be heard the grinding rattle of the Maxim gun, as a shower of bullets was poured into the assailants, the slaughter being terrific, as they were crowded together at close quarters.

The action did not last long.

The foes proved to be Free Staters and not Boers proper.

They had joined the standard of revolt raised by Kruger, and were acting in concert with Joubert.

Those who escaped ran for their lives, utterly demoralized and routed, leaving the broad surface of the veldt strewn with dead bodies, at least two hundred in number.

The peril was over.

Harkaway, who was a man of resources, placed some cushions in the furnace of the engine, and finding a can of oil, poured it over them.

A soldier is seldom without a match or two about him, for his pipe and other uses.

He had one, and speedily kindled a fire.

When steam was generated, he drove the engine himself into Durban, meeting with no more difficulties on the way.

Without losing a moment he delivered his message, and the guns were got ready with all speed.

Captain Scott, of the "Powerful," had manufactured some special carriages for them.

They were already in the trucks, with a large store of shells.

"I was only waiting for a message to go to the front," said the captain; "but, the wire being cut, I was in doubt. You have performed a feat, in getting here, which all must admire."

An hour after Jack's arrival, the men of the Naval Brigade embarked.

The train was armoured, and, fortunately, the line remained intact, so that by daylight the next morning they reached Ladysmith.

The guns were directly put in position, and shells were thrown, scattering death and destruction, filling the Boers with dismay, and silencing their fire.

"Thank Heaven," was the general exclamation. "The reinforcement of bluejackets has arrived just in time."

This was all the more important, because during Jack and Fred's absence, the English had met with a disaster.

In the battle which took place on the afternoon of their departure, two regiments, with the same number of batteries, were captured, owing to their mules stampeding, and carrying off the ammunition.

They fired the last cartridge before laying down their arms.

It was a heavy loss, and many people thought it was owing to the treachery of the mule drivers, who were supposed to be bribed by the Boers.

Fish was of this opinion, and remarked to Harkaway:

"I saw the division start; it was composed of Gordons and Gloucesters."

"Men who would not show the white feather so long as there was a ghost of a chance," said Jack.

"Certainly. I watched their movements through a field glass, and the drivers were beating the mules to make them run, acting in accord, as it seemed to me. You may think me mistaken, but I will swear that fellow Krause, from Mafeking, was one of the drivers."

"That explains it all. It is one more proof of Boer cunning. They hoist the white flag and then fire on us."

"They don't like our lyddite," continued Fish. "Joubert has just sent a messenger to White to say that the use of these new shells is barbarous and inhuman, and that we are not playing the game fairly. Good joke that, isn't it?"

"Rather," answered Jack. "They forget that they used rifles and big guns against the assegais of the Zulus."

"Last night," added Fish, "the police made a raid on a house in Fairmount Street, which was supposed to contain spies."

"Indeed! How did it result?" asked Harkaway, who at once became interested.

"No one was found there except a young and beautiful lady, who described herself as the widow of an Outlander, shot by the Boers. She is a Mrs. Steiner, and has an interest in some mine. I went with the police to see if I could pick up some news, and declare I never saw a more lovely creature in my life; and if there wasn't a Mrs. Fish in Cape Town, with several little Fishes swimming in the family bowl, Mrs. Steiner might——"

"What did she say?" interrupted Jack.

"He was, naturally, highly indignant at being suspected, and repudiated the charge, as it deserved. She's no spy. I'll champion that woman to the last, and should like to hear anyone say a word against her, I'd——"

Here the gallant Fish paused to take breath, and danced about, striking the air as if he were pummelling an invisible enemy.

"I'd give him lyddite, and make a dead Boer of him!" he shouted.

Jack did not take the trouble to explain that he knew a little more than Fish thought for.

He walked with Dawson through the lines.

The soldiers were silent; there was no singing.

The disaster of the previous day had cast a damper upon them; but the face of each man wore a look of grim determination, as if to say: "Wait till I get another shot at them!"

This mishap following upon the death of Symons, the evacuation of Dundee, and the loss of the Hussars, had a depressing effect upon rank and file.

The hospitals were full, and the number of wounded was being daily added to.

The enemy were as five to one, and the English were making as gallant a stand as they did during the famous siege of Lucknow.

"I shall go and help the Naval Brigade," said Dawson. "They are still keeping up a brisk cannonade, and their firing is very pretty. What are you going to do?"

"I shall pay Mrs. Steiner a visit, on my own," answered Harkaway.

"You had best mind what you are about," cried Fred. "I call that running your head into the lion's mouth. The police couldn't find Webb last night, because the cunning brute was driving us to Durban. Perhaps his assistant was Skiller, the German. How can you tell that they are not there now? The police ought to have taken possession of the house."

"There I quite agree with you, but the police are not a bright lot, and don't always do the right thing."

"Do you think you are a match for Webb and Skiller, with that charming Jezebel called Mrs. Steiner?"

"I consider myself a match for half-a-dozen ordinary men."

"Sampson and Hercules rolled into one," laughed Dawson. "All right, Jack, I'll forgive you for being a little cocky, for you are certainly a head and shoulders taller than most of us in dash and daring. Still, if you don't turn up at seven o'clock in our mess-room, I shall come to Fairmount Street after you. There is such a thing as a spider's-web, you know, and you may drop into it."

"I flatter myself I am a little too fly for that," replied Jack, making a pun upon the word; "yet if anything should happen to me and I don't turn up, there will be no harm in coming after me with three or four men, and I say, Fred, while I think of it I will give you the place of the mine in Rhodesia which Messrs. Webb and Krause so ardently covet. They think it a sure fortune, and so do I."

Unbuttoning his tunic, he took the parchment from a side pocket and handed it to Dawson, who promised to take care of it.

It was a long walk to Fairmount Street, but Jack arrived there before noon, and, counting the numbers, stopped before sixteen, which was a pretty little house with a verandah.

It had a small garden on each side and in the rear.

He was about to ring when the door opened, and a tall Kaffir appeared with a basket on his arm, as if he was going shopping.

He was the image of the one who had endeavoured to stab him on the veldt near Mafeking, and whom he had thought dead, when shot by Dawson.

"Dunko!" he exclaimed.

"Some mistake here, boss," replied the Kaffir, coolly, "that not my name at all. Me Bengula. Pas op, and let me go by."

"You're as like as two peas," said Jack, puzzled, "and if you are not Dunko, you're his twin brother or his ghost. Is Mrs. Steiner at home?"

"Gone out, boss. Nobody here but me. Call again, please, and move off smartly."

"Stand on one side!" cried Jack. "I'm going in whether you like it or not. You are Krause's nigger, Dunko, and this is a den of spies."

It was in reality Dunko, who had recovered from a serious wound. Dropping the basket he drew his knife, and regarded Harkaway with a vicious, defiant look.

At this critical moment for Harkaway, a loud scream in a woman's voice was heard coming from a room on the ground floor of the house.

Dunko was evidently alarmed, and turned his head as if to ascertain the cause. This was Jack's opportunity, and when the Kaffir again faced him, he saw the muzzle of

a revolver close to his ear, and the sight of it gave Dunko a terrible shock to his nerves.

"Don't shoot, boss!" he cried, much alarmed. "Me good Kaffir, and like the English, who know how to fight and kill the Boers. It made me laugh the other day to see them run and beg for mercy. All they can do is to wrap themselves up in the white flag."

"Give up that knife," said Jack curtly, "or I'll shoot you as dead as a door-nail. Confess who you are, and what kind of people live in this house. Come, no nonsense, speak out, or down you go, for I will shoot you as I would a dog. Come, speak out, now."

"Me Dunko, boss, that's right enough," replied the Kaffir, reluctantly giving up his weapon. "The man you knew at Mafeking lives here, and if you are wise you will go away. Dunko do you good turn if he can."

"Stab me in the back if you had the chance. Get out of my way, and think yourself lucky to be let off so cheaply."

Dunko grinned, showing his white, gleaming teeth, and, passing Jack, walked on to the stoep, muttering:

"This Kaffir's off, as the fly said, when he got out of the mustard-pot."

"Another shriek, more piercing than the first, was heard, and a female exclaimed in pathetic tones:

"Oh, Heaven! will no one help me, and save me from this cowardly ruffian?"

This was sufficient for Harkaway, who strode forward.

Traversing the passage he came to a room, the door of which was open, and did not scruple to look in, though he knew perfectly well that he had no business there, and that, in reality, his intrusion was an impertinence, but he thought the appeal justified him.

The apartment was elegantly furnished.

A coarse-looking man, with a low German type of face, was standing over a handsome woman, who was seated on a lounge.

Her countenance expressed extreme terror.

The man held in his hand a wine-glass, which contained a liquid of a dark colour.

"Consent to be mine," exclaimed the man, "or I will force you to drink the contents of this glass, which will speedily bring your earthly career to an end."

"Wretch, would you poison me!" demanded the lady.

"Marguerite Steiner," answered the ruffian, "you know my love and devotion for you. This is your last chance. Refuse me, and you die, as sure as my name is Franz Skiller."

"Assassin and spy! it can be no secret that I loathe and despise you. You know that I am one of the richest women in Pretoria, and it is my wealth you covet, not me. Once get command of my fortune, and you would poison me in my sleep, as you now threaten to do in the daylight."

"You call me spy," retorted Skiller, "forgetting that you are the head centre of the spy system, sent here specially by Kruger. The English would give something to get hold of you, if they knew as much as I do about you."

"What of that?" asked Mrs. Steiner, whose eyes sparkled with patriotic fire. "I am a Boer, and I believe our cause to be just. My husband was killed in the Raid, and I have been very bitter ever since. There is weeping and wailing all over the Rand, and I want to see the Rednecks driven into the sea."

"Stop that nonsense, it won't do for me," said Skiller, in a brutal tone. "I want your answer; and your fate depends upon it."

"You've had your answer."

Hearing this Skiller seized her by the hair, forced back her head, and was about to pour the poison down her throat, when Harkaway darted forward, and, with one blow of his fist, felled him to the ground.

"Scoundrel!" he cried. "I have prevented the crime you were about to commit, and if I treated you as you deserve, I should put an end to your miserable existence."

"Harkaway!" gasped the man, whom Webb had more than once pointed out to him. "By what right are you here? This is a private house."

"The right which every man has to protect a woman in distress," answered Jack. "Lie there, you hound! and if you dare to move until I have made up my mind what is to be done with you, I'll put a bullet in your cowardly heart."

Skiller glared at him.

The poison was spilled on the carpet, and any danger from that was over; but Skiller, who was as treacherous as a snake, moved his hand towards his pocket with the palpable intention of drawing his pistol.

Divining his purpose, Jack sprang upon him and banged his head two or three times against the floor until he was half stunned.

"Would you?" he exclaimed. "Not much, my man. I want that little toy, if you please."

He took from him his revolver and a knife, the man being too dazed to make any remark or offer resistance.

Mrs. Steiner rose and advanced to her deliverer with extended hand.

"I have often heard of you, sir," she said in a low musical voice, "and I thank you from the bottom of my heart for what you have done."

"Don't mention it, madam; I am only too glad to have been of service," replied Jack, with his best bow. "I hope you will pardon my intrusion on your privacy, but I have come here on police duty to look for an infamous fraud, named Webb, who is betraying our secrets to the enemy, and has more than once attempted my life, in conjunction with an equally vile specimen of humanity, called Krause, both of whom, I am convinced, are known to you; and I may be pardoned for adding that I am sorry to find you connected with such rabble."

"I am a patriot, like yourself, sir," rejoined the woman, drawing herself up proudly. "I cannot fight like a man, but with a woman's instinct I plot. Having overheard my conversation with Skiller, you will understand that I am no common adventuress. I am worth over a million, and risk all, even my life, to serve my country. By accident you have learned my secret, and I ask you as an English gentleman to give me twelve hours to leave Ladysmith and get back to Pretoria."

"That would be neglecting my duty, though, when a lady is in the case, I am inclined to make some allowance."

"My word is law in Pretoria," Mrs. Steiner continued, "and President Kruger will do anything I ask him. Do you see this armlet?"

She took a broad gold band from her left arm, and handed it to Jack.

On it was engraved a winged lion, which was trampling under its feet a curious-looking creature, resembling a dragon.

"Wear this for my sake," she said. "It is of very ancient workmanship, and was dug out of the ground. Some suppose it to be of Egyptian origin. The President gave it to me as a reward for services rendered to the cause, and, if shown to him, has promised to grant any request the wearer may make. If you are captured by our army, it will help you. Now leave me in peace. Say nothing, and to-morrow this house shall be empty."

"I will respect your wishes, though I know I am doing wrong."

"Oh, no, Mr. Harkaway; it is an unprotected lady you are assisting, and I am sure you will never regret that," Mrs. Steiner said, with a sweet smile, which would have disarmed a sterner soldier than Jack.

"Are you not afraid of this cur Skiller?"

"Not at all. He took me unawares. Foolishly I left my pistol on yonder table; if he persecutes me again, he will not escape with a whole skin."

"If it were not for fear of compromising you, I would run him down to the police barracks. Anyhow, I'll kick him out of the house for you."

He had slipped the armlet over his wrist, and turned to look at the German, whom he had left lying on the floor.

To his surprise Skiller had got up and gone to one side of the room, in which was a sliding panel.

This he pushed back, revealing an aperture large enough to permit of the passage of a man's body.

Suddenly he disappeared, and, in the heat of the moment, Jack rushed after him.

Mrs. Steiner seized him by the arm, trying to stop him; but he cast off her grasp, crying:

"Ha! There is some trick here. The fox has gone to his burrow, but I will unearth him."

"Stay!" said Mrs. Steiner, imploringly. "There are men on these premises who are hungering for your life. Oh! beware; you are too good and noble to die like a dog. Stay, I beg of you, for these wretches will have no mercy, and I cannot aid you, as they would kill me too."

Harkaway had passed through the panel, when her warning voice rang in his ears.

He was standing in a small, dark passage, which had a glimmer of light at one end.

For a moment he hesitated.

"Come back! Are you mad, to face an unknown danger?" Mrs. Steiner continued. "Your foes are desperate men, and will stop at nothing. Come back, I command you."

Convinced that he was pursuing a reckless and foolish course, Jack was about to do as she ordered, when, to his horror and dismay, the sliding panel shot back, and he was left in the dark.

Frantically he moved his hands up and down the woodwork, endeavouring to find the spring, but without avail.

The partition was as smooth as glass, and he saw that he was caught in a trap.

Outside he could hear the moaning voice of Mrs. Steiner, saying :

"Lost, lost! I owe him a life, and would have saved his, but he has rushed headlong upon his fate."

Groping his way along the passage, Jack stumbled over an impediment, in the shape of a block of wood, which had been placed there on purpose.

He fell on his hands and knees, and was all at once pounced upon by two men, who bound his arms behind his back, and pushing open a door, dragged him into a room, the windows of which were boarded up and thickly curtained.

A lamp hanging from the ceiling threw down a brilliant light, and he was able to look round, perceiving that his captors were Skiller and Dunko, the Kaffir, while at a table in front of him were seated Webb and Krause, playing cards, with a bottle and glasses before them, while the room was filled with the fumes of strong Dutch tobacco.

"Good-day, Mr. Harkaway," exclaimed Webb, with a cynical sneer. "You have saved us a great deal of trouble by your timely visit. Hitherto you have managed to escape when we laid hands on you, but now you must abandon hope."

"If you dare to injure me you will bitterly repent it," answered Harkaway. "My friend, Mr. Dawson, knows that I have come here to search for you, and if I am not back in about an hour's time, he will arrive at this house with a strong guard."

"In less than an hour the house will be empty," said Krause, looking up. "We are going to trek to the Boer's camp, and shall have the pleasure of taking you with us. I am glad you have told us of your friend's intention. He will search the house, and find no one. Your dead body would give us away, therefore your fate shall be a mystery to all."

"You will find it difficult to convey me through the town, as I am pretty well known."

"Not at all ; that is where you are mistaken," replied Krause, calmly. "I have a plan which will astonish you."

"What is that ?" demanded Jack.

"In a few minutes you will find yourself lying in a coffin. When out of the town we shall dig a grave and bury you alive on the veldt."

"That is a refinement of torture !" exclaimed Jack, struck with dismay. "Why not kill me at once, if such is your intention ?"

"Your body must not be found here," interposed Webb. "Ask no more questions, for time is precious. You are in our way, and we must get you out of it."

Seeing that it was useless to argue or expostulate with these men, Jack maintained a proud silence.

He understood that it would be dangerous for them to murder him in the house, for as soon as his body was found, a hue and cry would be raised.

There was faint hope of any rescue, but he did not show any sign of fear.

His life had been so often in jeopardy, that he had become hardened.

If he died, it was the chance of war ; but he would have rather fallen on the battle-field, with his gallant comrades round him, than be thrown into a nameless grave on the veldt.

At a sign from Webb, Dunko left the room, and was absent a few minutes.

When he returned, he brought with him a plain deal coffin, which he placed on the floor.

Skiller gave Jack a blow on the chest, and knocked him into it.

The next minute the Kaffir placed a perforated lid on the top, and, falling on his knees, began to nail it down.

At first Jack thought they might have been trying to frighten him ; but now he saw that it was a grim reality, and came to the conclusion that there was no hope for him.

There was a cemetery outside the town, where funerals were of daily occurrence, and it was not likely that any sentry on outpost duty would challenge men in charge of a coffin.

While this was being accomplished Krause had disappeared.

He came back looking much concerned.

"Marguerite has left us !" he exclaimed, in an excited manner. "A note lying on the table informed me that she is going to Johannesburg. Of course, she will have no difficulty in passing the Boers. She is off our hands, and we must look out for ourselves."

"Very good," replied Webb. "Perhaps it is for the best. A woman is always in the way when you are making a retreat. Skiller, help the Kaffir, and carry the coffin to the four-wheeled truck in the garden. You will find a square of black velvet in the ante-room, throw that over as a pall, put on a dark coat and hat, and we will do the same. Draw your hat over your face, and try to look as if you had lost a dear friend, or near relative. Webb and I will disguise ourselves with false hair, so that our own mothers wouldn't know us."

Skiller nodded, and in ten minutes the procession was in readiness for a start.

Skiller walked in front, Dunko wheeled the truck, while Webb and Krause brought up the rear, walking with sombre air and slow steps as befitted mourners.

The road which led to the cemetery branched off at the bottom of the street, and was quite lonely.

The main road led to the British camp, and naturally was lively enough, as men were always going up and down.

When they came to the junction of the two roads, they encountered Fred Dawson and Mr. Fish, at the head of six policemen belonging to the Natal Force, who were doing duty with General White.

Fred looked curiously at the melancholy procession, and stared at Skiller, making some remark to Fish, but pursued his way without interfering.

Little did he think that his chum Harkaway was so close to him.

As if prompted by some instinct, Jack cried for help, but the sound of his voice was smothered under the pall.

"I would have sworn that the Kaffir wheeling the coffin was Dunko if I hadn't shot him at Mafeking when we fell into Krause's ambush," said Fred, dubiously.

"All Kaffirs are alike, my dear fellow," answered Fish. "It's simply a walking funeral. People must die, you know, and it's the custom to bury them."

"I fancied I heard a sound coming from under the pall."

"Rats!" exclaimed Fish. "The dead don't talk. Hurry up; you seem to forget that Harkaway is in danger."

Dawson made no further remark, and they walked quickly up the street to Mrs. Steiner's house.

CHAPTER XII.

CHASING A COFFIN—BAFFLED ON THE VELDT —THE SMAUS AND THE PERUVIAN—DUNKO AND SKILLER AT BAY—A LUCKY ESCAPE.

THE astonishment of Dawson and his small party at finding Mrs. Steiner's house empty may be easily imagined.

There was every sign of a hurried flight. The lady had left all her clothes behind her, and the men their belongings.

The last room they searched was that in which Jack had been put into the coffin. Here they sat down and held a council of war, not scrupling to help themselves to the whisky which remained in the bottles.

"Spies gone," muttered Fish, producing his note-book. "'Consternation among the secret agents of the Boers.' 'Efficiency of Police system at Ladysmith strikes terror into the hearts of evil-doers.' Must send that by pigeon-post to Durban to-night. I say, Dawson," he added, "Buller will be sending troops up directly, and we may expect a big battle at Estcourt."

"Bother the fighting. I am thinking of my friend Harkaway," replied Fred. "What has become of him? I know for a fact that he came to this house, and the people haven't rushed off in a hurry for nothing."

"I should imagine that they have killed him," answered Fish, "and have gone off to avoid arrest. What a line that would make for a newspaper bill, 'Harkaway Killed by Boer Spies.' He has got his name up, and is well known."

"You cold-blooded monster," cried Fred. "All you think of is your infernal paper, a miserable rag, in which I wouldn't wrap butter for fear of insulting it."

"Draw it mild. I am the humble and undeserving representative of a highly influential and respectable family news journal."

"Bosh! Vootsack! as the Boers say; that means 'Get out!' The question is what are we going to do about Jack? who, in my eyes, is worth more than all the war correspondents in the world put together."

He looked enquiringly at Corporal Potts, a stout, middle-aged man, with a red face and blue nose, who was in command of the section of Natal Police.

"If you appeal to me, sir, I should say it was a case," said Corporal Potts. "Mr. Harkaway has been bottled up somehow. I'm not a detective—that is not in my line. I'm only an old soldier, having been twenty years in the army, and lately joined the police. If you ask me the difference between a Mauser and a Metford, I'm there, and I know shrapnel and case from common shell; but, in the present instance, it is no thoroughfare, so far as I am concerned. Perhaps they have buried him. It might be of some use to dig the garden or take up the flooring. Or they might have put the body down a chimney-pot. A water cistern, too, is a likely place. I've heard of such things being done."

As he spoke, the corporal, who was walking up and down the room, touched something with his foot.

"What is that?" demanded Fred, curiously.

"An officer's forage cap, sir, by the look of it."

Fred sprang eagerly forward, and picked it up.

Inside, written on a piece of tape, was the name of Harkaway.

"This settles it," he exclaimed. "Jack has been done away with, and we may put him on the roll of heroes who have fallen in this war."

"That by no means follows," interposed Fish. "We have not found a trace of blood in the house, and there are no signs of a struggle. Carry your mind back for half-an-hour or more. You fancied you recognised that Kaffir who was wheeling a coffin down the street!"

"What is your idea about that? Do you think Jack's dead body was inside? If so, we can pursue the wretches and revenge him."

"I cannot form any exact theory," answered Fish; "but I imagine that Webb and Krause passed us in disguise, and we did not know them. There is plenty of time to go after the party and overtake them before they have travelled far. Unravel the mystery, and if you want any help, I am at your service. I have a penetrating mind, and think that Harkaway was bundled into that coffin neck and heels."

"Still alive, eh?" ejaculated Fred.

"Certainly. The brutes mean to kill him on the veldt, and if we are smart, he may be saved."

"Bravo!" exclaimed Fred. "After all, Fish, you are a bit of a genius, and I am sorry to say I have been inclined to underrate your abilities. I apologise, and declare frankly that it shall not occur again."

"Stuff and nonsense, my dear boy," answered Fish, with a good humoured smile. "I admit that I vamp up all kinds of news for the Capetown Slasher, but you must remember that a newspaper man must be a good all round man, and know a little about everything."

"Drink up, boys," continued Fred; "if you are all game to go after Harkaway, we will make a start. Come, Corporal, another drop won't hurt you."

"I don't know whether I will or I won't, but I'd rather," replied Corporal Potts, who, after shaking his head two or three times, and looking affectionately at his glass, placed it to his lips, and drained it of its contents.

The phrase he had made use of was a favourite one of his.

He had a fatal fondness for drink, though he pretended that he did not care far it ; and those who knew him well always laughed when they heard him say, " I don't know whether I will or I won't, but I'd rather," for it invariably ended in acceptance.

Many a time had he interviewed his colonel in the orderly room, the result of the carpeting being the loss of his stripes.

He had shown himself a brave soldier in various parts of the world, and might have held a commission if he had been a sober man.

When he left the service he could not stay at home, and joined the police, only to find himself thrust into the middle of a big war.

In a few minutes Dawson and Fish were leading their men, armed with quick-firing rifles, along the road leading to the cemetery.

They made inquiries of the keeper, who informed them that no funeral had taken place that day ; but from a window of his house he had seen what he took to be a coffin going in the direction of the veldt ; and he imagined that it had about an hour's start of them.

They passed on, until they came to the open country, where they found themselves entirely at fault.

Experienced scout as he was, Fred Dawson could find no track, and could see nothing between him and the horizon.

The coffin might have been taken right or left or straight forward, he could not tell which, and did not know where to look for it.

Boulders were to be seen here and there, disturbing the line of sight, and he halted his men in perplexity.

"What is the next move on the board?" enquired Fish. "If you take my advice, you will divide us into three parties. Send three men to the left, another three to the right ; you, the corporal, and I will take the middle course."

"Union is strength. I don't like to separate," replied Dawson ; "but perhaps your suggestion is as good as any other."

The sound of a heavy cannonade was heard to the south of them.

"Joubert is pounding away at us again," added Fred ; "and, hark! our guns are replying to the bombardment. Confound it! I wish I was there, right in the thick, but I can't leave Harkaway in the lurch."

"Most decidedly not. That wouldn't do at all."

Fred acted upon the advice given him by Fish, and the police were distributed on either side, while he walked straight ahead with Potts and the correspondent.

They had not proceeded more than a mile before they heard voices coming from behind a kopje, which made them advance with the utmost caution, carrying their rifles at their hips, ready to fire at a moment's notice.

Being in front of his companions, Dawson peeped round a corner of the kopje, and perceived two men, who were comfortably seated on the sandy soil, eating some cold meat and Boer biscuit.

By the side of each was a large pack or knapsack, and a little way off was a horse and cart.

His knowledge of the Transvaal enabled him to perceive at a glance that one was a smaus (pedlar) and the other a Peruvian (illicit whisky seller).

The smaus was a Polish Jew, small, hairy, and dirty, his eyes full of cunning and sharpness.

His voice was oily and his manner cringing.

These pedlars journey the whole of South Africa, driving or riding over the veldt from one district to another.

They sell Birmingham cheap jewellery, pipes, mirrors, pencils, boot-laces, and oddments.

He wore high jack-boots, crinkled about the ankles, a long, dirty green garment, and his greasy curls were surmounted by a skull-cap.

He had no shirt collar or waistcoat, and his grey cord trousers were tucked into his boots.

The liquor-seller vended a vile compound of raw potato spirit, tobacco juice, and cayenne pepper, which the "boys," as the Kaffirs are called, drink greedily, being half their time unfit for work in consequence.

"Come on," cried Fred, "it's only a smaus and a Peruvian having a rest before coming on to the town or going into the camp."

Hearing this, Fish and Corporal Potts advanced at the double, and the wandering traders jumped up to meet them.

"Ha," cried the smaus, "English soldier very good chappie! What can I sell you to-day, captain? Will you buy a nice ring for your girl or a beautiful mirror to see your handsome face in?"

"Buy a bottle of the best Johnny Walker for a dollar-and-a-quarter, colonel?" said the Peruvian, asking five shillings for what cost him fivepence.

This request was addressed to Potts, who, as usual, shook his head.

"I don't know whether I will or I won't, but I'd rather," answered the corporal, who put his hand in his pocket and made the purchase, after which he sat down, took the cork out with a knife, and began to suck the monkey, as he termed it.

To propitiate the smaus and get all the information he could out of him, Dawson made a few small purchases, though he knew all the time he was being shamefully treated by the Polish vagrant.

"I say, you Pollack!" he exclaimed, "your eyes are small, but I daresay you can see well enough. Have you noticed anyone pass by here recently?"

"Only a boy wheeling a coffin, with three men following."

"If you will tell me which way they went I will give you a dollar."

"I lost sight of them behind that boulder, which is ten minutes' walk in front of you."

"Is that all you know about their movements?"

"Give me another dollar, boss, and I'll tell you some more," said the smaus, with a cunning look in his beady eyes.

"Here you are. Now, then, speak quickly," answered Dawson, who was burning with an impatience he could scarcely control.

"Two of the men, who wore long beards, walked away in the direction of the Boer line. The Kaffir and the third man remained with the corpse, as far as I know. What you buy now? Something pretty, I show you. Vos volen zie!"

"Give me a turn!" exclaimed the Peruvian, in his most persuasive tone. "It is good stuff. See, I drink to you. Gesuntheit. Very good; you feel it right down here."

He rubbed his stomach, and grinned approvingly; but Fred pushed him on one side and darted forward like a hare, calling upon his companions to follow him.

Good runner as he was, Corporal Potts, fired by the potato spirit, out-distanced him, and rounded the boulder first.

The next minute a couple of shots were heard, and when Dawson arrived on the scene, a startling spectacle met his view.

In the foreground he saw a wooden coffin, close by stood Dunko, with a spade in his hand, looking the picture of abject terror.

He had just finished digging a grave about three feet deep.

Near the boulder were lying Corporal Potts and the German Skiller, both apparently mortally wounded.

The ground near each was ensanguined.

It was clear that Krause and Webb had gone to the Boer camp, leaving Skiller and Dunko to complete the work they had commenced, and were satisfied in their own minds that at last Harkaway was done for.

Fish pointed his revolver at the Kaffir and was about to shoot him, when Fred knocked up his weapon, which exploded harmlessly in the air; but Dunko was so frightened that he fell on his knees and held up his hands, whining like a child for mercy.

"Let him alone!" exclaimed Dawson. "We may get a lot out of the fellow. Stand over him, if you like, to prevent his escaping, but don't hurt him."

"He's a thundering villain," said Fish.

"I know that the rascal isn't worth the powder to blow him out of existence."

"Me good Kaffir, boss!" cried Dunko. "Never do no harm to the Rednecks. You shot me once, and I don't want another hole in my skin. I'll come to your camp and serve you well if you let me off this time, and I'll never speak to Krause any more."

"Where is Mr. Harkaway?"

"I don't know who you mean, boss. Never heard the name before. Is he one of the Boers from Pretoria?"

"None of your lies!" exclaimed Dawson. "What have you got in that coffin?"

"A dead man, boss; very old friend of Krause. He caught the fever and died sudden; so, as no one should catch the disease, we bring him out here to bury him private."

"Knock the lid off and let me have a look. Quick, march! if you don't want me to blow your brains out. Set to work; no foolishness. You know me. If you haven't got a hammer and chisel, use your spade."

With evident reluctance Dunko, in a clumsy manner, began to loosen the nails, muttering to himself all the while, and perspiring freely with his ill-directed exertion; but he was obliged to go on with his task, as Fish walked up, and covered him with his revolver, while Fred bestowed his attention upon Corporal Potts, who was very red in the face, and breathed heavily.

"Are you much hurt, corporal?" asked Fred, feelingly. "Where is your wound? Surely you are not dying?"

"I have got it, sir," replied the corporal, dolefully. "My side pains me, but I believe the injury is internal. My inside burns as if it was on fire."

"No wonder after drinking that rot the Peruvian sold you. It's enough to kill a Kaffir, let alone a white man. Let me turn you over and have a look."

"Oh! Mr. Dawson, don't touch me!" moaned the corporal. "It's all over. I can't bear a finger laid me. Look at my blood streaming on the ground."

Undeterred by his remonstrance, Dawson rolled him over on his face, and found that the whisky bottle, which he had stuffed inside his jacket, had been broken by a bullet, and that a few pieces of glass had penetrated his skin, without breaking his ribs, so that in reality he was more frightened than hurt.

"Get up, you fool! There is nothing the matter with you. The Peruvian has done you one good turn, for the bottle saved your life," said Fred, pulling him up until he stood on his feet, scarcely able to believe the evidence of his senses.

"Thank goodness!" he exclaimed, heartily. "That spirit, sir, must be mighty strong to stop a bullet fired at short range. I wish it wasn't all gone, for I feel awful weak. Give that Peruvian a hail, sir, will you? I don't drink as a rule, but circumstances alter cases."

"Take a drop out of my flask," replied Fred, smiling, and kindly offering it to him.

"I don't know whether I will or I won't, but I'd rather," answered the corporal, with a greedy look in his eye.

Dawson now took a look at Skiller, who had been shot through the head by Potts.

The German was already stiffening in the embrace of death.

Suddenly a loud cry from Fish made Dawson turn round.

CHAPTER XIII.

DISCOVERY OF HARKAWAY—THE MAD BOER —JACK IS LEFT ALONE—THE YOUNG BUGLER COMES—CAPTURED—OFF TO PRETORIA.

SOMETHING of an extraordinary nature had evidently happened to disturb the serenity and upset the peace of mind of Mr. Fish.

Not contented with shouting at the top of his voice, he beckoned wildly to Fred Dawson, who ran up to see what was the matter.

"By jove," cried Fish, "this beats all creation. There is something alive in this coffin, which the Kaffir does not seem to be in a hurry to open."

"I'll see about that," replied Fred, giving Dunko a vigorous push, which sent him rolling on his back, and then kicking him in the ribs. "Speak out, you silly ape. Tell the truth. What's inside that deal box?"

"White man—no good," said Dunko, writhing like a worm, and wriggling himself out of reach, "heap too much plenty kick."

A low, faint voice issued from the coffin, and the words " Help ! help ! " were distinctly audible.

Fred's curiosity was now roused to the highest pitch, and, picking up the spade, he soon succeeded in wrenching off the lid, to his great joy revealing the pallid face of Harkaway, who was gasping for breath.

His long confinement had nearly resulted in suffocation, for the heat and the pall over the box had made it like an oven.

With the assistance of Corporal Potts and Fish, he lifted Jack's body on to the stunted grass, and fanned his face with his cap.

" Heaven send that it may not be too late to save him," Fred cried.

The Smaus and the Peruvian had come up, and the latter offered a bottle of his vile stuff.

In the absence of anything better, Dawson poured a portion of the spirit down Jack's throat.

" It is either kill or cure," he exclaimed, " though the rankest hummer in Cape Town would turn up his nose at this. It is worse than ' Cape smoke ' (brandy), or a glass of ' hard wood ' (Cape sherry). How are you, Jack ? " he added, bending over his friend.

" Still alive, thanks to you, old fellow," replied Harkaway. " Have you caught Krause and Webb ? "

" Unfortunately they have made their escape," answered Dawson. " One of your persecutors we shot, but we've got that son-of-a-gun, Dunko, and after what has happened to you, I think we shall be justified in putting it out of his power to do further mischief. I say, Fish, where's the Kaffir gone? Keep an eye on him."

" He's bolted, by Jingo ! " cried Fish, who, turning his head, saw Dunko running like a deer towards the enemy's camp. " Hang it all, what a set of duffers we are. I might have known he would show us his heels ; and there he is, cutting along like a springboek in a cloud of dust. He will give the alarm, and we shall be surrounded before we can get ' half - way home, unless our friend Harkaway can step out pretty lively."

" That is impossible, I am sorry to say," replied Jack, with a sigh of resignation. " I feel so weak and tottery, that I am afraid I can scarcely walk. If I can get something to eat, and have a few hours' rest, I shall be all right."

" The boss is all broke up," remarked the Smaus. " Playing at being a dead man doesn't seem to agree with him. If I were you, I should take him up to the farm, on the other side of that kopje. It is called Hoff-man's Farm. There is only the old man there now, and he is half out of his mind."

" What is the matter with him ? " enquired Fred.

" War, boss," rejoined the Smaus. He's got it on the brain, under his eyes, and in his heart. There are lots more like him in the Transvaal. The Burghers thought they were going to have a picnic as far as Natal when they joined the commandoes."

" Do you know him ? "

" Perfectly well. Every year I visit him, and he buys of me, but the rednecks have been too much for that family. Two of his sons were killed at Glencoe, and three more fell at Elands. His wife cut her throat, and old Hoffman has gone dotty ; but I know he killed a sheep yesterday, for I took a bit of his mutton when he wasn't looking. You might rest there for a time, though he has no liking for the English, and if you don't want that coffin, boss, you have just come out of, I'll take it up to the farm, and sell it to the old man, who is like the snuff of a candle, ready to go off at any time ; and it might come in handy, if he's got a neighbour to bury him."

" Look here," said Fred, " that's not a bad idea. Suppose Fish and the corporal take you up to the farm, Jack, while I go to our lines and get a horse for you ? "

" All right," replied Jack. " It is very kind of you to think so much of me. I fear I am a great trouble to you."

" Don't talk rot," cried Fred ; adding, " Now then, corporal, fall in."

" You buy of me just one more bottle before you go," said the Peruvian, persuasively, as he touched Potts on the shoulder.

" I don't know whether I will, or I won't, but I'd rather," replied the corporal. " I don't want to get muddled, but there's a lot of malaria about. They say whisky is good for a chill, and an ounce of prevention is better than a pound of cure."

Some money passed between him and the Peruvian, and the corporal stowed away a bottle inside his tunic, after which he offered Jack his arm, while Fish did the same thing, and they slowly marched towards the old-fashioned farmhouse ; while Dawson started at the double for Ladysmith.

They found Hoffman, the Boer farmer, seated on the stoop.

He was a very old man, with long, grey hair and beard.

His hard-featured face was furrowed with care, and his eyes were sunk in his head, making his high cheekbones look more prominent.

" Who comes here ? " he demanded, fiercely.

" Friends," replied Fish, airily. " We mean you no harm."

" By Heaven, if I thought you did, I'd shoot you down like a lot of dogs," he said, laying his hand on his rifle, which stood by his side. " You are English, that is enough for me. Curse you ; what do you come here for ? Can't you see it is a house of mourning ? There is death in the air, and the blood of my sons cries aloud for vengeance."

" Don't excite yourself, we only want rest, and refreshment, and are willing to pay for both," exclaimed the corporal. " My name is Tommy Atkins. You can see my identifica-tion card, if you like, and have a sup out of my bottle to cheer you up."

Potts thought this was quite introduction enough.

Every soldier carries, sewn up in the left hand corner of his khaki tunic, a card, on which is written his name, rank, regimental number, and the name and address of his next-of-kin, and he is also supplied with a small pad of bandages, for field dressing.

" Avaunt," shouted the half-mad Boer, " O Heavens ! the heathens are coming to mine inheritance. I can see what is before us.

My people will be driven from the Transvaal, but there is a Land of Promise on the banks of the Limpopo River, where we shall dwell in peace; and in our future home the wicked will cease from troubling. Away! false, covetous, blood-thirsty Roonecks."

"This is rather a hot reception, what shall we do?" asked Fish, who was becoming alarmed at the old man's vehemence.

"I can't go any further," answered Harkaway, sitting down, "so that settles it."

Hoffman pointed his gun at Fish, who seemed to be the special object of his aversion, and, without any further parley, fired, sending a bullet clean through the top of his helmet, and actually scorching his hair, which was thick and curly.

Quick as lightning the correspondent of the *Cape Town Slasher* retaliated by discharging his revolver, and landed a bullet in Hoffman's heart, causing him to fall back, with a hollow groan.

"Hookey Walker," cried the corporal. "I'm off. If the Boers catch us, we're sure to be hanged. What did you want to go and kill the old man for?"

"Didn't the maniac try to shoot me?" demanded Fish, indignantly, as he removed his helmet, and ran his fingers affectionately through his curls. "He took a little bit off the top as it is; I think I was perfectly justified; what more do you want? I only wish Harkaway could walk."

"Never mind me," replied Jack, cheerfully, "I shall come out all right, have no fear. It will be really best for you two to make tracks. Leave me to take care of myself. I shall be fit again directly. Don't think I have cried a go because I am down on my luck. Go after Fred, and come back with some horses; if anything *should* happen to me, tell Dawson to stick to the plan of the mine. We shall get to Rhodesia some day, when the war is over. He will know what I mean."

"I don't like to leave you," said Fish, "it looks cowardly, and——"

"Go," interrupted Harkaway, in as strong a voice as he was capable of. "I wish it. You can't do me any good now I'm landed. Go with Mr. Fish, corporal. I am your superior officer, and you must obey orders, you know."

By causing the death of the aged Boer farmer, Fish had certainly placed them in a dilemma, and their position was not at all to be envied, if a foraging party of the enemy should suddenly pounce upon them.

They were both anxious to save their skins as the saying is, but at the same time, to do them credit, we must admit that they thought they could be of more service to Jack, by going away for help, than remaining where they were.

Accordingly they departed, and Jack was left alone; while the sun, a fiery ball of red, was declining in the west.

Corporal Potts took the bottle affectionately from its hiding place, and regarding it kindly, removed the cork, muttering:

"I don't know whether I will, or I won't, but I'd rather," which remark was followed by a gurgle accompanied by a deep sigh of satisfaction; and, he added, "It's hard if a man can't have his lotion now and then. Where's the harm of a gargle? A man wants

a damper in this forsaken climate. I'll have another wet, and chance it."

A short rest revived Harkaway to such an extent that he was able to get up and explore the farmhouse.

In the kitchen he found some schnapps, cold roast mutton, and Boer biscuit, on which he did not hesitate to regale himself.

"Now I feel a king again, and as soon as it grows dark, if Dawson and the others don't come with the horses, I shall tramp it back to Ladysmith."

As he spoke, he heard the sound of a horse's hoofs outside, and a voice exclaimed:

"Hallo, inside there! Where are you?"

Jack rushed out, and to his infinite delight beheld his faithful boy, Andy the bugler, astride a powerful grey horse, which, from its heaving flanks and foaming mouth, seemed to have been ridden at speed.

"Glad to find you alive, sir," exclaimed Andy heartily. "I was exercising this horse just outside the camp, for Captain Garner, of the Lancers, when I met Mr. Dawson, who ordered me to come here to you. I should never have found the place if it hadn't been for a Smaus, who directed me.

"As it was, I nearly got shot by some foraging Boers on the other side of the kopje. I dropped one, for I can use the rifle now as well as anybody; and I fancy, from his appearance, that he belongs to a commando of Free Staters, who have come from the Orange River to join Joubert."

"Very likely," replied Jack. "Our scouts informed us that General Freider was expected. You have my thanks, Andy, for what you have done. Get off your horse and give him time to breathe."

"It won't do, sir. We cannot afford to lose a moment. Jump into the saddle, and I will ride behind you. If we make a circuit, instead of going as the bird flies, we shall be safe."

"What danger do you apprehend in staying here till sunset?" asked Harkaway. "I want to travel under cover of darkness."

"Be guided by me, and start at once," persisted Andy. "There are cattle and ricks on this farm the Boers would like to have, and——"

He paused abruptly, and an expression of alarm crossed his face, which was not to be wondered at, as he had suddenly noticed a body of some forty horsemen approaching at a rapid pace.

"The game's up," exclaimed Harkaway, stamping his foot impatiently on the ground. "My luck seems to be dead out."

So quickly had the Boers rounded the corner that Jack had no time to conceal the corpse of Hoffman, which he otherwise would have done, as he knew that the sight of it would give rise to awkward and unpleasant questioning.

"Shall we die fighting?" asked Andy with a cool courage which was surprising in one so young.

"No," replied Jack. "We are not combatants at present, and if they make us prisoners they are bound to respect us and treat us decently. Throw down your arms; as for me, I haven't any."

Andy complied with this request, and the next minute the horsemen drew up in front of the house, their leader, a tall, handsome man, dismounting, and advancing towards Harkaway, who maintained his composure.

"I am General Freider. What are you doing here? Are you alone? Who killed this old man lying on the stoop? Speak quickly, or I'll make you."

"He did not fall by my hand," answered Jack.

"You lie," thundered Freider; "anyone can see that you are a British scout. You have some deep design in coming here, and I mean to have it out of you. Do you hear? Be civil, for I can either make you a prisoner, and send you to Pretoria, or shoot you where you stand."

Jack looked defiantly at him, and preserved a disdainful silence, which greatly enraged Freider, who was a personal friend of President Kruger, and thought very highly of himself.

In a moment of passion he struck Harkaway over the shoulders with the scabbard of his sword, which caused the blood to rush to Jack's head, and made his ears tingle.

Weak as he was, he stepped up to the brutal Boer, and gave him a blow in the face, which sent him staggering back against his horse.

In a moment half-a-dozen troopers leaped from their saddles, and Harkaway's arms were firmly grasped by hands of iron.

Freider drew his revolver, and rushed furiously up to Jack, at whom he was about to fire, when he suddenly stopped short, gazing with wrapt attention at the armlet which Mrs. Steiner had given him that morning.

His coat-sleeve had been torn by his captors, and it was distinctly visible above his wrist.

"Where did you get that from?" he enquired. "The last time I saw it was in Pretoria, and the President himself was wearing it. This requires some explanation, young man."

"I have none to give you, and you are at liberty to draw your own conclusions."

"That armlet has saved your life, for, as there is a sky above us, I was going to shoot you dead, in return for the blow you gave me."

"It was only tit-for-tat. You struck me first in a most unsoldierlike manner; I am an officer, and can no more brook an insult than you. What is more, I am a gentleman, and I have yet to learn that a Boer understands the meaning of the word."

"Tut! Don't bandy words with me," cried Freider. "We are stubborn sons of the soil, and know how to defend our own, anyway. You will be sent to Pretoria at once, and this lad, who I suppose is your servant, will go with you."

"Bravo!" shouted Andy. "That's your style. When I get to Pretoria I'll give Oom Paul a bit of my mind. I'm a British lion, and he has been twisting my tail a little too much. If he is a good sort, I don't mind shaking hands with the old buffer."

His bugle was slung over his shoulder, and putting it to his lips he blew a loud, musical, cavalry call, which sounded something like "Come, water my horses; come, fodder, my men," and the Boers, in spite of themselves, were obliged to laugh at his audacity.

"Schwab," continued Freider, addressing one of his men, "take these two prisoners to the railway, and see that they are entrained with the batch of English soldiers who have fallen into our hands, and are to be despatched to Pretoria this evening. I shall remain here a few hours to see if the Rednecks turn up, and if they do, Heaven pity them, for I shan't, as I can hold this house with ease against five hundred of the enemy. Pay great attention to this prisoner, as I have an idea that he is of some importance."

"He shall not escape me, and I will see that no harm is done him," answered Schwab.

Harkaway and Andy were bound together with a rope, one end of which was held by Schwab, who started his horse in a northerly direction, compelling them to trudge by his side.

"Keep up your spirits, sir," said the boy. "It isn't our fault, but all the same we're in for it."

"I should say we are out of it," replied Harkaway, dismally. "If you like it I don't. You've blown your last note on the bugle, and I have killed my last Boer during this war, unless an exchange of prisoners takes place. I don't relish the idea at all. We may be shut up in Pretoria for months, without any of the amusements of garrison life. We shall get something to eat, drink, and smoke, and have a shake-down. I don't see where the fun comes in."

To this view of the case Andy was unable to make any reply, and they proceeded in silence until a siding on the line was reached, where a train of trucks was standing.

In these were distributed about three hundred men of the Gloucester regiment, and some of the Gordons, who had been captured a short time previously.

The locomotive had steam up, and the newcomers had arrived just in time.

In each truck were several surly-looking Boers, fully armed, ready to shoot down, at a moment's notice, any prisoner of war who attempted to escape.

Dismounting, Schwab unloosened his captives, exclaiming:

"Hurry up, and get on board somewhere; pig in with the rest of the Rednecks."

"Hurrah!" shouted several of the soldiers, who recognised Jack, and remembered how bravely he had fought. "This way, sir, we'll make room for you, Mr. Harkaway. Jump in here."

Jack smiled, and stepped up to one of the trucks with Andy.

The men stretched out their arms, and pulled them in bodily.

They found themselves among sympathetic friends, and met companions in misfortune.

The officer in command of the train was about to give the signal to start, when Webb appeared, holding a revolver in his hand, and driving two men before him, whom Harkaway, not a little to his amusement, recognised as Mr. Fish and Corporal Potts, who looked very dejected and cast-down.

They got on the wheel and clambered into the truck where he was, and for the time both of them were too crushed to speak.

Webb's eyes were as keen as those of a hawk.

When he saw Jack he started, and staggered as if he had been shot.

Rubbing his eyes, he looked again, and then was scarcely able to credit the evidence of his senses.

"Harkaway !" he ejaculated. "I thought we had buried you alive."

"Not exactly, my dear fellow," answered Jack, with a provoking smile. "You had a try at it, but the deal did not come off. I am a prisoner in the hands of the Boers, it is true, but you are powerless to injure me."

"Don't make too sure of that," retorted Webb. "Like a cat, I believe you have nine lives, but Krause and I will come on to Pretoria, and prove, to the President's satisfaction, that you are the worst kind of a dangerous spy, and if the hempen cord doesn't circle your sweet neck it won't be our fault."

"I defy you," said Jack, "and I tell you plainly, Mr. Webb, that I shall avail myself of the first chance I get to shoot you, for you have assailed my life so often, that I consider yours justly forfeited ; and if I had you in this truck, I wouldn't mind strangling you."

"Go it, Mr. Harkaway," cried one of the soldiers, "if that chap has done you any harm, we'll lend you a helping hand."

"And so say a' of us," chimed in a brawny Highlander. "Dinna yer fash yersel' aboot sich a sittin' hen like that, mon. We'll make Cockalukie of him. He's got the grin of yer, mair's the pity, but your turn will come, d'ye ken. Oot with the paltry loon ; he's got a white liver, and a paper face, which shows that he isn't worth a bawbee."

At this speech the soldiers burst into a roar of laughter, and Webb slunk away like a whipped hound.

But there was deadly malice in his heart, and Jack felt sorry that he had met him, as he would rather Webb had not known where he was going.

The signal was given, the whistle sounded, and the train moved away, carrying the captured, but not disgraced, soldiers to their destination.

CHAPTER XIV.

THE CORPORAL HAS A BOLD IDEA—GEISER THE BOER IS SUSPICIOUS—HARKAWAY AND POTTS MAKE A DARING ESCAPE AT JOHANNESBURG.

THE journey to Pretoria was a long, weary, uncomfortable one for the prisoners of war, and they were glad when they were told that they would shortly arrive in Johannesburg, for that city was the beginning of the end of their travel.

Fish occupied his time in writing specials for his paper.

Andy practised on his bugle.

The captives generally would not have cared a rap if they had not run out of tobacco ; but in many instances their guards kindly parted with some of their own.

The hot day was drawing to a close, and they expected to be in Johannesburg in an hour's time, where a halt was to be made for forty minutes.

Corporal Potts sought Harkaway, who was leaning over the side of the truck in a melancholy manner, and touched him lightly on the shoulder.

"Excuse me, sir," he said, "but I have an idea. It isn't often that kind of thing strikes me, but when it does it acts in a peculiar manner. I want to confide in somebody and ask advice."

"Don't bother me, my good fellow," replied Jack, petulantly. "I feel like a caged panther, and want to fly at somebody's throat, a Boer for choice, yet I could rend any person who upset me. I thought I should get the V.C. or die in the attempt, and here I am being taken to Pretoria as helpless as a baby in arms. It's enough to drive a man of my calibre clean out of his mind."

"Try a sup out of my bottle. It ain't all gone yet. A little of the Peruvian's stuff goes a long way, and I have been nursing it."

"Not for me, drink it yourself, and tell me your idea, if you want to. I daresay I shall survive the infliction. You can only add another lump to the burden I am bearing. Drink up, and air your eloquence."

"I don't know whether I will or I won't, but I'd rather," answered the corporal, who raised the bottle to his lips, and drank a dram.

The bottle was now empty, and he dropped it on the track, adding, as he lowered his voice—

"I've got a friend in Johnsberg, sir. He's a Jew, named Israel Malachi. He used to come to the Diamond City, as they call Kimberley, to transact business, and one night I saved his life from a couple of footpads, who had got him down and were going to bash his brains out, after robbing him. He swore he would do anything for me to show his gratitude. He keeps a restaurant, and, just before the war broke out, sent me his card. I have been in the town, and I know where his house is."

"Malachi !" repeated Harkaway. "That name recalls memories in my mind ; but no matter—proceed."

"I'll read the card first ; here it is," exclaimed Corporal Potts : " 'Israel Malachi. Cheap Well-cooked Meals. The Rest Café, 26, Pritchard Street (opposite the North-Western Hotel). Cannot be Beaten. No War Prices. Meals from One Shilling.' "

"I don't see anything in that calculated to interest me," snapped Harkaway.

"Mark time, sir. Don't be in such a deuce of a hurry. You should never bustle anybody's cattle. Now, look here ! It will be dark when we get into the station ; there is no twilight, and the sun sets at seven. If we could make our escape without being perceived, and get to friend Israel's, he would be bound to give us shelter until we could disguise ourselves and make good our flight. What are two of us among so many prisoners ? We shan't be missed. Buck up, sir, and have some life about you."

Jack's listless air vanished.

He saw in a moment that the idea was good and feasible, only requiring pluck and daring for its execution.

There was the risk of being shot, but what is that to a soldier in time of war, when every man carries his life in his hand.

"We'll do it, corporal," he cried, excitedly. "I'm your man."

"'WHAT PRICE MAJUBA!' CRIED HARKAWAY, CUTTING DOWN A BRAWNY BOER, OVER SIX FEET IN HEIGHT."

No. 4.

"Israel Malachi lives just round the corner by the station," continued Potts. "He does no business after dark, for he isn't in the high class supper-line, as you can tell by the price on his card. He can put us in a garret or a cellar, I don't care which, and it will be hard if we can't get back to our comrades somehow."

The dark shadow of a tall, burly Boer fell upon them, and a hoarse voice demanded:

"What's that you are talking about. It sounds to me as if you was plodding together. You had best mind what you are about. We caught a spy outside Ladysmith, and Freider cut off his ears and nose before he chopped him in half. I was told to keep a watch on you, mine fine fellows, so you will do well to stob your plods, if you have any, or you will catch it hot, as sure as my name is Geiser."

"How is the war going on?" asked Harkaway, carelessly.

"What is the war to you, my poor stool pigeon?" asked the Boer, curling his lip contemptuously

"Oh! I don't know. I take an interest in what is going on behind my back."

"You was oud of it, I tell you. Your comb is cut, your wings are clipped, and your tail feathers pulled. I call you a moulting bird, not worth to have a shot at. Ach! I have the skin of a fine bird in my tent. It is the petticoat of one of your Scotch soldiers. I catch oup with him, he fall on his knees for mercy, and pray, and while his lips move I shoot him dead."

"I should think you heard some bad news at the last station, or you wouldn't be so savage."

"Yes," said the Boer, biting his lips. "I will not tell a lie. Your men are pouring in from across the sea, and make tough work for us. It is bad business. Lord Methuen and your Guards beat us with the bayonet at Belmont. It is not a fair game, we do not fight that way."

"You like to hide behind stones," remarked Jack, sarcastically. "That's the kind of fighting you clod-hoppers understand."

"Wait and see, till we clear you all out; you will find that a Dutch farmer is not to be trifled with. We are a great nation. When the war is over, the Britisher will come here as a guest of the State, and we will teach him to behave himself, as a servant, and not as a lord of the Transvaal. You must all eat humble pie, and I hope you will like it."

The conversation was interrupted by the slacking up of the train.

The shades of night were falling, and some of the men had already thrown themselves on the floor of the truck to sleep.

"That chap, Geiser, has got his eye on us. We must dodge him," muttered the corporal.

"He is an ugly-looking customer, and as artful as they make them," replied Jack; "yet I think we can throw dust in his eyes, and give him the go-by. I shouldn't care if I had a weapon of some kind."

"I have a knife in my pocket, sir, if it is of any use to you. I hid it in my boot when I was made prisoner by Webb and his Boers."

"Give it to me quick, corporal!" cried Jack. "You are slower in your movements than I am. We shall be in the station in a minute or two. The first thing the Boers will do will be to shake hands with their friends and steer for a drink. We must drop out of the car in the darkness, and trust to our luck to get out of the station into the street. If it wasn't for our kharkies and helmets we should be all right."

"We can but try, sir; and I'll take my oath I'll do my level best," said the corporal, with a look of determination.

The train now glided into the dimly-lighted station, and came to a standstill.

There were several burghers on the platform, with whom the guards, jumping down, fraternized, and a Babel of talk arose.

The captive soldiers looked on, without any interest.

There was no one to say a kind word to them, or offer them anything.

They were down-hearted, worn, and weather-beaten.

"Come on, sir, now's our time," whispered Corporal Potts. "We must steal along to the east door; once through that and we are in the street, where I don't think anyone is likely to stop us."

Jack let himself down, without attracting any attention, and was closely followed by the corporal.

They crept along under the shadow of the cars, until they came to one in which several burghers had been travelling together.

It was deserted for the time, the door was open. They saw a heap of blankets and some overcoats.

Stretching out his hand, Jack seized a couple, one of which he handed to Potts, who slipped it on, Harkaway doing the same thing with the other.

Two white canvas, smooth-topped caps next attracted his attention. These they put on, in place of their own, and their disguise was complete, only their thoroughly British faces could distinguish them from Boers.

Skirting the crowd, they reached the door of exit.

This part of the station was in comparative darkness, and they were congratulating themselves, when a sombre form suddenly appeared and barred their way.

"Geiser, by jingo!" muttered the corporal, in dismay.

"Stand firm," replied Jack. "Stick to me, shoulder to shoulder."

"Who goes there?" demanded Geiser, sternly, as if he was on sentry go. "Show your pass."

Jack had one hand in the pocket of the coat he had taken, while the other was on the handle of the knife in his belt.

He did not want to use this except in self-defence, for the idea of fighting with a knife was repulsive to him.

All at once he felt a piece of paper in the pocket and produced it.

"Here it is," he said, in an off-hand manner. "Will that do for you? It is duly signed and perfectly regular."

"I have only your word for that," answered the Boer. "Hand it over, I want to look at it."

Jack gave him the paper, and Geiser, striking a match, examined it, reading the words: "Pass one to Pretoria.—JOUBERT."

"Humph!" growled the Boer, "this is formal enough, and no forgery, as I know the general's signature. Where are you going? You'll have to baas oop, or you'll miss the cars, which don't stay long here."

"We have some letters to deliver to a friend in the town," replied Harkaway, vaguely.

"That means a glass of good liquor, I'll warrant, and, with or without your permission, I'll come with you. Where did you get on board the train? I don't remember seeing your faces before, although they seem familiar to me somehow."

"Step out if you're coming," said Jack impatiently. "I never saw a man with such a jaw on him."

Geiser made no more ado, but walked out of the station, with the other two at his heels.

The latter saw that he suspected them, and meant to stick to them like a bird.

They could not do anything until they got rid of their tormentor.

Under the station wall Jack espied a short, thick piece of wood, which he picked up quietly and held behind his back.

Seeing the movement, Geiser exclaimed—

"Have you dropped anything?"

"Hold hard a minute," replied Harkaway. "I thought I saw a piece of money shining here."

"Our streets are not paved with gold, as the English think they are," replied the Boer, with a laugh. "All the same, some careless burgher may have dropped a pound sterling. Let me have a peep; finding is keeping, you know."

In his turn he stooped down, and as he did so, Harkaway gave him a whack on the back of the head which stretched him senseless on the ground.

Jack drew the body under the shadow of the wall.

He was as cool as a cucumber, but the corporal was trembling like a leaf, and muttered:

"I don't know whether I will or I won't, but I'd rather," from the force of habit feeling for his flask, and sighing deeply at not finding it.

"I thought that was the best way to get rid of him," remarked Harkaway. "I didn't mean to employ the knife unless I was compelled. Hurry up, and show the way to Malachi's. When Geiser comes to there will be a nice old hunt for us."

"Good old Geiser! Didn't he take his medicine nicely," replied the corporal, grinning. "You don't hit softly. He weighed in for a quiet spell, and I should like to sport a bit of gold that he doesn't wake up before the train goes. But here we are, sir; there's the Rest Café right in front of you. We've only to cross Pritchard Street, and there is the old Jew himself, just putting his shutters up. We've caught him finely."

They hurriedly crossed over, and the corporal touched the Jew, Israel Malachi, on the arm, causing him to turn round in profound astonishment.

Corporal Potts whispered a few words in the ear of the Jew, Israel Malachi, reminding him of their former acquaintance; and fully stating the position he and Harkaway were in, urgently implored him to give them all the assistance that was in his power, if it was only a night's lodging in some secret, and secluded part of his house.

The old Jew looked terribly nervous, for it was a dangerous thing to do, and he fancied he already felt the lash of the Boers sjambocks over his shoulders, but he extended his hand to both of the fugitives, and bade them enter.

The next moment they found themselves in a comfortable dining-room.

There was only one other occupant of the apartment, who was an Englishman.

"That is a friend of mine, by the name of Smart," exclaimed Israel Malachi. "Father Abraham, what a country they will make of this, when they have beaten the Boers. What is it now? Sheol let loose. A Hebrew cannot keep his shabbos. Sit down and I will get you something to eat and drink; then I will give you a nice dry cellar, with some straw, and you must do the best you can."

"Perhaps this Boer Geiser you speak of," Malachi continued, "is not much hurt, and will go on by the train, so you will be all right to skip away to-morrow."

Jack had his doubts about this.

He fancied that Geiser was an obstinate Boer, who would not leave the town until he had searched every house in the vicinity of the station, and fully expected to have a rough time of it before long.

However he was thankful for small favours, and glad enough to get in somewhere.

"Will you have a little drop of Kosher rum, which I know is a favourite beverage of yours?" exclaimed the Jew, addressing Potts, as he spread some cold viands on the table.

"I don't know whether I will, or I won't, but I'd rather," replied the corporal, accepting what at the Cape is called a big horn.

"Your hiding-place is ready for you. I will light you down, but you must have no lamp; and I will put you up to a little trick. On one side are a couple of hogsheads, which once contained wine, but are now quite empty.

"If you hear a noise of soldiers upstairs, you must climb up and conceal yourselves in those barrels, because they will hunt all over the dwelling, as if they were dogs after a rat. I know the hounds, for I am a suspect, and have had more than one domiciliary visit, and any moment I expect them to give me my walking papers, and I shall have to go, a ruined refugee, with the rest of the Outlanders to Lorenzo Marquez in the Portuguese territory."

"Excuse me, but your name is extremely familiar," said Harkaway. "I am a cavalry officer, but at present employed in the Intelligence Department, and was at Mafeking before I was made prisoner at Ladysmith."

"Ah!" exclaimed Israel Malachi, "that is where my poor brother Solomon went, and I have not heard a word from him since; I very much fear some evil fate has befallen him. It is bad business, for he had a paper on him which would have made his fortune some day; it was the plan of an old forgotten mine in Rhodesia, and there's millions in it. I think Sol must be dead and we shall never eat the Passover cake together again; but I have interrupted you, what were you going to say?"

"I scarcely like to tell you," said Harkaway, who felt some delicacy in the matter, "but your forebodings are right. I was with your brother when he died; he was killed for the purpose of a robbery, in spite of my efforts to save him."

"You make my heart very sad," answered the Jew, bowing his head, "but it is not for my will to be done. I told Solomon that he talked too much to strangers about the old mine. One night he was here, and he let it all out to a couple of men sitting at this very table where we are now. One was Webb, a traitor to the Union Jack; the other Krause, who was always for the Boers, and is paid by Joubert."

"Those were the very men who had him waylaid."

"His blood is on his own head. Holy Moses, what a fool he was to talk so loud. Have these men you speak of got the plan? If so they will be rich some day."

"No. Your brother gave it to me," replied Harkaway, "and it is now in the safe keeping of a friend of mine, named Fred Dawson, who is shut up in Ladysmith."

"We will be partners," cried Israel Malachi," eagerly. "I have money in the bank at Port Elizabeth, where I have another business; my manager there is the largest buyer in the Feather Market. As Sol was my brother, it is only fair that you should give me a share in what will be a big undertaking."

"Very well, I have no objection. Your capital will be of use. We will talk of it after the war."

The young man, Smart, had been looking steadily at Harkaway for some time; and at last, seeing a lull in the conversation, he ventured to speak:

"We are all friends here," he remarked, "and as I heard you say you were in the Intelligence Department, I don't mind admitting that I am a British spy, on my way to Kimberley from Pretoria."

"Let me test you," replied Jack, looking at him with suspicion.

He knew the latest regulation tests in such a case, and could easily prove whether Smart was an impostor or not.

"Will that do?" answered Smart, showing him a half-crown, with the head of George the Third, bearing the date in figures 1783.

"Good," ejaculated Harkaway. "Can you go any further?"

Smart took from his pocket a small Testament, which Jack looked over, finding that the fifteenth leaf was torn out, which was in keeping with the latest code issued by the chief of the office at Durban headquarters.

Jack put up his right hand to his ear, and then touched his left elbow; which was the sign that he recognised the man as an English spy.

These precautions are extremely necessary at all times, and perfect confidence being established, Smart began to talk freely.

"Bad news from the front has been received to-day by the general in command here, and the tide of invasion in Natal has been driven back," he said.

"Have we scored again?" enquired Jack.

"Lord Methuen has fought three battles, at Belmont, Graspan, and the Modder River, beating and driving the Boers back at the point of the bayonet. The Naval Brigade and the Guards suffered heavily. Kimberley is considered safe; and Buller is advancing on Ladysmith. We shall——"

He broke off abruptly, being startled by the sound of voices outside the dining-room.

"This way," whispered the Jew, "follow me, quick. The Philistines are upon us."

He took up a light, and hastily led the way along a stone passage, at the end of which were half-a-dozen steps leading to a cellar, in which, as the Jew had said, were two large barrels, between them being a heap of straw.

"Jump into the vats," exclaimed Israel Malachi, "and keep quiet as mice. Here is a revolver for you, Mr. Harkaway. If they should find you, do not hesitate to shoot."

"All right, I am not at all particular," answered Jack.

"Your detection," continued the Jew, "would prove my death-warrant; for the Boer skunks would hang me to the lamp-post outside my door."

Jack gladly took the pistol which was offered him, and nimbly clambered into the barrel, the capacity of which was sufficient to conceal him from view by sinking on his knees.

"Here is something for you," said the Jew, handing the corporal a flask. "I know your weakness for a drop of comfort when you are in a tight fix."

"That is where you make a mistake, my friend," replied Potts. "I never drink; I take it as a medicine. It is the hour of danger, and I accept it; but as to drinking —I don't know whether I will or I won't, but I'd rather."

He put the bottle in his khaki tunic, and the next moment he was lost to sight in the depths of his capacious barrel.

Malachi hastened back, and was just in time to hear a loud knocking at the door, which seemed to come from the butt ends of rifles.

He drew back the bolt, and opened the door, beholding Geiser, who was accompanied by two Boers.

"What is this knocking for?" he asked. "I was just going to bed. This young man lodger of mine and I were having a chat about the glorious victories of the Boers over the British, whom I hope will soon be swimming in the sea. Hurrah for the gay flag of the Transvaal! May it soon wave over London, and we have the pleasure of seeing the Queen in Pretoria Gaol."

"Talk's cheap, old man," answered Geiser, dryly; "you pretend to be very loyal to the Boers, but may I be hanged if I can trust a Hebrew Outlander."

"What you want now?" enquired Malachi, shrugging his shoulders, and holding up his hands.

"We are searching for two men in khaki, having over them Boer coats, which they stole, likewise caps. They are prisoners who escaped from the train and gave me the slip."

"They must have been clever indeed to do that; for I think I recognise you as Cornet Geiser, who belonged to a commando quartered here."

"Yes, they tricked me, and I got a blow on the head, but thank the stars my skull is thick, and can take a lot of walloping. We must search your house, and the sooner you show us a light the better I shall be pleased."

"With the utmost pleasure," replied Malachi; "go where you like. Make yourself at home, the house is at your service, from garret to basement."

The Jew, though not perfectly easy in his mind, hoped sincerely that his visitors would not be found.

It was unlikely that the Boers would look in the barrels.

"Ah! It is all right," he muttered, "they will not think of looking in the vats. Harkaway is labelled 'Port,' and that old soaker Potts is ticketed 'Sherry.' If it was full of wine, I believe the English corporal would drink his way out; he would keep on swallowing; until he got his head free, anyhow."

Holding a lamp, Malachi prepared to take the Boers over the house.

Geiser was in a suspicious frame of mind, and his temper had been very much ruffled by the treatment he had received.

His head ached, and like a rabid dog, he wanted to snap at somebody.

Stopping in front of Smart, he exclaimed, regarding him viciously:

"What is your trade, my friend?"

"I am travelling for a soap manufacturer in Capetown, but trade is bad; the Outlanders are all driven away, and I am going back to Natal, to see what I can do there."

"Show me your samples," continued the Boer, gruffly.

Smart produced from the pocket of his overcoat a small cardboard box, containing three cakes of scented soap.

"Have one?" he asked, curtly.

The Boer turned away with a look of disgust, as soap was a commodity which he and his countrymen never used, and he regarded the offer of some as an insult.

"It is no good," he remarked, shrugging his shoulders. "I would not soil my face with that greasy stuff."

The spy replaced his samples, muttering, "Thank you, old fellow, much obliged. I have my secret despatches from old friends in Pretoria to General Buller in those cakes of soap; you were very near the mark, but you have just missed it, my man."

The Jew conducted the Boers all over his house, which was a small two-storied building, and brought them to the cellar last.

"Humph," grunted Geiser. "I cannot see much in your house; but I say, what have you got in those barrels? Port is good, so is sherry to a thirsty man; suppose you draw us a mugful."

"I would gladly do so if I could, but the vats are empty. You have come too late for that vintage; upstairs in the dining-room I give you some out of the bottle. Ah, very fine wine; some of the best. It will touch the spot for you. Come on, do not waste any more time in this hole."

"You seem mighty impatient, and talk as fast as a Smaus. I must have a closer look at these barrels."

"Come away; what is the use of wasting your valuable time?"

"Tut, tut, keep your mouth shut, you old sheeny, you wag your chin too much," cried Geiser, giving him a push with his elbow in the stomach, which doubled him up and sent him staggering against the wall, where he stood trembling like a leaf.

"I'll make you sit up and gasp if you interfere with me," continued the brutal Boer.

Going up to the barrel in which Harkaway was hidden, he knocked the bung in with the muzzle of his Mauser rifle. No wine flowed, which convinced him that the Jew spoke the truth when he told him that the barrel had been run dry.

Still he was not satisfied.

"I'll put a shot into it, anyhow," he muttered, raising his rifle to his shoulder.

As he pressed the trigger, Malachi summoned up enough courage to rush forward and jerk his arm, which caused the bullet to go through the upper instead of the lower part of the barrel, and fortunately over Jack's head, or he would have been a dead man.

Turning round, Geiser clubbed his rifle, and knocked the Jew down with the butt end, making him lose his senses and lie helpless as a log on the floor.

"You Jew pig!" he exclaimed. "That action of yours has made me believe that after all there is something more than air in that coopered wood, so I shall take another shot, this time lower down."

These words were distinctly audible to Harkaway, who was in a quandary.

He felt certain that the Boer would shoot him, and shut up as he was, he had no chance whatever to defend himself.

Still, he must do something.

Acting on the impulse of the moment, he put through the bung-hole the muzzle of the revolver which the Jew had given him, and being unable to see, fired at random.

The ball struck one of the Boers standing behind Cornet Geiser, and the man collapsed with a wound in his leg.

At that identical moment the most horrible noises proceeded from the sherry cask.

They sounded as if someone was choking, and struggling for dear life.

Such was in reality the case.

A sad calamity had overtaken Coporal Potts.

Agitation and worry had engendered confusion in the brain of Israel Malachi, who, instead of giving the old soldier a flask of whiskey, as he intended, presented him with some crude petroleum.

Naturally the corporal took a drink, and swallowed a good quantity of the fiery stuff before he found out his mistake, the consequence being that he felt internal qualms, and fancied that a furnace was raging inside him.

"By thunder!" shouted the Boer, Geiser, "the secret is out now. That vile Jew has deceived me. Right wheel, Fritz. Get out of the line of fire, and pour in twenty rounds from your Mauser. You give one sherry, and

I'll give the other port. They don't play tricks with this Boer, not if he knows himself, and he thinks he does; that dodge was *sehr* goot, but I go him one better, you see."

Harkaway found himself in a corner, a second time, for the two Boers had moved out of the range of his pistol, and if he fired again it would be at the empty air.

"I'll hoist the white flag," he said to himself, sticking his white pocket-handkerchief in the muzzle of his pistol, and holding it up as high as he could, so that it waved above the top of the vat.

Then he shouted as loud as he could :

"Hold on, don't shoot, we surrender ; respect the white flag."

"All right," replied Geiser. "You come out, and I make you my prisoner, once more. Play the game fair."

"Certainly," answered Jack; "I'm coming Wake up, there, Potts, and show yourself. We are clean bowled, middle stump this time, and the bails flying in the air. How's that, umpire?"

The pair scrambled out of their hiding-places, Potts, pressing his hands to his stomach and groaning dismally, while the tears flowed from his eyes, murmuring :

"Oh dear, I'm worse than a sick Kaffir. I've been poisoned. Won't somebody kindly put me out of my misery?"

The surrender, so quickly arranged by Harkaway, had completety thrown the wily Boer off his guard.

He had placed his rifle on the ground, butt downwards, and was resting his hands on the muzzle ; the other Boer was attending to his injured comrade.

With a sudden dash, Harkaway seized Geiser's rifle in the middle, and raising it pointed it at his head, being only a few feet off.

"Down on your knees, or I'll blow your ugly head off," cried Harkaway, in a commanding tone.

"Nit. That was not a fair game for to play ; I call this a ferdomdy trick. I was taken in by that cursed white flag."

"So have lots of our brave fellows been, by your canting hounds," retorted Jack. "Down on your knees, I tell you, and swear that if ever you meet me again, you will treat me with civility and respect ; as to the white flag, I adopted your tactics, and if you don't like it, you must do the other thing. This cellar was the same as a battle-field, for you were going to kill me if you could."

The Boer went down on his knees, and took a solemn oath that he would always respect Harkaway, and treat him well whenever and wherever he met him.

"Very well done," observed Jack, approvingly. "Something can be made out of a Boer, after all, though I must say the raw material is very bad to work on. You have learnt your lesson quickly, and now I will teach you a bit more. Don't get up. Keep on your knees ; I like to see you that way. Now, follow me, pay attention ; say 'Rule Britannia' and 'God save the Queen.'"

"What!" cried Cornet Geiser, "you ask me to do that? I, who am a friend of Oom Paul, Reitz, Leyds, and Grobler? It would make their hair stand up to hear of that. Mind you, if I say it, you make me by compulsion. Ach! I never thought it would come to this. If the story gets about, how they will laugh at me, for I am what they call one big bug at Pretoria.

"Here you are. 'Rule your Britannia' and 'God save your Queen.' Ugh! there is a lump in my throat. You make me sick. That Queen sticks. She will choke me. I say it, but I don't mean it."

"Now sing it," continued Jack, putting the rifle a few inches nearer to his head. "I'll set you a go. Don't mumble, but raise it. Give us a chest note. 'Send her victorious, happy and glorious, long to reign over us, God save the Queen.'"

With the utmost reluctance, and making as many grimaces as a monkey with the spasms, the Boer followed Jack, and then rolled on the floor, burying his face in his hands.

"Hurrah! That's your sort. Bravo our side. 'Rule Britannia, Britannia rules the waves, and the Transvaal Boers shall never make us slaves.' Wake up, corporal, and have some style about you. Wire in and get your name up. Whatever *is* the matter with you, Potts? You look as if you have lost a shilling and found sixpence. You silly old boiled owl."

Saying this, Jack took possession of the rifles belonging to the other two Boers ; one of which he broke in half, by knocking it against a cask, and the other he handed to the corporal, who said, with a lachrymose air :

"I am very bad, sir ; I feel as if I had got what is known in my part of the country as the gripes, or mully-grubs, same as I had once when I was a kid, after pinching some sour apples in an orchard. It is all through something the Jew gave me, but I don't think he meant any harm, for if he is one of the chosen people he belongs to the tribe of Benjamin, which means that he is as good a Jew as they make now-a-days. It's passing off, sir, and I must give you a word of praise for the way in which you have conducted this campaign. What is the next move? Are you going to give them domino?"

"Bah!" said Geiser, who was recovering his composure. "I'll give you domino, some day, you old whisky thumper. What I said to your chum doesn't apply to you."

"Oh, doesn't it?" interposed Harkaway. "Then I'll make it my business that it shall. Take the same oath with respect to him, or I'll make a hole in your dirty hide that will let the daylight in.

Again the Boer, Geiser, was compelled to eat humble pie.

The dish did not exactly suit his palate, but he could not help himself.

He was a conscientious man as far as his religion went, and respected the virtue of an oath ; which he was undergoing his second humiliation, Harkaway examined the cellar door, and found a key in the lock, outside.

"Come on, corporal," he exclaimed ; "we'll take a walk, and get out of this blessed town as quick as we can. I shall lock the Jew and the Boers in here. They can stew in their own gravy ; or fight it out, like the Kilkenny cats, who were tied up in a bag, and fought till nothing was left of either of them, except their tails."

"No, no, I won't go back on good old Israel. He's proved himself our pal," said Potts, adding, with a knowing look and a wink of his eye, "he's got the key of the wine and spirit cupboard in his pocket; let me carry him upstairs, sir."

"I don't care. Please yourself," replied Jack.

The corporal took the Jew in his arms, and carried him into the dining-room, where Jack joined him, after locking the Boers in the cellar.

The movement brought Malachi to his senses, and when he heard what had taken place, he took up a handful of ashes from the stove, and cast them on his beard.

"I am lost and ruined," he moaned. "They will take it out of me for this. I dare not leave them in the cellar after you are gone, and I have nowhere to fly to at this time of night. Woe is me, I am undone."

"I don't think it is so bad as that," answered Jack. "If they can find any money they will take it, but the odds are they will let you alone."

"After beating me half to death, driving me into the street, and shutting up my shop; but I will not give way. My faith will support me; my consolation is, that I scattered seeds of kindness before you two. If there is anything in my poor place which will be of use to you, take it and welcome."

They made up a parcel of cold meat and bread, and a bottle of whisky was presented to the corporal, who shook his head dubiously, saying:

"I don't know whether I will or I won't, but I'd rather."

After which he drank a gill without winking, and coolly put the bottle in the pocket of his coat.

Wishing the Jew good-bye and good luck, Harkaway and Potts went into the street, and walked quickly along until they came to a corner, when they were accosted by a boy, who exclaimed:

"Where are you chaps going? You look to me like a couple of runaway Red-necks."

"Mind your own business," answered Jack, giving him a box on the ear, which rolled him into the gutter.

Getting up, the boy favoured them with some vituperative language, and threatened to send the police after them, but he disappeared in the darkness, when Jack threw a couple of stones at him.

Thinking they had got rid of the Boer urchin, who from his appearance and speech they knew was not an Outlander Jack and the corporal chatted together at their ease as they made their way out of the town, which, though it was not late, appeared to be empty and deserted.

This was owing to the fact that the President had ordered all the Outlanders to leave.

Most of the women and children had previously left; the men had remained to attend to business, but they were told that if they stayed any longer they would have to join a commando, and fight against the English.

A perfect reign of terror existed in Johannesburg, the soldiers and police doing pretty much as they liked.

Houses were visited in the middle of the night, and suspected people were dragged out of their beds, to be brutally ill-treated and taken to gaol.

At last they got out of the town, and a fairly good road going through a well-cultivated tract of country spread itself before their view.

The idea of Corporal Potts, who knew the country, was to walk to the railway line, and to go down a few miles to Fordsburg Station, and take the morning train, which, when it left the Transvaal, would convey them through the Orange Free State to Bloemfontein, from which place they would go to Durban, and report themselves to the staff officer in command.

This was a well-conceived plan, and if they could carry it out, all would go smoothly with them.

Feeling tired, they sat down under some trees to rest; and an inclination to sleep, which was irresistible, came over them.

It was an absolute necessity, and they gave way to it without any anxiety, because they thought they were in no danger, for when Geiser got out of the cellar he would not know where to look for them; but they would not have been so much at their ease if they had noticed the Boer boy, whom Jack had chastised, grinning at them from behind a low stone wall, above which his head was just visible.

They had unbuttoned their coats, and their khaki suits were plainly to be seen.

"As I thought," muttered the boy. "They are Red-necks who have escaped, and are trying to get away in the night. I'll put the police on to them, as sure as my name is Yawcobb Strauss."

With these ominous words on his lips, he hastily returned to the town, having a look of fierce determination in his eyes.

Harkaway was already asleep with his back against a tree, and the corporal, looking fondly at his bottle, said drowsily:

"I don't know whether I will or I won't, but I'd rather," and dozed off with it in his arms.

CHAPTER XV.

BOER TORTURE OF A JEW — SURPRISE AND CAPTURE OF HARKAWAY AND THE CORPORAL — THEY ARE TAKEN TO PRETORIA—A FRIEND TURNS UP.

As soon as the Hebrew had recovered from the shock to his nervous system, he bethought himself of those who were confined in the cellar; and with tottering steps advanced along the passage until he came to the door.

A tremendous shouting was going on inside. Geiser was demanding to be let out; his subordinate joined him, and between them they made noise enough to wake the dead.

Directly Malachi turned the key and threw open the cellar door, Geiser rushed upon him furiously, and seizing his arm shook him violently crying. "You are in league with traitors, and I will deal with you in a few minutes; meanwhile, sit down in your dining room, and Fritz will guard you."

His companion placed himself by the side of the unfortunate Jew, who did not dare to move.

Geiser went back for the wounded Boer, and binding up his leg, through which a ball had passed without touching the bones, stretched him on the floor until he could be taken to the hospital.

He then went outside, and the first person he encountered was the boy Strauss.

"Are you a soldier?" asked the lad. "If so, I want to tell you something which ought to be worth a shilling."

"You shall have two if your news is of any importance," replied Geiser. "Have you seen two suspicious-looking men of military bearing creeping along the streets as if they didn't want to be looked at?"

"That is just what I want to give you information about. I have seen two such as you describe, and they are now asleep under the trees on the Fordsburg Road. They have the uniform of the English under their coats, and one is nursing a bottle."

"The very men I'm after," cried Geiser, waving his arm with delight. "Here is your money."

He did not stay to receive the boy's thanks, but hurried to a stable in the same street, where he commandeered a waggon, and a span of six oxen, which was to be sent to the Rest Café.

He next went to the police barracks, and obtained the services of a dozen men, fully armed, and took a couple of rifles for himself and Fritz.

With this force he intended to capture Harkaway and the corporal, and bring them back in the waggon, bound hand and foot.

It may seem absurd for him to require so many men, and to make such elaborate preparations, but he fancied Harkaway had friends among the Outlanders who were still lingering in the town.

Like a good many other Boers, he could not forget Jameson's raid; and was always dreading some new surprise.

On his return, he found the waggon standing outside the door.

Nothing was to be seen of Smart, the spy, who had vanished as soon as he heard firing in the cellar, not wishing to run the risk of being implicated in the affair.

The moon was now up, and shining brightly.

Sending for a coil of rope, he had Malachi taken to the waggon, and bound tightly by his arms and legs to the off-side hind wheel, which was of considerable size, and the body was so arranged that when the wheel revolved neither the head nor the feet would touch the ground, but the man would go round and round in ceaseless and constantly increasing agony.

"Oh, Heaven, what have I done that this should happen to me? Let me go, inhuman monster that you are, or kill me at once, and put me out of my misery."

"It is a nice night for a moonlight ride," replied the Boer, with mocking laughter. "Ho, ho! we shall see some fun and hear some music. You shall have your Calvary in return for your treason. If you die, what do I care? It will only be one more skull for our Golgotha."

Geiser looked at the poor wretch with contempt; and getting into the waggon with Fritz, crouched down among the police, who could not be seen from the outside.

The waggoner was a common labouring man, who would not be likely to attract attention.

Waggons are seen everywhere in the Transvaal, and nobody turns his head to look at them; but had there been anyone about, the spectacle of the Jew on the wheel would have excited curiosity, and aroused sympathy.

Everywhere, however, silence reigned.

Lights were out and people indoors.

It was as if the Curfew bell had sounded, or they were going through a city of the dead.

At first Malachi uttered plaintive cries; but as the blood rushed to his head, and issued from his nose and ears, these died away.

The hour of midnight was striking from a clock outside the Municipal Building when the waggon came to the spot where Harkaway and the corporal were placidly slumbering, unsuspicious of the peril which environed them.

Stealthily Geiser and his men crept out of the waggon, and formed themselves in a circle round the Englishmen, each one having his rifle at his shoulder.

It was a critical moment for Harkaway and his companion, for they were caught in a trap.

The Zarps, as the policemen are called, had received strict orders from Geiser not to fire unless the word of command was given, as his desire was to recapture Harkaway and take him alive to Pretoria, thinking that Jack was a prisoner of distinction, and that he would be rewarded for doing so.

For the corporal he did not care so much, as he regarded him only as a common soldier.

To rouse the sleepers Geiser discharged his revolver in the air, the report causing Harkaway to spring to his feet with the rapidity of an indiarubber ball. The corporal, however, was too much under the influence of dop (Boer brandy) to hear anything, so that he did not move hand or foot.

Seeing the Zarps and a dozen rifles levelled at him, Jack gave himself up for lost, and folding his arms across his breast, looked calmly at Geiser, fully prepared to die, as a brave man should.

There was no weakening of the knees, twitching facial muscles, or blinking eyes about him. Jack was made of sterner stuff than that, and showed a bold front.

Geiser paused for fully half a minute before he spoke, as if he expected that the Outlanders still remaining in Johannesburg were ambushed somewhere, and would come to Jack's rescue.

Finding that this was not the case, his grim face relaxed, and a smile stole over it. At a sign from him a Zarp advanced, and seizing Jack, fastened his hands together with a rope.

Geiser gave the corporal a kick in the ribs, which only elicited a grunt; but another one made him murmur:

"Leave off your blooming larks; I've had enough, I tell you, and shan't be fit for parade to-morrow if I don't watch it. What do you say? Have another? Well, I don't know whether I will or I won't, but I'd rather."

With this he sank off to sleep again.

Telling one of the Zarps to stand by and bring him in when he recovered, Geiser turned his attention to Harkaway, saying :

"You think yourself clever, but you can't do me. You shall not escape again, I swear ; for I mean to take you in a wooden cage to Pretoria, like the lion Cecil Rhodes sent to Kruger. You forced me to sing your Queen just now, and you must sing Oom Paul, or I'll know the reason why. Say it after me— 'Oom Paul is a good fellow, by him the British are undone. He'll drown the Rednecks in the sea, and then he'll go to London.'"

"I should have that stuffed and put in a glass case; it would do for the Pretoria Museum. As for singing it, I'm not taking any, thank you. Bad verse doesn't agree with me, and I don't want any in mine," said Harkaway.

Geiser was about to make an angry retort, when a horrible groan came from the hind wheel of the waggon.

Turning his head, Jack was amazed to see the Jew lashed to the spokes.

His blood-stained face looked the picture of death ; and a more dreadful sight he had never beheld.

"You barbarian," cried Jack ; "is that how you treat a human being ? The Boers cannot be civilised ; they misuse the white flag, fire Dum-dum and explosive bullets, in fact they seem capable of any atrocity. Why don't you kill the poor beggar at once, you brute, and put him out of his misery ? "

"He is only an Outlander, and a Jew at that," answered Geiser, who, going up to Malachi, cut his bonds, letting him fall in the road, like a crushed, helpless worm.

Then he spurned him with his foot, and spat at him with contempt.

"You dastardly coward," Harkaway cried. "Don't I wish I could get at you. I'd spoil your beauty, my man ; and put a head on you like a zebra, when a lion has done with him."

"Shut your mouth, or I'll knock your ivories down your throat," vociferated Geiser, who shook with passion. "Bundle him into the waggon, and take him to the railroad depot. There is a large wooden crate there, which was used for earthenware. It's strong, and I'll warrant he doesn't get out until Kruger orders him to be shot."

Jack was pushed without ceremony into the cart.

The men followed him, and fearing to the last that Jack might elude him, Geiser stood over his captive with a revolver.

Malachi looked as if he had not long to live, if he was not already dead.

They left him to the charity of the first Samaritan who came by.

Corporal Potts was looked after by the Zarp, and his fate seemed to be renewed captivity.

Jack did not know when he would see him again, though the destination of both was Pretoria.

The station being reached at about two o'clock in the morning, Harkaway was promptly placed in the wooden crate spoken of by his captor, and the lid firmly tied down.

Its size was not sufficient to allow him to stand upright, nor to lie at ease, without drawing his legs up ; but he was unbound, and could use his hands, which was a great comfort, as the flies were numerous and irritating.

Only a single light burned in the station, which was deserted with the exception of Geiser, who sat on some mealie sacks vigorously smoking his pipe, which contained the Boer tobacco called "magaliesberg."

He drank a little dop now and then out of his flask, and watched the prisoner through the bars of his cage, which were about two inches apart.

"I am fairly cornered this journey," said Jack to himself. "It's all up the veldt with me unless I have a stroke of luck. Perhaps Mrs. Steiner will be in Pretoria ; she promised to help me. Maybe the armlet she gave me will be of some service if I can see Kruger. The old fox is superstitious, and I fancy he thinks there is some charm attached to it. It was of use to me at Ladysmith. It is well known to those in authority, and commands respect for the wearer."

Then his mind wandered to those he had left behind.

The unfortunate Jew ; the bibulous corporal ; his dear friend, Fred Dawson ; little Andy, the bugler ; Mr. Fish, the war correspondent.

The two latter he imagined to be already in Pretoria ; and, finally, he thought of the American, Cyrus Vanderbilt ; and, not without an inward tremor, of the truculent Boer Krause, and the vindictive traitor, Webb.

At six o'clock the officials made their appearance, passengers arrived, Geiser had the crate put in a truck, and, to be certain that Harkaway should not slip through his fingers, sat on the top of it.

The people stared curiously at Jack, and a leading citizen asked Geiser what he had inside the cage.

"That is a cross between the British lion and the Outlander jackal," replied Geiser, grinning until his capacious mouth opened from ear to ear nearly. "I was on the veldt, and I caught him on the hop. He will go well with the Polar bear in our museum after we have strung him up to a tree."

The whistle of the locomotive was heard, and the train started for Pretoria, which was not a long journey from Johannesburg.

On their arrival, Geiser had the cage deposited on the platform, and looked round for a porter, with a barrow, to take it and its living freight to the President's house.

He secured one, and looked round again, as if he expected to see somebody ; nor was he disappointed, for Webb, entering the station, rapidly approached him.

"Ha ! " exclaimed Webb, looking at Harkaway. "Well done. I see you have stuck to the prisoner. Where are you going to take him ? "

"To the President's, as you told me to do, if you were not here," answered the Boer. "I had to put him in this box, for he is as slippery as a greased black snake, or a Zulu Kaffir after a hard day's work in the sun. You don't know what a dance he's led me : but I haven't time to tell you now. I can only compare him to a flea, which is here, there, and everywhere."

Without any further parley Jack was conveyed through the streets, a tarpaulin being thrown over him to avoid a mob, and when within a few yards of the President's house, he was ordered to crawl out from his prison, and march between Webb and Geiser into a small room that served as an office, the door of which was open.

At a table sat Mr. Kruger, who was reading a long telegram just received from the front.

A small packet of papers tied with red tape was to be seen on his left.

He looked up as the party entered.

"Here is the spy, Harkaway, of whom I spoke to you, sir," said Webb. "We captured him at Ladysmith, and the general sent him on here, for you to deal with. He was on active service in Mafeking, and is a most dangerous man. His disguises are numerous. He has just penetrated our lines, and revealed our positions, causing us great damage and slaughter. I can swear solemnly to his being a spy for the British Intelligence Department. He should not be treated as an ordinary prisoner of war, but be shot at once, to prevent him doing further mischief to the Boer cause ; if you send him to the new prison at Waterfal he will most likely escape, or incite both the rank and file to open mutiny."

"What have you to say in response to charge?" asked the President, who looked worn and weary, his face telling of sleepless nights and bad news.

Harkaway pulled up his sleeve, and raised his right arm, pretending to smooth his hair, which was ruffled.

The President's eyes fell upon the armlet which Mrs. Steiner had given him, and he looked utterly dumbfounded.

"Retire," he said, hastily, addressing Webb and Geiser. "I wish to. question the spy in camera. The examination must be strictly private. Be good enough to close the door after you."

It was Webb's turn now to look astonished, for he thought he had got it all his own way, but he obeyed, and vanished with Geiser.

Jack's heart began to beat with hope again.

He drew himself up, until he was a couple of inches higher, and, twirling his fair moustache, indulged in a self-satisfied smile.

"Where did you get that armlet?" asked Kruger, betraying unwonted excitement. "It was mine, and I attach especial value to it. I had it from an old Kaffir woman, who was reputed to be a witch. It came to her through a miner, who found it in the ground, and thought nothing of it. It has brought me good luck, for before I had it I was very poor. I have shown it to all my principal friends, some of whom declare that it dates back to the days of King Solomon. I gave it to a particular friend, and naturally want to know how it came into your possession."

"It was presented to me by one with whom you are well acquainted," replied Harkaway, in his politest manner. "She is a most charming lady, of the name of Steiner, whose life I had the pleasure of saving a little while ago in Ladysmith. The ruffian who assailed her is dead. He was a friend of the man Webb, who has just left, and Krause,

who is one of your secret agents, and their hatred for me arose in Mafeking. It is partly a personal dislike, but I have something they which to get hold of ; if——"

"Never mind those details," interrupted Kruger, "let us deal with the armlet, which the old miner, Tati Jack, found in Kimberley. In return for services rendered, I gave it to Mrs. Steiner, and promised that if she sent it back to me, I would grant any favour the bearer wished, as I knew she would not return it without having an object in view. You cannot be an unworthy person. Mrs. Steiner must think highly of you, or you would not have the token of my friendship with her. She is at present in this city. I saw her only yesterday ; our interview was brief, and nothing was said about the armlet. I have only to ask what you require of me."

"Exactly," replied Jack, jauntily. "I am glad everything is clear, and you have come to the point. Please give me a pass through your lines to the other side of the Tugela River."

"Very well. I will write it out, and affix my seal of office to it. Excuse me for a few minutes while I go in another room to do so."

Harkaway bowed, and the President left him alone.

The first thing he did was to put the packet of papers tied with red tape into his pocket, muttering :

"They say I'm a spy, and by Jove I won't be called one for nothing. I bet this parcel will turn up trumps when I open it. General Buller will be at Durban by the time I get there, and he ought to give me a step for what I have been through and done."

"There is your pass, Mr. Harkaway," exclaimed the President when he returned. "If you are the dangerous spy that Webb alleges you to be, you can see that I am not afraid of you. The Boers are too powerful a nation to trouble themselves about one man. I wish you a pleasant journey, and hope I shall not see you again in Pretoria."

"If you do, it will be under different circumstances, as I am looking forward to eating my Christmas dinner with you ; and I will bring you a little British Union Jack to stick on the top of the Christmas pudding."

"Isn't that rather a proud boast. Perhaps it will be the other way, and you will see us in Cape Town. Is there anything else you have to say? My time is valuable."

"You have two prisoners here who are of no importance," answered Harkaway, thinking of his friends Andy Pearson and Fish. "One is a bugler, the other a newspaper man, Pearson and Fish. I am going to the nearest hotel for a few hours before I leave. Will you have them sent on to me?"

The President promised compliance with this request, saying he could refuse nothing to a friend of Mrs. Steiner, who was so good a supporter to the Boer cause ; and they parted in a very amicable manner.

When Jack opened the door, and let himself out, he saw Webb and Geiser, who were evidently expecting to be called in to take him away, and have him shot as a spy at one of the northern forts near Waterfal, which is the second station out of Pretoria ; this being the spot where military executions usually took place.

"Out of the way, you fellow !" exclaimed Jack, pushing Webb on one side.

"What do you mean ?" asked Webb, turning pale. "Aren't you a prisoner ?"

"Not by a long way," answered Jack ; "I'm going strong. Got a free pass to the Tugela River, my boy ; and old Kruger gave me his blessing into the bargain. I told him if he'd hang up his stocking at Christmas, I'd put something nice in it, when we come to stay here in force."

Webb looked at him in amazement, and seemed completely stupefied, for the issue was totally different from what he had anticipated.

CHAPTER XVI.

WEBB IS MADE A PUBLIC SHOW OF BY HARKAWAY—HE VISITS MRS. STEINER— THE BAFFLED ASSASSIN—BOER CAMP AT THE MODDER—JACK IS ROBBED OF HIS PASS.

IN spite of the declaration made by Harkaway, Webb and Geiser still continued to bar his progress.

"I don't believe a word of what you have told me," cried Webb, grating his teeth. "You must be a magician if you can get over the President, after the character I gave you. Get into your cage again ; I shall take you to the gaol."

"Will you, by jingo !" retorted Jack. "Not if I know it. Perhaps you would look as well inside that wooden arrangement as myself."

Fearing there was going to be a disturbance, Geiser drew his revolver, whereupon Harkaway flourished the pass in his face, and seeing the great seal of the Republic, the Boer recoiled.

"Take a back seat," said Jack, firmly, "and give up your gun. I am boss of the situation ; one word from me will settle the lot of you. It's wonderful how I do it, isn't it,· but I do."

Thoroughly cowed by this display of authority, Geiser gave up his revolver, which Jack presented at Webb, saying :

"Now, then, you slinker, crawl into that cage, and the sooner you do the better I shall like it, as I want to be off and join Buller at Maritzburg, or wherever I can find him."

Pale as death, clenching his fists impotently, and biting his lips until the blood came, Webb went down on his hands and knees and crawled into the cage, beaten and humiliated.

In a moment Jack fastened him in.

He always carried some paper and a fountain pen.

Quickly he wrote an inscription, as follows, and tied it on the side :

"British spy. With care. This side up. Not to be rotten-egged, poked with sticks, or ill-treated in any way."

He next hauled the crate into the middle of the street, and a crowd began to collect.

"What are you doing ?" asked Webb. "This isn't fair. Let me out, and I'll promise never to injure you any more. Refuse my prayer, and I will haunt you to your dying day."

"Shut up ! You might as well talk to the wall as to me. You may think yourself lucky I didn't punch your wicked head for you ; but that's a pleasure to come, if you don't let me alone," replied Harkaway.

Since the war began, the good people of Pretoria were prepared for anything.

If they had seen a procession of monkeys on the backs of hippopotami they would not have marvelled, for had they not beheld our captured Hussars and our gallant infantry who lost their way at Elands Laagte.

But one citizen, more curious than the rest, asked, pointing to Webb, "What is it ?"

"I am not a showman," said Harkaway ; "but I am able to inform you that this animal is a dangerous English spy, who has been capturing Boers and roasting them whole on the veldt ; he has also put out the eyes of several Kaffirs, and has a fancy for scalping women and children, like a Red Indian."

A thrill of horror and indignation ran through the crowd.

"Do not be rash, ladies and gentlemen," continued Harkaway. "I do not wish to rouse your wrath against this miserable wretch ; pray do not ill-treat him. He may have a sorrowing mother at home. By no means pelt him with offensive missiles. Do not throw dirty water at him. The guards will take him to prison presently, and he will pay the penalty of his crimes."

Instead of pacifying the mob, these words only inflamed their passions to fury, as he intended they should.

There was a corner grocery hard by, which they raided for eggs, vegetables, paint, syrup, liquid dyes, red pepper, which they cast at Webb, until he was bruised and stained all over.

Then they got brooms and made him uncomfortable with the handles, howling and screaming like demons, the women being as bad as the men ; but above the din Webb's yells and execrations were to be heard.

At last some of the more savage and determined tore the cage to pieces, letting Webb loose, and he ran wildly up the street, with the ramping throng behind him.

Harkaway now inquired his way to the nearest hotel.

Going into the dining-room he sat down to an excellent repast, and showing his pass to the proprietor, coolly told him to send his bill in to the President, as he had no change about him.

Scarcely had he finished his bottle of wine when he was delighted to see little Andy and Mr. Fish walk into the room.

The bugler shook him cordially by the hand, expressing his joy at seeing his master once more.

"Wonders will never cease," exclaimed Fish, "taking out his note-book. "Here you are, enjoying yourself like a lord, right in the heart of the enemy's stronghold. The god of war seems to favour you. By the way, I hope the bottle isn't empty ; if so, you can send for another, and I will drink your health, whilst I jot down your adventures in my note-book."

They had a long talk together, and were surprised to hear of Jack's trials in Johannesburg.

They were very glad that they could go back to the English army, instead of remaining prisoners in Pretoria.

Jack determined to pay Mrs. Steiner a visit before he left.

He enquired for her address.

She was well known, and he got it.

He then found out that the train he wanted would leave at six, so that he had about three hours' time on his hands.

Telling Andy and Fish to meet him at the station, he walked to Mrs. Steiner's house, and rang the bell.

It was one of the finest mansions in the town, and showed that she was a woman of wealth and importance.

He was slightly astonished when it was opened by Dunko, whom he had last seen at Ladysmith, running away on the veldt; but as Dunko was mixed up with the spies, it was not strange on consideration.

Dunko smiled in the most civil manner, and said:

"It was not my fault, boss. I have to obey orders, and I didn't half bury you, after all. The English are losing so many officers in this war, I thought they couldn't afford to spare you."

"Hang your impudence, you Kaffir dog!" cried Jack, angrily. "Where is the mistress?"

"Go right through, Mr. Harkaway. At the end of the passage you will come to the garden, and Mrs. Steiner is in the grotto under the gum-trees. If you like, I will announce you. If I'd got a horn, I would blow it in your honour."

"Stand on one side," answered Harkaway. "If there is one thing I hate more than another, it is a cheeky nigger. You must learn to behave yourself when you are in the presence of a white man. I suppose the Boers have taught you that a Kaffir is as good as an Outlander."

"Heap plenty better, boss. Outlander no good, Kaffir sehr goot."

Harkaway bestowed a look of disgust upon him, and, not wishing to make an unseemly disturbance in a lady's house, walked through the passage indicated by Dunko, and, gaining the garden, had no difficulty in placing the grotto by seeing the luxuriant trees in which it nestled.

It was prettily built in the shape of a bee-hive, with chunks of rugged rock, among which flowers and creepers were growing.

It was just the spot for a lady to rest in of an afternoon, doze or read, as the fancy took her.

When Mrs. Steiner saw Harkaway, she got up and extended her hand, while her face wore a pleased smile of recognition, saying:

"I knew you would come; my dreams told me so. Your image has been in my mind ever since we parted at Ladysmith. I can guess all that has happened. There is no need to tell me anything. You have been brought before Kruger by Webb, and you have a pass to go to your own people. May prosperity go with you and Heaven be your guide in all things; though I wish you were one of us. What a gain you would

be to our cause. There are few so noble, brave, and true as you; but your honour would never allow you to leave your flag. Pardon the few rash words I have uttered. I recall them, and it is for you to forget them, as I know such a gallant gentleman as you are, and a British cavalry officer of distinction, cannot help feeling insulted."

Jack was surprised at her tone, and his cheek flushed slightly as the suspicion that this beautiful and singular woman loved him crossed his mind.

His flirtations at balls and in drawing-rooms, garden parties, and picnics had not touched his heart, which was entirely devoted to his country and the army.

He did not know what love, in the real sense of the word, was.

He loved a handsome woman or a pretty girl as he did a flower, a horse, or a work of art; but nothing more.

"I am afraid we have hard and trying times before us, Mr. Harkaway," she continued. "The Boers are an ignorant nation, who do not know the might of Great Britain, and, dearly as they love their homesteads, their wives, and children, will fight to the last for independence, struggling on as long as the faintest scintilla of hope remains; but you have come to pay your respects to me, and to say farewell. Your time is short, and I must not moralize."

"I'm glad to see you are so jolly here, Mrs. Steiner!" exclaimed Jack, who did not know exactly what to say, feeling slightly bashful, as all young men do, in the presence of a woman of the world older than themselves. "Oh, I must tell you; I had an awful lark with Webb this morning. He'll never get over it, poor beggar. I made him look such a fool right in front of Kruger's house.

As he spoke a Kaffir servant, not Dunko, came up, with a gentleman's card, on a silver salver.

She looked at it, and in a tone of annoyance ejaculated—

"Mr. Webb!"

"This is unfortunate," remarked Jack. "Not that I am alarmed, but you cannot expect me to be civil to him."

"Certainly not. Yet I suppose I must see the man, because we are mixed up in the Secret Service, in which he has played an important part. Do you know, Mr. Harkaway, I dread him, and fancy he will do me some injury, as Skiller tried to do when you interposed."

"Let me hide myself behind a tree," said Jack. "If he tries any nonsense on, I shall be ready for him. As you say, there is something sinister and chilling about him. Whenever I come in contact with him I feel as if someone had slipped a lump of ice down my back."

Mrs. Steiner nodded her head.

She told the Kaffir that she would receive Webb, and Harkaway hid himself behind a tree.

He was in his khaki uniform, having left his Boer coat at the hotel; and it struck him all at once that his revolver was in the pocket, and that he had no weapon of any kind, not even a knife big enough to pare an apple.

Webb was not long in making his appearance.

He had changed his clothes and washed himself, but he looked morose and sullen.

He had a black eye, and a piece of plaister concealed a cut on his cheek.

"What brings you here?" asked Mrs. Steiner. "I suppose you know that I start for Kimberley to-morrow on business with which you have nothing to do."

"Yes," replied Webb. "I am aware that you intend to assume the disguise of a nurse, and under the protection of the Geneva Cross get into the tower on pretence of nursing the wounded Boers. But I have come to tell you that you are a double-dyed traitress, and cannot be trusted any longer ; for you have got this man, Harkaway, off in some mysterious manner. He has fooled the President, and obtained a pass to go to the Tugela. I am satisfied it is through your means, and death is too good for you. If you love the beardless young English officer, why don't you say so, and go over to the enemy?"

"How dare you talk to me like that?" cried Mrs. Steiner, with flashing eyes. "You are no man to do so. Get out of my sight, you are loathsome. I would sooner see a scorpion than you."

"Not so fast, my lady. I have telegraphed to Krause about you. He has consulted others belonging to the Secret Service like ourselves, and it has been decided that you must die. You have been judged by a Vehmgericht (self-constituted tribunal), and I have been selected as your executioner."

In spite of her courage, Mrs. Steiner was speechless with terror, but she contrived to raise a cry which she knew would reach Harkaway's ears. Webb seized her by the throat, forced her back in a chair, and raised a dagger, which gleamed in the sunshine.

Jack ran from his place of concealment, snatching up on his way a garden hoe which was lying by the side of a flower bed, and with this he dealt the assassin a blow on the head just as the point of the dagger was grazing the alabaster skin of the lady just above the bosom.

Webb staggered back, and, throwing his long, sinewy arms round Jack, grappled with him. He could not have used the dagger, for Jack would have kept him at a distance with the hoe. As it was, they engaged in a trial of strength.

Webb suffered from dizziness caused by the blow he had received, but he was the more powerful of the two, and by sheer strength, born of desperation, forced him on his knees, and in another minute it would have been all over with Harkaway had not Mrs. Steiner come to the rescue, which she did by grasping the hoe Jack had let fall, and desperately attacking Webb from behind. He fell senseless to the ground, and Jack drew a deep breath of relief.

He was unhurt, but he noticed that Mrs. Steiner's swan-like neck was bleeding, and the front of her white blouse was stained crimson.

"How can I thank you?" he cried. "But you are hurt. The wretch has stabbed you."

"It is a mere scratch," she replied. "I am not such a child as to be frightened by the sight of my own blood. Leave this coward to recover as best he can. and kindly come with me into the house. It is useless to prosecute Webb. He is too much thought of by the powers that be. In future, however, I will never allow myself to be without a revolver, for the villain will certainly kill me if he gets a chance."

Entering the house, her maid put a bandage round the wound.

She was greatly upset by what had happened, and Jack did not stay long.

In fact, he could not do so, as it was time for him to go to the station if he wished to catch the train.

They parted in the most amicable manner, and leaving the house, Jack caught a tram-car, which conveyed him to the depôt.

He found Fish and Andy waiting for him.

Jack showed his pass, and they were given three seats in a carriage, which soon filled up with other people.

The journey was an uneventful one until they got near Kimberley.

The line was in the hands of the Boers as far as the Modder River, and the train stopped close to an extensive laager.

It was growing dusk.

There were few passengers left, these being soldiers and officials.

It was known that communication was interrupted, and réfugees had been put off at a station higher up.

Numerous fires were to be seen in the Boer camp.

On the right of the line the Kimberley searchlight could be distinguished.

Jack looked out of the window, and half-a-dozen crowded behind him to see what was going on.

One of these pushed rudely against Jack, who felt his hand gliding over his tunic.

He was tall, and had a long beard and side whiskers ; his peaked cap was slouched over his eyes, and in the ever-increasing darkness it was difficult to see his face.

Jack felt nervous about his pass and the packet of papers he had appropriated, which he had read.

They contained the full strength of the Boer forces, the number of guns possessed by them, and the tactics which had been settled upon by the commandoes, as well as other details of great importance.

"Do you want to pick my pocket?" demanded Jack, giving the man a shove, which caused him to slink away with an indistinct apology.

Scarcely were the words out of Jack's mouth, than the door of the carriage was thrown open by a big, burly Boer, who demanded tickets, or something to prove identity, before the travellers were permitted to alight.

"I have a pass," exclaimed Jack, "which includes these two persons who are with me."

He pointed to Fish and Andy, and the Boer, holding up a lantern, ordered him to produce it.

Harkaway felt in his pocket, and to his utter consternation found that, though the packet was there, his pass was gone.

"By Heaven!" he stammered. "It has been stolen from me. I'll swear that man with the bushy beard did it, when he was crowding me at the window."

"Can't help that," replied the Boer, with a grin. "You must come with me, before General Cronje."

"Stop that man with the beard."

The Boer turned his lantern, but the stranger had evidently slipped out of the carriage, for he was nowhere to be seen.

CHAPTER XVII.

MR. CECIL RHODES GIVES A MASKED BALL AT KIMBERLEY—SMART AND CORPORAL POTTS—THE SPIES' NEST—WEBB MAKES FRIENDS WITH MRS. STEINER, AND IS BAFFLED.

KIMBERLEY had stood a long and wearying siege, but the spirits of the brave garrison and the inhabitants were as high as ever.

Mr. Cecil Rhodes, who was called the Diamond King, of the Diamond City, gave a grand masked ball in the large house he occupied, and a number of prominent people were present in various costumes.

The spacious ball-room, adorned with flowers, was illuminated by the electric light, and the band belonging to a crack regiment was in attendance.

The giver of the ball was dressed as Charles I.

He wore a collar studded with the finest gems, and a crown set with diamonds, which were worth a huge fortune.

When the dancing was at its height, two masqueraders entered, one being attired as an English barrister, with wig, gown, and white bands; the other as a non-commissioned officer in khaki, which had seen some service, and he carried his left arm in a sling, as if he had been recently wounded.

Seeing a vacant chair, they sat down together and watched the dancers.

These two were Smart, of the Intelligence Department, whom we last saw at Malachi's house in Johannesburg.

The other was Corporal Potts, whom we left in the same town, guarded by a Boer soldier, after the capture of Harkaway.

"Here we are at last, Potts, safely landed in Kimberley, listening to the strains of the band, and watching the gay dance."

"I little thought it a week ago, sir," replied the corporal. "It was lucky you came up as you did and knocked that Boer on the head who was guarding me, or I should have been in a prison by this time, where, I suppose, Lieutenant Harkaway is kicking his heels. I owe you a debt of gratitude for bringing me here, and I hope I shall have a chance of fighting again before long."

"This campaign will last longer than most people have any idea of. But here comes the King—I mean Mr. Rhodes—and I want to have a word with him."

"Don't forget supper, sir. There's sure to be something good here, and I am as dry as an Arab in the desert."

"Go into the room by yourself, don't wait for me. I'll find you somewhere," replied Smart. "Though you did not put on any costume, you are easily recognised. It was a good idea of mine for you to sling your arm over your soldier's dress, for there is no one like you, and you attract the attention which a supposed wounded veteran deserves. Have a bottle to yourself, and enjoy it."

"I don't know whether I will or I won't, but I'd rather," replied the corporal. "It's better than shivering and shaking with ague on the veldt."

Smart went up to his host; they shook hands, exchanging a peculiar grip, like that of a Freemason.

"I heard you had arrived, Smart," said Mr. Rhodes. "I have seen the despatch you gave Colonel Kekewich, and we are deeply indebted to you for the information it contains. If General Cronje detaches part of his force to meet Lord Methuen this side of the Modder River, all the better for us; but I fear he will have a hard task when he meets the Boers in the neighbourhood of Spyfontein, for the hills are dangerous, and will take a lot of storming. I hope to see you often as long as you stay here. Have you any particular business in the town, or do you move on elsewhere at once?"

"I want to run down a famous female spy of the Boers, Mrs. Steiner, who, I am told, has left Pretoria to come here, acting on express orders from Kruger and Cronje."

"Of course," continued Smart, "they want to find out where your mines are placed. Do you suspect anyone of being a spy in Kimberley, and capable of giving shelter to our enemies?"

"If I did, and could prove it, he or she would soon be in confinement," was the quick rejoinder. "But now I come to think of it, one of the Intelligence here this morning informed me that suspicious characters had been seen going into the shop of a French barber, named Borlaise, who lives half-way up Main Street. That is all I can tell you. Come and see me again. Excuse me now—I have so many people to speak to. And everybody knows who I am, in spite of my mask."

He passed on, and Smart was left standing alone, feeling utterly lost in the crowd.

It was very warm, and he lifted his mask to wipe the perspiration from his face; and at the same moment a voice hissed in his ear:

"So you are in Kimberley? Beware."

With a start, Smart turned, and beheld a tall, thin man in front of him, dressed as Mephisto, but who he was he could not for the life of him divine.

"Who are you?" he asked, curiously.

"His Satanic Majesty, as you perceive. Do you not notice the sulphurous fumes which surround me? Perhaps you will make my better acquaintance after your decease,' was the grim reply.

Saying this, Mephisto gave Smart a brisk tap on the shoulder with his pitch-fork, and vanished from view, leaving the spy utterly bewildered.

He was annoyed also, for he did not wish his identity to be known.

Mephisto went on, threading his way through the giddy throng.

A smile curled his lip, and he muttered— "I am glad I discovered Smart, for he is a man who hates me as much as I detest him, and he would no more mind putting a rope round my neck than he would drinking a glass of wine. I only wish I could find out Mrs. Steiner as easily. That she is in this room I feel certain, and I am longing to tell her that Lieutenant Harkaway, who she evidently loves, has been shot by this time.

"I played him a nice trick when I rubbed up against him in the train, and stole his pass. It will require all my diplomacy to make her forgive and forget the attack I made on her in the garden at Pretoria. By Heaven! What a magnificent woman she is; and how rich!

"If she'd have me, I'd marry her like a shot, when the war is over. I know she dislikes me; but women at best are a contradiction, and worse men than I have married better women than she. It will not do to fawn upon her. I must make her afraid of me. She is like a high-spirited horse, and must be ridden with a tight curb."

So engrossed was he with his own thoughts that he did not see where he was going, and as he spoke, pushed somewhat rudely against a tall lady, beautifully dressed as Cleopatra, who was unattended by any cavalier.

The shock caused her mask to fall off, and she, with difficulty, caught it in her hand, but before she could replace it Mephisto recognised her, and was unable to refrain from laughing.

"I beg pardon," he said; "the collision was unintentional on my part. A fiend such as I represent is not supposed to have much manners or delicacy, yet my dear Mrs. Steiner, I apologise, and assure you it shall not occur again."

"I need not ask who you are, for I know your voice only too well," answered Mrs. Steiner in a vexed tone. "Am I always to be haunted by your shadow, Mr. Webb?"

"Fate seems to ordain it so, and I could not wish for anything better. When in your presence I feel as if I were on enchanted ground, and forget all the ills that flesh is heir to," said Webb, in his suavest and most polite tone.

"Have you been here long?" she asked, carelessly, as if she had not heard his flattery.

"I am here on special business, and the authorities believe I am a Natal refugee. I only came in a few hours ago from Cronje's laager, disguised as a mule-driver," replied Webb, "and am on the look-out for an English Intelligence spy, named Smart, whom I saw by accident just now. He is regarded by the Boers as a remarkably dangerous man, and my orders are to put him out of this world as quickly as possible. I have an introduction to a friend of our cause—Borlaise, a French hairdresser."

"That is strange, indeed, for I am staying in his house. Do you bring any news from the camp?"

"I am delighted to hear what you say, for I shall have the pleasure of meeting you, which, I assure you, is the essence of celestial bliss."

"Don't, for goodness sake, talk to me, Mr. Webb, as if I was a silly schoolgirl! I asked you what news there was!" cried Mrs. Steiner, impatiently.

"Not any of much importance," rejoined Webb, slightly abashed. "Cronje went yesterday to the hills about Magersfontein, and is preparing a nice little trap for the British. When Methuen advances from the Modder River to relieve Kimberley, the British will find twelve thousand Boers hidden among the hills, and if they make a frontal attack they will be nearly annihilated; but you will be gratified to hear that your friend, Lieutenant Harkaway, will not be among the attacking party."

"How is that?" she asked, becoming interested.

"Cronje is expected back to-morrow evening, and on his arrival, Jack Harkaway will be shot as a spy!"

"How can that be possible, when the President gave him a pass?" gasped Mrs. Steiner, much agitated.

"I have no particular liking for that young gentleman," replied Webb, "who has come out here full of martial ardour, to help wipe the brave Boers off the face of the earth; and to tell you the truth, Mrs. Steiner, I stole his pass, and the last I saw of him and his two companions, the bugler boy and a newspaper man, was when he was led off by a Boer sentinel, and I am certain, from what is known about Harkaway, that after Cronje has set the trap at Magersfontein, he will be shot."

"According to that statement, he has not more than twenty-four hours to live," remarked Mrs. Steiner, recovering her composure with admirable presence of mind. Of course, Harkaway takes his chance, the same as we do. If you or I were detected in this locality, what would our fate be?"

"Death!" replied Webb. "But we will not anticipate such a gloomy conclusion to our mortal career. I never give up until the last. If I were in prison now, under sentence of death, I should be thinking how to escape."

"Perhaps Harkaway will elude his captors. However, that is a matter of indifference to me," continued Mrs. Steiner. "We are all taking war risks. I shall have a little supper in my rooms at the Frenchman's after the ball. Two men you know are coming, and I should be glad of your company."

"With pleasure. Whom may I expect to meet?"

"Carl Hymer and Wallach. They were both Pretoria dandies before the war, wearing patent leather boots, high silk hats, and frock coats. Now one is working as an ambulance man, and the other as a mule driver. No one knows who they really are except myself."

"What duty have they assigned them by the Secret Bureau of the Transvaal?"

"One has to cut off or injure the water supply of Kimberley, and the other is ordered to explode one of the big mines on the Spytfontein Road."

"We part to meet again," exclaimed Webb. "You are really the goddess of war, and spread a halo over this black business; but we shall all have our reward when the English are conquered, and we can dictate the terms of peace in Cape Town. We are gambling for a high stake, but, by the powers above, it is worth playing for."

"Yes," answered Mrs. Steiner, her eyes lighting up with enthusiasm. "We shall sound the death knell of the British Empire, and found a mighty Dutch Republic in South

"DAWSON RAN BACK AND JUMPED INTO THE TRUCK, JACK AND ANDY FOLLOWING QUICKLY."

No. 5.

Africa. Adieu! Be true to the cause, and all will go well; I shall expect you."

With a sweet smile that thrilled his blood, the lady took leave of Webb, who walked towards the refreshment room, meeting on his way a Fool, with cap and bells, holding a stick with a bladder tied to the end of it.

This was filled with peas, which rattled as he swung it in the air.

Whether by accident or design, he struck Mephisto on the head, laughing loudly.

Whereupon Mephisto attacked him with his pitchfork, and a merry fight began, which made the onlookers laugh.

Webb got the best of the contest, and drove his opponent into the supper room, where he sat down at a small table, and taking off his mask, begged for a cessation of hostilities.

"Is it you, my dear Carl?" asked Webb, who saw before him his fellow spy, Hymer. "I see you combine pleasure with business, and have contrived to visit the ball. We shall have good news, I expect, before many days are over, and if you attend to your part of the work, there will be an early surrender, for people cannot live without water."

"Hush!" cried Carl Hymer, nervously. ' Don't you see there is a wounded Redneck behind you, who can hear every word we say?"

"I stand corrected," replied Webb; "it shall not occur again, but as to this wounded soldier, let us remove him. There are plenty of other tables where he can sit. Give him a rap on the head with your bladder, and I will make him acquainted with the prongs of my fork."

It happened that the person selected as the recipient of these favours was Corporal Potts, who was waiting for Smart.

The bladder rattled on his head, and the pitchfork started him off his chair.

"Hi! hi! stop it. Who are you playing the fool with? Don't bash me about the head as if I was of no account, and prod me in the stomach like a truss of hay."

"Didn't you think you were at the Modder River with Long Tom making music for you?" sneered Webb.

"It's my opinion you are a couple of spies, and I'll call for help if you don't leave me alone. You are here for no good purpose that I swear," said the corporal.

Webb became alarmed at this threat, as he did not want his personality inquired into too closely.

"We did not mean any harm, my friend," he explained. "This is a festive occasion, on which we all give and take. Buck up, and have a glass of something with us."

"I don't know whether I will or I won't, but I'd rather," rejoined the corporal.

And they were soon clinking their glasses together.

The wine had the effect of making the corporal good-tempered, confidential, and talkative; when asked by Webb what he was doing at Kimberley, he told all his business, to the amusement and satisfaction of his hearers.

"You are the kind of man I like to come across," exclaimed Webb. "Quite a treat, I assure you, that one doesn't often meet with. You are a friend of Harkaway's, and want to find him, and are here with Smart, the

English spy, who is on the look-out for a dangerous woman named Steiner; and you think Kekewich is going to make a sortie, to draw the Boers away from Methuen, on the Modder. Are there any more secrets you have to tell me? If not I will say good-night, as your company is not particularly entertaining."

He had altered his tone, becoming positively rude.

Receiving no answer, he and Carl left the corporal staring blankly at them, and murmuring—

"I don't like that demon with the pitchfork. Look how his tail curls up; and what a glare there is in his eyes. I'll give him beans if he comes back, and dares to talk to me again."

"What's the matter, corporal?" asked Smart, joining him at last. "Has something occurred to ruffle your feathers, my old warrior?"

"I've been talking to a fellow representing the king of the lower regions. He asked me a lot of questions, and I answered them."

"What did he say, and what did you?" inquired Smart, who appeared to be very uneasy.

"Upon my word, I don't recollect exactly," said the corporal, with a puzzled air. "This champagne wine has got into my head. First of all, he and his friend were talking about the Kimberley water supply, and I said my name was Steiner, and I was after a Mrs. Smart—I mean I was Smart, and you were Steiner, and she was after me. No, that isn't it! Mark time, I shall get it right in a minute. I wasn't Smart——"

"No, I'll be hanged if you are, or ever will be, if you go on like this," interrupted the spy. "You've made a pretty mess of it, and given the show away."

"How is that, sir? I am sure I am always very careful what I say. You wouldn't catch me opening my mouth to let out anything I ought not to. The two gents were perfectly harmless, and felt a little bit spreeish. The waterman was a turncock, I expect."

"Fool!" cried Smart, in a harsh voice. "You ought to go out in the trenches and get shot by a dum-dum bullet, which would explode inside of you, and blow you to atoms. You can travel by yourself after this, I don't want any more of you."

"Don't ask me to have a drop more, sir," replied the corporal. "But still, as you are so pressing, I don't know whether I will or I won't, but I'd rather."

He stretched out his willing hand for the bottle, and Smart, with a look of disgust, left him to enjoy his carnival.

The absent-minded beggar looked lovingly at the wine in his glass, and forgot all about his companion.

Smart had an idea that something serious was brewing among the Boer spies who infested the town, and as Cecil Rhodes had mentioned the shop of Borlaise, the Frenchman, suggesting that it was a likely spot for spies to harbour in, he determined to watch it.

Going to the cloak-room, he changed his clothes, and left the ball-room.

It was now half-an-hour past midnight.

The moon was shining.

Though the day had been very warm the night was extremely chilly, which is a peculiarity of the South African climate.

He buttoned up his coat, drew his hat over his eyes, and strolled towards Main Street.

On his way he came to an open space, and stood still, bending his gaze towards the Boer entrenchments.

Suddenly a jet of flame burst from one of the hills, which was followed by a sound like thunder, and a shell came hurtling through the air in his direction.

Being accustomed to this sort of thing, as he had been an artilleryman at Woolwich in his young days, he watched the shell calmly, taking shelter in a hole which had been excavated for building purposes.

The shell struck the ground, in which it buried itself without exploding, as was the custom with many of the Boer shells, which were imperfectly charged.

"The enemy are trying to wake us up," muttered Smart. "It amuses them and doesn't hurt us. It will take a better shell than that to make this town bump."

Climbing out of the pit and resuming his way, he had not gone far before he overtook a man whose contour resembled that of Webb.

Slipping over to the dark side of the street, he kept him in view, and, after going some distance, tracked him into a shop in Main Street, over which was inscribed the name Borlaise, hairdresser and coiffeur.

The shop was closed, as might have been expected at that hour of the night; but a light could be seen in the first floor window.

Webb gave a mystic rap at the side door, and in a very short time it was opened.

Smart lighted a cigar, and sat down on a doorstep opposite, determined to watch the house until morning dawned.

Webb, who was entirely unconscious of being followed, shook hands with Borlaise, a dapper little Frenchman who had let him in, and asked if Mrs. Steiner was upstairs.

"Ah! yes," answered the Frenchman; "the grand woman is in her parlour. Supper is on the table, and she told me she was awaiting you. I have to go to a friend's house, where there is some sickness, but I will join you later.

"Did she not look superb at the ball? Ah! I tell you she will reign queen of the earth when the English bullies are beaten. As a military nation the English are done for. No more victories for her; no more empire. South Africa for the Dutch, India for the Russians, Canada for the Americans, Egypt and Australia for the French! How does that sound to you, my friend? Great Britain shall sink to be one little Holland. John Bull think too much of himself for me. Hark! Madame is playing the mandoline!"

With a smile, the lively Frenchman put on his hat and went out in the street, leaving the door slightly ajar, so that he could come in without any noise or trouble.

Smart did not forget to notice this action on the part of Borlaise, and chuckled to himself.

He saw his opportunity, and did not neglect to seize it.

No sooner was the shopkeeper's back turned, than he glided into the house, like a thief in the night, and went upstairs as lightly as he could tread.

The door of the drawing-room was only partially closed, and he could hear the sound of voices.

On the landing was a table, on which stood some flowers in porcelain vases, and, thinking it a good place for hiding, he crawled underneath, and, sitting down, made himself as comfortable as he could, listening intently to catch every word which was uttered in the room.

Mrs. Steiner was the first to speak, saying, in a gracious voice :

"So glad you have condescended to visit my poor little room. It is nice to have someone to talk to; and we are old friends, you know. Pray, sit down. If you have no appetite to eat, we will gossip together. There are wines and spirits. Shall I wait on you? It will be a pleasure, for I assure you the past is forgotten. We are both working for the Boer cause, and that is enough to bind us together."

"Champagne, if you please; I never mix my drinks," replied Webb, throwing himself into a chair, and adding to himself : "What the deuce does the cat mean by all this civility? If she is a spy, so am I, and I'm not taken in easily. That woman is up to every move on the board, and I must be on my guard. She isn't so sweet and charming for nothing. However, I will take her as she is, and play my part like a star actor. I am a quick study. Is it tragedy, comedy, or melodrama? What shall we call the play? 'Spy against Spy, or the Fooler Fooled.' Mrs. Steiner discovered. Enter Webb the mystic. We only want the villain of the piece."

"I am here," muttered a voice under the table on the landing.

"You don't look comfortable," observed Mrs. Steiner, with a look of tender solicitude. "Allow me to help you off with your overcoat and hang it in the passage. Do pray make yourself at home. You know you can lodge in the same house; we have a lot to talk about, and I expect Carl Hymer and Wallach here before the night's out. We form a nest of conspirators. Isn't it charming? I call it quite a sporting kind of life."

Webb drank a glass of wine which she poured out for him, into which she carefully and unobserved dropped a small crystal, which in a short time would have the effect of producing sleep, more or less prolonged, according to the vigour of the recipient's constitution.

In a lamb-like manner he allowed himself to be divested of his outer garment, which she took to the landing and hung on a peg, at the same time taking the liberty of hurriedly ransacking the pockets, in one of which she found a paper.

The landing was illuminated in a pretty and effective manner by a dozen fairy lamps, which gave a subdued light of various hues, but it was sufficient to enable her to read.

She held it up, and burst into an exclamation of delight.

"The pass, the pass," she murmured, wildly excited. "Jack Harkaway shall be saved, or I will perish in the attempt."

CHAPTER XVIII.

WEBB IS CAJOLED BY MRS. STEINER, WHO GETS THE PASS—SMART ALLOWS HER TO DEPART, BUT CAPTURES HYMER AND WALLACH.

THE words uttered by Mrs. Steiner were heard by Smart, who up to this time was not aware that she was acquainted with Harkaway, whom he well remembered meeting at Malachi's restaurant in Johannesburg, and he began to take an interest in her at once, though he had previously heard enough to convince him that he would be justified in arresting both her and Webb.

For the time he did not move, being anxious to hear as much as he could.

"That wretched Webb has betrayed Harkaway to the Boers," continued Mrs. Steiner, talking to herself, little dreaming that Smart was so near her. "It is lucky, indeed, that I met him to-night, and have wormed his secret and the pass out of him. Jack has saved my life twice, and I will not prove ungrateful."

She paused, as she heard Webb moving in the room.

"What are you doing out there?" asked Webb. "You invite me to supper, and it is not very good manners to leave a man alone. Directly, we shall be invaded by our two spies who are going to disturb the water supply, and blow the big mine up. You know whom I mean, Hymer and Wallach. I want to have a little quiet conversation with you, but confound it all, I've come over so sleepy I can scarcely keep my eyes open."

"I'm coming," replied Mrs. Steiner, smiling, as she saw that the drug she had given was taking effect on him.

While the lady went inside to talk to Webb, Smart emerged from his place of concealment, and was bold enough to look in at the half-open door.

Webb's head had fallen back in the chair, and his eyes were closed, while he snored profoundly.

"She has settled him somehow," muttered Smart, "or else he has taken too much wine. I could easily arrest her, although I daresay she has a shooting iron in her pocket; but I want to bag those two fellows she was speaking about—Hymer and Wallach. They deserve to be executed, and it is quite time we shot a few spies as a warning to others."

All at once he was surprised to see Mrs. Steiner open a door, through which she disappeared into another room.

He did not think she was trying to escape, because she had no danger to apprehend, so he watched and waited for a few minutes.

At length Mrs. Steiner reappeared, dressed as a man, wearing a false beard and moustache, while her hair was tucked up under her broad-brimmed felt hat.

She was evidently prepared for a journey.

Smart at once entered the apartment, and, levelling a revolver at her, cried "You are my prisoner. I am an English spy by the name of Smart, and have been shadowing you for some time. Stand still, while I slip the handcuffs on your wrists, madame. One move, and you are a dead woman. I have got you at last, Mrs. Steiner."

"For Heaven's sake let me speak," she replied. "If you do me any harm, my friends in Pretoria will promptly avenge it. I am going to leave this town on an errand of mercy."

"Explain yourself; I am willing to listen."

"You may have heard of your compatriot, Lieutenant Harkaway, whose name has often figured in dispatches and newspapers for distinguished gallantry and deeds of adventure."

"I have had the pleasure of meeting him, and may say that he is a friend of mine."

"His life is in imminent danger, and I alone can save him," Mrs. Steiner went on, full of nervous energy. "I am only a poor, lonely woman, but I can do it. Will you let me go, Mr. Smart, and save your countryman?"

"We shouldn't like to lose Harkaway, that's a fact, and, as a rule, I don't make war against women; but you are one of the tip-top spies, and now I've got you I want to keep you."

"He had a pass given him by Kruger. It was stolen, and I have recovered it. If I can only get to the Boer lines before Cronje comes back from the Modder to-morrow evening, all will be well. Harkaway's fate and mine hang on your decision. Have pity, Mr. Smart. Be noble, be grand, and on my word of honour, you shall never regret it. You may want a friend at court, some day; you may have to travel the same road yourself. Don't be hard. It won't hurt you to let me go."

"Your pleading and eloquence disarms me. Go, and may you be lucky, Mrs. Steiner. Say nothing about my leniency, for you may compromise me with my superiors."

"Not a word; I would rather cut my tongue out. God will bless you. Good-bye. I shall ever have you in my thoughts. I have a golden wand, and will shower the precious metal upon you."

"I believe you are a good woman, and I can't blame you for doing the best for your country, and it is especially good of you to think of Harkaway in this, his darkest hour of need. I pay homage to you."

Saying this, he raised her hand to his lips, and kissed it.

She smiled upon him, and hurriedly left the room to undertake an anxious ride over the veldt.

Smart breathed a deep sigh.

Being a man of the world, he did not blame himself for what he had done.

Lighting a cigar, he drank a glass of wine, and had scarcely done so, when Hymer and Wallach walked into the room.

"Who are you?" demanded Hymer. "I suppose it's all right though, as Webb is here. Where is the lady?"

"She hasn't come back yet; we are expecting her every moment," answered Smart. "Sit down, and make yourselves at home. This is Liberty Hall."

The men did so, and began to eat and drink as only Boers can.

"Have you heard the news?" asked Carl

Hymer. "I have been at the club playing billiards, the click of the balls keeping time with the music of the Boer shells. By heaven, it is glorious!"

"What is it?" enquired Smart.

"Cronje has beaten Lord Methuen at Magersfontein, cutting nearly the whole of the Highland Brigade to pieces. That was the news from one runner. Now for the other."

"Go on," said Smart, feeling as if his heart was about to stop beating.

"The second runner says that General Buller crossed the Tugela River yesterday, and has been utterly routed by Schalk Burgher, who inflicted great loss on the British, and captured eleven big guns. The Rednecks will soon be in the sea. Hurrah!"

"Hoch! hoch!" grunted Wallach.

"I don't think it will make much difference to you, gentlemen," exclaimed Smart, recovering himself, and threatening them with his pistol. "I am an English detective, and you must surrender to me."

The Boers regarded him with amazement, and their countenances fell, while Smart indulged in a smile of triumph.

CHAPTER XIX.

HARKAWAY PLAYS THE BOERS A SMART TRICK — THE BALLOON — THE SHELL — DEATH OF KRAUSE AND GEISER — DOOM OF THE PRISONERS.

THE night was cool, even to chilliness, though no breeze was blowing.

The various laagers which formed Cronje's camp, on the hills between Modder River and Kimberley, were illuminated by the pale beams of the moon.

The forms of the Boer sentries could be seen standing, shadowy and ghost-like, at different points, which commanded a view of the surrounding country.

These sturdy burghers are not trammelled by severe discipline.

They sat down when they liked, and smoked their pipes stolidly.

There was no bustle and excitement, and, as the scouts reported no danger, a slack watch was kept, though they were ready to spring to their arms at the first alarm.

In a tent by themselves were Harkaway, Mr. Fish, and Andy, who had been marched from the railroad to the camp, where they were confined.

Whatever may be the faults of the Boers, they were kind to their prisoners, although they were told that the English had come to steal their farms.

An old man over sixty years of age was on guard outside the tent, calmly smoking and reading the Old Testament.

This was the second night of the prisoners' detention in the laager.

They were held as spies on a charge made by Webb.

The papers which Jack had taken from the president's office were found in his pocket, and went directly against him, though no judgment could be passed until the return of General Cronje.

Andy did not seem much concerned at what had befallen him.

He took things as they came, and trusted to his luck, putting in plenty of sleep, as he said his system required it.

Jack and Fish, however, were nervous and restless.

They had not been robbed, and they bought tobacco and some brandy from their sentry.

Fish had a pack of cards, which enabled them to while their time away.

At about three in the morning they woke up, being aroused by the sound of heavy firing in the direction of the Modder; this was the beginning of the fight in which Methuen received a check.

"Our fellows are keeping the Boers busy," observed Harkaway; "but they will find it hard to storm miles of entrenchments like these; and Schalk Burgher is stronger on the Tugela than Buller has any idea of. He has thousands of men, and the Boers' guns are better than ours. They have been buying in the best and cheapest market, while we have been standing still. I got splendid information out of Kruger's papers, and it is trying to be cramped up here, when I ought to be revealing it to our Staff."

"It is worse for me than it is for you," replied Fish.

"How do you make that out?"

"My dear sir, you seem to forget that I am a special correspondent. A war special is far above generals. He enlightens the world. Think of the eager millions who buy extra editions, and here am I with two note-books crammed full of stuff that all the nations would give their ears to read, and I can't get a wire. It is sickening, maddening. I am bursting with knowledge, and, like a damp musket, it won't go off."

"It is hard times, but you must buck up, a time will come."

"A bullet, you mean," said Fish, with a deep sigh. Tapping his head, "It is a pity, for there is something here. That's the worst of war. Such a lot of good clever fellows like myself get killed; but it all comes through keeping your company, Harkaway. You lead me into perilous paths, and I shall cut you dead in future, if I get out of this hole."

"Dry up and give us a rest," answered Jack. "Hire a hall if you want to air your mournful numbers. Stop your croaking. I'm going to wake these sleepy-headed Boers up."

"Don't do anything rash; though it doesn't matter much if we die a few hours sooner than we expect. It's a rotten world, and I don't care how quickly I get out of it."

Jack stepped out of the tent.

His guard was sitting on a stone, looking so solid and motionless that, if it had not been for the smoke coming out of his pipe, he might have been taken for a part of it.

Some distance off was another sentinel.

Jack had resolved to use a little ventriloquism, be the result what it might.

Throwing his voice into the air, he shouted in a gruffly-excited voice:

"On guard; the English are upon us!"

The Boer in front of him sprang up and brought his rifle to his shoulder.

Just then the moon went under a cloud, and it was difficult to distinguish anything a few yards off.

"Fire!" continued Harkaway. "Fire, you dunderheads; the Rednecks are coming!"

The bewildered Boer discharged his rifle, and by accident shot the sentry in front of him, who, before he fell, fired his gun and hit another Boer who had rushed out of his tent.

The alarm spread like wildfire.

The Boers came out of their tents, firing at random, and Jack's guard got a bullet in the head.

There was a panic in the camp, during which half a hundred Boers were either killed or wounded.

Jack retired to his tent, just as the moon showed itself once more, and the Boers began to recover from their surprise.

Keenly they looked for the enemy, but, seeing no sign, they calmed down, collected their dead and wounded, and came to the conclusion that someone had blundered.

"Capital," laughed Fish. "That's the best ruse I ever heard of."

Out came his note-book, and he jotted down:

"'Fooling the Boers at night. Harkaway's great joke. A false alarm in the laager. Boers shooting one another. Heaps of killed and wounded.' Something for the *Diggers' News.*"

"Boy," he called out, "take this to the telegraph office, and transmit it to Cape Town at once. Hang it all," he added; "what am I talking about? I forgot I was a prisoner."

Fish burst out laughing at the mistake he had made, Harkaway and Andy joining in his merriment.

"Hein!" exclaimed a voice at the entrance of the tent. "You dogs are laughing at our misfortune. You will laugh the other side of your faces when Cronje comes back victorious."

It was now daylight, and, looking up, Jack beheld his enemy, Krause.

"Can't you leave us alone?" replied Harkaway. "Surely prisoners ought not to be wantonly insulted."

"If you say another word to me, I'll pistol you!" hissed Krause, savagely. "You are a dirty spy!"

"That epithet applies to you more than it does to me. What were you in Mafeking when the English ran you out?"

Krause, who had been drinking, lost his temper, and, drawing his revolver, was about to fire at Jack, when Field Cornet Geiser, who happened to be on the ground, stepped up and held his arm.

"*Nien*, my friend!" he exclaimed. "None of that. It is contrary to the usages of civilised warfare. Drop your gun and come with me. Wait till the general returns. Harkaway once made me sing his Queen, but I do not want him killed like a pig for that."

Krause allowed himself to be led away, and Jack was relieved, for he thought that his last hour had come.

Suddenly the Boers began firing again, but this time they fired into the air, which caused Harkaway to look up, and to his surprise he perceived a balloon, in the car of which were two persons.

At first he thought it was sent up by Methuen, to make observations; but, taking his field-glass from his pocket, he looked at it more closely, and perceived the American flag flying from the car.

The Stars and Stripes convinced him that it was his old friend, Cyrus Vanderbilt.

The car was too high for the bullets to reach it, but Vanderbilt, incensed at being fired at, dropped a small hand shell into the midst of the laager.

By a strange fatality it fell a few yards from the spot where Krause and Geiser were standing, bursting with a loud noise, the splinters flying in all directions, and the pair of them were killed, being terribly mutilated, in addition to which a score of Boers were seriously injured, and a fragment flew into Harkaway's tent, which fortunately was empty, the inmates being outside gazing at the balloon.

Cowed at this display of force, the Boers left off firing, and hid themselves like a lot of hares, under any cover they could find.

Jack knew how to Helio, and taking a small mirror from his pocket made a few flashes, which, as he had expected, were replied to by those in the car, after which the balloon was carried on by the air current.

"Who are they, and what do they say?" asked Fish.

"Our old friends, Vanderbilt and Fred Dawson, doing a bit of sky scouting for the British. I told them we were here and our position. They promised to help us if they could, but I don't see how. Confound it! If I only had that pass we should be all right."

"I had a dream last night that you held it in your hand," said Andy.

"Oh, bother dreams! I don't believe in them," replied Harkaway. "Realities are the things for me, and I like the one I see in front."

He pointed to the mangled remains of the villain Krause and the consequential Cornet Geiser, whose power for wickedness was happily at an end.

As he spoke, a small party of Boers came up, carrying pieces of wood and spades.

Harkaway watched them curiously.

They dug a hole, in which they placed a stout post.

On the top of this they nailed a beam, at the end of which a rope with a noose in it dangled.

Then the conviction flashed upon him that they had erected a gallows.

Stepping forward, Jack addressed the man in command of the party, saying, "What is your name?—if it is not an impertinent question—and what are you going to do here?"

"Hang your friend and the boy," replied the man, with a grim smile; "as for you, it is our intention to send you back to the British."

"That is very kind of you," answered Jack, who could scarcely believe what he heard; "but may I venture to enquire why my friend and the boy are to be hanged, while I am to be liberated?"

"My name is Lauberg, and as I am on the General's Staff, you may credit all I tell you. Cronje is away, and I have taken the matter into my own hands."

"Isn't that rather exceeding your power?"

"Not at all. Don't bandy words with me," replied Lauberg. "I am an old and particular friend of Krause, who was killed just now by the hand-shell thrown from the balloon. He has told me much about you. He says you can talk behind your back, and utter any sound, and make an old boot speak like a man. In fact, you have magical power."

"That is true enough," replied Harkaway, calmly. "I can make a snake twine round your leg, if I like. Look out for yourself, old son."

As he uttered these words, a long black snake wriggled itself out of the dry earth at the Boer's feet.

It rapidly coiled round his right leg, and fixed his fangs in his flesh.

It was not poisonous, but the pain was great, and the Boer capered about like a monkey on a hot plate, his face being comically contorted, while he uttered the most diabolical yells, and, drawing his knife, slashed at the reptile below his gaiters, until he cut it in half-a-dozen pieces.

The simple-minded Boer thought that this occurrence really did savour of magic, but Harkaway had seen the snake coming out of a hole at his feet before he made his assertion.

"Do you want any more of it?" asked Jack, simply. "If you do, I can give it you. Do you see that dust-cloud behind you? It is full of poisonous vapour."

The Boer naturally turned his head to have a look, and Jack, who a little before borrowed Mr. Fish's snuff-box, threw the contents in the air, and when Lauberg again faced him, he found himself enveloped in it. It got into his eyes, and half-blinded him. It went into his mouth, and half-choked him. It penetrated his nostrils, and made him sneeze, until his whole body shook.

"A-chew! a-chew!" gasped Lauberg. "Oh, my poor head!—a-chew!—to—a-chew! —get over this—a-chew! Boo—hoo! Ferdomdy!—a-chew!"

"You had better stop it, boss," cried Andy, laughing until he grew red in the face, "or else you will sneeze your bloomin' old head off; but if you do die of sneezing, there will only be another dead Boer; so keep the pot a-boiling. Go it, guv'nor! You've got your encore! Keep it up lively, and show us what you can do!"

Recovering himself slightly, Lauberg ran towards Andy, raising his hand to give him a box on the ear, but the boy artfully fell flat in front of him, and the Boer, tripping over his body, plunged headlong against the post of the gallows, receiving a blow on the forehead which stunned him for a minute.

His men picked him up and wiped the blood away from a gash, but he leaned against the post, being unable to walk.

All the same, he had strength enough left to shake his fist at Harkaway.

"My bitter curse upon all of you!" he cried. "I'll have my revenge! You don't suppose I shall wait for the General. The English are marching to attack us, and you shall meet them half-way, Harkaway."

"I'll start now, if you have no objection," replied Jack.

"By thunder! you shall, and in a way you don't expect, my man. Give me some Dop, and do as I told you just now."

One of the Boers gave him some brandy, which braced him up and gave him nerve.

Some others bound the arms of Fish and Andy behind them, and made them stand on an empty cartridge-box under the gallows.

Two more brought a powerful black horse from the rear of a waggon.

It had no saddle or bridle, and from the way in which it pawed the ground, the animal seemed to be wild and untame.

It was led along by a halter round the neck, and the men had difficulty in holding it in.

Much to his astonishment, Harkaway was seized by half-a-dozen Boers, and was placed face upwards on the horse's back.

Ropes were bound round his body and under the belly of the steed, so that he could not fall off, and was unable to move hand or foot.

"When you hear the first shot fired by the Rednecks, start the horse down the hill," exclaimed Lauberg. "He shall go to his friends, but it will be through a storm of bullets. To madden the horse, tie some mimosa bush to his tail, and he won't hesitate to face the guns, for he'll think there is a pack of fiends behind him. Then string the other man and the boy up."

It was a striking scene. The horse was tightly held, the men being ready to let him loose at a moment's notice.

Fish and Andy were on the scaffold, while Harkaway gazed vacantly at the clear, blue sky above him, and the vindictive Boer smiled in triumph.

CHAPTER XX.

AN EXCITING TIME AT THE FRENCHMAN'S— EXECUTION OF THE SPIES—WEBB DISAPPEARS—CORPORAL POTTS GOES TO THE ENEMY'S LINES.

THROUGH his clever action, Smart had got the two Boer spies entirely in his power, but he was not completely satisfied until he saw them securely handcuffed, which feat he accomplished without difficulty, as they were afraid of being shot if they resisted.

It was an important capture, and he knew it.

If they had been allowed to have their way, they would have ruined the town by poisoning the water and blowing up the principal mine which the engineers had been weeks in constructing. It contained tons of dynamite, and was capable of blowing the Boer invaders to atoms.

Being a far-seeing man, Smart had taken the precaution of slipping a hastily-pencilled note into the hand of Corporal Potts when he left him at Cecil Rhodes' fancy ball.

In this he instructed the corporal to be outside the Frenchman's house in a couple of hours with half-a-dozen men of the Natal Police. If he opened the window and blew a whistle it would be a signal for them to rush in.

The corporal was under the influence of wine at the time; but he was an old soldier, and, however absent-minded he might be, he knew how to pull himself together when duty called him to order, therefore Smart thought that he could rely upon him.

Hymer and Wallach were dumfounded and crestfallen ; they did not utter a word.

Webb moved uneasily in his chair.

His eyes opened, and he looked vacantly around him, starting as if he had been stung by a snake when he saw Smart and noticed the condition of the two spies.

"What ho! my friend," exclaimed Smart. "You are coming to your senses. Your hostess no doubt gave you a sleeping draught, but it was not strong enough to keep you quiet long. I think you had better join your companions in misfortune. Hold out your hands, I have another pair of bracelets in my pocket, which will fit you."

While he was speaking the form of the Frenchman Borlaise appeared in the doorway, but the English spy did not notice him.

Borlaise was quick of apprehension, and took in the situation of affairs at a glance.

He saw that his friends were captured, and that Webb was in danger.

He could not understand the disappearance of Mrs. Steiner, but that was a mere detail to him at such a juncture.

The lamp which lighted the room was standing on a table near the door.

In an instant he extinguished it, and the apartment was plunged in darkness.

Alarmed at this sudden event, which foretokened danger, Smart ran to the window, threw it up with a bang, which fractured the glass, and sent splinters flying into the air.

Having accomplished this, he blew his whistle three times in quick succession.

The signal was answered from the outside by Corporal Potts, who cried in a loud voice :

"All right, sir ; I'm coming, with six men good and true."

"Look sharp!" replied Smart.

He turned round, and struck a match, intending to rekindle the light, for he was afraid of treachery on the part of someone.

Perhaps Mrs. Steiner had returned with people of her own class to aid her, but he scarcely thought that.

His suspicions turned principally upon the Frenchman who kept the house, and the events proved that he was right, for, as soon as he had got a light he felt the prick af a dagger in his back, and had he not slipped nimbly on one side, he would have been mortally wounded.

Instantly he turned round fiercely, and grappled with his assailant.

A desperate struggle ensued between the two.

Smart's revolver was knocked from his hand, exploding harmlessly on the floor.

Exerting all his strength, Smart threw the Frenchman to the ground, and fell on the top of him.

"Die, you wretch," he hissed in his ear, as he seized him by the throat with both hands. "I will strangle the life out of your cowardly heart."

"Mercy, mercy!" whined the Frenchman, in almost inarticulate tones.

It would have gone hard with Borlaise had not Webb crept up in the darkness to the scene of the encounter, and dealt Smart a severe blow on the head with his fist, which stunning him, made him roll on his back.

"Off for your life," cried Webb, "I'm going. Follow me! We shall be pounced upon directly by others outside."

"Leave me," replied Borlaise, faintly. "I cannot stir ; save yourself! You know your way out by the back door, and this is not my fault."

"I do not blame you, and wish you well out of it."

With these words Webb vanished, managing to get down the stairs in time to avoid the corporal and those who were with him.

The next moment Corporal Potts and his men entered the room, carrying lanterns in their hands.

Smart had recovered from his knock-down blow, and was sitting up.

Hymer and Wallach were standing in a corner together, watching the course of events.

Both of them seemed resigned to their fate, whatever it might be.

Manacled as they were, they could do nothing for themselves.

"Seize that Frenchman, and look after my other two prisoners!" were Smart's first words. "I have had a pretty tough tussle, but have come out all right. Webb is gone, I see. Confound it! that fellow has the devil's luck and his own, too. He no sooner gets into a scrape than he scrambles out of it. However, we have three big fish in our net, and we will make an example of the Zachenrollers."

"What for you take me?" asked the Frenchman. "I let lodgings in my house, and do not know who the people are I accept. I am a man of business, and cannot afford time to hunt up people's pedigrees."

"You have harboured well-known spies, and that is quite enough for us," answered Smart. "Mrs. Steiner and Webb are sufficient to give you away, and the sooner you take a back seat on that ground the better."

Three of the men who had accompanied the corporal took charge of the Frenchman, Wallach, and Hymer, the latter protesting loudly against being taken into custody.

"It is an outrage!" he exclaimed. "What proof have you against me? If anything happens to us, Cronje will hang a hundred Englishmen in revenge."

"Tut! tut!" answered Smart ; "don't gas so much, my man. We have ample proof of your villainy and sinister designs. You have been planning to let the enemy into Kimberley, and kill the lot of us. It is another Boer trick, and, God knows, we have had enough of them in this campaign."

"I want to be heard," said Wallach. "This is a high-handed proceeding. I can prove my perfect good faith and respectability. It is——"

"Keep your mouth shut," interrupted Smart. "You are in my hands now, and you will soon be as harmless as a dried snock or a stuffed cablejaw (popular South African fish). Before ten o'clock you will be down among the dead men. March away with them!"

The police roughly compelled the spies to leave the room and accompany them to the gaol.

Smart and the corporal were left together. They relighted the lamp, and thoroughly searched the house, which they found entirely empty until they came to the basement.

Here, before the kitchen stove, which was throwing out a good heat, they saw a long-legged Kaffir stretched out, wrapped in a blanket, and sleeping serenely.

"Get up, lazy bones; what are you doing here?" cried Smart, giving him a rousing kick in the ribs.

The Kaffir sprang to his feet in a state of alarm.

"Me good man, boss," he said, rubbing his eyes. "Don't you hurt me, because you make a big mistake if you do. I'm just handy man here—do the cooking, make the beds, answer the door; and all I get is a dollar a day and my food. What you want here?"

"We've made a raid on this house," rejoined Smart, "and I reckon we'll have to take you as well as the rest of them, unless you can give a good account of yourself."

"It's Dunko!" exclaimed the corporal. "Don't trust him, Smart; he's a wrong 'un— I may say a villain of the deepest dye."

"His skin wouldn't take any more colour, for he's as black as the ace of spades already," remarked Smart.

"His heart is darker than his hide," continued the corporal. "He tried to bury Harkaway alive on the veldt, and has been guilty of other crimes. I know the beggar well, and so does he me. He's a friend of Mrs. Steiner and Webb, and was employed by a Boer scoundrel named Krause."

"All a mistake, boss," replied Dunko grinning. "You've got hold of the wrong man. That fellow you're speaking of was my brother. We're just as much alike as two beans in a pod; no one can tell the difference between us. His name's Dunko, my name is Bunko. Our mother don't know which is which; Dunko and Bunko very much alike, especially Bunko."

"You'd like to do a bunk, but we don't mean to let you," said the corporal, sarcastically. "You will have to come with us."

"Who told you so?" asked Dunko, insolently. "It would take more than an old beer barrel like you to arrest me. Wait till I get hold of my assegai, and you'll see what a Zulu can do."

The Kaffir pretended to look round for a weapon, but suddenly lowered his head and butted the corporal full in the pit of the stomach, doubling him up, and rolling him like a bale of goods into a corner.

Then he made a dart for the door, rushing away like a whirlwind.

Smart fired a couple of shots at him; but, owing to the darkness which reigned in the passage, he missed his mark, and the Kaffir escaped.

"Oh, lor!" groaned the corporal, as he scrambled slowly to his feet, panting for breath, "that Zulu has completely knocked the stuffing out of me, and I fear I shall never be the same man again. It was Dunko right enough; he's double-faced, and you can't trust him."

"Let him go; I don't suppose he's particularly dangerous. He's nothing more than a servant, just as all these Kaffirs are; they will work for anybody who pays them. Have a drop of something. There is a bottle of Boer brandy on the table. What do you say to a thimbleful of Dop?"

"I don't know whether I will or I won't, but I'd rather," answered the corporal, stretching out his hand to receive a glass, which Smart filled to the brim.

Shortly afterwards they quitted the house, and went to their lodgings, where they snatched a few hours' slumber.

After a hasty breakfast they went to headquarters and made an accusation against Borlaise, Hymer, and Wallach, who, after a brief court-martial, were condemned to death.

The three men were taken out of the town, and compelled to dig a large grave, which they did, under a sweltering sun.

Twelve men were told off as a firing party, Corporal Potts being in command, while Smart stood by his side.

When the grave was sufficiently deep, the three condemned men were made to stand at one side, their arms being bound behind them, and their eyes blindfolded.

For fully a minute an awful silence reigned.

Then the corporal gave the words:

"Make ready! Present! Fire!"

Instantly a volley was discharged, and as the crack of the rifles was heard, the miserable wretches fell head foremost into the trench.

"Thus perish all traitors," remarked the corporal, as he walked slowly from the blood-stained spot with Smart.

"There is an end to those ruffians," said the corporal. "Webb and Dunko are free, and so, as far as I know, is Mrs. Steiner. What will be your next move, Mr. Smart?"

"If I can manage it, I want to pass the Boers, and join Methuen, for whom I have instructions. As he has not come to our relief, his force must have met with some unfortunate reverse. As for Mrs. Steiner, I may inform you that she has gone on a special mission of her own to save the life of Lieutenant Harkaway."

"Is he in danger?" asked Potts.

In a few words Smart told him of the very critical position in which Jack was placed, through the treachery of Webb, who had stolen the safe permit, or pass, given him by the President.

"Heaven save her!" exclaimed the corporal. "She is a splendid woman, and I admire her pluck; but I don't see why I should be left out in the cold in this adventure. I am proud to say that Harkaway is a friend of mine, and I would risk my life at any time for him. I'll beg, borrow, or steal a horse, and be off at once."

"Where on earth are you going, and what good can you do?"

"I don't know; I'm all in a fog. But I'm going to get into the Boer lines somehow, and do my level best for Mr. Harkaway, who is a whole-souled man, and one of the best. I don't care where the next comes from."

"Isn't it a fool's errand? It strikes me that way."

"I don't care. I'm going to get there somehow. I shall be in the saddle in less than half-an-hour. Farewell, old friend; you can't stop me when my mind is made up. I tell you, I'm a terror to snakes."

"Good luck to you, old boy," exclaimed Smart. "I daresay we shall meet again before long. If not, we shall find a nameless grave in the arid soil of the Transvaal, where much precious English blood has already been shed; but it is only proper that a man should die for his country when called upon."

"Quite right, sir," responded the corporal, waving his cap. "Hurrah for old England! I have been pretty nearly all over the world, and you can bet your boots you can't beat her."

"Have a smile, corporal?" asked Smart, handing him his flask.

"I don't know whether I will or I won't, but I'd rather," said Potts, in his usual dubious style. "On reflection, I think the occasion requires it. We'll have a couple of drinks, sir, what in the service we call a 'parter' and 'binder.' We may never meet again, but all the same, old acquaintance should never be forgot. Here's my hand, and give me a hand of thine.'"

They shook hands.

The corporal took the flask and drank twice.

He handed it back to the donor, who followed his example, and observed:

"We'll call this the Queen's Chocolate, and say 'God bless Her Majesty,' which sentiment, I think, deserves another refresher. Wet the toast."

The corporal did as requested, and in a thoroughly absent-minded manner put the flask, which was yet half-full, in his pocket, and giving Smart a friendly nod, hurried away to prove his loyalty to Jack Harkaway, who, if he had enemies, could also boast of staunch friends.

CHAPTER XXI.

A TRAP FOR THE REDNECKS—HARKAWAY'S WILD RIDE—A FIGHT WITH AN AFRIKANDER—AN ALARMING THREAT—SAVED BY A WOMAN.

HARKAWAY awaited his fate calmly, but not without some degree of hope.

He was more anxious about his companions than for himself, being afraid that nothing could save Andy and Mr. Fish from being hanged.

The plan conceived by Lauberg the Boer, respecting him, was transparent.

When the English attacked, the horse to which Harkaway was bound would be driven down the hill, and started on his wild career.

The Boers, concealed behind their entrenchments, would then open fire upon their foe, and it was quite fair to suppose that Jack and the horse would be riddled by bullets.

This was a new way of executing a supposed spy, but it appealed to the tragic side of Lauberg's nature.

Those men who were holding the horse laid down flat on the grass.

The Boers ensconced themselves in their rifle-pits and behind stones, without showing a head.

On their right flank were their big guns, also hidden from sight, which, being of the most modern European make, by Creusot and Krupp, were capable of throwing a shell further than any piece of artillery possessed by the British army; which fact Methuen's men soon found out.

Six batteries of artillery made their appearance at the bottom of the hill, and began to shell the Boer position, which they quickly unmasked, the fire being replied to with damaging effect.

Disregarding the artillery duel, several regiments of British infantry rushed to the assault; the foremost among them being the Highland Brigade, consisting of the 42nd. or Black Watch, and the Argyll and Sutherland, these being supported by a brigade of Guards, all being told to hold their fire until they could see the enemy.

It was at this moment that Lauberg waved his hand, as a signal for the horse to be let loose.

The ropes were allowed to drop, and the animal, being lashed with sjambocks, snorted loudly and plunged wildly down the hill.

The next moment the Boers opened a withering fire with their rifles and Maxims, which was answered by the British, who, being taken by surprise, fell in heaps, without doing much harm to their sheltered enemies.

Harkaway was enveloped in a storm of bullets; but his position on the horse's back did not afford a good target.

He escaped unhurt, but the horse, receiving a bullet through the head and others in various parts of the body, fell heavily forward, and rolled on its side, dead.

Jack received a severe shock, and narrowly missed having one of his legs broken.

The ropes did not break, and he was as much a prisoner as he had been before.

The men in charge of Andy and Fish, while attempting to execute their orders, were shot down near the gallows.

At this juncture a lyddite shell, discharged by a naval gun, burst some distance above them, scattering death and destruction around.

The young bugler contrived to free his hands from the cords which bound them, and at once released Fish.

"This was the hottest corner I ever was in, and I wish I was out of it," gasped the correspondent. "It is all very well to describe it from a distance, but the grim reality of war is—bah! A bullet grazed my ear; and I shall lie down flat until it is over. My paper does not pay me to stand and be shot at."

"Don't do that," replied Andy; "let's make a dash for liberty. Our men are in retreat. The bugler is sounding the recall. The 'Sandys' have tumbled into a hornets' nest. We can only die once. I'm off."

"There is twice as much of me as there is of you, and I am more likely to be hit. All the same, if you lead I will follow, though it is a thousand to one chance."

Away they went.

The Boer fire had slackened, and the men in khaki were forming up under shelter of their guns.

It was a sad story of an unreliable, or treacherous, guide, who had led the British into an ambush carefully prepared for them.

In the whole of the brief encounter they scarcely saw the enemy, who were hidden in skilfully-prepared pits.

Methuen had been betrayed, and we lost many valuable lives in consequence.

We were not fighting a handful of farmers, but skilled marksmen from their boyhood days, who outnumbered us by at least three to one.

They were led by officers trained in the best military schools of Europe, among whom was an Afrikander, named Hartz, a man born of white parents on South African soil, who had been a staff officer ten years for in the Austrian Army.

He bought the guns, organised the tactics, and directed the strategy of the Boers.

The fight was practically over when Andy and Fish made their bold attempt; and, luckily for themselves, the Boers did not try to snipe or pick, them off.

Owing to this carelessness, they passed by the dead and wounded, gaining the retreating Highlanders, who were anxious to renew the fight.

Without knowing it they almost touched Harkaway in their headlong flight.

He could just see them, and called out, but they heard him not.

Their ears were filled with the hissing sound of the flying bullets, with the roar of the cannon and the bursting of the shells with the cries of the dying, and the moans of the maimed.

It was a devilish din, and seemed as if two legions of fiends had been let loose to work their wicked will on one another.

There was only one chance for Harkaway; and this was, that when Methuen's men, under the Geneva Cross, came to collect the soldiers who had fallen in the battle, he would be picked up among the rest, and taken care of by his friends.

For an hour he remained bound to the horse, until the thunder of the big guns died away.

The hot sun was beating down upon his uncovered head, and a feeling of faintness came over him.

His eyes closed, and his brain became dizzy, for he had been once more passing through the valley of the shadow of death, and the black pall of the grave was still hanging over him.

One enemy had gone to his last rest; that was Krause, who, ever since the early days in Mafeking, had been bitterly hostile.

Another one, Webb, remained; he was a fiend in human shape, and more to be dreaded than the Boer Krause, because he was artful and suave, bold and treacherous, and capable of being all things, to all men.

Webb knew the secret of the Jarkin Mine in Rhodesia, which Jack hoped to own and explore at the termination of the war, if he was fortunate to survive, and he was always afraid that Webb would get the best of him in this matter.

From his foes his mind turned to his friends.

He thought of Fred Dawson, and the rich, accomplished, and beautiful Mrs. Steiner; and then his mind reverted to honest Corporal Potts.

There is an old saying, that if you think of anyone, he is sure to appear; and he had no sooner cast his thoughts upon the corporal, than a man, mounted on a grey horse, coming from the direction of Kimberley, approached him.

One glance was sufficient to convince Jack that the strange horseman was no other than Corporal Potts; and in a frenzy of delight he shouted at the top of his voice, though his tongue was almost cleaving to the roof of his mouth through thirst and dust.

"Hi! Corporal! Stop! Where are you off to?" cried Jack. "Come here and lend a fellow a helping hand; the Boers have played me a dirty trick, and tied me to a horse. I believe I am bullet-proof, or I should have been potted long ago, for Mauser balls have been as plentiful as blackberries in autumn."

The corporal stared in surprise at the strange spectacle. It seemed to him that Mazeppa, the hero of his youth, had come to life again.

He managed to rein in his steed close to Jack, and just as he did so, a Boer sentinel fired at him, and his horse fell with a broken leg.

"Never mind," exclaimed Potts, extricating himself from the saddle by a nimble movement, "they can't hit you, because you are under the belly of your horse, and I'll protect myself in the same manner. Hold on for a spell, and we'll have the best of them yet, although we are in a tight fix. What has happened here?"

"Our fellows were trapped," answered Jack, "and we have met with a check, or whatever you like to call it. A deuce of a lot of officers have fallen, as far as I can see, and there are a heap of Tommies lying about; but though we couldn't reach them with our bayonets, the naval guns have touched them up a bit; and the dead Boers will take some counting."

"We'll lie low until it is dark, sir," continued the corporal. "When I heard that you were in danger, sir, I swore I'd find you, and give you a shove up, if I possibly could."

"Thank you," answered Jack. "What I want at this particular moment is a knife, in the hand of a friend, to cut me free from the horse corpse, to which I am tied. If I could only reach Lord Methuen, I could tell him what would prevent further calamity and bloodshed. He must have more men, and better guns, before he can dislodge the Boers, and relieve Kimberley. Why, man alive, their entrenchments are twelve miles in length, and near Colenso they are planted on mountains which are impregnable. We want to draw them from their holes, like a lot of badgers, and smash them up in the open."

The corporal crawled round to where Jack was lying, and with his clasp-knife cut him loose, in return for which courtesy, Harkaway offered him his pocket-flask.

Potts took it, shook his head, as if the idea of such a thing was abhorrent to him, after which there was heard:

"I don't know whether I will or I won't, but I'd rather."

And Potts added:

"This sort of thing is needful in campaigning, Mr. Harkaway. There is a waste of tissue in the human body which requires renewing; and after that sip of dop, I feel as if I could fight half-a-dozen Boers with my right hand tied behind me; one down and the other come on. I'm not mean, and I don't want to sub on anybody, but when a gentleman offers me his flask I can't refuse it. Do you blame me?"

"Not at all. I applaud your sentiments; but for Heaven's sake don't talk so loud. Some Boer ghoul, prowling about to rob the dead and wounded, as is their custom, might overhear us."

"Bring on your Boers. Who's afraid?" demanded the corporal, valiantly. "I should like to get hold of that Afrikander officer, Hartz, who is training and directing the Boers under Cronje. I'd give him beans."

Unperceived by them, two men had approached from the Boer camp, and were standing close to the dead horses, having overheard the conversation between the two Englishmen.

They happened to be Lauberg and Marshall Hartz, as he called himself, though that was not his real name, who ten years before had been a well-known character in Pretoria.

He suddenly vanished, and during this period was lost sight of by Kruger, Rietz, Leyds, and other leading Boers, but now he had come back to point out the road to victory to his former friends.

Lauberg carried a rifle slung over his shoulder; clubbing it he advanced to Corporal Potts, and was about to brain him, when Hartz stepped in front, saying:

"What would you do to these unarmed Rooinecks?"

"You heard what this insolent fellow uttered," replied Lauberg. "Does he not deserve death? As for the other, he is a notorious secret agent for the English. He knows all our positions, as well as our strength, and can do us great harm."

"Not he," exclaimed Hartz, with a gesture of contempt. "We wish these invaders of our soil to bring their bodies within reach of our bullets. Spurn these two with your foot, if you like, but do not kill them without formal trial, according to the law of Nations."

As he spoke, he gave Harkaway a kick in the ribs, which was more than his fiery temper could stand.

Springing to his feet, with flashing eyes, he dealt him a blow in the face, which spattered him with blood, crying:

"Coward and bully, take that!"

Hartz was staggered for the moment.

He was a man of fifty, and not bad-looking.

His body was thin, and devoid of muscle.

As he was fond of telling his friends he worked with his brain, and not with his hands.

Wiping the blood from his face with a clean pocket-handkerchief, which was a rarity among the Boers, he looked at his assailant with a demonic smile.

Lauberg had drawn his revolver, with which he covered Harkaway, at the same time glancing at Corporal Potts to make sure that he did not attempt to escape, every moment expecting that he would receive an order to shoot; but to his surprise no command was given him, though he knew that the indignity from which the Austrian officer was suffering, could, according to the code of honour, only be washed out with blood; and he wondered what course Hartz was likely to adopt.

He was not long kept in suspense; both Hartz and Lauberg carried swords.

"I have received a blow from you, which it is impossible for an officer in my position to forgive," exclaimed Hartz. "I understand that you hold a cavalry commission in the British Army. Lauberg will lend you his weapon. I challenge you to fight a duel on the field of battle. It is not my wish to take any advantage of you. All I ask, is to kill you in a fair and honourable manner. I could shoot, or hang you, whichever pleased me best, but I want to have the pleasure of killing you with my own hand, and at the same time give you a chance of defending yourself. Mind you, it is a duel to the death, and if you beg for mercy you will not receive it."

"I never beg," answered Harkaway, proudly. "Put yourself on guard. Mr. Lauberg, may I trouble you for your sword?"

"That is a strange way to do business," grunted the Boer. "A man shall hit you on the nose, and you give him the opportunity of running you through the body. If that is what they do in Austria, it is not Boer custom. I should club him with a rifle, or cut his head off. Suppose he runs you through; what you do then. Let him go home to his friends to tell what a fool you were."

"If he vanquishes me," rejoined Hartz, calmly, but enigmatically, "I will promise to let a part of him go."

"What do you mean by that?" asked Lauberg. "Are you going to cut him up, and send off his head in a bag?"

"Wait, and you will find out. Don't be in a hurry, my friend. There are more ways than one of killing a dog."

Lauberg shrugged his shoulders, as if the Austrian officer was a mystery which he could not fathom.

He handed Harkaway his sword, who promptly faced Hartz.

They saluted one another, and then their swords crossed.

The duel had commenced.

Lauberg and the corporal stood by, being silent spectators.

Not knowing how his opponent could fence, Harkaway at first acted on the defensive.

The latter had carefully studied the sword exercise at Sandhurst, and was not at all afraid; though he soon found that he was matched against a clever and dangerous foe; all his skill being required to parry his thrust, and it was very difficult to get within his guard.

Lunging in carte, Hartz wounded Jack slightly in the shoulder; it was only a prick, but it roused Jack's blood, and he pressed his foe closely, beating down his guard, and grazing his side in a painful manner.

Hartz stepped back, renewing the fight with vigour.

Their swords clashed, producing sparks, and they fenced very prettily, and with extreme caution, until Harkaway beat down his enemy's guard, and making a clear volte, jerked his sword out of his hand and sent it flying in the air.

Hartz was now entirely at his mercy, and folding his arms, awaited the death thrust, which he expected every instant.

But it did not come.

Jack gave Lauberg back his sword, and bowing politely, said :

"If you are satisfied, gentlemen, I can assure you I am."

"Bring the two prisoners into laager," Hartz exclaimed, biting his lips, while a look of vexation crossed his face.

Saying this, he walked hastily away ; and Lauberg commanded Harkaway and the corporal to follow him.

"You have been a little bit too clever this time," he remarked to Jack. "He can't forgive you for the blow; and this sword business will make him more savage than ever. I wonder what he'll do. You are a lucky fellow. I thought you were settled when I put you on the back of that horse; but I don't see how you can get out of it this time, my bold Briton."

"There is a kind little fairy who always watches over me," replied Jack, with a forced laugh, though he felt the reverse of merry.

Corporal Potts did not utter a word.

He had nothing to leave to anybody.

Had it been otherwise he would have made his will, for he frankly confessed afterwards that he thought the game was up.

When they reached the camp, they found the Boers busily engaged in picking up their dead, which they threw without ceremony into a deep hole.

Scarcely any of them had been struck by bullets, the fatal work had been done almost entirely by the shells.

Outside a tent they beheld Hartz, who was talking to several of the leading Boers about the surprise they had given the English, and what a number they had killed, with only trifling loss to themselves.

Before him, lying on a flat stone, was a steel axe with a very sharp edge.

"Have you any orders for me, general?" enquired Lauberg.

"Wait," rejoined Hartz, in a tone of authority.

He continued his conversation with the Boers for fully another ten minutes, without bestowing the slightest attention on Harkaway or the corporal.

"I do not think that the English will attack again to-night," he observed, "but I should advise you to place your two biggest guns on the tramway which runs between the two kopjes, and arrange them so as to command the valley. The enemy know that we are very strong here, because they have unmasked us, and should they assault us to-morrow, it will be in a place where they think we are weak. I should also move a couple of thousand men in that direction as soon as darkness comes on. It will be best for me to remain here and direct operations until Cronje comes up from the river."

The Boers agreed to this proposal; having the utmost confidence in their instructor, who, with others from foreign countries, was turning their undisciplined levies into a well-organised army, containing the best mounted infantry in the world.

When they had gone away, Hartz beckoned to a couple of sentries, whom he ordered to seize Harkaway, which they did by each arm.

Clearly, they had previously received their orders, and knew exactly what to do without being told.

They marched him to the flat stone on which the axe was lying.

With a knife one of them ripped the sleeve on Jack's right arm, baring it to the elbow ; and exerting his strength, forced his prisoner to place his open hand upon the stone.

Then, with stolid mien, his face being as implacable as fate, Hartz stepped forward and took up the axe, which he raised in the air.

"That hand of yours, sir, shall strike no more," he exclaimed, in a low, guttural voice, which showed that his whole frame was deeply moved. "In a minute it will be a dead hand, for I mean to cut it from your wrist."

"That is monstrous!" cried Jack, looking appalled. "Shall it be said that the Boers torture their prisoners in such a cruel, relentless way? The nations will call you down, and history will point the finger of scorn at such brutality!"

"I am doing this deed on my own authority, and nobody can blame Joubert, Cronje, Schalk Burgher, or their Boers," responded Hartz.

"But I gave you your life just now."

"That only makes the burden I have to bear more oppressive."

"Hang it all, man or beast, whichever you call yourself, think of what you are doing. Of what use is a soldier, without his right hand?"

"Precisely. That is my point; I intend to render you useless as a moonbeam lying on a shutter, and harmless as a dried snake."

Beads of perspiration stood on Harkaway's forehead.

He was so securely held by the burly Boers that he could not move.

The axe flashed in the sunlight, and almost blinded his eyes.

Corporal Potts was horrified, and could only murmur in a confused tone :

"This isn't a fair deal, mate. Blow me tight, if it is. Look here. It won't bump, I tell you, and we can't get our money back. I'd rather you'd cut both my hands off, and feet too, if it comes to that, than touch the boss, who is one of the best."

"Silence! Your turn will come next," said Hartz, in a voice of thunder.

Suddenly a woman riding a black horse dashed into the camp.

The animal was covered with foam, and staggered, rolling to and fro, as if his endurance was exhausted, which was actually the case; for without any warning he dropped to the ground, gasping in the throes of death.

His rider alighted on the ground without being hurt, and rushing with hair flying over her shoulders, and a face which was ghastly white, to the spot where Hartz was standing, shouted :

"Stop! I command you, in the name of the President of the Transvaal. I have a free pass for Harkaway and his friend, which none of you dare disregard."

Harkaway looked up thankfully, for he saw that Mrs. Steiner had saved him at the eleventh hour.

Once more his luck had turned, and, as the soldiers released him, and Hartz dropped the axe, he gracefully sank on one knee, raised Mrs. Steiner's hand to his lips, and kissed it.

Hartz stood like a marble statue, gazing intently at Mrs. Steiner, from whose face he never took his eyes.

Corporal Potts was intensely delighted.

He laughed and cried by turns, rolled on the grass, and tried to stand on his head.

"We're saved!" he cried. "I feel like a Salvation Army cove. I think there's a drop left in the guv'nor's flask; I don't know whether I will or I won't, but I'd rather. Here goes, and may Old Nick take the Boers; which is all the harm I wish them, except that I might be their stoker down below. Oh crumbs! Wouldn't I keep a good fire burning."

As for Lauberg, he merely shook his head, and said, with a grieved look:

"There should be no womans in war. Wherever the womans come they spoil the fun. We was all right before she turned up, and now that ferdomdy, Harkaway, has slipped through our fingers. Ah! Pshaw, womans is not fit to ride for sour apples."

"Make haste," whispered Mrs. Steiner to Jack. "Why are you lingering? You are free. Take the pass and hurry away. Do not fear me. I am at home among the Boers. Up to this time I was in your debt, but what I have done now makes a settlement. The debt is repaid."

"A thousand times over," replied Jack. "For what is a life without a right hand! I've got it in for that Austrian fellow. What does he come over here and fight us for?"

"Because the Boers pay well. Soldiers of fortune are always ready to fight on any side; and you must recollect that Englishmen are hated by foreign nations on account of their pride, their wealth, and their arrogance. Say no more. We shall meet again."

Harkaway beckoned to Corporal Potts, and disappearing behind a kopje, they descended the hill together.

CHAPTER XXII.

A STRANGE INTERVIEW BETWEEN MRS. STEINER AND HARTZ—SHE DEFIES HIM, AND IS PLACED UNDER ARREST—SHE IS BANISHED—A DARK PLOT.

THE manner in which Hartz continued to regard her, somewhat confused Mrs. Steiner, although she returned his gaze boldly.

She tried to carry her mind back into the dim and misty past.

Where had she seen that man before?

His face was certainly familiar to her, though it was furrowed with care, and his hair was white.

He did not speak, and at length the silence became painful.

"I want a tent," she said, addressing Lauberg. "If you have not that, you must get me some accommodation in a wagon and something to eat, for I am hungry and weary. I left Kimberley in the early morning and have been riding ever since. Two of the Cape Mounted Police chased me for half-a-dozen miles, but I shot one and killed the other's horse. Why don't you men clear the English out of Natal and make peace in Cape Town.?"

"Give us time; you was in a hurry, I should think," snarled Lauberg. "We are very well here; why should we go down to meet the English? Let them knock their heads against our guns until they haven't any brains left; but you can rest contented, I will go and do what you ask."

He departed, leaving Mrs. Steiner and the expert from the Austrian Army together, which appeared to embarrass both of them.

"Are you aware, madame, that in spite of your well-known Boer proclivities, you have laid yourself open to grave suspicion by what you have just done?" exclaimed Hartz, at length, without removing his evil glance from her face. "This man, Harkaway, to whom you restored his lost pass, which one of our spies, Webb, told me he stole from him, is in the English Intelligence Department. He calls himself a secret agent, and comes among us to find out what we are doing. What is that but a spy? We don't reckon him an ordinary fighting man, though we know he was in the ranks against us at Elands Laagte. Why should you befriend him? If I do not have a satisfactory answer to that question, I shall order you under arrest. It is ten to one that you are playing into the hands of the English, and deceiving us."

"It is nothing of the sort," answered Mrs. Steiner, indignantly. "I have been true as steel to the Vierkleur. I have never played the four-coloured flag false. You are a villain to accuse me of such a thing. Lieutenant Harkaway saved my life on two occasions, and I have done him a good turn for it."

"Talk Taal (Boer dialect). That is more in your line. You are a rich woman, now, Belle Steiner, but I knew you when you were a girl, without any shoes or stockings, selling fruit outside the old Volksraad (Parliament House) in Pretoria, which was not then, as now, a city of twelve thousand people, with fine buildings, and a splendid suburb, called Sunnyside. An uncle educated you, and left you his money, but he was nothing better than a miner at the start.

"Then when you were quite young, you married a politician named Steiner, with whom you lived a miserable life, until you separated. Since then your money, which you always took care of, has grown by leaps and bounds, until you are one of the richest women in the Transvaal. You call yourself a widow, and tell people that Steiner died abroad, but you have no proof of it, my lady."

During these remarks the woman had become pallid, rigid, statuesque, a small hectic spot burning on each cheek.

She drew her breath quickly, as her bosom heaved and fell, while she clenched her hands together until the nails ran into her flesh.

"What else do you know about me?" she asked, in a stony voice.

"Simply that you have offered your services to Kruger, as a society scout in the besieged towns. Not because you love the Boers ; you are fond of money, and you are working for yourself. This war has really nothing to do with the franchise of the Outlanders, as England pretends. It is a war of capitalists and financiers. We have the control of the diamonds and the gold, and the English, backed by the Jews, want to get the minerals and the mines away from us. Their victory would make you poor. We parted because you would not give me money. I am Steiner, though I go under the name of Hartz. Yes, madame, I am your lawful husband ; and if I don't know you, who should ? "

"You are an artillery officer in the Austrian Army," said Mrs. Steiner, trembling, though she was not surprised, for her heart had told her what was coming.

"That makes no difference. Not a pin's point. I have been waiting for an opportunity to disclose myself. You have put yourself in my power by realeasing Harkaway. I care not by what intrigue he got the pass. In this camp I can prove him a traitor. He was under martial law. I received a blow from him, and you baulked me of my revenge. Gratitude, you say, inspired you to this act ; I should say that love was at the bottom of it. But let that pass. Love has long ago died out between you and I. All I want is your money, and if you refuse to buy my friendship, I will be your bitter foe. You must acknowledge me as your husband, and swear to hate Harkaway as much as I do."

"What is the alternative ? " she asked.

"Your immediate arrest, and subsequent execution as a vile traitress. Don't think you will get off because you are a woman. The Boers are in the humour to shoot anyone just now. In fact they are getting tired of shooting Englishmen, and want a change," Hartz replied, sarcastically, adding, " Come, your answer. Quick, madame! I have no time for dallying. Do not imagine I am trying to impose upon you, for I can easily prove my identity, and take you to the church where we were married. Decide! Your life hangs upon your response."

She looked at him with withering contempt, as only an injured woman can look when her face is flushed with indignation and her soul is filled with loathing.

"Do you call yourself an officer and a gentleman?" she enquired, her lip curling with a scornful smile, which made him cower before her beautiful disdain. "I am glad Harkaway struck you ; such as you deserve to be kicked out of the society of all decent men."

"Your answer! Speak!" hissed Hartz.

"Is an emphatic negative, sir," replied Mrs. Steiner, firmly. "I would rather die a thousand deaths than be again connected with you in any way."

Hartz put a whistle to his lips and blew it, whilst his face was black and convulsed with rage.

Three men from an outlying picket came to his side, and receiving instructions from him, took Mrs. Steiner away and confined her in a tent by herself.

She did not utter a word ; bearing herself erect and defiant, an attitude which, as she was dressed in male attire, made her look every inch a soldier.

Hartz paced the ground impatiently.

Belle Steiner had saved Harkaway, but she had ruined herself ; for her brutal and mercenary husband was fully capable of having her shot, and intended to do so as soon as Cronje returned and he had mentioned the case to him.

He was only afraid that she might somehow send a telegram to Pretoria, where she had powerful and influential friends, who would intervene on her behalf.

Walking towards the telegraph office to stop this contingency, he met Webb, and Dunko the Kaffir, who had just come into the laager from Kimberley, meeting accidentally on the road.

They shook hands, and Hartz related what had happened, for he was always confidential with Webb.

"By all means shoot her before the sun goes down," said the latter. "She has been false to us ever since she met this zachenroller, Harkaway. I came to look for you. Cronje has come back, elated at the Boers' success. Methuen won't attack again in a hurry. Come to his tent. His tastes are very simple ; he is recruiting himself with a bit of biltong and some mealies, washed down by dop and water, and as busy as a bee, talking to half-a-dozen commanders."

They repaired to headquarters, and having listened to the charge against Mrs. Steiner, the general decided it right off hand.

"I can't take it upon myself to shoot the woman," said Cronje ; "for various reasons, that would not do. I will confiscate her property, and banish her from the Transvaal for ever. She is no longer worthy to be called a Boer."

Cronje was a man of determination, who did not allow his decisions to be commented upon or interfered with.

Hartz and Webb were disappointed at Mrs. Steiner's escape from death, but they were satisfied in so far that they had brought about her downfall.

She would no longer be a great power among the Boers, and she could hope for little sympathy from the English, who were not at all likely to trust her.

Her property would be taken from her and divided among the general and his friends, which would make her a poor woman, and compel her either to work for her living or beg her bread.

This, however, was not enough for Hartz, who hated his wife with a deadly animosity.

He knew that in a few minutes her sentence would be communicated to her, and she would be bundled out of the camp without ceremony, possibly to take her chance as a refugee at Lorenzo Marquez or Cape Town.

When he and Webb left the general's tent, they walked up and down along one of the trenches, gratefully inhaling the cool air of the evening.

The sun had set, and the sky was studded with a myriad of glorious stars.

Camp fires were burning as the men cooked their suppers.

"'NOW FOLLOW ME, PAY ATTENTION,' SAID JACK, SAY RULE BRITANNIA, AND GOD SAVE THE QUEEN.'"

No. 6.

Sentinels paced to and fro, though there was no expectation of further fighting at dresent; as the tide of war had turned against the English, who were held in check throughout Natal, awaiting reinforcements and guns from far across the sea.

It was only breathing time however; bravely had our gallant men fought against enormous odds, attacking entrenched positions on the Modder River and at the Tugela.

The Highlanders and Marines, for instance, losing fifty per cent. of their companies.

"Am I to be baffled in this way by that woman?" demanded Hartz, suddenly stopping in his walk. "I thought I had her in my clutches, but she has escaped me and is free to roam about at will. If we lose this war, the English will give her back her property, and she will be more powerful than ever. Great Britain is a fair dealer, and does not rob people. If I dared, I would shoot her with my own hand, but that would bring about trouble between the general and me. Then again, there is that man Harkaway; he has given me the slip. As I deserted her, she could easily get a divorce. It makes me mad to think that Belle and he might join their lives together. Perdition seize the pair of them."

"I will settle them for you," replied Webb, confidentially; "and no one shall be a bit the wiser. All you have to do, is to give me that diamond you wear on your finger. It is one of the finest the De Beers Company ever unearthed, and is a fortune to any man."

"Take it," said Hartz, removing the gem and handing it to Webb, whose eyes glistened as he put it in his pocket.

"Thanks," exclaimed Webb. "It is a pleasure to work for a man like you. I have an account to settle with Harkaway. I'll poison him, and shoot the woman. My Kaffir, Dunko, will come with me. We will follow Mrs. Steiner down the hill, and if you send some scouts into the valley to-morrow, I swear that you shall find her dead body."

"Enough," answered Hartz. "I rely upon you to do all you've promised. Make haste. Away with with you, or the cat will evade us."

Webb gave him an intelligent nod, and sought Dunko, who was busy watering some horses, the Kaffirs in camp having to make themselves generally useful.

"Follow me," he exclaimed. "I have some important work in hand."

"This Kaffir has done enough running for one day," replied Dunko. "Can't keep his eyes open now. I know I'm your Kaffir, now Krause has gone; but you send me out like a dog to get my own dinner. You haven't given me a drop of squaro all day."

"Take that," rejoined Webb, "throwing a small bottle at him. That's warranted to kill at a thousand yards, and if it doesn't take the starch out of your hair, I can't help it."

"Hi! Hi!" laughed Dunko. "You heap better man than I thought you. Listen, boss, I'se that dry, you'll hear it hiss as it goes down; and now, as the Rednecks say, what's the bloomin' racket?"

In a few words Webb told him what he was going to do, and after hearing all he had to say, Dunko shook his head, shut one of his eyes, and scratched his ear.

"Don't like this job, boss!" he exclaimed, thoughtfully. "Mrs. Steiner has been a very good woman to me; and I can tell you, she can shoot for a prize. You might give her a bullet in the back, but that's cowardly. I'm a Zulu, but we don't kill women. Harkaway is a hard nut to crack; he is one of the toughs, and I should think you have had enough of him.

"That man takes a lot of killin', and don't you forget it. You're after the plan of the mine in Rhodesia, without which you can't locate it. Mark me, Harkaway has hid that away; you'll never find it in his clothes."

"I mean to have a try, anyway," replied Webb, "so you can shut up your mouth. Come with me, and don't forget your rifle. We must follow Mrs. Steiner, and settle her hash between this and midnight."

The coward glided along silently in the semi-darkness, until he came to the place where Mrs. Steiner was confined.

As he came up, he saw her leave the tent, guarded by two Boers, one on each side of her.

These men conducted her out of the camp, and accompanied her to the bottom of the hill, Webb and Dunko following at a distance.

Arriving in the valley, the Boers left her; and she sat down, as if in deep thought, possibly wondering what she could do.

Desolate as her position was, she did not neglect to be on the alert, for she continually turned her head in different directions, as if looking for some lurking foe.

This compelled Webb and the Kaffir to hide themselves under the shelter of a rock.

Webb was in no hurry to kill the woman, and could afford to bide his time.

His opportunity would come, sooner or later.

Being turned out by the Boers she must seek refuge in the English lines on some pretext or another, or starve.

He thought she might sleep where she was until daylight, when she would continue her enforced journey.

They had not sent her away without arms, for they could see the gleam of a rifle on the small boulder against which she was reclining.

Webb dared not fire at her where she was, for to do so would have been to arouse the Boer camp, and bring retribution on himself, so that he had to remain quiet until she made a move.

It was a relief to him to get out of the Boer entrenchments.

The hills on which they camped were between three and five hundred feet high; these were covered with loose stones, with which each man had built for himself a little fort breast high.

Here he lived, night and day, with a supply of biltong and mealies, plenty of cartridges, and an overcoat to sleep in at night.

The Boers were small farmers or labouring men, wearing their ordinary dress, taken from their work at a moment's notice by the field cornet, inconceivably dirty, shaggy, and unshaved

The officers and rich men were different.

They wore good clothes and kid gloves.

When our men got at them with the bayonet, they jumped on their fleet horses and galloped away.

All was silent in the neighbourhood of Kimberley.

As he looked in that direction he could see the flashes made by the searchlights; and turning his head, saw them answered by Methuen on the Modder.

His experience as a spy had taught him the meaning of those dots and dashes, which were strangely like the electric telegraph.

Methuen was saying:

"Waiting for reinforcements; the same as Buller on the Tugela. Roberts and Kitchener are coming out. Have heard of good sortie from Ladysmith last night. Fort captured, and Long Tom blown up with cordite. Heavy fighting at Mafeking, but all well. Am afraid we shan't eat our plum-pudding with you on Christmas Day."

Webb smiled, and Dunko asked him what he was thinking about, and he replied:

"Sir George White has been talking to Methuen. I got hold of the signalling code, and can read the flashes you see in the air."

"White man heap too much clever for me," replied Dunko, with a puzzled air. "Hullo!" he added, "what's that up in the air, boss?"

Several of the bright stars, notably the Southern Cross, had become suddenly obscured.

Both of them were much puzzled.

All at once the moon rose, making everything almost as clear as day; and to their amazement they beheld a balloon, which was quite near the earth's surface.

It was sailing slowly before a gentle breeze in the direction of the river.

Two men were discernible in the car.

They were in a dangerous position, because their altitude was not great enough to enable them to get away from the Boers' guns.

The unthought-of appearance of the moon had betrayed them.

One displayed a white flag, the other hung over the side of the car the Stars and Stripes.

"I'll bet a hundred to one those are Cyrus Vanderbilt and Fred Dawson," cried Webb, much excited. "The balloon doesn't belong to us, and here goes for a crack at it, anyhow."

He pointed his rifle in the air, and fired.

As he did so a volley rang out from the kopje, followed by a Maxim, from which the Boers kept on pumping dozens of balls.

A big long-range gun was also discharged.

The utmost consternation prevailed in the camp.

As a matter of course, the unfortunate balloon was completely riddled with bullets, being made a sieve of, but strange to say the car was untouched.

This rapidly began to descend like a lump of lead, but the two men within it were quite equal to the occasion.

Without a moment's hesitation they leaped from the car into the air, each one holding a parachute, which opened out over their heads like an umbrella, and the wind blew them gradually away from the hill, out of range, though they were fired at, like two strange birds.

Taking advantage of the din and excitement, Webb took deliberate aim at Mrs. Steiner, who had not moved from her position, and fired.

A piercing shriek rang through the air, and her form disappeared behind the stone.

"That settles it," said Webb, complacently. "We've done the trick, Dunko, and we'll go back to the Boers' burrow. I shan't make any move until to-morrow."

All at once the moon went under a cloud, Webb and the Kaffir returning to camp in the half-light which had previously prevailed.

He found Hartz and two other commanders in a tent, playing cards, smoking cigars of the best London make, and drinking champagne which was worth a guinea a bottle, for the Boer generals were always supplied with luxuries.

"There is nothing left of the balloon," remarked Webb, "yet the occupants got off."

"That does not interest me," replied Hartz, testily. "Did you do what I told you to?"

"Yes," answered Webb. "If you go down the hill on the Magersfontein side, you will find it lying by the side of a long stone."

"Good!" ejaculated Hartz. "If these gentlemen will excuse me for half-an-hour, I should like you to take my hand at cards, as I have to go on duty."

He vacated his seat, which Webb occupied, to play the game for him, during his temporary absence.

With a grim smile of gratified malignity, Hartz quitted the tent, and walked in a thoughtful manner through the laager, and descended the hillside.

The consternation caused by the appearance of the balloon had passed away, and the lethargic Boers had once more curled themselves up in their little forts, and gone to sleep.

He could hear the groans of the wounded, who had been placed in the hospital tents, English and Boers being cared for alike.

The battle had taken place on the other side of the hill, so that no trace of it was to be seen where he went.

For over an hour he searched for the corpse of Belle Steiner, but could see nothing of her.

At a certain spot he noticed some blood splashed upon a stone, and peering down upon the sandy soil, distinguished further marks, which indicated that some tragedy had occurred there, but he could see neither man nor woman.

At length he gave up the search; and greatly disgusted at his ill success, went back to the camp, and reaching the tent, beckoned to Webb, who came out.

"You have lied to me," he said, in a sibilant tone. "I am not a man to be fooled with, and I would as soon put a bullet in your miserable body as look at you. Give me back my diamond. You can't expect to be paid for failures."

"Certainly not," answered Webb, submissively. "All the same, I can assure you that I have earned the ring you were kind enough to make me a present of. I shot the woman in cold blood, as I would a bird on a tree. I saw her fall, and heard what I took to be her dying shriek. But here is your stone. Take it ; I am not the poor beggar you take me to be, and could buy one equal to it, if I wanted."

"Keep it," said Hartz, struck by his tone. "You have yet to give an account of Harkaway ; and there may be some truth in what you have told me, for I saw a considerable quantity of blood on a stone where there had been no fighting. Solve this mystery, and do your best."

"Rely upon me. I shall be in the English camp to-morrow, under some disguise, and will not fail you," rejoined Webb.

With this assurance, Hartz was satisfied, and Webb departed to snatch a few hours, sleep before he began his adventurous journey.

CHAPTER XXIII.

HARKAWAY IS WELL RECEIVED AT HEAD-QUARTERS — THE ARMOUR - CLAD MOTOR CAR — A FRESH MISSION — DAWSON IS ROBBED OF THE MINE PLAN.

HARKAWAY and Corporal Potts were cordially received, when early in the morning they entered Lord Methuen's camp near the Modder River.

They were cared for by Captain Preston, of the Coldstream Guards, who was an old friend of Jack's ; but the first thing they asked for was water, which precious commodity they had not tasted for twelve hours by the clock.

Their lips were dry and parched, and they were half choked by the all-prevailing dust, while the pitiless, blazing, South African sun had blistered their skin.

After breakfast Jack related his adventures to the officers of the mess, and then made himself as respectable as he could for a visit to the general, with whom he had a long conversation.

The information he brought from Pretoria, and also from Kekewich at Kimberley, was very valuable, and he was thanked for his services.

"Your experiences have been lively in the extreme, Harkaway," said Lord Methuen. "If we had more men like you in the Intelligence Department we should be better off. I think from what you have told me, I shall be able to get round the Boers, with whom we have had some terrible fights."

"I should like you to give me a cavalry command ; if it is only Volunteer Horse," replied Jack, "unless I am wanted in another direction."

"In time of war there is no rest for the brave. I cannot give you a command, but I can attach you to the Colonial troops, who are at Belmont, the Canadians, Toronto Company, and Queenslanders. You and your friend, Dawson, know the country. I will give you a line to Colonel Ricardo, and order an advance on the Boer commando at Sunnyside, which is a hostile camp on my left flank. By the way, where is Dawson ? He has not reported himself lately. When I last saw him he was going with a friendly American, Mr. Vanderbilt, in a balloon to take observations."

Jack declared his ignorance of Fred's whereabouts, and adding that he would help the Colonials to give a good account of the

Boer laager at Sunnyside, quitted the general, much pleased at his reception, and the exciting duty which had been assigned him.

As he was walking back to the Guards' mess-tent with the corporal, he encountered Mr. Fish and Andy, the young bugler, who were both in high spirits and pleased to see their old friends.

"Bravo ! Here we are again, as the clown says," exclaimed Fish, taking out his note-book. "We had a narrow squeak for it, but we bolted and managed to get through somehow, though I shall never forget the constant pump, pump, of the little Maxims the Boers have. It rained bullets."

"It was a terrible day," replied Jack "We did not see half of the fight. I hear that one battalion of the Guards fired two hundred thousand rounds.

Briefly Jack proceeded to inform the correspondent of what he and the corporal had gone through, and the generous behaviour of Mrs. Steiner ; all of which Fish dotted down in his book.

"Harkaway as Mazeppa," he muttered. "A fiery steed very much under fire. Boer savagery. Harkaway nearly loses his right hand. The mysterious Mrs. Steiner to the rescue. That will do. Won't I astonish the readers of the *Cape Town Slasher*. Good-bye."

"Where are you off to ?" asked Jack. "Don't be in such a hurry ; we are just beginning to like you."

"I'm off to the telegraph station to write my despatch, and pass the censor. Excuse my impatience, this is the first chance of sending a wire that I have had for weeks. I assure you, I feel chock full of electricity, and bursting with news."

He ran off as fast as his little legs would carry him.

Before he had time to move on, Jack met with another surprise.

He was close to one of the hospital tents, over which the Geneva Cross flag was flying.

Two men carrying a stretcher approached ; behind it walked Cyrus Vanderbilt and Fred Dawson.

Something impelled Jack to take a nearer look at the stretcher.

He started back with horror at beholding the blood-stained face of Mrs. Steiner.

Her thick glossy hair was dabbled with blood.

Her eyes were closed, and she appeared to be unconscious.

The stretcher disappeared in the tent, and he knew that she was only wounded ; for if dead, she would not have been taken there.

Vanderbilt and Dawson welcomed Harkaway as if he had come back from the grave.

He had indeed escaped from the jaws of death.

They explained that when the balloon was shot by the Boers, they descended safely to the earth, by the aid of their parachutes.

Hearing groans close by, they made a search, and discovered Mrs. Steiner lying under a rock, a bullet having hit her ; but as she still lived, they did what they could in a surgical way, until they met some English bearers who were collecting the dead and wounded in the recent battle.

A field doctor extracted the bullet, and they went with her to the camp, having the surgeon's assurance that as she had been struck by a Mauser bullet, she was likely to recover, but she must on no account be disturbed.

She had Jack's best wishes, but in the hurry and bustle of war, there is little time for sympathy.

He told Fred about the new mission which had been given them.

"After an hour or two's sleep," he said, "I will see about a horse. We will ride to Belmont, and make the acquaintance of Colonel Ricardo."

"If it will be of any service to you," exclaimed Vanderbilt, "I can give you a lift, as I am going in your direction."

"How is that?" asked Jack. "Your balloon is done for. Have you got another in your pocket?"

"I provided for such an event," answered Vanderbilt, "and have had my new, patent, armoured automobile, or veldt motor car, sent up here from Cape Town. It is capable of going up and down hill, and big enough to hold a dozen men, though I do not propose to take more than half that number.

"There is a chance for you, Dawson, the corporal, little Andy, and Fish, if he likes to come. The 'Dart,' as I call it, will stand any amount of shot; and I have the latest machine guns. Everything works by electric power, which I alone control. I could go from Cape Town to Cairo, if I wanted to. Say the word, and I will have it ready for you an hour after noon to-day."

"I think you can count us all in," answered Jack. "It will be a novelty."

"You are right there. It is the first of its kind. No one has ever seen an armoured motor car before, and I guess the Colonials will stare some. We went over their camp in the balloon yesterday, and in my opinion they'll do. They are well built and can stick it. You can have a look at the 'Dart' now, if you please, and I can give you a drop of sparkling."

The proposition was gladly agreed to.

Fish rejoined them, and jumped at the invitation, remarking:

"This will be more copy for me. I am in luck to-day. Harkaway shooting Boers from an armoured automobile. How will that strike the intelligent public?"

As they were about to walk off, a young officer, not more than twenty years of age, having a very effeminate and blasé air about him, came up, and twirling a scarcely preceptible moustache with his thumb and fore-finger, presented a despatch to Jack.

He was dressed in khaki, and according to the new regulations had laid aside his sword.

Our officers now are not to be distinguished from the private soldier.

"You are Lieutenant Harkaway, I believe?" he exclaimed with a languid drawl. "Fancy I have met you before somewhere; I am Lieutenant Listless, of the Grenadier Guards, you know. Deuced hot, isn't it? Enough to bake an elephant, as my friend Twaddles of the Blues says. Awfully nice fellow, Twaddles; but he can't stand this beastly climate, you know. I breakfasted with him just now, and Twaddles said there was sand *à la* Modder in everything we ate, and that made us moderate eaters. That's not my joke, you know; it's Twaddles'."

"Very good," replied Jack, with a smile, looking at the despatch which had been sent to him for transmission to Belmont.

Lieutenant Listless informed him that he also was ordered to Belmont, and would, if he had no objecttion, accompany him.

Hearing this, the American asked him to take a seat in the motor car, which the young Guardsman made no objection to, though he suggested that it would be safer to go by rail, as they might meet with prowling bands of Boers on the veldt.

Not that the little dandy and pet of London drawing-rooms was afraid.

Far from it.

If there was fighting to be done, he was ready; but he did not like unneccessary exertion.

In all the battles that had been fought, he had displayed conspicuous gallantry.

At the Modder he had been ten hours under fire, and was one of the first to cross the river to the island, at the head of his men.

"Boer killing is not bad sport," he observed, "but as my friend, Twaddles, says, I rather prefer grouse-shooting. The difficulty is to get at these beggars. The Guards routed some of them out of their holes yesterday, and we hit them up in splendid style. When beaten, they certainly make good sprinters, but as Twaddles says, they do not retire gracefully, and are not much to look at."

The party now made their way to the motor car, which was outside the camp, guarded by a Kaffir, called Slimpiet, who had been engaged as cook and odd man generally.

They all went inside, with the exception of Jack and Fred, who remained to exchange a few words in private.

Slimpiet was talking to another Kaffir, but the young men did not take any notice of them, and the second Kaffir turned his back, as if he had a purpose in concealing his face.

"So we meet again, Fred, after a long separation," exclaimed Harkaway. "What a lot we have been through; if, please Heaven, we live, we may expect to see a heap more; for with Buller stuck on the Tugela, and Methuen anchored here, it will be some time before we get into Ladysmith or Kimberley, let alone Pretoria."

"The more the merrier, dear boy," answered Fred. "I have been through my baptism of fire, and am game for anything. The sight of blood doesn't affect me now any more than water, and the rattle of the guns is just as good as the music of 'The Belle of New York.'

"Fighting is born in an Englishman, and even that little chap, Listless, wakes up when he hears the ring of a rifle. He fights like a Turk, and the men will follow him anywhere, although he curls his hair, uses perfume, and thinks everything too much trouble, don'tcherknow; but you wanted to say something to me?"

"Yes," replied Jack, at once becoming serious. "I hope you haven't lost the plan of that Rhodesian mine. Without it, no one will ever be able to find the spot, and what has lain buried for centuries will remain so. We must think of our future, remember, Fred. These are the days of millionaires, and I mean to be one if I can. As we are partners you will share my prosperity."

"The map has not been out of my pocket ever since you gave it me," replied Fred Dawson. "I'll take it out, and show it you if you want to look at it. Perhaps the sight of it will reassure you. I know it is a dead-sure thing for us, and it isn't likely I'd lose it."

Fred unbuttoned his tunic, and diving into an inside pocket, produced the parchment, which Jack eagerly glanced at.

He knew it again in a moment, and was satisfied.

"That will do," he said, "stick to it, for it is safer with you than with me. Now Krause is dead, I've only to fear Webb, who is always on the lookout. Whenever I fall into his hands, the first thing he does is to run through my clothes, like a zarp with a zachen-roller. He'd rather have that bit of parchment than all the books in the free library at Pretoria."

He had scarcely finished speaking before Vanderbilt appeared at the door of the automobile, and cried out :

"Harkaway, we have filled the flowing bowl, which awaits your presence."

In a moment Jack nimbly set his foot upon the step, and disappeared inside the large, ugly-looking, iron-clad waggon.

While Fred Dawson was replacing the plan of the mine in his pocket, he received a blow behind the ear, which made him sit down on the grass, under the influence of a stunning sensation.

Bells rang in his ears, and a mist came over his eyes.

The person who had hit him with his fist was Dunko, who had been talking to the Kaffir, Slimpiet, employed by Vanderbilt.

Dunko had heard all that had passed between Jack and Fred, and his motive for the attack was to possess himself of the mine plan, which he did.

Directly afterwards he ran away as if a snake was after him.

Naturally, Dunko had been sent into the camp by Webb to see what was going on, and find out anything he could about Harkaway.

Kaffirs were always going to and fro like a lot of flies, offering themselves to the British, proving at times very useful.

Dunko had not even been challenged.

The motor car attracted his attention.

Slimpiet was a friend of his, and he was asking questions about the automobile when Harkaway came up with the others.

Instantly he turned right about face, and waited his opportunity with the result we have described.

Fred Dawson came to himself in less than a minute, and looked round.

No one was to be seen, except a few soldiers who had strolled up to have a peep at the car, into which Slimpiet had retreated, it being his game to pretend ignorance of what had occurred.

Fred's first thought was of the parchment, for which he looked in vain.

He uttered a cry of dismay when he found it gone.

"Confound the luck!" he exclaimed. "I have been robbed! This is Webb's doing. I might have known we were spied upon. Vanderbilt's Kaffir must be in league with him ; but I might as well question a brick wall as to get the truth out of one of these blooming Kaffirs. We are done unless we can get hold of Webb, who must be looked after as soon as this affair at Belmont is over."

Appearing very disconsolate, he entered the car, which was long, high, and broad, being divided into four compartments.

The first was the arsenal, where the arms and ammunition were kept; the second, a living-room, comfortably furnished; the third was the sleeping apartment; and the fourth, a cooking and store room ; and at its extremity was the motive power.

Each division was loop-holed for rifles and the machine guns ; all being supplied with the electric light.

The party were standing round a table, each holding a glass of wine in his hand, while Jack was proposing success to the "Dart."

Slimpiet was holding a box of cigars in his hand for the guests to help themselves.

Going up to him, Fred Dawson tapped him on the shoulder, saying :

"Who was that Kaffir with you, and why did you allow him to knock me down and rob me ? No lies. Out with it, boy."

"Ikona, baas," replied Slimpiet, elevating his eyebrows, and looking the picture of injured innocence and astonishment.

This phrase, "Ikona, baas," was a complete denial, and intended as an emphatic negative ; and though Fred spoke to him again and again, he could get nothing else out of the lying rascal, whose moral sense as to telling the truth was either completely blunted, or had never existed.

So Fred had to give it up as a bad job.

Not for the first time in his life he felt puzzled how to act.

He knew that it would grieve Harkaway to hear of the loss of the plan, and after some deliberation, he thought it best to keep it a secret.

They certainly could not start in search of the mine until the war was over, and as things were going at present it was impossible for anyone to tell how long that would last ; and perhaps neither of them would live to see the end of it.

He determined to leave no stone unturned to capture Webb and get back the plan.

Feeling confident that Dunko would give it to him, and that Webb would part with it on no account whatever.

Krause being dead, Webb had no rival in the business, except Harkaway and Dawson ; which would make him all the more anxious to hold what he had got.

A few hours had to elapse before the car started on its journey.

Jack, Fred, Fish, and Andy retired to the sleeping-room, as they were half-dead with fatigue.

Vanderbilt busied himself with his machinery.

Slimpiet had plenty to do in the kitchen.

The corporal and Lieutenant Listless sat together in the saloon.

War had placed the officer and the non. com. on an equality.

There was little difference between the duke's son and the cook's son at Table Bay.

"Have another glass, corporal," said Lieutenant Listless. "You do not often come across a luxury like this; as my friend Twaddles, of the Blues, says, imagination has to go a long way in Natal, and bai jove, there is more truth than poetry in his remark, don't-cher-know."

"Thank you, sir," replied the corporal, taking up the bottle. "I don't know whether I will or I wont, but I'd rather."

"We may fully expect to be attacked by the Boers before we reach Belmont. Twaddles told me so, and he knows everything. Where he gets it from, I can't imagine. The country is full of Kaffirs, watching our movements, and they run to the Boers directly they see anything. Baden Powell at Mafeking had to release a villainous horse thief and spy, named Viljohn, in exchange for Lady Sarah Wilson."

"Viljohn," repeated the corporal. "I know him well, for I helped to capture and bring him a prisoner into Mafeking. He's a desperate ruffian, and a great pal of Cronje's."

"Exactly. Now you've hit it. Viljohn is said to be in our neighbourhood, with a small commando of his own, composed of gaol birds and the scum of Johannesburg, whose main object is loot."

"Then they'll be a mark on this haughty mobiliar, or whatever you call it," said the corporal with emphasis.

"That's what Twaddles thinks, and I'll back his opinion against anyone's. Deuced clever fellah, is Twaddles. I wish I'd gone by rail, now, for I don't half like the look of this perambulating fort on wheels. Vanderbilt is a scientist, yet, as Twaddles says, he has got too much inventive gas in his noddle, and it will be a wonder if it don't explode some day and blow the roof off."

They continued to talk until Vanderbilt rang a bell, and a whirring sound denoted that the car was in motion, the latter however being scarcely perceptible, unless the ground was very uneven, when some jolting was unavoidable.

CHAPTER XXIV.

THE ATTACK ON THE MOTOR CAR BY VILJOHN —DEATH OF VANDERBILT — MACKAY'S FARM — THE FLEIDERMANS — WITH THE COLONIALS.

OWING to the tropical heat of the sun, the interior of the automobile was like an oven, the armour-plates attracting the solar rays.

Mr. Vanderbilt opened the hatch, as he termed it, by moving a sliding panel in the roof, but this did very little good, and the travellers were glad enough to get outside and walk.

With the exception of Lieutenant Listless and Corporal Potts, who appeared to care no more for the heat than a salamander, all preferred marching; but the two we have mentioned, after going a couple of miles resumed

their former positions, Listless remarking that if he must perspire he would rather do so sitting down than standing up, while the corporal kept Slimpiet busy bringing him cooling drinks.

Fish smoked his pipe, and made occasional notes in his book.

Andy took pistol shots at the little birds that fly about the veldt.

Harkaway and Fred had much to say to one another.

Dawson was rather downcast at the loss of the plan of the mine, though he gave his friend no inkling of it.

The Dart did not require steering, as it rolled steadily on in a straight line, climbing the small hills as easily as a traction-engine.

Its owner, Mr. Vanderbilt, walked by himself, apparently plunged in deep thought, while he now and then looked at a plan of the country, as if he was not quite certain of his reckoning.

Now and again he raised his field-glasses to his eyes, searching the veldt in all directions.

All at once he beckoned Jack and Fred to his side.

"Is there anything wrong, commodore?" asked Harkaway. "If so, I shall be glad to help you out of the difficulty."

"I am afraid that no one can give me any assistance," replied Vanderbilt. "When we started on this journey I forgot a very important consideration."

"What is that?"

"My motor car is not amphibious; if it were, all would be well. I can see in front of us a small river, which, as far as I can make out by the map, is the Vaal. There have been recent rains, and these African rivers, though their beds are perfectly dry one day, will be in flood the next, as they will sometimes rise thirty and forty inches in a night. Most of them are fordable, if you only know where to find the spot, but the Dart would be sure to stick in the mud."

"What do you propose to do?" inquired Jack.

"I must beat a retreat," replied Vanderbilt, "I am sorry to say; and you fellows will have to get on the best way you can. I reckon we are sixty miles from Belmont now, where you want to go. The nearest towns are Sunnyside and Douglas, both occupied by the enemy, who swarm thick as bees round here. I will see you to the banks of the river, and then, to my great sorrow, we must part."

"It can't be helped," answered Harkaway cheerfully, "and I daresay we shall meet again before long. You need not go any further; turn back at once."

The American thought this a good course to adopt, and he moved towards the car to change his direction, when he suddenly came to a halt.

"Christopher Columbus!" he cried, "look over there. We are caught in a fix. On guard, all of you."

The young men turned, and saw a body of at least thirty mounted Boers galloping towards them; and as well as they could see, through the cloud of dust which they raised, there were more behind these.

Little Andy perceived the danger at the same time, and putting his bugle to his mouth, blew it shrilly, causing Listless and the corporal to look out of the door.

"What's up?" asked the guardsman, with his usual languid air.

"The Boers are upon us," replied Vanderbilt. "We shall have some fun directly."

"Hang the brutes. I wish they had kept away until night. It's too uncomfortably hot to fight. That little beggar, Andy, must have brought them down upon us through popping away at the birds. Sound travels an awful long way in this dry air. My friend Twaddles says you can hear a snake hiss a mile off."

"Inside, all of you," said Vanderbilt, in a voice of authority.

The order was instantly complied with, and each man was assigned his position.

The door was securely fastened, and the machine stopped.

"Gentlemen," continued the American, "we must defend this fort to the last gasp. Fire only when I give the word of command. Harkaway, take charge of the Maxim."

This gun was fixed on the left-hand side of the car, and as Vanderbilt finished speaking a commotion arose between Andy and Slimpiet, whom the bugler seized by the arm, and, young as he was, forced on his knees, snatching a long chisel out of his hand.

Slimpiet looked terribly alarmed, and gazed with longing eyes at the door, as if he wished it was open, and he could make a dash for liberty.

Then he cast his eyes up to the ventilating hole in the roof, but he would have to stand on a table to reach that.

"Do you see this, sir?" cried Andy, holding up the tool. "This rascally Kaffir has been tampering with the machine gun. I caught him in the act, right under our very noses."

"Is that so? I didn't think he was such a traitor," replied Vanderbilt.

"Try the gun, sir. I bet it won't work."

Harkaway did so, as he was the nearest, and found it impossible to move it.

"The lad is correct," he said. "The action of the gun is entirely ruined."

Cyrus Vanderbilt's face assumed a grave air.

"The penalty of treachery in a community like ours, and at such a critical juncture, is death," he exclaimed. "The Maxim was our strong point, and it is done for, being put out of action when we most wanted it. There is no time for repairing. The loss is great, and I think you will all agree with me that the wretch who did the deed should be shot."

There was a murmur of approval from everyone present, while the American took his revolver from his belt.

"Stand on one side," he added. "I will be the executioner; and I am sure that no one ever deserved death more than this Kaffir does."

"Mercy, baas," whined Slimpiet. "I was only trying to see how the gun went off, feeling that I should like to make myself useful when the Boers come. Slimpiet is your Kaffir, and would die for you."

"That won't wash," replied Vanderbilt, who advanced with a handkerchief, which he intended to tie over the Kaffir's eyes. "Your defence is a little too thin, my boy."

"I know he's a traitor," exclaimed Fred Dawson. "It does not matter how. I've no time to tell you now, but you will be very foolish if you spare him. It will be no act of mercy to let him live."

"Just so," said Vanderbilt. "The rascal deserves to die."

Quite unexpectedly the Kaffir made a spring in the air, and climbing up Harkaway's back like a monkey, stood for an instant on his shoulders, from which elevated position he sprang through the hole in the roof of the motor car, thinking to escape by letting himself down the side.

He was, however, sadly disappointed in his calculations.

No sooner had he gained a footing on the roof than the mounted Boers, who had come within range of the motor car, commenced to fire.

They made no distinction between Kaffirs and white men.

Seeing Slimpiet on the top of the automobile, they made a target of him, and the unhappy wretch fell back through the hole, with a dozen bullets in him, tumbling on the top of Andy, whom he knocked down as flat as a pan-cake, and covered with blood.

His body was dragged on one side.

A storm of bullets flattened themselves against the armour-plates.

A deadly hail continued for more than a minute, but seeing they had not to deal with a structure of wood, the Boers left off firing, discovering that they were merely wasting their ammunition.

During this time, those inside had not been idle.

Everyone fired as quickly as possible, and, as their bandoliers got empty, Andy brought them a fresh supply of cartridges.

The destruction among the Boers was great, the plain being studded with fallen men and horses.

There was a look-out hole at the end of the car, at which Vanderbilt placed himself, Fred Dawson looking over his shoulder.

The Boers who remained alive had taken shelter behind such stones as they could find, and were waiting for a chance to get a shot at someone visible. They were evidently puzzled and baffled, but they did not mean to give up the fight, possibly relying on some support from their rear.

Those who had fallen seemed a ragged set of rascals, not on a par with the ordinary Boer farmer, who has a look of solid respectability about him.

"That is Viljohn's lot, or I am greatly mistaken," said Dawson. "I should know that fellow again in a moment if I saw him, through my acquaintance with him at Mafeking. The fellow has been in Pretoria Gaol several times, but Cronje values him for some reason."

As he spoke, a man got up from behind a boulder, and displayed a white flag tied to a stick.

"There he is. That's Viljohn," cried Fred. "If you look closely you will see a deep scar on his left cheek."

"I'll get out, and go and speak to him!" exclaimed Vanderbilt. "If I explain that we are non-combatants, I should think he would let us alone. There are more behind him, and if they bring up a machine gun we are done for, as we cannot expect any help from our side."

"Don't be so rash and foolish," said Harkaway, who heard his intention. "It is impossible to trust a character like Viljohn, or, indeed, any of the Boers when they show the flag of truce. You will get shot to a moral certainty."

"I don't think so," replied the American, who was fond of having his own way. "At present we are hard pressed, and in a desperate tight fix; unless these men are robbers they are bound to respect my neutrality, or the United States Consul at Pretoria will have something to say about it."

It was in vain that Harkaway and Dawson endeavoured to restrain him.

He would not be dictated to or listen to advice; and opening the door of the car, stepped out on to the open ground, unarmed, and advancing leisurely with his hands in his pockets, to meet the notorious and dreaded Viljohn.

"There goes a man who can write out a cheque for a million without hurting himself," remarked Harkaway. "He could not stay at home because his love of excitement and adventure is too strong."

"He may be right," observed Fred, "but I call him a decided crackpot. He must be a little bit luny."

Without exposing themselves, they watched Cyrus Vanderbilt, who was as brave as a lion, betraying no concern.

He might have been walking along Broadway, so indifferent did he appear.

Before he had gone twenty yards, Viljohn dropped the flag of truce, and swiftly raising his rifle, villainously fired point-blank at the American.

A bullet crashed through his skull, and he fell back a corpse.

Harkaway, who was standing at the loophole, witnessed this dastardly act, and his blood coursed wildly through his veins, while he trembled with rage and indignation at the loss of so good and true an ally, who had always been devotedly loyal and generous to a fault.

With the quickness of thought, he put his rifle through an embrasure, and fired at the cowardly Boer, who was just sinking down into his former position, chuckling to himself over the cowardly murder he had committed.

Luckily Jack aimed low, and hit the miscreant in the stomach, causing him to fall with a loud cry, which roused his marauding gang, who began to fire again at the automobile.

It was a day of disaster for those inside.

A chance shot came through one of the firing holes, and struck Lieutenant Listless in the breast.

The unfortunate young guardsman fell back with a gasp into Harkaway's arms, and he was laid by the side of the dead Kaffir.

Corporal Potts now performed a brave deed, in conjunction with Andy.

The two went out on the plain, and in spite of the bullets which rained around them, succeeded in bringing in Vanderbilt's body, closing the door behind them.

"Bravo! Well done!" exclaimed Harkaway. "We will give it these fellows yet. I only wish poor Vanderbilt had taken my tip. If he had he would have been alive and well now."

"The Boers are too wicked to be trusted," said Dawson. "Downright wicked, I call them; but our friend's is only one of the precious lives which have been and will be lost in this terrible war, which Kruger truly declared would stagger humanity."

Fish was making notes, and did not join in the conversation.

He left the fighting to others.

Lieutenant Listless was beyond human help.

The corporal was busily engaged trying to repair the Maxim.

Andy was only a boy, and all he could do was to keep a look out, so that the command devolved entirely upon Jack and Fred, whose resources were severely taxed to find a way out of the dilemma in which fate had placed them.

"Hurrah!" cried the corporal, turning the Maxim, and sending out a rattling volley. "I've got the gun all right again, and it will work like magic. The Kaffir had only got a screw loose, and I've fixed it. That's one to me. Aren't you going to say something? I was born with a mouth, you know, and it's jolly hot in here."

Jack tendered him his flask, which he took with apparent reluctance, saying—

"There's no label on it. Is it Kola or lemon squash? I don't know whether I will or I won't, but I'd rather. All fermented liquors are poison, but——"

"It's a wonder you weren't dead long ago," interrupted Jack, who, touching a lever, set the car in motion, and turned it round to face the enemy.

"What are you going to do?" inquired Fred.

"Dig these beggars out of the rocks. I'll kill everyone of them in revenge for what has happened. Vanderbilt's spirit wouldn't rest unless I did."

He carefully steered the motor car to the spot where the Boers were hiding.

Seeing this move on the part of their foe, they got up and fled, being shot down like a number of rabbits, only two or three escaping to tell the tale of their defeat.

Whether they had friends behind them or not, Jack was unable to discover; but the automobile was not again molested, and they were free to bury their dead, which they did in a hurried but solemn manner.

The Boers they did not trouble about, leaving their bodies for the vultures to prey upon.

As Cyrus Vanderbilt had been taken from them, Harkaway decided that he was at liberty to use the car in anyway he liked.

It was useless to try and cross the Vaal river, as it was in flood; so, after studying the map, he proceeded in the direction of a town named Sunnyside, situated between Belmont and Douglas, to which we have previously alluded.

It was Jack's hope that they would find the house of some loyal farmer, where they could leave the car, and obtain some horses with which to continue their journey.

The farmer would no doubt be able to tell them where to find the nearest ford, and they would have to rough it, as they were accustomed to do.

Nor was he disappointed in this expectation, for, after travelling about six miles, he came to a substantially-built farmhouse, from which a stalwart Scotchman came out to meet them.

Perceiving nothing to be alarmed at, they opened the door, and alighted.

"I'm Angus MacKay, born north of the Tweed, and for some years past have been a Natal farmer. Who are you, my friends? and what are you doing with that steam-roller out here?"

Jack gave him the desired information, and a conversation ensued between them.

MacKay stated that his farm had been looted by the Boers, and most of his stock driven off.

All the farmers who refused to serve under the Transvaal flag had been badly treated by the Boers, and he had sent his wife and family to friends at Sunnyside.

"My wife's father, who is an old man, refused to leave me," added Angus MacKay, "and he met with a strange fate last night at the hands of the Fleidermans."

"Who is he?" enquired Harkaway.

"Haven't you heard of the mad Boer, called the Fleidermans?" responded the Scotchman. "He is an incarnate fiend, and his name strikes terror to every heart in this region."

"Tell me something about him."

"His name is Van Heller; he comes from some place near the Basuto territory. When the war broke out he went mad, and swore a fearful oath that he would not rest until he had killed a thousand Britishers. He is a short, thin man, and wears a black cape, which swings over his arms like the wings of a bat, which is English for Fleidermans. Hence the name. He creeps upon his victims in the dark, or when they are asleep, and round their foreheads he ties a label, on which he writes certain figures indicating the number of Englishmen he has slain. My father-in-law's number is 137, which shows that the vampire is getting on with his foul work; and if he isn't stopped, he'll kill his thousand, as he swore he would."

"Does he touch women and children?"

"No. For his credit's sake let it be said that he does not, as far as I know. The old man, Fergus McIvor, slept in the next room to me. I heard a sound of footsteps. I piled out of bed, and was just in time to see the Fleidermans departing in the pale moonlight. Rushing back for my gun, I hunted everywhere, but the ghoul was gone. I tell you, my flesh has been on the creep ever since. I didn't mean to sleep here to-night; I was off to Sunnyside as soon as I had done a few little jobs about the farm."

"Can you let us have some horses? We shall want five."

"Yes," replied MacKay; "the Boers are well supplied with horses, and did not touch mine. I have half-a-dozen in the yard; one will do for me."

His curiosity about the motor car was so great that it could not be gratified until he had gone all over it, expressing his admiration at everything he saw.

"I'll sink it in the river for you if you like!" he exclaimed. "It's too good for the Boers to capture."

Harkaway made no objection to this course, as the car was only an encumbrance to him.

The party expressed a wish to see the body of McIvor, and the farmer took them into the house for that purpose.

The victim of the Fleidermans was lying stretched out upon a camp-bedstead.

He had been stabbed to the heart with a knife, which was the way in which the homicidal Boer treated all those he murdered.

The bed was stained with blood, which had trickled down into a pool on the floor.

On the forehead was the label, with the figures which every week were increasing in magnitude.

It was an awful sight, calculated to appal a man of the strongest nerve, and Harkaway quitted the room with a shudder.

When they gained the stoep, they were surprised to see a large mounted force approaching the farm, with two guns and a horse battery, behind which came some light infantry, marching on foot, and an ambulance.

"This means something," said Fred Dawson. "They belong to our side, and must have come from Belmont to do a little bit of night work."

"They look like the Colonials," answered Jack; "the very men to whom we are despatched. They must have anticipated the order I had to give them, which will save us a lot of trouble."

A scout who was in advance of the main column galloped up.

Words were exchanged between him and Harkaway, who ascertained that the force coming from Belmont consisted of two hundred Queenslanders, commanded by Colonel Ricardo, one hundred Canadians, and two companies of the Cornwall Light Infantry, the whole under the command of Lieutenant-Colonel Pilcher.

After leaving Belmont, they marched westward, and had covered twenty miles when they reached Angus's farm.

"We shall encamp here for the night," said the scout, "and in the morning attack a rebel laager, reported to us at a point not far from this farm."

"That's right enough," replied Angus MacKay. "There are a lot of Boers to the west, in strongly entrenched kopjes."

"You will all have to fall in with us," continued the scout, "for fear some of you might give information to the enemy."

"Nothing will suit us better," exclaimed Harkaway. "I should like to lead some of you fine fellows. What part of Australia do you come from?"

"A little way from Brisbane," rejoined the scout. "We haven't been in Africa long, and I'm just itching to have a bout with these Boers."

The next minute Colonels Pilcher and Ricardo rode up together.

Jack and Fred saluted, and the corporal came to attention.

Andy drew himself up to his full height, which was about four-feet-nothing; and Mr. Fish produced the inevitable note-book, looking as wise as an owl in an ivy-bush.

The despatches were delivered, and Lieutenant Harkaway was soon on familiar terms with his superior officers, who were conducted into the sitting-room by MacKay, and such refreshments as could be hastily procured were placed before them.

The soldiers watered and attended to their horses, after which they prepared their own suppers.

They were to sleep on the ground that night, which was nothing new to these hardy volunteers from our Colonies.

The strictest silence was preserved, and a guard was kept over several Kaffirs who had been picked up on the way, as these natives could run like ostriches, and were very fond of selling information to the enemy.

"I thought it advisable to let the Boers know that we were alive," remarked Colonel Pilcher, "and I am glad the general is of my opinion. We have been too tame lately, but I hope in a few hours we shall teach them a lesson. This war should be conducted with vigour. You will fight with us to-morrow, Harkaway."

"Certainly," replied Jack. "What do you suppose I am made of? I will join Colonel Ricardo, if he has no objection. When this affair is over, I want to help in the relief of Kimberley, which I expect Lord Methuen will effect before Buller shakes hands with White in Ladysmith. None of the generals have got men enough. It is the old story of a War Office breakdown. The men at home didn't know the strength of the enemy, and we have harder work to do than we thought for."

"Quite right," answered Colonel Ricardo. "It is a shame that we should be checked for want of men and guns. We are a nation of forty millions of people, with unlimited resources, and the Boers only number four hundred thousand all told."

"Never mind," said Jack, cheerfully. "All we want is a long pull, and a strong pull, and a pull all together. We shall corner Kruger yet, but it will take a bit of doing."

Jack introduced his friend Dawson, and also trotted out the corporal and Andy.

Mr. Fish also paid his respects to the colonels.

"So you are a correspondent, sir," observed Colonel Pilcher, "and are seeing a little more of the night side of nature than you bargained for? I have read your letters in the *Cape Town Slasher* with great interest, and am extremely glad to make your acquaintance."

"You behold me, sir, shorn of my glory," replied Fish. "My camp equipage is equal to that of any correspondent in the field. The London *Times* could not beat me. I have a splendid trap, a couple of horses, a well-furnished tent, which the King of the Persians might have envied; but I left all that in Mafeking, and it will become the spoil of war if some of you gallant gentlemen do not hurry up and come to the rescue of poor Baden Powell."

"Have you been making notes?"

"Oh, yes; I never neglect that, but they have not been of much use to me lately. I have been led astray by Harkaway, and have not been near a telegraph office for weeks until recently; but I have got a fine description of the Colonials. Splendid fellows, full of go and glee."

"That's right. Put in a kind word for us. We have come a long way to help you, and there are more at our back if you want them," said Colonel Ricardo.

The party took their leave, and Jack went for a stroll with Andy through the lines of the soldiers, to have a look at them before it grew dark and they cast themselves down on mother earth for a brief sleep.

Very fine, pleasant fellows he found them.

They did not seem to think they were on active service, with a chance of getting a bullet next day.

They laughed and chatted as if they were out for a picnic.

As they were returning to the house, Andy asked Jack where he was going to sleep that night.

"Angus MacKay has got the horses all ready for us, so we shall be able to ride with the troops in the morning," he said. "I only wanted to know were you were going to doss down, because I should like to be with you."

"Don't worry about me," answered Harkaway. "I'll pitch anywhere."

"It isn't that, sir," continued the little fellow. "I heard Angus say that he had got a room for you in the house, and if you rest there, I am afraid you will come to grief."

"How is that, my little man!"

"There is something very uncanny about that story of the Fleidermans. I believe the assassin is hanging about these farm buildings."

"What makes you think so?"

"When I went to see after the horses I fancied I saw a thing like a bat on two legs darting behind some ricks. The man may have been hiding during the day, with the intention of attacking MacKay in the night, thus adding another victim to his already long list; and, perhaps, if you sleep in the house, he might select you. So I thought I would sit up and see that you come to no harm."

"Really, Andy, you are quite too precious," replied Jack, laughing. "You only want a pair of wings to be a guardian angel. If you want the distinguished honour of watching over me, I shan't say no. I had an idea of sleeping in the motor-car, to tell you the truth. Where is it?"

"I took it upon myself, sir, to run it into one of the barns, so that the soldiers should not get at it, as I thought there might be a thing or two you would like to have out of it before Angus sinks the car in the river."

The bugler led the way to the barn, the door of which they opened carefully, stepping lightly inside, both of them on the alert, for there was no telling where the Fleidermans might be.

It was necessary to be cautious.

A sudden spring, a stab in the dark, and all would be over.

To their astonishment they perceived that the electric light was burning in the car;

and, going a little closer, they looked in at the half-open door, where they saw Mr. Fish and Corporal Potts hobnobbing together over some wine, a couple of empty bottles on the the floor showing their capacity for that beverage.

"This is what I call cosy," remarked the corporal. "You sung that ditty very well, sir. Many a time have I marched to the tune of 'The girl I left behind me.' God bless her pretty face. I hope she'll be alive when I go home. I've had a good many sweethearts, but she's the best of them all. She answers to the name of Polly, and her parents keep a ham-and-beef shop in the Blackfriars Road. Here's your health and song, sir. By George, the bottle's empty. Sit still, I'll bring on another. Anything to oblige a gentleman."

The corporal got up with a very unsteady gait.

He took a couple of steps towards the storeroom, when he lost his balance and fell down upon the floor.

"That'sh funny thing," he said, with an imbecile smile. "Don't think I mished my pitch; I'm as steady as a marine in a storm. I wanted, you know, to see if she'd bump; but I can mark time as well as our generals in South Africa."

"That's high treason, Potts," remarked Fish. "You shouldn't say anything of that kind above a whisper. What do you know about tactics and strategy? Leave all that to the Staff College and the War Office. Tommies are only paid a shilling a day to be shot at."

Not understanding the full significance of these words, the corporal, with a supreme effort, picked up an empty bottle, and, in an absent-minded manner, put the bottom end to his mouth, murmuring softly:

"I don't know whether I will or I won't, but I'd rather."

The next minute he cuddled it in his arms and fell asleep.

"This is no place for us," whispered Harkaway. "Let us go to the chamber that Angus MacKay has prepared."

They did so, each of them thinking, more or less, of the dreaded Fleidermans.

CHAPTER XXV.

ANDY KILLS THE FLEIDERMANS—WEBB SHOWS HIS HAND—HARKAWAY AND THE COLONIALS—HOLDING THE FARM—THE STRANGE HIGHLANDER.

As Harkaway returned to the farmhouse with Andy the bugler, he shivered.

It might have been through the cold, for the air was very keen, but the feeling undoubtedly arose partly from nervous apprehension, for there was something so ghostly and weird about Van Heller, the Fleidermans, that he could not get the mad Dutchman out of his mind.

After inspecting the room which Angus MacKay had assigned him out of compliment, he could not make up his mind to rest.

Though tired and exhausted by the events of the day, he was ill at ease, having an undefinable dread of something which was to happen to him in the near future.

The apartment was spacious, being dully lighted by an old-fashioned oil lamp; the floor being covered with a sort of silver sand.

A mattress and a blanket had been thrown in one corner; a couple of chairs and a deal table formed the only furniture.

The stars shone into the uncurtained window, cold and lustrous.

To his heated imagination, the chamber seemed full of dancing shadows, and it was altogether chilling and repellent.

"What I have gone through lately has upset me a bit," exclaimed Harkaway, "and I will take a walk round the camp to steady my nerves. If you like to stay here alone, you are at liberty to do so, but I should advise you to keep your eyes open after what we have heard about MacKay's nocturnal visitor."

"I shall not risk going to sleep," replied the bugler. "You need not be alarmed about me; I have picked up something since I've been in South Africa on active service, and know how to take care of myself. I'm not a boy on a farm now."

"Perhaps you had better come with me, I don't half like to leave you here, though I can hear Angus MacKay snoring in the next room. He wanted to go to Sunnyside, but Colonel Pilcher will not allow anyone to get in advance of the troops."

"If it's all the same to you, sir, I would rather remain here," said Andy, firmly. "I mean to have a bout with the Fleidermans if he comes in this direction. It doesn't matter about sleeping, as we shall be in the saddle at daybreak. As for me, I can't sleep before I am going into action."

"Don't fire your rifle, or you'll rouse the whole camp. Hide yourself in a corner, and use your bayonet if you see anything suspicious. Should you want me, I shall be found with some of the outlying scouts of the Queenslanders."

With these words Harkaway left the bugler alone, and went outside.

Pulling his helmet over his brow, and carrying his rifle on his shoulder, he walked slowly towards the camp of the Colonials.

Andy had conceived an idea which he proceeded to execute.

Hanging on a nail behind the door was a suit of farmer's clothes, and in a corner he perceived a bundle of hay.

Taking down the clothes he stuffed the hay into them, making them resemble a man.

In a cupboard he discovered a pair of high-topped boots and a farmer's smashed hat, with which he ornamented the extremities, placing the effigy when completed on the mattress, as if it was lying with its face to the wall.

Then unfixing his bayonet, he held it in his hand, and concealed himself in the cupboard to await results.

Half an hour passed.

The lamp began to burn low and flicker, making the surroundings look still more dismal and dreary.

All at once a shadowy figure glided into the room, wearing a black cape, such as the Scotchman had described, which, when the arms moved, made them look very much like wings.

The face was thin and bronzed, the nose short and pudgy, the black hair was cut close, the ears stood out from the side of the head, and there was a stoop in the back.

Altogether the singular creature looked like a bird of prey, and Andy did not doubt that the Fleidermans was before him.

For a moment the figure remained stationary, glancing with eager, vindictive eyes at the dummy stretched out on the bed in the corner.

Then the man glided up to it with cat-like tread, and bending over what he supposed to be the body of a human being wrapped in slumber, plunged a long knife into what he took to be the heart.

The knife penetrated easily through the hay, causing the wretch to utter a cry of surprise and lose his balance, falling forward over his imaginary victim.

Rushing from his hiding-place, Andy did not scruple to attack the would-be murderer, driving his bayonet into his back before he had the opportunity of withdrawing his knife.

Though mortally wounded, the Fleidermans was for a moment possessed of a terrific power born of despair.

Gripping Andy by the throat, before he could repeat the blow he endeavoured to strangle him, but he was unable to accomplish his evil purpose, for his strength gave way, oozing out at his finger's ends, and with a final effort he threw him on the floor his head knocking against the boards with a stunning sensation.

The little bugler knew no more.

Both of them lost consciousness at the same time.

Blood from the dying Boer streamed over Andy, but save for the heavy breathing of the Fleidermans, all was still.

Then came the death rattle, a spasmodic contraction of the limbs, and the assassin had ceased to exist.

At this juncture Harkaway returned from his walk through the camp.

He had been excited by what he had heard from some of the Queenslanders.

Two men of an outlying picket had been stabbed from behind, by an unknown hand, and one Canadian had suffered the same fate; over the foreheads of the three were found the fatal numbers of the Fleidermans, who had lost no time in adding to his terrible score.

This information proved conclusively to Jack that the murderer was at work in the camp, and would most probably pay a visit to the farmhouse during the night, and fearing danger to his friend Andy and the worthy Scotchman, he hastened back to put them on their guard.

His horror can be imagined when he saw the bugler stretched on the ground covered with blood; the Fleidermans lying by his side, stone dead.

From his bottle he dashed some water into the little fellow's face, and helped him to his feet, greatly revived.

When he heard what had happened, Jack complimented Andy highly upon what he had done.

"Bravo!" he cried, "you're the boy for work, and you're the boy for play. It was time somebody wiped this Boer fraud out, and your dodge was extremely clever; he has been killing sentries."

"I hope he has not injured anyone in the house," replied Andy.

"That is all right, I looked in the rooms as I came along the passage; he must have entered this one first, whatever his ulterior designs may have been."

They were startled by the sound of a bugle, which was the signal for all hands to get up, though the grey dawn was only just breaking.

"By Jove," continued Jack, "how this night has passed I don't know. Just time to get a bite of something, and then boot and saddle, mount and away."

They went into the kitchen where Angus MacKay had prepared coffee for the officers.

Here they obtained breakfast.

The news of Van Heller's death gratified the Scotchman, who felt that he could now remain safely in his home, and hope for better times when Natal was cleared of its Boer invaders.

Going to the yard, Jack and Andy mounted their horses, and were joined by Fred Dawson, who had found shelter with a Canadian; Fish and Corporal Potts came up yawning, and looking as if a little more sleep would have done them good.

Mounted men were to be seen in all directions.

The force consisted of two hundred Queenslanders, one hundred Canadians, two guns, and a horse battery.

In the rear was the New South Wales ambulance.

Fish had decided to join the surgeon-major, as he thought he could better help the wounded than fight.

Andy went with the artillery; Jack, Fred, and the corporal fell in with the Australians as previously arranged, commanded by Colonel Ricardo.

At six o'clock the force proceeded to a point where a rebel laager was reported.

They marched in silence, not a word being spoken.

The position proved to be a line of strong kopjes.

Colonel Pilcher, who was at the head of the expedition, detached the Canadians to work towards the right and make a turning movement, while he himself with the Queensland contingent moved slowly towards the southern end of the enemy's position.

A halt was called, and a patrol of four men, under Lieutenant Adye and Harkaway, were sent forward to report if the veldt to the right of the enemy was clear.

After riding a mile in advance, the patrol came suddenly upon a dozen Boers, hiding behind stones, who opened fire.

Lieutenant Adye, and those with him, immediately replied, killing five of the enemy, when a bullet severely wounded the lieutenant, while a trooper received a ball in the calf of the leg, and his horse was killed.

He attempted to rise, and another shot killed him.

The three remaining men of the patrol retreated, firing as they did so.

The lieutenant stretched out his arm, as if asking for help, and seeing that he was not dead, Harkaway dismounted amidst a shower of bullets, picked up the wounded officer, and placing him on his horse, leaped into the saddle, and galloped back unhurt, holding the lieutenant with one hand, while he guided his horse with the other.

It was a splendid action, and Jack was greeted with a burst of cheers as he carried Lieutenant Adye to the ambulance, directly after resuming his place in the ranks. The Boers encountered were only an isolated party, and Jack reported the veldt to the right clear, whereupon the guns were ordered to advance at a trot, and arrived within 1500 yards of the laager unmolested.

The guns were unlimbered, and in five minutes they planted two shells among the enemy's laager and tents, which was the first intimation they had of the presence of the force.

Immediately the Boers were seen streaming up the kopje.

When the shells fell among them their surprise was complete.

They lined the kopje, however, and opened a well-directed fire on our guns, bullets flying right and left.

Colonel Pilcher now sent an order to the Queenslanders to double into action.

The order was received with great satisfaction all along the line.

They had not been under fire before, and exclamations of "At last!" were heard.

The company rushed forward to within 1000 yards of the enemy's position, from whence they opened a hot fire on the kopje, completely subduing that of the enemy.

The guns shelled the Boer position with wonderful accuracy, while the Canadians worked completely round and opened fire on a portion of the enemy who were ensconced among some bushes.

The Queenslanders rode steadily and quietly on, adopting the Boer tactics, taking advantage of every cover, shooting only when they saw the enemy.

The Boers were soon completely defeated, their camp captured, and a number of prisoners taken. Then Colonel Pilcher pushed on to Sunnyside, which the Boers evacuated.

There he stopped for the night, being well received by the inhabitants, proposing to advance on Douglas the next day, where he would be on the extreme right of the Boer force, which confronted Lord Methuen at Modder River.

The neighbouring country was hilly, affording capital shelter for the Boers, and although some good scouting was done in the afternoon, it was impossible to ascertain where the enemy were hiding, the presumption being that they were broken up into small parties, because shots were exchanged. Our friends had got into a hot corner.

The colonel deemed it advisable to hold Angus MacKay's farm at which they had camped on the previous night; for which purpose he detached twenty-five men belonging to the Queenslanders, and as Lieutenant Adye was badly wounded, he gave the command to Harkaway and Fred Dawson, allowing Corporal Potts to go with them.

Mr. Fish also formed one of the party.

They were supplied with a couple of Maxims, and considered themselves well able to hold their own against any number of Boers, as the farmhouse stood on an elevation commanding a good view of the surrounding country, and was well adapted for defensive purposes.

Jack knew all the men who were going with him, and invited them to dine with him at the "Open House," a well-known restaurant in Sunnyside, before they started to occupy the farmhouse, where they would have to remain until further orders.

The men were highly delighted at the prospect before them, for they were likely to have some hard fighting.

The Boers had lately been raiding a quantity of cattle, which were reported to be grazing in a valley not more than five or six miles from the farm.

Jack's orders were to get possession of these cattle, if he could, and drive them into the farm enclosures, as they would be a valuable acquisition to the British commissariat, but it was not likely that the Boers would part with the oxen without a struggle.

Already Jack had become on friendly terms with two of the Queenslanders in his party, Dunstan and Lewis, who were fine specimens of our Colonial cousins.

They honoured him for the noble way in which he had saved their lieutenant.

All were anxious to do something worthy of notice.

Successful skirmishes were better than nothing while Methuen and Gatacre were at a standstill, and Buller had been beaten back at Colenso.

They sat down to a good repast in a private room, and wine was not wanting.

It was the first square meal they had partaken of since they left Belmont, and they were all in high spirits.

Harkaway considered it a great compliment to be placed at the head of this detachment, and he liked the idea of spending a short time with the Colonials, though he was anxious, as soon as he could, to join the headquarters staff with General Buller at the Tugela, and be in time to assist at the relief of Ladysmith, where General White was being so hard pressed by the Boers.

"Gentlemen," said Harkaway, raising the glass of wine to his lips, "I am bound under the circumstances to propose the Colonials'; you will therefore be good enough to drink your own healths."

The men laughed and emptied their glasses in silence, while Jack sang "For they are jolly good fellows," in which time-honoured festive ditty he was ably supported by Fred Dawson, the corporal, and Mr. Fish, who made an entry in his note-book:

"Colonials entertained at Sunnyside by Harkaway. Made them drink their own healths. Comical idea, but seemed to take their fancy."

Jack looked round and missed Andy the bugler, whom he had invited to partake of his hospitality, and he could not help wondering why he was absent.

The room in which they were dining was on the ground floor, and the large window looking on the street named Adderley, after the well-known one in Capetown, was open.

All at once a tall Kaffir appeared in front of it, and looked inside with a scared face.

"Help ! Murder !" he cried.

This was enough for Jack, who was always ready for action in the hour of danger.

Without ceremony he rose from his seat, and running to the window, put his hand on the sill, vaulting into the street.

"Who are you, and what's the matter?" demanded Harkaway, accosting the Kaffir.

"Me friendly native, baas," replied the man. "My name is Yaberoon. Oh, yes, me all right. Excellent character; before the war I was working in Lorenzo Marquez. I was waiter at Levi's Kiosk; he will give me first-class recommend. When the war break out I come to Natal for a job."

"Hang your pedigree and particulars. Why did you shout 'Murder' ?"

"Somebody tried to kill one of your soldier boys close by here. He stab him with a knife, and when I try for to stop him, he trip me up and I fall on the back of my cocoa-nut. There is the little fellow lying by that door-step, with all the people round him."

Hearing this, Jack hastened to the spot, and pushing through the crowd of spectators, saw Andy lying on his back, with the blood streaming from a wound in the shoulder.

"Andy, my poor fellow, who did this?" he asked, bending over him.

"Somebody you know too well, sir," replied the bugler, faintly. "It was Webb. I was coming to the banquet. He stopped me just here, and asked where you were, and because I wouldn't tell him he stabbed me."

A rush of blood came to his mouth, nearly choking him, and he was unable to say any more.

An ambulance was brought, and he was taken away; the surgeon saying that his life was not in danger, but it would be some time before he recovered.

This affair broke up the gathering.

Jack could not feel at ease while he knew Webb was lurking in the town, and he was anxious to take his men to MacKay's farm.

The small party was soon in the saddle.

The sun was setting, and the air getting cooler.

The sky was streaked with dark clouds ominous of rain.

In fact, the rainy season had set in, and a river which was dry to-day might be in flood to-morrow.

Harkaway was riding at the head of the column, with Fred Dawson on one side of him, and Dunstan, the Australian, on the other.

Most of the Colonials had nick-names, and Dunstan was known as Cornstalk.

He was a giant in stature, and as brave as a lion.

Behind them were a Canadian and a New Zealander, who had obtained permission to be on Harkaway's staff, as they called it.

Frank Fearless, the Canadian, was named Kanuck, which is a term applied to Canadians in America.

Dashley, the New Zealander, was commonly alluded to as Maori, which is the name for natives in Tasmania.

Dashley was a little man, but as quick as lightning in all his movements.

Fearless did not talk much, but was a great thinker, and a dead shot.

These three, Cornstalk, Kanuck, and Maori, had conceived a great friendship and admiration for Harkaway, although they had only known him such a short time, and swore that they would follow him anywhere.

This was not to be wondered at, for they had seen what he could do, and were aware that he did not fear death any more than they did themselves.

As there were only about thirty in the whole force, it was easy enough for them to find quarters in the farmhouse, the horses being stabled in the barns and guarded by sentries.

Angus MacKay had not yet deserted his homestead, and was able to give his visitors better rations than they expected.

He had a carefully concealed cellar under his kitchen-floor, which could only be reached through a trap-door.

This the artful Boers had not been able to discover.

Here he had a good store of cheese, hams, bacon, biscuits, and other luxuries, added to which he had that day killed a sheep.

After supper he entertained Jack, Fred, the corporal, and the three Colonials, in his parlour, placing a demijohn on the table, at the sight of which the corporal's eyes began to sparkle.

"You seem rather down on your luck, Angus," remarked Jack.

"I'm nae soldier," replied MacKay, "but a puir Scotch body farming in Natal. My bairns are awa', and the Boers overrun the Colony. I am thinking of the brave men at Ladysmith, where I lived twa years, in Main Street. I ken the Klip River and the Drakensberg Mountains. It's a bad war, but I hae one comfort; I buried the Fleidermans to-day, and the wind whistled the coronach."

"Cheer up, Angus, there's a good time coming," said Jack.

"I hae my doots," replied MacKay, shaking his grizzled head. "It's mair likely we shall a' be driven into the sea."

He had scarcely spoken when Mr. Fish, the correspondent, entered the room, waving his arm.

"Here you all are, enjoying yourselves, while you thought you had left me out in the cold," he cried. "But I have brought you good news. Buller and Warren have crossed the Tugela, and are outflanking the Boers, within ten miles of Ladysmith. We shall hear great news before long."

"There will be some tall fighting, I guess," observed Kanuck.

"You can bet your boots on that," replied Cornstalk. "If the general gets face to face with a mob of Boers he will make them skip like kangaroos."

"I'd like to be there, and give them some of our Tasmanian apples plugged with lead," remarked Maori.

Mr. Fish sat down by the side of Harkaway and whispered in his ear:

"As I rode along after you from Sunnyside I saw two men sitting by the side of a boulder. They were eating and drinking as fast as they could, just as if they hadn't tasted anything all day, and they were so busy that they did not appear to notice me, but I had a good look at them, and I'll swear that they were Webb and Hartz."

"WEBB SEIZED HER BY THE THROAT, AND CLUTCHED A DAGGER WHICH GLEAMED IN THE SUNSHINE."

No. 7.

"That bodes me no good," replied Jack. "They are clearly on my track. Did you notice which way they went?"

"After going some distance I turned my field-glass on them; the ground is unusually level about the spot where I saw them, though there are a range of kopjes in the distance."

"Did they make for the hills?"

"Yes, they did, but they didn't arrive there. Now comes the curious part of my story," said Fish. "When half-way between the road and the kopjes, the beggars disappeared, vanishing as if the earth had opened and swallowed them up."

"Come! Come!" exclaimed Jack, laughing, "don't tell me any fairy tales; you are not writing for the *Slasher* now, you know. You are good at romancing, as I am aware, for I read your last letter to your paper, in which you stated that our gunners at Magersfontein attempted to field the cannon-balls which fell amongst them, and merrily cried out : 'How's that, umpire?'"

"That was a fact, my dear fellow; I was there."

"In your mind. I am afraid that your imagination is too vivid. We were prisoners in Cronje's camp."

"Don't be foolish; I know what I'm talking about," protested Fish. "I took up a shell myself one day which fell at my feet without exploding. Lighting the fuse with the end of my cigarette as I picked it up, I hurled it back at the enemy with all my force, and succeeded in killing twenty Boers and wounding forty others."

"Give us a rest; that's a bit thick, isn't it?" replied Jack.

"Oh, that's nothing to what happened to me one day at breakfast. A shell burst in my tent and blew the tea-pot to atoms without touching me or anything else."

"Drop it," said Jack, "and come to business. Do you really mean to say that Webb and Hartz vanished as you have described?"

"I give you my word; you may believe me, I never told a lie in my life, and am too old to begin now."

"Then the Boers must have an underground hiding-place, a series of subterranean caves perhaps, which accounts for us not seeing anything of them since the action this morning."

"Shouldn't wonder," answered Fish; "they are artful enough for anything."

"Whereabouts did this occur?" enquired Jack.

"Two-and-a-half miles up the road from this farm. Halt there, turn to the left, and walk another mile over the plain; I can give you no other direction. Don't think it was an optical delusion, like a mirage; I saw them go down."

"No offence, old boy, but I can't quite credit your story. Boers aren't moles; they more resemble aasvogels, or birds of prey, in the rocks. The moon will be up directly; will you go with me to settle the matter?"

"Not for a pension," replied Fish. "You couldn't hire me, Jack. I know your playful ways. You want to put me in the front of the battle, but in my opinion the pen is mightier than the sword. and I will stick to it. You do the deeds of gallantry, boy, and I will write them for the printer and the public. You have your directions. Judge your distance, and go straight ahead. If you tumble into a Boer trap it will not be my fault."

"Then I will go alone, for this mystery must be solved at any cost. There is a lurking danger in the air, and I cannot rest."

"Ah me!" said Fish, with a deep-drawn sigh. "Some fellows never know when they are well off, and love to meet trouble half-way. Thank goodness, that is not I. We have a quick-firing gun at the back and front of the house; sentinels are posted to protect us from surprise. We form a merry little party. I find my surroundings quite comfortable, and I shall call upon our friend, Potts, for a song. Corporal!"

Potts looked up, thinking he was asked to take a drink.

The jar was at the other end of the table, and he had been looking wistfully at it for some time.

"I don't know whether I will or I won't, but I'd rather," he replied, stretching out his hand.

"I didn't ask you to gargle your throat," said Fish, "but I'll push the stuff over to you, though this won't last long if it gets before you."

There was a roar of laughter at this sally, which made the corporal look somewhat indignantly at the Colonials.

"Gentlemen," he exclaimed, "this is quite contrary to my usual custom, as everybody who knows me can verify. I have been fifteen years in the service, don't know what the inside of a guard-room is, and was never brought before my colonel, yet, as it is a new thing to be with Colonials, I don't mind stepping over my rule for once. Don't ask me to do it again, that's all. I'm not an abstainer, but I respect myself."

"Take a long drink while you're about it, corporal," said Kanuck. "It will save a lot of trouble in crooking your elbow. I'd like to have you enjoy yourself; it isn't often you get a good time."

"Please keep your remarks to yourself, sir; I am drinking with this gentleman, Mr. Fish, just out of compliment, in a manner of speaking, and after that I shall smoke a strictly sober pipe."

The corporal put four fingers round the glass, so that they should not see how much he took, and with one gulp swallowed the contents without winking.

"That is a satisfying swig," was the Kanuck's comment. "Four fingers, by the living jingo, and it hasn't even raised a blush to his face. He must be ironclad. It would knock spots out of a Quebec loafer. Corporal!"

"Sir, to you," replied Potts.

"Have another with me?" continued Kanuck. "Fire in a second ball for luck; I'll blow you off this time."

"I don't know whether I will or I won't, but I'd rather," answered Potts, forgetting himself.

He repeated the dose with the same unflagging energy, and was greeted with a roar of laughter louder than the first, amidst which Harkaway quitted the room, unnoticed as he thought.

But he was mistaken.

Cornstalk had noticed a look of care and anxiety on his face, and followed him to the stoep, where he found him examining his rifle.

Thinking he was bent on some expedition, he offered his services.

Jack wanted a companion, though he did not like to ask for one.

In a few words he told him what he had heard from Fish, and of his resolve to find out the secret, if there was one.

"He is a queer Fish, but I don't think he is a fish out of water in this case," exclaimed Cornstalk, as they walked on together. "I reckon these beggarly Boers have made themselves a cave, where perhaps five hundred men are hiding, only waiting for a dark spell to swoop down on us."

"That is precisely my idea," answered Harkaway, "and if I could only find a few of their holes I would drop some shells down which would astonish the Krugerites. What do you think, Dunstan?"

"That's the ticket for soup," answered Cornstalk. "I should like to see a few Boers' heads flying about. You show the way, and I'll teach you how we do a scout in the Queensland bush."

"Agreed! I've had a little practice since I was ordered south, but I give in to you."

Of a sudden the stars became obscured, and a dense darkness fell around them.

Fearing that something was going to happen, they crawled to a boulder which had an overhanging ledge, under which they crouched for shelter.

It was lucky they did so, for in less than a minute a terrific hail-storm came on, the stones being as big as pigeons' eggs, and in some cases larger.

They hammered against the stone with a rattling noise like volley-firing.

It did not last long.

When it was over the stars shone again and the moon came out, but the land was covered with stones of ice for some distance, but strange to say, the storm was local, for after walking half-a-mile they could see no trace of it.

They heard the powerful, alarming screech of the goat-sucker, which bird, like the bat, is a flyer by night, and also the melancholy note of the hornbill.

All at once Cornstalk put his hand on Harkaway's shoulder, whispering the word, "Halt."

The Queenslander pointed to a large stone in front of them, before which stood what appeared to be one of the Argyll and Sutherland Highlanders, with kilt, sporran, and bonnet.

"One of the Scotch Brigade, lost after Magersfontein," said Jack. "Let us take the poor fellow back to MacKay's farm."

"Don't be so sure of that. I want to know more about the fellow first," replied Cornstalk.

"Do you mean to tell me I don't know a Highlander when I see one?"

"Easy now. Who's scouting, you or I? Lie down in the grass, and leave the rest to me."

Reluctantly Jack did as he was ordered, and Cornstalk went on alone, keeping his eye fixed on the Highlander all the time, the latter advancing as if to meet him.

Without any warning there was the crack of a rifle, and as Cornstalk fell on his knees a bullet whizzed over his head.

CHAPTER XXVI.

A NEW BOER TRICK—CRUEL TREATMENT OF A NATIVE—HARKAWAY VANISHES UNDERGROUND—TEUFELSKINT, THE HUNCHBACK OF THE HILLS—PLANS FOR JACK'S RESCUE—CAPTURE OF DUNKO—FORCING A CONFESSION.

As soon as the man in the kilt had discharged his rifle, Harkaway saw that he and his friend Cornstalk were intended to be the victims of a Boer trick.

The fellow had no doubt stripped one of the Highlanders killed at Magersfontein, and dressed himself in his clothes, the plan being to go out sniping, as it is called.

He thought, no doubt, that the disguise would throw any Englishman off his guard.

The Kaffirs were the Boers' spies, and the latter had probably heard of the occupation of MacKay's farm, and this particular Boer had come out of his hiding-place to shoot any too adventurous scout.

Directly the Queenslander fell on his knees Jack took a quick shot at the Boer, and dropped him as neatly as if he had been a pigeon on a post.

"Who was right, you or I?" asked Cornstalk, rising to his feet. "You were going to shake hands with the impostor, but I told you to be wary."

"I ought to have known better," replied Harkaway, as they advanced towards the Boer. "Upon my word, these Boers are like conjurors, everyone has a bag of tricks with him."

The Boer had received a mortal wound, but he had strength enough left to ask for water, and Jack, again in his good-natured way, made a false move, by unslinging his water-bottle and offering it to him.

While he was in the act of doing so, the Boer raised a revolver, and was about to fire at his benefactor.

Fortunately Cornstalk saw the action of the miserable wretch, and brought the butt of his rifle down on his head, smashing his skull, and the coward expired without a groan.

"That takes the cake!" exclaimed the Queenslander. "You ought to have eyes in the back of your head to deal with these chaps. They are as treacherous as an Australian black; in fact, I would rather deal with a bushman."

"It is impossible to be too cautious," answered Jack. "I admit that I am foolhardy, which is not really true courage, as it is born of reckless impatience; but I'll take care it does not occur again. Two escapes in ten minutes are quite enough for me; I will be more prudent."

"Not you," replied Cornstalk, laughing; "you're not made that way. If there is any danger ahead you are bound to run into it."

"True; yet I manage to get out of a hole somehow when I tumble into it. Sometimes I wonder if I shall make old bones; but we won't waste time in moralising—let us get on our way. The Boers are not far off, or this joker would not have been cutting his Highland fling. Keep your eyes peeled."

They proceeded on their scout, stopping every now and then to look round and take their bearings.

They had been travelling over a bit of table-land, but they suddenly approached a small hill, which caused them to moderate their pace, and go slowly.

At the left side of the hill were some stunted trees.

From these came loud cries, which induced them to think that some cruel deed was being committed.

A man was shrieking with pain at one minute, the next was begging for mercy.

"This is some dastardly outrage," whispered the Queenslander. "The Boers are torturing a captive—possibly one of our fellows."

"We will soon put a stop to that," answered Jack. "Down on your hands and knees, and crawl through the grass as if you were stalking a wild animal."

"Don't teach your grandmother how to suck eggs," replied Cornstalk. "Haven't I lived in the bush for six months at a time? A 'possum would have to climb up a very tall gum-tree to escape me."

"Don't be offended; I am perfectly well aware that you know as much about this sort of thing as I do—possibly more."

"Very well. Follow my lead," said the Colonial. "There is not much danger ahead of us; we aren't going to fight the whole Boer Army."

"How do you know we have not a commando in front of us?"

"There are only two Boers among those trees," replied Cornstalk. "Perhaps you are curious to learn how I found that out. I will tell you. Under the bluff of the hill are two horses, and I put down one man to each animal. Creep along and see if I'm not right."

Complying with this request Harkaway, in a few minutes, discovered that the Colonial's statement was correct.

Lashed to the trunk of a tree was a tall Kaffir, who was being flogged by two Boers, wielding heavy sjamboks.

His back was torn and bleeding from the effect of these formidable whips, the yells, prayers, and entreaties of the wretch being dreadful to listen to.

He turned his head round, as if looking for assistance, and his countenance bore an expression of agony.

"It is Gaberoon, the Kaffir I saw in Sunnyside," whispered Harkaway to his companion. "I wonder what he has done to incur their resentment. As far as I know, he is not in our pay."

"It matters little what he has done," rejoined Cornstalk, "the Boers are lamming the life out of the poor beggar, and I think it's our duty to save him. Let 'em have it."

"They may have friends close by, whom our shots will rouse," suggested Jack.

"We must chance that. The two horses will be ours, if we want them. Take a pot-shot for the off-side Boer, and I will take the other."

"Good enough," replied Jack. "I have covered my man."

Their rifles were discharged almost at the same time, and the Boers fell to the ground.

"Lie low," cried Cornstalk. "Not a move yet. We shall soon see if there are any more of the enemy about."

They remained motionless and hidden for the space of five minutes.

No one came upon the scene, so they advanced fearlessly to the Kaffir, and, cutting his thongs, placed him on the grass.

The Boers had half killed him with their merciless sjamboks.

The action of his heart was weak, and he could scarcely speak.

"What made the Dutchmen beat you like this, boy?" asked Cornstalk. "You must have done something, or they wouldn't have laid it on so thick. They have made your flesh fly and no mistake."

"I have been working for the Boers against my will, boss, since they have been in Sunnyside," replied Gaberoon. "If I had refused, I should have been shot, for they treat a Kaffir like a dog. I helped a soldier boy to-day in the town, and that got me into trouble. Two hours ago I went to their camp, and was accused of being a traitor. They are going to attack MacKay's farm, and thought I was going to give them away. A Boer was going to run a knife into me, but I knocked him down and escaped in the darkness. The two Boers you have killed got on their horses and pursued me. I am a good runner, but they rode me down close by these trees."

"Why didn't they put a bullet in you, if they thought you were so dangerous?"

"They said shooting was too good for a son of a gun like me, and, after a little talkee-talkee, they decided to flog me to death; and they have done it, baas, for I feel I am breaking up fast and going home just as quick as I can."

"Nonsense!" exclaimed Harkaway. "You are worth a dozen dead men yet, boy. I remember you, and made up my mind to do you a good turn if I could. Get up to MacKay's farm, and you will be well cared for"

"Curse those cowards for cutting me up like this!" cried the Kaffir, tearing the grass up by handfuls in his pain, and squirming like a worm.

This paroxysm exhausted him, and he remained perfectly still on the flat of his injured back, gasping for breath, and looking as if he was battling for life.

"Say, boy," observed Cornstalk, "you're in a bad way, but if you can, I should like you to tell us where the Boers are?"

Gaberoon tried to speak, but was unable to articulate; only a few incoherent sounds issuing from his lips.

With a feeble effort he raised his hand, and pointed to the ground.

"What does he mean?" asked Cornstalk.

"I can guess," replied Jack. "The Boers are burrowing somewhere; and this idea just fits in with what Fish told me about the two men he saw. Try the Kaffir again, and see if you can get anything more out of him."

Jack was particularly anxious for information.

It was dangerous to move from the farm to collect the cattle they were after, unless they could locate the position of the Boers, who might sweep down upon and destroy their little party.

If a commando hidden in underground caves were to suddenly come out of the earth without any warning and confront the Colonials, the latter would have no chance at all with them.

Cornstalk in vain tried to get a word or two out of Gaberoon.

The poor fellow wanted to tell him something, but was too far gone, and all at once closed his eyes in a dead faint.

"He's done for," said the Queenslander; "but it takes a thundering lot to kill a Kaffir, who's generally got as many lives as a cat is supposed to have."

"He evidently knows the Boers' secret, but if he is dead it has died with him, so we must find it out for ourselves. Come on!"

They continued their way for another mile without seeing anything to arrest their attention.

"It's a wild goose chase," said Cornstalk; "we may as well give it up, unless you want to keep on the tramp all night, and then there's the getting back again."

Harkaway seemed reluctant to adopt this course, and his face was filled with a grim determination.

"If you like to part company, you can," he answered. "I'm going to see this thing through."

He went on alone, and Cornstalk, not to be outdone, followed him; though he did not see what object there could be gained by doing so, as their scout up to the present had been a blank, and the Boers appeared to be as safely hidden as foxes.

The next minute he was startled by a loud shout which came from Harkaway.

Fixing his eyes in the direction of his friend, he saw him throw up his arms, and disappear through a hole in the ground.

Cornstalk ran after him, but stopped short, as if he had been shot.

"By gum!" he exclaimed; "what a fool I am! This won't do at all. I must be over the underground caves, and of course there are more holes than one. Harkaway has gone clean through into the enemy's hands, and I expect this is the last I shall see of him. Poor chap! I had hoped to ride to victory with him; but it is all up, and I may share the same fate if I am not careful. This spot must be like a rabbit warren."

Anxious as he was to make an effort to save his companion, he felt that it would be useless to attempt to do so.

There were subterranean mysteries which one man, single handed, would be an idiot to face.

And he was about to retrace his steps in the pale moonlight, sad and forlorn, when an elfin chuckle behind him made him jump half a foot in the air.

"Confound it," he muttered. "What's that? Is this place haunted?"

"Ho! ho! ho!"

He started again as this blood-curdling laugh fell upon his ears, and he felt a creeping sensation come over him.

The crack of a rifle he could understand, or the bursting of a shell; but there was something forbidding, and he feared ominous, about this merriment, and the stout-hearted Queenslander slightly trembled as he turned round, with the cold night wind blowing in his face.

"Ho, ho! you're out late, when all good people should be in bed. Know you not that danger lurks around you, and if you value your safety you will fly from this spot as if a legion of fiends were at your heels. I like your face, and would help you. Tell me that you are not a Boer."

"I can honestly swear that, thank goodness!" replied Cornstalk. "I am an Australian, that is to say, British."

"It is good to hear that. I want your side to win this war. You must drive the Boers out of the Transvaal. Ho, ho! I knew I should live to see it."

The voice seemed to Cornstalk to come out of the earth, but this was a mistake on his part.

Looking down, he saw a stunted specimen of humanity, whose head scarcely came to a level with the Queenslander's waist.

He had the face of a man, with the body of a boy; and a terribly ugly face it was. The nose was flat, the eyes small, like those of a pig, and the mouth stretched from ear to ear.

The forehead was low, the ears abnormally large and protruding, while his black hair hung in cork-screw ringlets round his head.

But this was not all which made him repugnant.

The unfortunate wretch was deformed; he had a huge hunch on his back, and was bandy-legged.

"Well I'm blest!" ejaculated Cornstalk. "It's a freak. I've seen baboon monkeys, and once had a squint at a gorilla in a show, but this thing beats the lot. However, I suppose there's no harm in him if he's against the Boers. I'll talk to him, though you must look out for lies when you are dealing with a hunchback. I say, you freak, what's your name?"

"I thought everybody knew me," was the rejoinder.

"I'm one of the favoured few who don't, allow me to observe."

"Ho! ho! ho!" roared the hunchback, as if he was mightily amused. "You haven't been long in Natal if you don't know me. I'm Teufelskint, the hunchback of the kopjes. I don't stop long in one place. I'm here, there, and everywhere. I never sleep in a house; I live on the hills."

"I should like to hear the story of your life. Where did you spring from just now?"

"Out of the ground," answered the hunchback dwarf. "I was talking to Villebois, the French general who is leading the Boers, when a gentleman in khaki dropped through one of the holes into the cave below, and I came up to see if there were any more soldiers about."

"If you hate the Boers so much, how is it you are friendly with them?"

"My hatred goes a long way back," replied the hunchback. "I am forty years old now, and have lived for thirty on the veldt.

When I was a boy, they drove me from my mother's side, and swore that if I was seen in a town they would shoot me like a dog. I was a thing of evil, they said; but since the war broke out, they have been civil, thinking I bring them good luck. They will pay a shilling to stroke my hump, after which they are certain that no Redneck's bullet will hurt them."

"We'll see about that," Cornstalk said.

"I've heard of their ignorance, but Great Cæsar! I didn't think it went so far as that."

"They don't stop there," continued the hunchback; "they will give me gold for a lock of my hair. Before the war it was a foot and a half long, but it has been snipped until it does not reach to my shoulders. There is not an armed Boer who would hurt me; but if I went into a town or a farmhouse, the women would shriek themselves hoarse, and the children begin to cry; even the very dogs bark at me."

"How do you manage to exist on your hills?"

"If I want any food I go to a farmer's," replied Teufelskint. "I have only to stop within a quarter of a mile, and give one of my demon laughs. Ho! ho! ho! Food is placed on the stoep, the people retire inside and shut the doors; but don't linger here, the Boers may come out of their holes and shoot you. I will see you to your comrades at the farm."

"How do you know we are there?"

"Villebois and a man named Webb are acquainted with all your movements; and when you come after the cattle, they intend to shoot you to the last man."

Cornstalk was glad of his offer, as he wanted to ask him some more questions, and get all the information he could out of him.

They were a strange contrast.

The perfect man and the monstrosity did not seem to belong to the same species; but Cornstalk's first aversion passed off as they went along together.

It was not surprising that the Boers had named this misshapen being Teufelskint, which means the devil's child; but after all he did not appear to be wickedly inclined.

Cornstalk gave him some money, and the hunchback told him all he knew about the Boers under Villebois.

The commando consisted of 400 men, who had been driven from the hills by the Colonials, and they were hiding themselves in underground chambers, which had been previously dug out for their reception, in case of defeat.

They were well supplied with provisions, and had plenty of cartridges.

Their orders were to cut to pieces all small parties of Rednecks they could meet with.

They got air through shafts, such as the one Jack had tumbled down, and passed their time in smoking, playing cards, or singing hymns; but they had scouts out, and were watching MacKay's farm.

When asked what he did with money, Teufelskint replied in a simple manner that he had one vice, which was drinking.

Once a fortnight a smaus visited the kopje on which he had built himself a small stone house, and left him a supply of liquor, on which he would revel for days, making himself an incapable sot.

It was all the pleasure life afforded him, and he looked forward with childish expectancy to the coming of the smaus.

"That's all right," remarked Cornstalk, looking with pity at the dwarf. "It's a queer way of enjoying yourself; but I suppose you know best. I say, Beauty, what do you think the Boers will do with my friend, Harkaway?"

"I heard Webb say he would peg him out on the ground, and drive a stake through his body; but they daren't hurt him until one of his leaders named Hartz comes back tomorrow. He has gone to Douglas to warn the Boers of the Rednecks' approach. He will be absent till mid-day; then you may say 'Good-bye' to the man you call Harkaway."

"Could you save him, do you think?" asked Cornstalk, eagerly.

"If I made a request for his liberty, I don't think they would dare to refuse me," replied Teufelskint; "and I'll tell you why. The Boers believe in the power of my curse. Before the Battle of Belmont, two Free Staters made fun of me. One placed a fool's cap on my head, and the other threw a pail of water over me. I cursed them. Next day they were shot by the Rednecks. Give me gold, and I will bring back your friend."

"You shall have all the money that us chaps can pull together. It won't be much, as we are on a campaign, but it will be enough for you to get drunk on, you bet. Don't fool me on this deal. I want you to act on the level. Daylight isn't far off. Our men will be on the move directly, and I'll trot you around. Each man will give something to save Harkaway; and I know Maori and Kanuck will plank down their bottom dollar for him."

Teufelskint declared solemnly that he was to be trusted, and said that he would not take a shilling of the money until he appeared among them with Jack, uninjured; but as he had come so far, he would like to rest himself, and begged a glass of spirits might be supplied him, a request which his conductor promised to comply with.

Passing the sentries, they entered the farmhouse, the Colonials regarding the hunchback with wonder.

In a room they found Kanuck, Maori, and Mr. Fish at breakfast.

They were early risers, and the first streak of dawn had stirred them.

They had slept in their dust-covered khaki suits, and did not trouble themselves about soap or water.

"Hallo! What have you got there, mate?" cried Maori. "Is it a new sort of animal?"

"Don't be afraid of him; he won't bite," replied Cornstalk. "It is a friendly hunchback. Give him a drink, one of you."

Fish placed a bottle and glass on a table close to Teufelskint, who eagerly seized it, knocked the glass on the floor with disdain, and began to drink out of the bottle, gulping it down as if it was milk.

"Bless my soul, what a curiosity!" observed Fish, taking out his note-book to do some descriptive writing for the *Slasher*:

"A Colonial to-day brought in a remarkable specimen of the Transvaal hunchback. He is more ugly than sin, but is quite tame. He is not much taller than an ant-heap. If he wanted to kick a dog he would have to stand on a good-sized stone.

"He has a marked liking and marvellous capacity for whisky, which he drinks like a horse. He would make the fortune of a showman, and is the greatest living wonder I have yet seen in these regions. He has just opened his mouth to take breath. I cannot call it a mouth in the common sense of the term. It is a chasm—a yawning abyss. I thought his head was coming in half; it looked just as if it was cut in two and set on hinges.

"A swarm of flies came by at the time, and the dwarf with the hump must have swallowed a gross. Mem.—Can any of our readers inform me if flies are a common diet with this class of hunchback?"

"I didn't sleep more than an hour," remarked Maori. "We got in a funk about you and Harkaway. Fish told us he thought you had gone on a dangerous scout. About midnight Fred Dawson and the corporal started out after you."

"Is that so?" said Cornstalk. "I saw nothing of them."

"Where is Harkaway?" asked Kanuck.

"Gone, I am sorry to say. It wasn't my fault. No one can blame me. I'll take my dying oath that I would have laid down my own life for Harkaway."

"We all know that, my lad," replied Kanuck. "You're about as good as they make 'em, eighteen carat, Hall marked. But what's happened to Harkaway? Have they sniped him?"

"No. He was walking a little in front of me, some distance from the farm, when he went wallop down a hole, into a Boer cave. While I was rubbing my eyes in surprise, up came this funny little man from another hole. Give me a cup of coffee, and I'll tell you the whole story."

He took a seat, and related all that Teufelskint had told him; whereupon Kanuck and Maori took from their pockets two little wash-leather bags, tied round the top with tape.

These they placed on the table; it was their spending money.

"There's my little lot, I wish it was more," observed Kanuck.

"Pass the hat," said Maori. "I'm in this sweep for all I'm worth. Give it to Teufelskint, and start him off to bring back Jack. I'll make a collection among the men for him when he comes back. Don't keep him here too long, time is precious, and Hartz may turn up sooner than you think."

"Where has the creature got to?" asked Cornstalk.

Teufelskint was nowhere to be seen.

"While listening to your talk, I lost sight of the imp," observed Mr. Fish. "When I last saw the curiosity he was like a baby with the feeding-bottle."

A crash was heard outside on the stoep as if glass was being broken, and, looking that way, the Colonials saw that the hunchback had thrown away the first bottle, and was calmly beginning to empty a second, which he had coolly taken from a shelf.

"That licks everything," exclaimed Cornstalk. "There wasn't a word of a lie about what he told me. The beggar will drink himself silly, and be unable to move. He has got a skinful already; having emptied one bottle, the hog is starting on another. It won't do. Harkaway will be left to his fate. I'd snatch it out of his hand if I didn't think there would be ructions."

"Who's afraid?" cried the New Zealander. "Leave the little beast to me. If he tries any game on, I'll cut his hump off."

Advancing to the stoep with a quick stride, Maori went to the side of the dwarf and said, in a commanding tone: "Give me that bottle."

Teufelskint glared savagely at him, and, making a dash past, grasped the side-post of the verandah, and climbed up out of reach.

He seated himself on the top, and began to drain the second bottle, when he suddenly collapsed.

The bottle slipped from his hand, he sank on his back, his eyes closed, and to all appearances he was insensible.

"That's bad luck," said Cornstalk. "We must get a ladder, carry him down, and duck him in the water-tank."

"Yes," chimed in Kanuck. "All depends on getting the varmint sober. I was kinder scared when he tried to freeze you up with that look. His eyes were worse than a grizzly bear's. I thought you'd have to pass in your checks, Maori."

"Go on, what are you giving me? I don't want no ladder. I'll bring him down on my arm."

Saying this, the Queenslander placed a chair on the stoep.

He stood on it, and, stretching out his hand, grabbed the hunchback by his thick hair, and swung him down.

Teufelskint fell with a dull thud, which, however, failed to rouse him.

He was carried to the water-tank and soused several times, but they could not get any life or motion into him.

Maori pricked him with a bayonet, but it did no good.

Cornstalk fired a couple of shots close to his ear, yet he did not budge.

Kanuck rolled him over the grass, swung him round by his heels, and stood him on his head; the hunchback remaining as helpless as a log.

He was dragged into a sheltered spot to be out of the sun, and there they left him.

Fish felt his heart and his pulse; the beating was regular.

"Most extraordinary case of alcoholic poisoning I ever came across," he exclaimed. "The mind is dead, but the body's alive. How long the trance will last no one can tell."

"The imp can be of no use to Harkaway," said Cornstalk. "Time glides by rapidly, and the Boers will have their victim."

"It is very annoying, and enough to make a cat swear, for I believe the dwarf would have saved him."

"I wonder which way the commandant, Hartz, is coming?" remarked Fish. "If you fellows could intercept him before he reached the caves, it would give our friend Jack a respite. Suppose a couple of you ride out in the direction of Douglas?"

"Not a bad idea that," replied Maori "I'll make one."

"Count me in," said Cornstalk. "We'll leave Kanuck to look after the garrison."

"I have a plan of my own," exclaimed the Canadian. "We know where the Boers are hiding, and are sure they will not show themselves until they think they can shoot us down in the cattle-valley. How would it be to drop a lyddite shell down one of their holes and smother the lot of them?"

"Tut, tut!" answered Fish. "That's a silly way of going to work. You're too eager, and don't give yourself time to reflect. Of course we should kill the Dutch rats, but Harkaway would have to go too."

"By George, I didn't think of that!" responded Kanuck, who was despondent at the breakdown of his brilliant conception.

"It is a very difficult matter," continued Fish, thoughtfully. "If we draw the Boers and provoke a fight, they will put their prisoner to death. We are tied hand and foot."

Everyone was silent.

A feeling of sadness came over the scouts, who would gladly have laid down their lives for their leader if they could have been of service.

They were roused from their apathy by a trooper, who made his appearance, leading a Kaffir by a rope, which he had put round his neck like a lasso.

The latter looked vicious, but dejected.

"I have come to make my report," said the private. "Being out on patrol duty, I saw a Boer approaching on horseback, this Kaffir running by his side. The spot where I was is close to a kopje, where there are some trees. I made my horse lie down, and concealed myself. Not far off was the body of a dead native, who seemed to have been flogged to death; his back was raw, and there were some sjambocks on the ground. Further on were the bodies of two Boers."

"Quite right," said Cornstalk. "That is where Lieutenant Harkaway and I left Gaberoon. Proceed. What did you do?"

"I drew a bead on the rider, and bowled him out of the saddle; then I covered the Kaffir, and called upon him to surrender, which he did. I had a bit of rope with me, which I put round his neck, and brought him here, thinking you might get something out of him, for he wouldn't answer any of my questions."

While the man was speaking, Mr. Fish had kept his eyes riveted on the captive, and suddenly exclaimed:

"I know that fellow. He is a bad native, and the worst traitor in Natal. He is mixed up with all Kruger's swell spies. I have written about him frequently in my paper. His name is Dunko."

The prisoner looked up with an air of assurance, and said glibly:

"No, baas; that is a mistake. I am a camp-follower for Lord Methuen, and was coming to this farm with a message for you. That boy you speak of——"

"None of your infernal lies!" interrupted Fish. "I know you, and that is sufficient."

"Can you swear to him?" asked Cornstalk.

"Most decidedly; I would swear in any court of justice that it is Dunko."

"So will I!" cried a voice on the verandah.

They turned round, and beheld Fred Dawson, accompanied by Corporal Potts, who had just returned from an ineffectual search after Harkaway.

The state of affairs was quickly explained to him by the Queenslander, and he was deeply depressed to hear of Jack's peril, but this feeling gave place to one of strong resentment against Dunko.

He snatched the rope out of the private's hand, and with a fierce jerk brought him on his knees, half choked and gasping for breath.

"I could hang you myself, you brute," exclaimed Fred Dawson, with an unusual display of temper. "Where's that paper you stole from me at the Modder Camp?"

Dunko hesitated.

"Answer," proceeded Fred, "or, by heaven, I'll tighten this rope and kill you!"

Dunko saw that he was recognised, and did not try to conceal his identity any longer.

"What do you want to know, baas?" he asked.

"More things than one. What have you done with the stolen document? How many men have the Boers in the caves? Who was the person travelling with you when the trooper fired?"

Though he heard these questions distinctly, Dunko remained obstinately silent.

There was an iron bar in front of the window, on which a curtain had been hung by the farmer's wife in her prosperous days before the war.

Over this Fred Dawson threw one end of the rope.

"Lend a hand, boys," he cried. "As he can't find his tongue we'll string this beggar up."

The three Colonials seized the rope with a will, and hauled Dunko on to his feet, which rapidly began to leave the ground.

He waved his arms frantically, and his lips moved.

"Hold on," said Fred Dawson; "lower him a bit. I think he wants to speak."

CHAPTER XXVII.

JACK IS HELD AS A PRISONER—WEBB'S DESIGNS FRUSTRATED—THE DYNAMITE CELLAR — A DARING ESCAPE — THE TERRIFIC EXPLOSION.

WHEN Harkaway fell through the hole in the ground, he dropped down a dozen feet, and was deposited unceremoniously upon a table formed of a few deal planks resting on stones.

It was in the centre of a small sort of square cellar, dug out of the earth, lighted by a lamp attached to the wall.

There were passages on each side leading to other caves, from whence the voices of men proceeded.

At the table were seated two persons, these were Webb and the French general, Villebois, while in a corner the hunchback, Teufelskint, was squatting like a monkey on his haunches.

The men were playing cards, with a bottle and a box of cigars before them.

They darted to their feet as Jack appeared, and regarded him with amazement as he sat with his feet dangling over the side of the table, looking at them with a comical smile.

They also saw the absurdity of the situation, and could not help laughing.

"Redneck!" ejaculated the hunchback, "I will go and see if there are any more of them."

He scrambled up some steps cut in the earth, and soon emerged into the open air, where, as we have stated, he met the Queenslander.

It was always Jack's plan to look on the rosy side of things if he could find one, and leave the seamy side to others less mercurial than himself.

His rifle had been jerked out of his hand as he lost his footing, but he still had his revolver in his pocket, which circumstance cheered him, as he knew he could sell his life dearly.

The only thing that caused him apprehension was the presence of his enemy, Webb, whose diabolical nature he knew full well.

He could see that Webb's companion was an officer, for he had a gold star on each shoulder, and wore a piece of blue ribbon in his buttonhole, which Jack surmised was the French order called the Legion of Honour.

From this man he hoped to obtain protection.

"How are you, Mr. Webb?" he exclaimed cheerfully. "I must apologise for visiting you so abruptly, but we do not use cards and kid gloves in the Transvaal. If I intrude, I shall be very glad to go back again."

"I daresay you would," replied Webb, sarcastically, "but now we have got you, depend upon it we shall keep you."

Webb could not accuse him of being a spy on the present occasion, as he certainly had not intended to come into the Boer caves, but he resolved to tell Villebois all he knew, and make the case as black as he could against him.

Hartz, who had the command of this detachment, was absent on business, and nothing could be done in the way of the death penalty until he came back the next day.

Still his heart throbbed with savage joy at having Jack in his power; and he thought that if his body was found with a knife in it the next morning, no one would trouble themselves to ask how it got done.

"He shall not see to-morrow's light if I can help it," he said to himself, knitting his brow.

Jack could read his evil thoughts in his face, and, knowing him as he did, resolved to be on his guard.

"Who is this man?" enquired Vilbois. "You seem to have met before."

"He pretends to be a British officer, but he is only a secret agent," replied Webb. "A very low type, I assure you. He has played the Boers several scurvy tricks. Cronje was going to execute him once, but he slipped through his fingers. Hartz knows him as well as I do, and will verify my statement."

"What have you to say for yourself?" asked the Frenchman, addressing Jack.

"All that your colleague has stated is false," was the answer, "except that I escaped from the Boers. I am a cavalry officer, and you will find my name—Harkaway—in the Army List. At present I command a squadron of Colonials, who hold the farm on your right. I demand to be treated as a prisoner of war."

"That is a fair request," rejoined Villebois. "Let him be put under a guard in one of the empty caves. His case shall be gone into when I see Hartz."

This angered Webb, who could not control his temper.

"Can't you take my word?" he asked. "Verdomdy! I am as good a friend of the Boers as you, if I am an Outlander. Remember you are only a foreign mercenary fighting for your pay!"

"Do you intend to insult me?" shouted the Frenchman, hotly.

"If you like to take it so. I say this rascal ought to be shot."

"Touch him if you dare! The Boers use you as a spy, but they don't respect you as a soldier, as they do me. I am for fair play in war. If I know that you injure this man, you shall rue it. I don't say that Hartz won't shoot him; he probably will, but he must be properly tried first."

"Shake hands. I didn't mean what I said!" exclaimed Webb, subduing his resentment. "I don't care whether the man lives or dies. It was only for the good of the cause I spoke. Take the prisoner away, and we will go on with our game."

"Very well. See to it."

Webb called a couple of Boers from an inner cave.

They placed themselves on each side of Jack, who was conducted into a long chamber filled with Boers sleeping on the floor.

Webb followed at their heels.

Threading this apartment, they came to another which was similarly occupied.

The air was close and confined.

Each man slept with his Mauser by his side and his bandolier round his body, ready to spring up at the least alarm.

A smoky oil lamp relieved the gloom, casting a feeble gleam of light into a small chamber, in which Jack could see a couple of large tin cases, one standing on the top of the other.

On each of these, was painted in black, the word "Dynamite."

"Get in there," said Webb, gruffly, giving his prisoner a push, adding to the guards who were with him, "keep watch, and see that he does not attempt to escape."

Harkaway entered, and took up a position behind the tin cases.

A smile came to his lips, and showing his revolver, pointed with the other hand to the dynamite.

"Confound it; I forgot to search him," muttered Webb.

This was an important omission, and he bit his lips with vexation.

"Like the weasels, I sleep with one eye open," said Jack, quietly. "If any attempt is made on my life, I shall blow this part of your hiding-place to the winds, if I go too.

I shall have the pleasure of knowing that I do not die alone."

"You cannot be so mad as to carry out such a threat as that."

"Why not? I may as well die one way as another. Talk the matter over with General Villebois and Hartz, when he returns. Don't you think it will be best to let me out, and fight the game on the square?"

"I will talk to you to-morrow," replied Webb, who was completely baffled.

He retired in disgust, for the stand taken up by Jack had altered matters altogether.

The guards assumed a sitting position, and lighted their pipes, but kept their eyes open.

Jack made himself as comfortable as he could to rest his limbs, but there was no suspicion of sleep about him.

Twice in as many hours he was positive that he saw the dark eyes of Webb glaring at him, like a tiger's, through the imperfect light.

A steel dagger was visible.

Their eyes met, and his visitor vanished.

This made him feel uneasy, for he was certain that Webb wanted to kill him in his sleep.

Slowly passed the time.

It was an agony of suspense to the captive.

He was in a pit, hot and stifling.

Nothing was heard but the snoring of the Boers.

Now and then a long snake glided by him.

His limbs were stiff, and his mouth parched with thirst.

All at once a ray of light came down from above.

It heralded the break of day, and to his delight Harkaway saw a hole in the roof of the cavern.

He rose to his feet and examined it.

It was one of the manholes used by the Boers.

He looked at his guards, who, forgetful of their charge, were as fast asleep as their companions.

He judged his distance, and reckoned that if he got on the top of the dynamite tins, he could reach the top of the shaft with his hands and draw himself up.

Now or never, he murmured, setting his teeth together.

Climbing on the tins very cautiously, he got up the shaft, and was soon in the open air, exultant and joyous.

Pausing for a moment with his pistol in his hand, he looked down into the pit from which he had escaped, and his eyes fell directly on the dynamite.

The Boers had not intended to show him any mercy, why should he extend any to them?

He had only to fire a shot, and numbers of his enemies would be hurled into eternity.

Click!

Taking aim, he pulled the trigger of the revolver, and turned to run as fast as his legs would carry him.

A terrific explosion and gigantic upheaval took place.

Enormous quantities of earth being thrown up into the air, and a rumbling noise like that of thunder was heard, followed by the appalling cries of wounded and horror-stricken men.

All at once a cloud of earth, flying like scud before the wind, overtook Harkaway and threw him to the ground, where he remained senseless, his body being partially hidden in the débris.

CHAPTER XXVIII.

DUNKO TELLS ALL—CAPTAIN ALLEN BRINGS NEWS FROM THE CAMP—JACK'S PROMOTION—"THE WAR SCOUTS"—A BATTLE AND ROUT OF THE BOERS.

THE execution of Dunko was stopped at the last moment, as Fred Dawson had ordered.

Before the Kaffir could speak, they had to give him some dop, Potts being sent for the bottle, some of the contents of which he poured down his throat.

"That will do," said Fred. "He has had a couple of go-downs, and if he won't speak now he shan't have another chance."

The corporal turned his back, and, looking at the bottle affectionately, whispered:

"I don't know whether I will or I won't, but I'd rather. It's early in the morning, but it don't matter. These scenes affect my nerves."

More than once was the bottle raised to his lips, with a gurgling sound, before he put it on the shelf.

Meanwhile, Fred Dawson repeated his questions to Dunko, who now responded freely.

The horseman who had been shot by the trooper was Hartz.

Fred did not regret his loss; it was another foe removed from Harkaway's path, and Mrs. Steiner, when she recovered from her wound, would be set free from a villain.

The number of Boers in the caves had been exaggerated; there were not more than a hundred, all told.

Finally, in abject dread of losing his life, Dunko produced from the inside pocket of an old soldier's coat he was wearing, a vellum envelope, which he handed to his questioner.

The sight of it made Fred's eyes flash.

He knew it well.

It was the one the Kaffir had stolen from him.

Opening it, he found inside the plan of the Rhodesian mine, without which no one could find the spot which was supposed to contain untold wealth.

With a cunning leer, Dunko explained that he had never given the plan to Webb.

He knew it must be of value, and kept it, thinking he might make something out of it for himself.

"You shall live," cried Fred. "I will spare your life, as you have done me good service. You must stay here for a time, but can go where you like when our operations are over."

Hearing this, Dunko ran out of the room, laughing to himself, and frisking about like a young spring buck at play.

"I propose that we hold a council of war," said Cornstalk, addressing his companions. "Harkaway is our leader, but for the time we are deprived of his services.

"We will get him back somehow," exclaimed Maori, "and I must impress on you that anything we do ought to be done quickly."

"Quite so," remarked Kanuck. "Has anyone a suggestion to make?"

"I have been here a bit longer than you fellows," answered Fred Dawson, "and am really one of Baden-Powell's Mafeking scouts. I vote that we leave five men here to guard the farm, with the two machine guns, though an attack is not likely, for I don't see where it is coming from, with Colonel Pilcher on the North, and Methuen to the South-West of us. Let us take a score of men to the caves, and provoke an attack. They will come out of their holes like rabbits, and we shall have them at a disadvantage. I think they will be afraid to injure Harkaway, because they know if they do, and we take any prisoners, they will be shown no mercy. Afterwards we can drive the cattle to the farm, and our mission will be practically accomplished. If you approve of my idea, hold up your hands, and we will get into the saddle."

All hands were uplifted, and Fred had the satisfaction of knowing that his plan was adopted by the colonials.

A trooper who had been out scouting all night among the kopjes at the back of the caves, walked into the room.

"Any news?" queried Cornstalk.

"We shall not get the cattle so easily as you expected," replied the man.

"How is that?"

"About thirty Boers left their caves during the night, and marched to a kopje overlooking the valley where the bullocks are. Here they have a trench, and their horses are grazing in a sheltered spot, so they can mount at any time."

"That looks as if they expected us," observed Fred Dawson, thoughtfully. "It's a deep-laid scheme. While these men engage us in front, those who are hiding attack us in the rear. We shall have to be cautious."

"The Boers are a curious people to fight," replied Cornstalk. "They rely upon trickery, and the rocks Nature has provided them with."

"Anyway," said Kanuck, "we know what they are doing this time; and the sooner we face the music the better."

They were again interrupted; this time by an orderly, who came from Colonel Pilcher's camp.

In his hand he held a despatch, which had come through Methuen's camp on the Modder from General Buller on the Tugela.

He was an officer in a hussar regiment, with which the colonials had been brigaded, and his name was Allen.

"Haven't you fellows got those cows in yet?" he enquired. "You are rather slow hands at foraging. You should have my soldier servant to put you up to a wrinkle or two."

"Send him along," replied Kanuck; "we are always willing to learn, especially in a strange country."

"The other night rations ran short. We hadn't enjoyed a square meal for two days, and I chanced to remark in chaff that I should like a ragout. Three hours after my man came in with a soup-bowl full of something giving a capital smell."

"What's that?" I asked.

"Your raggoo, sir," answered my man, who was unsteady on his pins, clearly having been drinking; in fact, he was horribly intoxicated. "It's an extra up-to-date raggoo, sir. I was on picket, and strolled into a farmyard, where I saw a Boer hen and a Boer duck, an Orange Free State turkey, and a couple of Natal pigeons. I held out a bag, and they got into it somehow. When I got to the mess-kitchen they had broken their necks, and I thought I would cook 'em, with a Transvaal onion, for you."

"Don't you know that looting is against Lord Roberts' general orders? You found some brandy at the same time, if I am not mistaken."

"Never mind that, sir," was the answer I got. "Wire into your raggoo, and enjoy it. Yu're a rattling good soldier, sir."

Saying this he slapped me on the back, lurched up against the tent-pole, and fell head-over-heels on the sand outside.

"But I didn't come here to tell you that yarn. Where are Harkaway and Dawson?"

"I am here," replied Fred, who had escaped the captain's notice. "Our lieutenant, I am sorry to say, is in the hands of the Boers, and we are going to get him out if we can."

"Allow me to go with you on an errand like that. I have not killed a Boer for the last two days, and am feeling rather rusty."

"Your rank entitles you to lead our company, and I know the Colonials will follow you."

There was a murmur of assent from Cornstalk, Kanuck, and Maori.

"Thank you," exclaimed Allen. "I may tell you, without breach of confidence, that Harkaway is looked upon as one of the most promising youngsters in the service, and the Horse Guards' people have made him a captain."

"Hurrah for Captain Harkaway!" cried Fred Dawson, who was not at all envious of his friend's well-earned promotion.

The cheer was taken up by the colonials in a most hearty manner, and echoed by some troopers who were grouped on the verandah.

"This dispatch which I carry in my hand," continued Captain Allen, "comes from General Buller. Harkaway and Dawson are commanded to join him at once at his head-quarters on the Tugela River. They are requested to bring with them a force of one hundred colonial and Natal volunteers, who will be called "Harkaway's War Scouts."

"What will their duty be?" asked Fred.

"They will be the nose of any force they are attached to. That is to say they must find out where the enemy are; also make raids for forage and, other supplies, burn houses and towns, scout, ravage, harass, destroy, and think nothing of riding fifty miles in a night."

"He won't have much trouble in finding volunteers for this corps of War Scouts. I'll go for one," exclaimed Cornstalk.

"And I," joined in Maori and Kanuck.

Corporal Potts pushing himself forward, said, "I won't be left out in the cold; you must put my name down on the roll of honour."

"It will be my delight," observed Fish, "to be attached to the War Scouts as special correspondent of the *Cape Town Slasher*, and I shall wire my proprietors accordingly."

"Ain't I to have any decoration for all the hardships I've gone through, and the gallantry I've displayed?" asked Potts.

"My friend," replied Fish, with the air of a patron, "we will decorate you with the order of the pump-handle, for we all know that you are a total abstainer."

There was a merry twinkle in the correspondent's eyes, and his remark evoked a burst of laughter.

"We have all heard of your stainless record."

"Quite right, sir," replied the corporal meekly. "I have always tried to set an example to the other Tommies. When I was only a little tot I belonged to the Band of Hope."

"What did you hope for, you old humbug? Here, it's a dry morning, and we have got some rough work before us, which will try even a colonial tough. Have a drop of this?"

Fish jerked his flask out of his pocket, and handed it to the corporal, who, thrown off his guard, said: "I don't know whether I will or whether I won't, but I'd rather."

And raising it to his lips, drained it to the dregs—an exploit which provoked more merriment.

Captain Allen drew Fred on one side, and whispered to him:

"Do you know Mrs. Steiner—a very beautiful woman? Quite a toff in her way. Has the air of a Cleopatra, and brings a fellow down like a shot with one look of her lustrous dark eyes."

"By Jove! captain, you seem hard hit," answered Fred Dawson. "Of course I know Mrs. Steiner. She is a very dangerous woman. But what about her?"

"Hearing somehow that I was going to visit Harkaway, she sent a hospital nurse for me, and asked me to give him a message to this effect: She has got well of her wound, and was that day going to leave the camp for Cape Town, where she intended to stay for a few weeks at the Victoria Hotel, where all letters should be addressed. If I fall, just be good enough to tell Jack this, will you?"

Fred nodded.

The bugle sounded. Cornstalk shouted "To horse!" and the colonials lost no time in getting into the saddle.

They rode over the plain in two lines. There was only a handful of them, but they were fine dashing fellows, full of life, pluck, and endurance.

When they arrived within half-a-mile of the caves, the dynamite explosion caused by Harkaway took place.

To them it looked like the eruption of a small volcano, and was all the more terrible in the early dawn.

The Boers came pouring out of their holes like rabbits, beginning to scamper over the ground to the kopjes.

The Colonials fired at them as they rode, shooting them down, and only a few joined their friends on the hill.

Arriving at the caves, the Colonials halted their horses.

Dense fumes were rising from the holes, threatening anyone with suffocation who ventured too near.

The Boers sleeping in the apartment near the dynamite had been destroyed.

It was only those at the other end of the diggings who had escaped, and the whole of the caves were now full of smoke.

It was considered useless to look for Jack, and shaking his head mournfully, Captain Allen waved his sword in the air, and shouted:

"Forward!"

The troop galloped on towards the valley, and when they rounded the kopje, behind which the cattle were grazing, the Boers in their trench opened fire upon them.

The troopers quickly dismounted, and, sheltering behind stones, crept up the hillside, returning shot for shot, whenever they got a chance.

Captain Allen and two Colonials were hit, rolling down the kopje, but the others pressed on until the ridge was reached, when they fixed bayonets and charged the Boers.

A desperate hand-to-hand conflict ensued in which the Boers were routed, the majority being killed.

Only half-a-dozen avoided death by flight, and the Colonials were left masters of the field, having only lost five men killed and wounded, Captain Allen—Fighting Allen of the 10th, as he was called—being among the former.

The dead were roughly buried in the valley, the wounded sent home on horseback, carried by a companion, while Dawson, Cornstalk, Maori, and Kanuck, assisted in driving the herd of cattle to the farm.

It was a complete triumph, but their hearts were sad when they thought of Harkaway, about whose fate they had no doubt whatever.

CHAPTER XXIX.

JACK IS SAVED BY THE HUNCHBACK—FORMATION OF THE WAR SCOUTS—SENT TO THE FRONT—BATTLE OF SPION KOP—ON ACTIVE SERVICE.

THOUGH the Colonials were unaware of the fact they twice passed close to the spot where Harkaway was lying, insensible, and partially covered with the scattered earth.

Gladly would they have extended a helping hand, had they known it; but coming and going back, they went silently by.

As soon as the last of the cattle, driven by the horsemen were out of sight, Webb, Vilbois, and the few Boers who had escaped the carnage, crept up to their old hiding-place.

The smoke had disappeared, and the air below in the unruined caves was pure.

Webb went down one of the shafts, and was absent some time, Villebois calmly smoking a cigarette meanwhile.

When he emerged from the underground depths, Webb said:

"I can find no trace of the missing article."

"It is a great loss to me," replied the Frenchman, in a tone of vexation. "I had fifty diamonds in a gold box, which I placed in our treasure chest. The latter was in the last cave, near the dynamite. These were choice diamonds from Kimberley, worth thousands."

"There is no sign of the chest; all is a perfect wreck. I could only see heads, and limbs, and trunks of dead Boers. It is a chaos. No wonder the diamonds are lost."

He pointed to a yawning chasm in the ground, which showed the destruction which had been wrought by the explosion.

The Frenchman eyed Webb with suspicion, and the latter read what was passing in his mind.

"If you don't believe me, go down, and look for yourself. You know the way," he added, insolently.

Webb's coat was buttoned tightly over the breast, and something in the pocket made it bulge.

"*Pardieu!*" cried Villebois. "If I thought you were cheating me, I'd have it out of you."

"What do you mean?" demanded Webb. "You may as well call me a thief at once, and have done with it. If you do that, I shall know how to treat you."

"What have you got in your pocket? Come, unbutton your coat, if you are an honest man."

"Certainly not, at your dictation. I consider such a request an insult," retorted Webb.

"You stand self-condemned by that very answer."

Uttering these words, the Frenchman made a sudden grab at Webb's coat, tearing off the buttons, and by his violence jerked out a square gold box, which fell upon the ground.

"How now?" vociferated Villebois. "You have tried to rob me, villain that you are; but I have regained my own, so we will let the matter drop, but I shall be careful how I trust you in future."

He stooped down to pick up the casket, when Webb, reversing his rifle, treacherously gave him a blow on the head with the butt-end, which sent him staggering forward like a drunken man; and Webb, coolly taking up the diamonds, put them once more in his pocket.

The Boers stood by, silent and passive.

Only one word escaped their lips, and that was zachenroller.

It was a quarrel between two above them, and they did not consider it any of their concern.

At length the Frenchman fell down, stunned and bleeding, upon a heap of earth thrown up by the dynamite.

Muttering, with a curse, "I'll finish him," Webb strode after his unconscious victim, when a singular event occurred.

Villebois had tumbled on Harkaway, the result of the shock being to rouse the latter, who recovered from his stupor, and rising to his feet, looked vacantly around him.

Webb could scarcely believe the evidence of his senses.

"By Heaven! it's Harkaway," he exclaimed," showing the wildest excitement. "Seize him! Hold him in a grip of iron! Don't let him go, under pain of death! He

has not long to live, but I must taunt him before I send him to the grave."

Before he could offer any resistance, Jack found himself in the grasp of four strong Boers, and his revolver fell from his hand.

"Death to the traitor," cried the Boers grimly.

With his usual luck, Jack had only escaped one danger to fall into another.

He was held by four men, two more were standing by, and Webb, rifle in hand, was in front of him.

What possible means could there be of getting out of this entanglement?

All at once a harsh mocking laugh was heard.

"Ho! Ho! Ho! Is this how you welcome your true friend, Teufelskint?"

"The hunchback of the mountain," muttered Webb: "I could wish him far away. The Boers reverence him. He is no friend of mine, and may mar my plans."

"Back," continued the hunchback, in a voice of thunder. "Release your prisoner, or my bitterest curse shall fall upon you. Your limbs shall be rent asunder by the Rednecks' shells, and you shall grope about without eyes."

Alarmed at this terrible threat, the Boers, abashed and trembling, slunk away from Jack, who promptly picked up his revolver, and faced Webb.

"I never did a dirty action in my life," he exclaimed, "and I'm not going to begin now, or I should shoot you. You can go. Beware how you cross me again."

Webb and the Boers hastened to the hills.

Teufelskint explained his power over the superstitious Dutchmen.

He had recovered from his stupor; his first thought being to redeem his promise, and help Jack, but he would not return to the farm.

The kopjes were his home.

He could not live anywhere else.

Jack went back by himself.

His appearance was hailed with delight by the Colonials, who that night left MacKay's farm and rejoined the main column.

The following day was occupied in organising Harkaway's War Scouts, the number required being speedily found.

They were the most intelligent men that could be selected, used to life in the bush, on the prairie, and the hills.

The officers were Captain Harkaway, the lieutenants being Kanuck, the Canadian; Cornstalk, the Australian, from Queensland; Maori, the New Zealander; Corporal Potts retained his rank; Special Correspondent Fish was a supernumerary; Little Andy, the bugler, was to join them as soon as he got over his wound; Fred Dawson took the position of adjutant.

They were well mounted and full of enthusiasm, feeling fit to go anywhere and do anything.

They arrived at the Tugela River soon after General Buller had crossed it, on his great flanking movement, to relieve Sir George White and Ladysmith, and were sent to act with Sir Charles Warren's army, being attached to the South African Horse, under Major Childe.

It was nearly dark when they reached Warren, and they had not been in camp two hours before they received an order to make a night attack upon the key of the Boers' position, a tall hill, called Spion Kop.

In conjunction with the F Squadron of the South Africans the War Scouts scaled the hill, dislodging the Boers from their trenches, the enemy being surprised in the darkness, but offering a stubborn and desperate resistance, which continued for some hours.

Harkaway was the first on the summit of the kop, and hoisting his helmet on his blood-stained bayonet, shouted wildly :

"Hurrah ! for old England."

The battle was won, but our casualties were heavy.

Harkaway's War Scouts had received their baptism of blood, and won their spurs at the battle of Spion Kop.

Further hard work was in store for them.

Ladysmith had to be relieved.

There was a distance of sixteen miles between General Buller and the besieged garrison.

The intervening country swarmed with Boers.

It was important to locate their positions.

Harkaway had lost thirty of his men in the assault, but he was promptly sent, with the remainder, on a scouting expedition, which was full of risk and danger.

CHAPTER XXX.

TWO SCOUTS BELONGING TO HARKAWAY'S HORSE ARE SURPRISED ON THE VELDT— DUNKO THE SPY—IN DANGER OF DEATH —THE HUNCHBACK OF THE HILLS.

"HANDS up ! rifles down !"

It was noon on the veldt.

The sun was high in the heavens, and its burning rays made even the rocks hot to the touch.

The grass drooped, and the insects hummed drowsily.

Here and there large boulders were lying about as if scattered by a giant hand.

Behind one of these—which afforded a slight shelter from the rays of the sun—two men were lying on their sides, taking a brief midday rest.

They were Corporal Potts and Kanuck, the tall, wiry Canadian, who belonged to a force of irregular cavalry called Jack Harkaway's War Scouts.

The main body was camped at the base of the Drakensberg Mountains, whose tall, rugged peaks could be seen in the distance.

Thirty miles behind this range was the long-beleaguered town of Ladysmith, so gallantly defended by Sir George White and his brave army.

Harkaway and his men had received orders to swoop down upon and destroy a large farmhouse, known as Shalker's, which was situated on the veldt.

It was a dangerous task, as the neighbouring country was over-run by small parties of Boers ; but the English general placed great importance on the position, because Shalker's farm had been reported to be a base of supplies, containing large quantities of canned provisions, biltong, biscuit,

and, above all, cases holding half-a-million of cartridges and a considerable weight of shell, all of which was supposed to be stored in the cellars.

It was important for Harkaway to know by how many men Shalker's farm was protected.

He did not imagine there were many, as an attack could not be expected by the English, White's force being shut up in Ladysmith and Buller's troops being occupied in trying to force their way through the mountain passes near the Tugela River.

If the stores and ammunition at Shalker's could be destroyed, it would inflict a heavy blow upon the enemy, consequently Captain Harkaway had sent out the Canadian and the corporal to bring him all the intelligence they could obtain.

It was during their noon-day rest, when they were only about five miles distant from the farm, that they were pounced upon by two prowling Boers.

Their clothes were worn and dirty, their broad-brimmed hats battered and rain-soaked, their beards long, and their faces had a half-starved look, showing the effect of a prolonged campaign.

The speaker who had ordered the scouts to lay down their arms was Constrad, a Transvaal Boer, who formed one of the garrison at the farm.

He had come out with his companion on a scouting expedition because a Kaffir had brought them information that a small party of English Horse had been seen at the foot of one of the Drakensberg Hills.

In this war, the Boers rely upon the Kaffirs for their news, the latter being quick-sighted and remarkably fleet of foot, traversing many miles of country in a few hours.

Their kraals are to be seen everywhere, and they are always on the alert.

The Kaffir who had intimated to the Boers the proximity of a hostile force, had been in the pay of Joubert and other generals for some months, and was well known to Corporal Potts as a treacherous and designing native, generally acting with two well-known spies of Kruger's, Webb and Mrs. Steiner, who, before the war, moved in the best society at Pretoria.

His name was Dunko, and he had acquired the nick-name of Funko, because he always got out of the way when there was any firing going on, and he could hear the splur of a shell more than a mile off.

Dunko was with Constrad on the present occasion.

His hawk-like black eye had first seen the two scouts, and after pointing them out, he said a few words in Taal, and discreetly hid himself in the long grass, not knowing which way the coming encounter would result.

The Canadian and the corporal were taken completely by surprise.

The muzzles of two guns were pointed within a few feet of their heads.

To resist was useless, and cursing their ill-luck, they dropped their rifles, sprang to their feet, and held up their hands.

Taking up the arms that the prisoners had let fall, the Boers grinned, evincing the most lively satisfaction.

"I hope you have enjoyed your morning walk," said Constrad. "It is a nice day for Boer sniping, but you should never go to sleep, my friends, in the enemy's country."

"We are simple travellers," replied the Canadian, "and were going to visit some friends."

"That won't do. Travellers do not carry rifles and wear khaki; we know that you belong to a party of horse, camped at the base of the hills. Tell me the truth about this horse, and you will be treated well."

"I repeat that we are not fighting men," protested the Canadian. "Your commander will soon let us go when we show him our papers, and then you will get into trouble for detaining us."

An incredulous smile came over Constrad's face.

He whistled shrilly, and Dunko sprang up from his place of concealment in the grass.

Nodding familiarly to the corporal, the Kaffir exclaimed:

"Glad to see you, baas! How was Captain Harkaway when you left him? You will know all about Shalker's farm presently. There is a nice place for prisoners."

Corporal Potts looked angrily at him, and ground his teeth with rage at being outwitted by one who had been a thorn in his side on previous occasions.

"You viper!" he replied, "I only wish I had you within arm's length; wouldn't I knock some of those shining ivories down your throat. Are you always to be hanging on our flank, and harassing us?"

As he spoke, he rapidly stooped, and picking up a chunk of rock, hurled it with all his force at the Kaffir.

It struck Dunko full on the forehead, making an incised wound, which caused him to sink to the ground like a bullock poleaxed in the shambles.

"Take that, you miserable dirty cur," he added. "I hope I have killed you, for, by George, you deserve it. I don't think you will interfere with me again, Mister Dunko Funko."

Constrad's brow lowered, and his face assumed a satanic expression of hatred and spite.

"What did you do that for?" he cried. "How dare you touch one of our friendly Kaffirs? Suppose I treat you the same way; how'd you like that? None of your ferdomdy tricks for me, you bad Rooinek."

"We are your prisoners, and you have no right to ill-treat us," replied Potts.

"Don't talk to me," thundered the Boer. "I could shoot you if I chose."

Constrad raised his rifle, and Kanuck, fearing that he would do some rash thing, seized the muzzle of the weapon, and forced it up in the air.

"Fire on him, Hans, shoot them both down," exclaimed Constrad," addressing his companion. "This is mutiny, and they shall die. What are two Rednecks more or less, and who is to tell of it? The Asvogels will pick their bones. Bah! shoot, shoot."

It was a moment of imminent peril for the two scouts.

It looked as if nothing could save them from the merciless fury of the Boers.

Hans was about to obey the command, when a burst of mocking laughter rang in their ears, startling and causing them to turn round.

"Ho! ho! ho! No blood shall be shed here," said a shrill, harsh voice. "Do you hear me, Constrad, and you, Hans, or shall I speak louder? Do you want me to put my bitterest curse on you and your families, who are pining in their homesteads? Do you wish your cattle to die of the rinderpest, and your corn to be eaten up by locusts? Shall I dry up your springs, and strike down your little children with the fever?"

The Boers were astounded and abashed.

Hans grounded his rifle.

Constrad feebly allowed Kanuck to snatch his from him.

"Great heaven," he muttered, "'tis Teufelskint, the hunchback of the hills!"

CHAPTER XXXI.

TURNING THE TABLES ON THE BOERS—GENEROSITY OF THE SCOUTS—A RUN FOR LIFE—FIRING AT A THOUSAND YARDS—CONSTRAD ESCAPES.

TEUFELSKINT was a poor, stunted, misshapen specimen of humanity.

He lived in the hills, first in one place, then in another, for he could not rest long in one spot.

He was hump-backed and hideous.

Towns knew him not; but he could always get food at the farms, for the Boers held him in superstitious reverence, thinking he could do them harm if they incurred his displeasure.

He had met Harkaway, for whom he conceived a liking, and, seeing the letters H.W.S., which stood for Harkaway's War Scouts, on the tunics of the prisoners, he determined to befriend them.

Teufelskint, which means the devil's child, had arrived just in the nick of time to be of service to Corporal Potts and the Canadian, who, at the moment of his coming, were in sore straits.

The hunchback had changed all this, as if by magic, for Kanuck had taken Constrad's rifle and picked up his own.

Seeing the consternation of the foe, Corporal Potts made a sudden dash at Hans, and, knocking him down with a blow of his fist, put himself on an equality with his friend, by repossessing himself of his own weapon and that of the Dutchman.

This action entirely turned the tables on the Boers, who were at the disposal of those whom a few minutes before they were going to shoot.

"That's one for you, fathead!" exclaimed the corporal. "If you want any more, get up and face the music like a man. Oh! you won't. Had enough, eh? Well, I don't blame you; you're not the first one who has disliked a blow from this Tommy's fist. What are you going to do with them, sir?"

This remark was addressed to the Canadian, who was looking on in a thoughtful manner; while Teufelskint, like an evil genius, stood on the summit of the rock, the wind blowing his elfin locks until they looked like small flying snakes.

"'I AM AN ENGLISH DETECTIVE, AND YOU MUST SURRENDER TO ME,' SMART EXCLAIMED."

No. 8.

"Ho! ho! ho!" he laughed; "there is blood in the air—I can smell it. What a feast the vultures will have this afternoon ! I can see them hovering overhead, for they scent their prey afar off."

Kanuck had a coil of rope round his waist, which he unloosed. With this he bound the arms of the two Boers behind their backs, and made them stand side by side.

They looked very dejected, sullen, and morose, but they said nothing.

It was the fortune of war, and they were always prepared for the worst.

"The lives of these men are justly forfeited," said Kanuck. "If this hunchback dwarf had not appeared as he did, we should not have been alive now."

"That means you intend to execute them, and I concur in the sentence. But, at the same time, with your permission, I should like to move an amendment, as they say at a public meeting," replied the corporal.

"Your amendment shall be attended to. What is it ? "

"We can get all the information we want about Shalker's farm from Dunko Funko when he comes to his senses. I'll make the beggar speak the truth for once in his life, if I have to prod him with the point of my bayonet. Shoot these Boers by all means, but give them a chance for their lives. Let them have a run for it."

"What do you mean ? " asked the Canadian, who was rather puzzled.

"Let them cut across the veldt, and give them a thousand yards start before we begin to fire at them."

"That's what I call noble magnanimity, which they don't deserve, as they certainly would not have done it for us. However, I am not a bloodthirsty chap, and for once we will forget that we are at war. They shall have the chance you suggest."

At hearing this the eyes of the Boers sparkled, for with a thousand yards start they hoped to get off.

"Baas oop, brother Hans," whispered Constrad. "We are not dead yet ; maybe we shall see our frous and kinterin once more."

"It is possible," answered Hans. "These Rooineks are not so bad after all. We must run like ostriches."

"That's settled," observed the corporal with the complacent air of a man who feels that he has done a good action.

"It's a long time between drinks, corporal," said Kanuck. "What do you say to a drop out of my flask ? "

"I don't know whether I will or I won't, but I'd rather," answered Potts, who pretended that he objected to drinking, but always wound up by accepting an offer.

The corporal handed back the bottle, largely depleted of its contents, and, helping himself, the Canadian remarked :

"It's a bad habit, but under the circumstances I reckon it may be excused. What do you say, mate ? "

"Not for me, sir, not a drop more, thank you," replied the corporal, artfully, for he had noticed that the flask was empty. "You might have offered a taste to the imp of darkness with the hunch on him."

This observation caused Kanuck to look up.

Teufelskint had disappeared.

Directing his eyes down again, Kanuck saw the dwarf scudding across the plain in the direction of the mountains.

"The little beggar is gone," exclaimed the Canadian. "We have to thank him for saving our lives. We will now turn our attention to the captives, who are indebted to you for still being in the land of the living."

"When you let them loose, and we judge that they have gained a thousand yards, I will fire at the big one, while you take Hans," said Potts.

"Just as you like. I am going to have a little Boer-shooting, and it does not matter much which one I hit."

"It is rarely I wager a bit of gold ; but I will bet you half a sovereign that I drop my man."

Kanuck made no reply to this boastful challenge, though he knew that Potts was a good marksman, having once been musketry instructor at Hythe.

Unbinding the Boers, he said :

"You can walk until you have measured off a thousand yards, for which I shall allow you ten minutes. Then you can start for home on the run."

"You'll give us a fair chance ?" replied Constrad, looking up in his face with suspicion.

"Well, I should smile," exclaimed Kanuck, drawing himself up proudly. " I guess this isn't a Boer trick ; I am strictly on the level with you fellows. Death's door is open before you, but it does not follow that you are bound to step in. You may find a way round. Now, then, no more nonsense. Off you go."

" My thanks to you," answered Constrad. "If I can do you a turn, I will. I've got something here."

He tapped his side in a significant manner.

"What's that, old hoss ? " asked the Canadian.

"A heart," rejoined the Boer. "I am only doing my duty to my country, the same as you are to yours. If you hadn't come over here we shouldn't have troubled you. Fare-thee-well. If we meet again, you will be always welcome to a bit of this old man's biltong. Step out, comrade ; put your best leg forward."

Thus admonished, Hans commenced to walk over the veldt, his leader putting himself by his side.

They could not avoid a nervous tremor ; that was only to be expected.

They strode along, measuring the ground honestly, reckoning each stride as three feet, or one yard.

Kanuck and the corporal sighted their rifles at a thousand yards, and stood in readiness to fire when the time allowance had expired.

Kanuck looked at his watch, Potts raised to his eyes his field-glasses, with which all Harkaway's War Scouts were provided.

The minutes flew slowly by.

Suddenly Kanuck replaced the watch in his pocket, and ejaculated " Time's up."

"Right you are," answered the corporal. "Blaze away. A pound to a penny I kill."

Saying this, the corporal threw himself down flat on the grass.

He always fired in a reclining position if he could.

The Boers had reached the limit allowed them, and began to run.

But they did not go straight.

They doubled about like hares, went in eccentric circles, and sometimes fell down, to dodge the shooting.

The corporal fired three times at his man and missed him, much to his disgust and vexation.

Kanuck sank on one knee, and waited fully a minute before he was satisfied that his aim was correct.

Then he discharged his weapon, with the result that Hans leaped up in the air, uttering a wild, weird, terror-striking death cry, and fell to rise no more.

Constrad was now well ahead.

He turned for an instant when he heard his companion, whose fate only gave him wings, adding renewed vigour to his flight, and though the corporal discharged five more shots after him he escaped unhurt.

The Canadian bit his lips with annoyance.

He knew that the Boer would prepare the garrison of Shalker's farm for the attack Captain Harkaway intended to make upon it.

This was a very serious thing, as they could no longer hope to take the enemy by surprise.

CHAPTER XXXII.

DUNKO IS MADE TO CONFESS—THE SAND-STORM—CAPTAIN HARKAWAY ARRIVES ON THE SCENE—HE SCOUTS ALONE — A SURPRISE.

CORPORAL POTTS threw his rifle on the ground, and using his field-glasses, watched the flying Boer, who, in spite of his boasting, he had failed to bring down.

Constrad was out of range now, and though they might have done so, they did not consider it advisable to follow him up, as Shalker's farm was so close, and they did not know what they might have to encounter.

It was a disappointing scout, so far.

If Constrad had not got away, they would certainly have gone on to the farm, and made the reconnaissance they had been sent out to achieve.

The great point which troubled Harkaway was the means of defence.

Had they big guns or quick-firing ones; easily-moved Nordenfeldts, on light carriages, or Maxims? That was the question on which much would depend.

It was computed by the Intelligence Department that nearly half a million pounds worth of provisions and ammunition were stored at this apparently harmless and unimportant farm, to blow up which would be a grand *coup*.

All at once, the corporal perceived that Constrad had come to a halt.

He bent over, as if looking at his leg, and then sat down on the grass, seemingly unable to go any further.

"I believe I hit him, after all," remarked Potts. "He wouldn't stop in his run like that for nothing. I tell you, he's a lame dog."

"Ten to one he's resting, you silly old crackpot," replied Kanuck. "Don't blow about your shooting any more. You couldn't hit a haystack if it was as close to you as I am. You can't shoot for sour apples, and have given the whole show away."

"How is that, lieutenant?" inquired the corporal. "It takes a bit of doing to hit a man at a thousand yards when he is cavorting about like a March hare."

"You make me tired with your everlasting talk," answered the Canadian. "I am real sick of gasbags since I've known you. It is useless to proceed further, we shall have to go back to camp. If we only had our horses we might ride up to the Boer, and give him his death blow. What will Captain Harkaway say to us? You bet, he'll be just jumping mad."

At this moment their attention was roused by a deep, guttural sound, which proceeded from the prostrate Kaffir, who was coming to.

"Dunko, by Jove!" cried the corporal. "We'd forgotten him. He's a Boerite, and knows the ins and outs of the farm. Let me tackle him."

"Stand aside," cried Kanuck, "I'm the man! Just allow me to do a bit of tall talking to this varmint."

"All right. Go your own way. I suppose I have lived in Natal some years for nothing. You get anything out of that Kaffir that's worth having. I wouldn't like to give you much for what you obtain."

"Hush up," said the Canadian, "I'm from Winnipeg, and I know the Red Indians of the Satskachewan. A Kaffir can't be more crafty than a Red, and I can beat the latter at their own game every time, and don't you forget it."

With these words Kanuck went to Dunko, and gave him a drink of water out of his bottle, after which he asked him how many Boers there were at the farm, and what guns they had.

Dunko got up, and, leaning against the rock, remained in a thoughtful attitude for quite the space of a minute, as if he was slowly recovering from the blow he had received, but in reality he was puzzling his brain to find the means of baffling his interrogator.

At the same time he was playing nervously with a knobstick he held in his hand.

It was in vain that Kanuck plied him with questions.

Assuming an innocent air, he evaded everything, declaring that he had only just met the Boers, and, being tired of the war, was on his way to Maritzberg.

"This pump's dry, I guess," said Kanuck. "I can't get anything out of the well."

"Didn't I tell you to leave him to me?" exclaimed the corporal, in triumph. "I've got these Kaffirs down to a fine point. It takes the likes of me to get over the likes of them. What you've got out of the well is a pack of lies, but they say truth is at the bottom. Let me have a go at him. Give this counsellor-at-law a turn with the pump-handle. I'll astonish the native with a little bit of lyddite."

The corporal advanced to the Kaffir and gave him a dig in the ribs with the butt end of his rifle, which doubled him up and made him gasp for breath.

"Now, then, Dunko Funko," he cried, "wake up, and have some style about you! How many men and guns have they got at Shalker's farm? Speak the truth, or I'll blow your brains out."

"Hold on, baas." responded Dunko, becoming alive to the situation; "don't frighten a man into fits. There's one thousand Boers in laager and twenty quick-firing guns."

"That will do," said the corporal. "Prepare to die. I hate a liar, and I'll be hanged if you don't take the cake—I may say the entire bakery."

He raised his rifle, and, looking Dunko full in the face with a determined air, was about to pull the trigger, when the Kaffir exclaimed piteously :

"Don't shoot, baas! I'll never tell a lie again. Promise to let me off, and you shall know all about Shalker's."

"Go ahead; I'm watching you. No fear. I've got my eye on you, crawling, scorpion reptile that you are."

"There are only fifty men at the farm, and they have one gun, a Hotchkiss, which goes thump, thump, thump, and pours out the shots like winking. They were practising with it this morning, and it brought down all the peaches off the trees, and a couple of hundred little birds dropped dead. We had peaches and veldt birds for dinner."

"Lying again, are you? I'll be shot if it isn't born in you. What have you got in your right boot?"

"A foot, I reckon, baas. You don't suppose I put my head in a boot?" answered the Kaffir.

"No trifling with me, Dunko Funko; none of your larks," said the corporal, sternly. "You are asking for a dose of lead, and you'll have it if you don't give me that despatch you've got. Take off your boot and give it to me."

Reluctantly the Kaffir did as he was told, and took from his boot a sheet of paper, on which was written :

"From Constrad to General Joubert. The Kaffir runner Dunko has brought your letter. We are aware that Harkaway's War Scouts are in our vicinity, and you may depend that we shall be on the look-out for them. Reinforcements not needed. My fifty men, with one gun, can keep off all intruders. To-night six waggons shall trek to you, with the ammunition and supplies you require."

"That's a little bit of all right," observed the corporal, when he had finished reading the letter to Kanuck. "Now tell me you are not a spy."

"I work for pay," replied Dunko. "If you pay me better than the Boers I'll be your spy."

"Not you," rejoined the corporal, sceptically. "I wouldn't trust you further than I could see you, because you are too well in with Kruger's lot. Where is that villainous friend of yours, Webb, now?"

"He is with Joubert," said Dunko, who saw that he could gain nothing by telling more falsehoods. "Want to know any more? Well, I'll tell you, just to show that I am a good Kaffir. The Frenchman, Villebois, is at the farm, and Harkaway's friend, Mrs. Steiner, has come back from Cape Town quite cured, and is with the Boers on the Tugela.

I heard her say that she was coming to the farm to visit Mr. and Mrs. Shalker and their daughter, Gretchen, though I think it is more likely she wants to be near Captain Harkaway. Ha, ha! Dunko knows a thing or two. That Dutchwoman loves the young Redneck officer, and he don't know it. Oh, my! wouldn't I like to make her Mrs. Dunko, and take her to a kraal in Zululand."

"Dry up, you ugly ape. What white woman would look at you. We're going back to camp, and you'll have to come with us. Your life is in no danger, but it won't do to let you go and tell tales until we have made our midnight attack on the farm, and blown it to glory. March alongside of us."

Dunko made no opposition. He did not care so long as his life was safe, and was just as ready to spend a few hours in the camp of the War Scouts as anywhere else.

"Stop a moment," added the corporal, eyeing him critically. "What's that you've got bulging out of your tunic?"

"That's square-face, baas. This Kaffir never travels without it. I bought it off a Smaus, who called it Sudden Death. It takes a man to drink that and live. Better be careful, sir, but you're welcome if you want it."

"I don't know whether I will or I won't, but I'd rather," said the corporal," with a melancholy sigh. "It's a weary world, and a vale of tears. Hand the jug over."

Scarcely had Corporal Potts taken the bottle of vitriolic stuff from the Kaffir than a sudden rush of wind tore it from his hand, and dashed it against the rock.

The next minute there was a screeching, howling, rattling, grinding sound, and the men were enveloped in a storm of sand, such as is of common occurrence at a moment's notice in the Transvaal.

It blinded, it choked, it blistered their skins, and nearly suffocated them.

Groping like men in the dark, they reached the rock, and crawling round it, obtained shelter from the furious blast whch was hissing and whizzing round them.

It lasted fully twenty minutes, when the sky cleared, and the veldt resumed its former appearance.

Looking round for Dunko, they found that the Kaffir had vanished.

"More trouble," said the corporal. "I was wrong again. It doesn't do to be merciful in war. We ought to have shot the Boers on the spot, and brained Dunko as soon as I had got all I could out of him; but it's no use crying over spilled milk. Let us make tracks for home."

"The object of our mission is fulfilled," replied Kanuck. "We know exactly the state of affairs at the farm; but Constrad will, no doubt, have put them on their guard, and we shall meet with a hot reception. I guess Dunko will go back to Joubert."

"You needn't make so sure about Constrad," continued the corporal. "I believe I hit him in the leg, and he sat down because he couldn't get along. By this time he is covered with a heap of sand, as big as an ant-hill."

"That sounds too good to be true. We want to catch the Boers napping."

"We'll do that, safe as houses, sir," rejoined the corporal. "Plague take that sandstorm, it was the worst I ever saw. Just as I had got that bottle of square-face to my lips, away it went, slap-bang, and its contents were wasted on the desert air. There is both truth and poetry in that remark. Not that I wanted it. I'd never touch a drop of liquor again if it would do anybody any good, but this climate is very trying."

They stepped forward to march to the camp, when they beheld a solitary horseman galloping over the plain.

He was coming towards them from the direction of the Drakensberg.

For a few minutes they were puzzled to make out who he was, but as he drew nearer they distinguished the noble, commanding physique and magnificent athletic form of Jack Harkaway.

"The captain!" exclaimed Kanuck. "By Jove, it's our leader. Now I suppose we shall get a jacketing for letting those fellows go. Mark time, corporal, and let me do the talking. I can explain better than you, for you are small potatoes on a job of that kind."

"I am an eloquent speaker if anyone will listen to me," replied Potts, "but the trouble is they won't. I am a flower."

"Weed, you mean, you silly old fool," interrupted the Canadian.

"Flower, I say," persisted the corporal. "Born to blush unseen."

"Give us a rest on that," said Kanuck, laughing. "I don't think anything would alter your colour; but keep your mouth shut —here comes our gallant captain. Attention!"

The words were scarcely out of his mouth when Jack Harkaway reined in his horse and brought him to a standstill, with quivering flanks and dilated nostrils.

"How is it you fellows haven't got any nearer the farm than this? You've been all day at it," exclaimed Harkaway. "The sandstorm couldn't have delayed you long. I rode right through it. Anybody would think you were salt or sugar."

"We've had a bout with the Boers," replied Kanuck. "Let me explain, captain."

In a few words he related all that had happened, which did not altogether please their commander.

"You're a couple of bunglers," he said. "I send you out to do a certain thing, and find I have to do it myself, which isn't very pleasant. In the first place, you shouldn't have taken a sun-bath under the rock, with your eyes half shut. Secondly, when you had a chance of shooting this Constrad, and especially that thief Dunko, you should not have neglected to do so. When we attack to-night, we may expect that the Boers will make it warm for us. I shall have to go and take in the bearings of this farm myself. You two can remain here until my return."

"Look out, sir, for a heap of sand with a man under it, which, in my opinion, will be Constrad," replied the corporal.

Jack nodded his head, and, putting spurs to his horse, was soon again careering over the plain.

His energy was indomitable.

He never seemed to tire, and the activity of his body was only rivalled by that of his fertile brain.

He saw nothing of any mound, nor did he discover any trace of the Boer Potts thought he had shot, and he came to the conclusion that he had rejoined his comrades.

When he was near enough to distinguish the faint outlines of the farm building he dismounted, and with one word made his horse lie down.

He then crawled on his hands and knees through the grass towards a clump of trees which overshadowed a vlei, or glassy pool, thinking he would be from observation and able to take a full survey of the surroundings.

Having gained the cover he desired, he was about to resume his erect position, when he heard a woman's voice exclaim:

"It is cowardly to persecute me thus. You are a stranger to me, and will always be so. Remove your hand from my arm, or I will scream for help. You, Van Shalker, will know how to protect his daughter Gretchen."

Peering cautiously through the trees, Harkaway saw a strikingly handsome girl, whose arm was held in a tight grip by the Frenchman, Villebois, who was assisting the Boers in their resolute invasion of Natal.

CHAPTER XXXIII.

JACK HAS A FIGHT WITH A BOER LEADER . HE RESCUES GRETCHEN—THE GOLDEN KEEPSAKE—PURSUED BY BOERS—A RIDE FOR LIFE.

THE Frenchman, in spite of the protestations of the girl, Gretchen Shalker, was not to be shaken off.

He declared that if she would not return his affections he would kill her, adding that he had spoken to her father, who favoured his suit.

Always ready to protect a woman in distress, no matter what the risk might be to himself, Harkaway advanced fearlessly, and made himself visible to the couple.

Villebois, with the vanity peculiar to his countrymen, always wore a sword buckled round his waist.

He only took it off when going into action, for fear that it might attract the attention of the enemy.

"Liberate that girl, sir," exclaimed Jack; "and give an account of your outrageous conduct to me."

"To you!" repeated the Frenchman, with a sneer. "Who are you? We have met before, and I hear that you are in command of a body of Irregular Light Horse. Such a man we regard as a guerilla, and not a regular fighter."

"You're entitled to your own opinion, but I hold the contrary to be the case. We form a part of the regular British army, and are under the same discipline, subject to the orders of our commander-in-chief."

"Do you know what we do with such men when we catch them?"

"You and the Boers you serve for pay—not from patriotism—are capable of any atrocity. You are only fit to loaf about the taverns of a French garrison town or prance on the boulevards of Paris."

Villebois was a short, thick-set, bull-headed, fussy little Frenchman, with a red face and a spiked moustache.

Harkaway's uncomplimentary retort angered him extremely, and he danced about like a bear on hot bricks, releasing Gretchen, and gesticulating wildly.

"We hang them. sir," he cried. "That's what we do with Buller's Irregular Horse; so you had best look out for your precious neck if you value it. I command you to place your rifle at my feet; if you refuse, I shall run you through with my rapier."

He drew his sword as he spoke, and flourished it in the air, making rapid passes and thrusts at nothing in particular.

The scene was so ludicrous that even Gretchen could not refrain from smiling, and the Frenchman was compelled to stop his capering when he saw his image reflected in in the pond.

"Let me put the case in another way, Monsieur," said Jack calmly. "Suppose you hand over that sword of yours, to avoid getting a bullet in your thick head."

"What! You threaten to shoot me—me! General Villebois of the Boer Army. I never heard of such audacity."

"Perhaps not; but I'm going to do it all the same, if you do not comply with my request. Look sharp; I can't waste my time here."

The sight of Jack's rifle raised in the air, and the barrel gleaming in the bright sunshine, convinced Villebois that the intruder on his privacy was in earnest.

Reluctantly he unbuckled his sword, and was about to hand it to his antagonist, when a treacherous idea seized him.

Thrown off his guard by the apparent submission of the Frenchman, Jack had dropped his rifle on the grass.

Seeing his advantage the Frenchman ignobly lunged at Harkaway, intending to spit him through the body like a bird; but the scout, perceiving his design, stepped nimbly on one side, and, coming to close quarters with the Gaul, struggled fiercely with him for the possession of the sword.

While the issue of the contest was hanging in the balance, Gretchen Shalker pluckily picked up Jack's rifle.

She was deeply interested in the handsome young Englishman, who had so gallantly come to her rescue, and was resolved to save him at all hazards.

She put the muzzle of the gun close to Villebois' breast, which alarmed him to such an extent that he fell back, leaving his sword in Harkaway's hand.

"I'll teach you a lesson for this, my good fellow, and you richly deserve it, for you basely attempted to take my life when you saw I was unarmed," exclaimed Jack, setting his teeth firmly together.

"Mercy! mercy!" pleaded the Frenchman. "It was only a little trick to frighten you. I will not play any more like that."

"I don't think you will," replied Harkaway. "It is my turn to do a bit of acting. I'm going to cut off one of your ears, so that I shall know you again when we meet. Which shall it be, right or left?"

"Oh, horror! You will spoil my beauty. Do not do a thing like that."

"I shall also give you a prick in the right arm, to render it useless for a while. You will be a Boer ornament until it gets well, and draw your pay for doing nothing."

Harkaway was an expert swordsman.

The weapon flashed twice in the air, with the rapidity of lightning.

At the first stroke the Frenchman lost his left ear, which was sliced off close to his head; the second wounded him in the right arm above the elbow, and he sank to the ground, bewailing his fate.

The blood flowed freely.

Jack tore a piece of stuff from his tunic, and bound up his wound, but the little man collapsed, and fainted away like a woman.

Now Harkaway had time to turn his attention to Gretchen, who smilingly and blushingly presented him with his rifle, thanking him for what he had done on her behalf.

"I think I have to thank you," said Jack. "Your presence of mind did me a good turn. You never know how to take a Boer or a Frenchman. They'll have you in some way if they can."

"Take this ring, and wear it, for my sake," exclaimed Gretchen, drawing a plain gold ring from her finger set with one diamond, which, from its lustre, was a stone of price. "It has my name engraved on it, and, when you are far away, you will perhaps bestow a thought upon the humble Boer maiden whom you saved to-day from a man I detest the sight of."

Accepting the ring, Jack put it on his finger, feeling rather proud of the present, and reflecting that, if he had done nothing else, he had made a friend.

"I have nothing to give you in return," he remarked. "Soldiers in war-time don't wear jewellery, but it shall be a keepsake, and in return I will give you a valuable hint."

"What is that?" asked Gretchen, adding: "Oh, how I wish this terrible war was over!"

"I am Captain Harkaway, of the War Scouts," continued Jack. "You must not betray my confidence. I am going to attack your father's farm to-night and blow it up. If you and any females you have in the house are wise, you will leave on some pretext before sunset, and seek shelter elsewhere."

"There is a place a few miles off, called the Lodge. Our cattle graze close by; we make butter and cheese there. It will be a good refuge. But hark!"

Harkaway put his hand to his ear and listened.

"Do you not hear the tramp of horses, Captain Harkaway?" queried Gretchen, in alarm.

"Most distinctly, and I must be off at the double," answered Harkaway. "Farewell, fraulein."

Their hands met in a cordial grasp, and Jack, inspired with the gallantry of a soldier, could not resist the temptation of pressing his lips to hers.

It was a parting kiss, to which the girl made no objection.

The next instant he was bounding over the plain like a deer, to the spot where he had left his horse lying on the ground.

"Up and away, my beauty!" he cried, springing lightly into the saddle.

He was satisfied with what he had done.

His quick eyes had taken in the bearings of Shalker's farm, and he had seen the exact position of their machine-gun; he knew its size and its firing power.

He had made Villebois a one-eared man, and secured the gratitude of the Boer maiden.

Suddenly loud shouts were borne towards him on the breeze, and he heard the ping of a bullet as it whistled past his ear.

He patted his horse's neck, and leaning forward, said in her ear:

"Keep it up; this is a ride for life."

The animal seemed to understand his words, for it quickened its pace, and went on at racing speed.

Dropping the reins, Harkaway unslung his rifle, just as another bullet tore through the brim of his hat, and making a half-turn, he saw that he was pursued by half-a-dozen well-mounted Boers.

Without slackening speed he took a quick aim at the leading horseman, and had the satisfaction of seeing him throw up his arms and fall from the saddle.

It was a difficult feat, but Jack could fire as well on the back of a running horse as he could on foot.

The chase was not yet over, for the remaining Boers urged on their horses, undeterred by the fate of their comrade.

CHAPTER XXXIV.

JACK'S HORSE FALLS, AND HE IS AT THE MERCY OF HIS PURSUERS—CORNSTALK AND MAORI COME TO HIS AID—A TRAITOR IN THE CAMP—DEFIANCE.

THE ground over which Harkaway was travelling happened to be uneven.

He had to avoid boulders which were lying about, so that he could not go in a straight line as the bird flies.

Still he was better mounted than the Boers, and succeeded in getting out of range.

The bullets no longer reached him, and he was congratulating himself, when his horse put its foot into a small hole, and stumbling, fell to the ground.

Being a rough rider, Jack was accustomed to this sort of thing, and alighted on his feet.

He took a rapid glance at his pursuers, who had gained upon him, and were once more within range.

It was an awkward situation, which he did not like at all.

If he remounted, there was the danger of being shot before he could get the horse into its stride once more; so, instead of making the animal get up, he told it to lie still, and crouching down under its belly, prepared to receive the onslaught of his foes, they being now only five in number.

There was nothing to be seen of Jack except his helmet, and a pair of eyes gleaming underneath, his rifle resting on the side of his horse.

The Boers were not riding all together.

One was ahead.

Three rode side by side, and the fifth brought up the rear.

Bang! Whiz!

The foremost Boer was firing as quickly as he could, but owing to the rate at which he was going he could not take accurate aim.

Thinking it time to reply, Jack favoured him with a ball from his Lee-Metford, and brought down his horse, the rider being hurled to the ground with great force.

Before the Boer could struggle to his feet, he received his death wound, and sank like a log by the side of his steed, both of them dyeing the sandy soil with their blood.

Undaunted, the other Boers pressed on, firing as they came.

Jack succeeded in killing one, when a couple of bullets in quick succession struck his horse, mortally wounding it.

In its dying agony the unfortunate beast kicked Jack on the side of the head, partially stunning him.

He sat dazed, still holding his rifle, but unable to use it.

It was a terrible position for the scout to be placed in.

Three Boers were riding down upon him, firing every quarter of a minute.

He knew what was going on, but was nerveless from the effect of the blow, and gave himself up for lost.

"Oh, for a little strength!" he gasped. "I feel half paralysed. That kick from the horse did it. But I will not give in like this; the mind and the will shall triumph over the body, and conquer pain."

His pluck gained the mastery.

Crouching as before, he sighted his rifle and fired, covering the foremost Boer, as he thought.

His eyes were misty, however, and his hand trembled, which made it no wonder that he missed his mark.

The dead horse was riddled with bullets, but its body protected the captain of the War Scouts.

This could not last long.

Jack kept on discharging his rifle; but it might as well have been a toy gun, for all the harm it did the enemy.

He could not shoot with any effect, and he felt that the moment was slowly and surely coming when he would be laid low by a ball from a Mauser.

"Fortune has failed me," he murmured, sadly, "but I will keep on firing so long as I have a cartridge in my bandolier, and when the end comes, they can only say I died fighting."

Immediately after he had made this speech to himself, a shaggy-haired, bearded Boer appeared before him.

His horse had stopped, his rifle was in his hand, and he cried in a loud voice:

"Surrender!"

The other Boers could be seen riding up, and Jack knew that if he hit the one in front of him, those behind would revenge his death.

"All right, old chap," said Jack, who was beginning to recover himself. "I suppose I must give in; but I haven't shown the white flag."

"Ah!" replied the Boer, with a grim smile, "you left that in camp, eh? A rooinek should always carry his white flag about with him. Your men find it so useful. We learnt the trick from you at Majuba."

"Don't be insolent. You would not talk to me like that if we met on equal terms."

"It is not for you to talk at all. You are my prisoner. Hands up!"

The Boer had only time to utter these words before the sharp crack of a rifle was heard, and a bullet crashed through his brain, knocking him out of his saddle as clean as a whistle.

Other shots followed, coming from the south.

Venturing to look up, Jack saw two more Boers fall, while the last turned round and galloped for home with the utmost speed.

It was an unexpected deliverance, and for the life of him he could not tell from whence it came, until he got up, reversing his position, and beheld two of his scouts.

One a New Zealander, who was known as Maori; the other a Queenslander, called Cornstalk.

They were both tall, splendidly - made fellows, strong as giants.

Each held the rank of lieutenant in the War Scouts, and were so devoted to Harkaway that they would follow him anywhere.

Brought up in the wilds of their native lands, they were as cunning as foxes in the matter of scouting.

"Cor-ee-ee!" shouted the Australian, uttering the peculiar call of a man who is lost in the bush.

"Come on," replied Harkaway. "Hurrah for the flag!"

In a few minutes the Colonials were by his side, and they shook hands together.

"Did the beggars hit you?" asked Cornstalk, perceiving that his leader's face was spattered with dry blood.

"My horse kicked me," replied Jack, explaining what had happened. "What made you leave the camp?"

"Nothing much," answered the Queenslander. "The horses wanted exercising, and we thought we'd have a ride just to give them a bit of a pipe-opener. We met Kanuck and the corporal going home, and they told us that you had gone on to take in the farm, so we thought we'd follow you, to see fair play."

"Nothing wrong in that, captain, I hope?" remarked Maori. "It wasn't disobedience of orders."

"Say no more about it," replied Harkaway. "I don't like free scouting, and you might have waited until I came back. Your horses will want all their wind to-night."

"We are all there when we are wanted, cap," continued Cornstalk. "You will never find us behind in the hour of danger, or when duty calls."

"I know that," said Jack cheerfully. "Better or truer men never lived. Which of you two will give me a ride? Your horse is big enough to carry double, Cornstalk."

"Get into the saddle, and I'll lay hold of the tail," answered the Queenslander, politely.

Jack would not accept this offer.

He jumped up behind, put his hands on Cornstalk's shoulders, and the horses started at a trot for the camp under the Drakensberg.

As they rode along Jack detailed his plan of attack on the farm.

The Boers would no doubt be awake and awaiting their coming.

They could no longer expect to take them by surprise, for recent events would put them on their mettle.

He intended his men to dismount when they got within range, and creep up under such cover as they could find, taking advantage of every stone and boulder.

They would make a feint in front to draw the Boers' fire, but the actual assault was to be made in the rear, and would not take place until near daybreak, when the Boers would be worn out with watching and suspense.

"That is all very well," exclaimed Cornstalk, "but I heard something from Corporal Potts which I think will induce you to alter your plan."

"Indeed? Has anything happened which is of importance? If so, let me hear it."

"He had not time to tell you, for you were in such a deuce of a hurry, and busy in calling him and Kanuck down for blundering. Potts caught a Kaffir named Dunko, and found in his boot a letter from Constrad to Joubert, saying that a lot of bullock waggons containing supplies would be sent to him after dusk, and I think it would be as well to waylay them."

"Certainly," replied Jack. "A dozen men will be enough for that, as the Boers can spare few to escort the convoy, which will be principally in the hands of natives. I will leave you to see to this duty."

"There is another thing I should like to mention."

"Name it. I know you always keep your eyes and ears open : if you saw a hair on a bullock's tail twisted the wrong way, you would make something out of it."

"That's true," said Cornstalk, stroking his chin. "I got on to a nest of Boers at the Modder in a funny way. I spotted a trail on the grass leading to a kopje, which seemed to be deserted. Following it up, I saw a leaf from a gum-tree on the ground. There wasn't a tree to be seen for miles around.

"'Hallo!' said I to myself, 'where did this come from?' and I remembered being told that the women at the farms bring beer in jugs at night to their men in the hills. It is their custom to cover the top of the jug with leaves; and I felt sure that the hill was occupied.

"True enough, it was. I went back. We brought up a Naval gun, and the lyddite unearthed a whole commando, out of which we killed and wounded a couple of hundred. That's scouting. Now I'm going to tell you a bit more. You know Bracken, of ours : a tall, thin, sallow-faced man, with a saturnine, not to say sinister, face."

"Yes," replied Harkaway. "He is a Natal Volunteer, and had been previously in the Mounted Police. I never liked the cut of him ; but he was recommended to me, and I took him."

"This afternoon I watched him climb up the hill behind the camp. He had no gun with him, so I knew he wasn't on the hunt. I followed, without his seeing. When about two hundred feet up he met a man who was hiding behind a rock. They greeted one another, and I heard Bracken call the strange man Webb. The wind was blowing pretty rough, and I could not catch all they said; but I heard Bracken say distinctly: 'It will be all right. I have a dark lantern, and I'll flash a warning signal to the Boers when we approach Shalker's farm. That's straight.'"

"He is a traitor," said Jack, hastily, "and must be dealt with at once. Webb I know to be one of the most dangerous of the Boer agents. I met him first in Mafeking, and again in Kimberley. He has a personal hostility towards myself."

"Death is too good for him; he intends to lead us into some infernal ambush," remarked Cornstalk.

"That is the curse of this war," continued Harkaway. "We are surrounded with spies, and don't know whom to trust. I'll deal with Bracken in a way that will be a warning to others."

They had, by this time, reached the camp and dismounted, picketing their horses.

They had no tents; each man slept in his blanket, and carried his mess-tins.

They lived on what they could find during their foraging excursions.

That day they had captured some sheep, and the men were cooking the mutton over their fires, while the sentinels kept a look out.

Going to the mess to which Bracken belonged, Jack found him reading a newspaper called the *Pretoria Times*, which was an extraordinary thing to discover in the hands of a British soldier.

"Where did you get that from?" demanded Harkaway, snatching it from him. "And how comes it that you were seen just now speaking to a Boer agent? Stand up and let me hear your defence."

A dark scowl settled upon Bracken's face, which had a cadaverous appearance.

He was sitting when spoken to, but he sprang to his feet in a moment, and presented a revolver at Harkaway's head.

"By heaven," he cried, "if you touch me I'll make a corpse of you. Let me go, and we'll say quits."

Jack did not flinch, for, like Nelson, he did not know what fear was.

He stood his ground like a man, erect as a dart, and, folding his arms, looked the traitor boldly in the face.

"Now do your worst, you scoundrel," he said, defiantly.

"There's no hurry," said Bracken. "You are in my power."

CHAPTER XXXV.

BRACKEN MEETS WITH HIS DESERTS—THE ATTACK ON THE WAGGONS—BOERS CAUGHT IN THEIR OWN TRAP—THE ADVANCE ON SHALKER'S IS CHECKED.

PERHAPS Jack would not have been so much at his ease, if a side glance had not shown him that the Queenslander, Cornstalk, was creeping up behind the villain who had defied him.

The other war scouts looked on, as if they could not understand the nature of the disturbance which had so suddenly arisen between their captain and the Natal man.

"Now," continued Bracken, imprudently, "which is it to be, boss, peace or war? I am

willing to walk right out of this camp, and cry a go, if you are. Give me your word, that's all. I know you are a gentleman, and I can rely on it. If you refuse, I'll shoot, and I don't care a rap if I get a dozen bullets in my carcase the next moment. That's the kind of a settler I am."

Harkaway made no response.

"Are you deaf?" continued Bracken. "Why don't you speak? I want to know just how we stand. No fooling; don't gamble with your life."

At this moment the long, sinewy arms of Cornstalk twined round his body with a force which made him gasp for breath.

The revolver dropped from his palsied hand, and he was thrown to the ground with a crush and a jerk which broke three of his ribs. His eyes glared.

"You've got the whip-hand on me this time. Curse you!" he hissed. "Shoot, and put me out of my misery."

By this time the spot was crowded with the War Scouts, to whom Harkaway addressed a brief speech.

"My lads," he said, "this fellow has been in communication with the enemy, and intended to lure us to our doom to-night. Being discovered and taxed with his crime, he threatened my life with a pistol; but, thanks to this brave Queenslander, he has been overpowered, and is now harmless. I think that you will agree with me that he deserves death."

There was a unanimous chorus of approval and assent.

"Death to the traitor!" roared the scouts, furious with indignation. "Hang him! Shoot him! He's a wrong 'un. Chuck him on the fire!"

Jack whispered to Cornstalk, who forced the traitor on his knees, bound his hands and legs, and tied a handkerchief over his eyes.

It was a weird scene.

The scouts fell back on each side, standing in two lines.

Bracken was as hard as iron, and knew that his hour had come.

He neither whined nor begged for life.

Though in great bodily pain, a sarcastic smile curled his lip, as if he was laughing at death and making sport of the grave.

Five minutes elapsed in dread silence, this time being allowed the wretch to prepare for the other world.

Then Harkaway raised his hand.

Cornstalk, who acted the part of executioner, stepped up to the condemned man, and, halting a dozen paces from him, put a bullet in his heart.

There was a spasmodic quivering of his frame, and all was over.

The body was carried away by two men, and buried under a heap of stones, a stake being driven into the ground to mark the spot.

Mr. Fish, the special correspondent of the *Capetown Slasher*, who was with the War Scouts, and Corporal Potts had been interested witnesses of the dismal drama enacted at the foot of the Drakensberg.

"Discovery of a traitor," jotted Fish, in his notebook. "Exciting scene. Pistol pointed at Harkaway, calm as a snoek when in danger of death. Clever device of the Queenslander.

Tried, sentenced, and shot in ten minutes. Surely the quickest work ever done in history. Harkaway thoroughly up-to-date. Colonials in touch with him."

"You've got something to write about at last," observed the corporal. "We shall educate you before you have been long with us."

"My dear fellow, it has been all education for me since I came out as a special. It isn't all honey-pots and roses. Three days out of seven my stomach goes empty. I wake up every night with the cramp. There is nothing to drink but water, and that's half sand. I am blistered by the sun. All the music I get is shot and shell, and all the colour I see before my eyes is a gory red. But stay ! a word in your ear, corporal. While you were out scouting to-day a smaus paid us a visit, and from the itinerant pedlar I bought a couple of bottles of that kill-you-quick stuff they call dop, or Boer brandy. What do you say to a taste, my worthy friend ? "

"I don't know whether I will or I won't, but I'd rather," answered the corporal. " This tragic affair, and the uncertainty in which we exist, is enough to knock spots out of an abstainer. Pass the bottle quietly, and don't let anyone see you, as I have a reputation to keep up."

He got the bottle to his lips, and Maori, who was passing by, said :

"What ho ! my ancient. Up to your old tricks, are you ? "

"Only toast and water," replied the corporal, "with an infusion of lemon to give it a flavour. Quite a teetotal drink, I assure you. I have heard they are very fond of it in New Zealand. Isn't that so ? "

"Go on, you old humbug," answered Maori. "We can fight without getting up Dutch courage."

As he spoke, the sound of a bugle was heard, which was a signal for the scouts to get ready and mount.

The sun was already setting, and some miles had to be traversed before they reached the farm.

Harkaway had changed his plan, and meant to attack early, in order to intercept the waggons going to Joubert with supplies.

"That's little Andy, the famous bugler of Elands Laagte, who was afterwards stabbed by some villain in Sunnyside," remarked Maori. "He joined us this afternoon coming from Colenso."

"He is a brick," said Potts. "I knew he would never leave Captain Harkaway."

The scouts were always ready for duty at a moment's notice.

They were soon in the saddle.

Harkaway, in command, rode at the front, and they proceeded leisurely to their destination.

It was dark and cold; only a few stars being visible.

Arriving within two miles of the farm, Harkaway called a halt, and sent out Fred Dawson and Kanuck as vedettes.

Half-an-hour elapsed, when Jack's old and trusted friend, Fred Dawson, and the Canadian came galloping back.

They had gone in different directions— Fred scouting to find out if the waggons had left the farm, and, if so, ascertain their exact position.

Kanuck, on the other hand, had penetrated as near as he could to Shalker's, to see if the defenders were keeping a good look-out.

"I will hear from you first, Dawson," exclaimed Jack. "What have you to report about the waggons ? "

"There are ten of them left unattended on the veldt, three miles from the farm on the main Colenso road," answered Fred.

"Do you mean to tell me there is no one with them ? That is a most extraordinary thing, and I cannot make it out. Are you sure your eyes did not deceive you ? "

"There was not a soul about, as far as I could distinguish. The oxen had been outspanned, the Kaffir drivers had gone away, there was no Boer guard, and each waggon was covered over with a tarpaulin, to keep the contents dry, I suppose, if it should rain.

"The loads must be valuable, and my opinion is that some spying Kaffir has notified our advance to Shalker, Villebois, and Constrad, who had them halted, and called back the Boers to protect the farm, which is their main object."

Jacked looked at the Canadian, whose turn it now was to speak.

"I can't agree with Lieutenant Dawson ; his view of the case is not mine," Kanuck said. "I have ridden close up to the farm, where there is not a light to be seen, nor a voice to be heard. Shalker's, to-night, is as desolate and silent as the grave."

"Very well," continued Dawson, "I may be right after all. What you have told us does not prove anything. I suggested that the Boers with the waggons had been re-called, and your report makes it feasible that Shalker has taken the alarm, abandoned the position, and retreated south under cover of the darkness."

"You would not wait to hear all I had to say," exclaimed Kanuck, sharply. "Captain Harkaway told me it was my turn to speak, and you pulled me up short."

"By all means go on if you think we shall be any wiser when you've done. We know your sagacity, and value it highly ; but I was a scout under Baden Powell before you came from Canada."

A keen rivalry existed between the two, and they frequently had a difference of opinion, Fred thinking himself far superior to the volunteer scout from Canada West ; but they were really good friends, although they tried to outvie one another.

"Listen here, captain," exclaimed Kanuck. "I'm not given to blowing, and I don't talk tall ; but I am willing to bet a silver dollar against a brass button that those ten waggons our friend speaks of are filled with armed Boers, who have loop-holed the sides, perhaps armoured them, and are ready to fire at us as soon as we come within range."

"That's a startling theory," said Harkaway, thoughtfully.

"I'll go further than that, captain, and say that the farmhouse is just bristling with Boers, lying low. You just try to run those waggons up to our camp, and see what you'll get for your rashness. Approach the farmhouse, and look out for the deadly hail of the Maxims."

Fred Dawson could not conceal a smile; but Jack thought there was a good deal of sense in what had been advanced by the Canadian.

"We must proceed very carefully," he said, calling up Maori and Cornstalk, who, as staff officers, had been listening to the conversation, but without making any remark, adding—"Take twenty men, and run a couple of the quick-firers we brought with us down to the waggons on the left. Dawson will show the way. Pound and rake the waggons thoroughly. If they contain stores, I don't care if you burn them; if they hold men, as Kanuck suspects, do not allow a man to escape, if you can help it."

"It will be a waste of time, if I may say so," expostulated Dawson. "There is no Boer trap in that direction. Still, all I have to do is to obey orders."

"Do so, if you please, and as promptly as possible," rejoined Harkaway. "You will be ably supported by our colonial friends from Queensland and New Zealand. I will go to the rear of the waggons with the rest of the force, and cut off the retreat to the farm."

The movement was carried quickly into execution.

The scouts advanced within a thousand yards of the waggons, which, as no shot was fired from them, they began to think were harmless, as Fred did.

However, to carry out their instructions, they opened fire, and were astounded to find it instantly replied to; the sides of the waggons blazing with flashes of fire.

The scouts lost no time in seeking such shelter as they could find.

Several of their number were wounded, and for some time the action waged hotly.

The machine-guns were splendidly handled, and the cries that came from the waggons indicated that they were being rapidly turned into slaughter-houses.

At last, unable to bear the terrific and death-dealing fire poured into them by the scouts, those of the concealed Boers who remained alive leaped from the waggons, and ran for the farm, pursued by Dawson's small force.

Unfortunately for the defeated Boers, who, to their dismay, had been surprised in their own trap, they were cut off in their retreat by Harkaway.

Caught between two fires, they were shot down to a man, though they fought valiantly to the last.

The battle was not yet over, although the scouts thought that they had disposed of their foes.

While the firing was going on, a party of Boers had crept out in silence from the farm-house.

They were mounted on fleet, wiry ponies, and, completely surprising the scouts, began to fire upon them.

Harkaway rapidly reformed his men, some of whom had dismounted and lighted their pipes.

"Forward!" he shouted, "to death or victory!"

With a wild hurrah the scouts followed him, and dashed furiously at the Boers.

Kanuck's penetration had saved the scouts from a great disaster, and if they were able to defeat the fresh force brought against them, there was little doubt they would in a short time call Shalker's farm their own.

———

CHAPTER XXXVI.

A TIGHT CORNER — JACK AND THE BUGLER ARE HARD PRESSED — BOERS DEFEATED — FARMHOUSE TAKEN — THE CAPTAIN MISSING — A STRANGE COFFIN.

THE rifle-firing, which had commenced, continued on both sides. Bullets flew thick and fast, and the conflict waged furiously.

The scouts, adopting the caution of the Boers, did not expose themselves more than they could help, and so hotly did Harkaway repel the attack that the enemy were obliged to fall back, a diminution in their firing showing that many of them were badly hit.

Always anxious to be in the front, Jack galloped in advance of his men, and getting amongst some boulders, found himself surrounded by half-a-dozen of the foe. Shooting two men, he fell on the others with his bayonet, killing one and wounding another. His clothes were torn and his helmet pierced by balls, but he escaped unhurt.

His horse was not so fortunate. It had a leg broken, and fell to the ground.

Jack was fighting on foot. A bullet struck his rifle, knocking it from his hands.

Not in the least daunted by this mishap, he drew his revolver and disposed of another Boer, when his foot slipped in a pool of blood, and he rolled over on his back.

The remaining Boer darted forward, and standing over him, lowered his rifle to give him his death-blow.

It was a critical moment for Harkaway, who was entirely at the mercy of his antagonist.

"Die, you British dog!" hissed the Boer. "I have you now, accursed rooinek!"

A mist came over Jack's eyes, and everything swam before him.

In this desperate crisis of his fate, a friendly hand came to his aid.

Andy, the bugler, always kept as near Harkaway as he could. On this occasion the little fellow had lost sight of his officer for a while, but by the help of the stars he had seen him fighting among the stones, and hurried up as fast as his legs could carry him, arriving just in time to discharge his pistol at the Boer, who plunged forward with a cry of agony and never spoke again.

But Harkaway's troubles were not yet over.

Some more Boers, who were in full retreat, passed by them, but seeing that Jack and Andy were alone, they halted and began to fire at them.

Close by was a boulder, about four feet high, which formed a natural breastwork.

Crawling behind this, Jack took refuge.

Andy kept close to him.

The bullets of the Boers spattered against the rock, but without doing any harm.

Infuriated at the escape of their foes, they were bold enough to come round one corner.

Here they were met by a deadly fire.

In a minute Jack and Andy had emptied every chamber of their revolvers.

It was a fight for life, but Jack Harkaway knew that he and Andy could not hold out long against such tremendous odds.

"Run for dear life!" cried Jack, throwing his empty pistol at a Boer, and fracturing his skull. "If we get shot in the back, we can't help it, for there isn't a cartridge left."

"All right, sir," said Andy.

They made a rush for another stone.

A dozen bullets whizzed past them, but they gained shelter without being hit.

Here they found a couple of dying Boers, whose rifles and cartridge-belts they at once seized.

This enabled them to carry on the fight, and whenever a Boer showed his head over the opposite rock, they made a hole in it.

"Keep it up lively!" said Harkaway. "We are holding our own finely. These Boers must be Free Staters—they're awfully bad shots."

As he spoke a bullet from behind went so close to his ear that it made him jump.

"Down, sir!" exclaimed Andy. "We're outflanked. There is another lot of them peppering us. Fox them a bit. Pretend you are hard hit, and I'll do the same."

This advice was too good to be neglected, and the pair of them sank to the earth.

More Boers appeared upon the scene.

They were flying from the scouts, who had driven them back on all sides.

They made a last stand close to the spot where Harkaway and Andy were lying concealed.

In a minute the scouts were upon them, dealing death and destruction.

The Boers could not stand against them.

Their wild cries filled the enemy with alarm, causing them to break again and fly, Jack and Andy joining in the pursuit.

It was a dreadful night for the defenders of Shalker's farm.

They lost very heavily; two-thirds of their number being killed or wounded, as the bodies found on the veldt next day proved.

Nor did the scouts escape, as the roll proved when their names were ticked off.

Maori, the New Zealander, was wounded in the leg; Cornstalk had two flesh wounds, but Kanuck and Fred Dawson were untouched.

The enemy made no attempt to hold the farmhouse, retreating in a southerly direction.

They had laid a very cunning plot, but it had failed.

It must be admitted that the waggons were a good lure, and the flank attack was well planned, but badly executed.

The superior sagacity and irresistible dash of the scouts had been too much for them.

The scouts surrounded the farm, and Kanuck, the Canadian, volunteered to find out if it was occupied, coming back with the intelligence that it was entirely deserted, and that no sign of Boers was to be discovered in the vicinity.

Harkaway was looked for, but could not be seen.

In his absence Fred Dawson took the command, and ordered the scouts to pile arms and bivouack for the night on the veldt, being afraid that the enemy might have laid a mine in or about the house, which would blow them all up.

It was necessary to be on the look-out for every kind of artifice and stratagem.

Rain fell during the greater part of the night, making the condition of the men very uncomfortable.

But Harkaway's were used to that.

They were not feather-bed soldiers, but went to war in grim earnest, all of them declaring that camp-life, with all its dangers and hardships, was much better than being at home.

When day broke, Shalker's farm was entered, and formally taken possession of.

A search of the premises was made, but nothing whatever could be found.

There were no stores of any kind, no provisions, or munitions of war.

The large sheds which had contained them were empty, and there was no doubt that the Boers had taken them away to a safer and more convenient spot before the scouts could attack.

The Boer cunning had triumphed, and it was a great disappointment to all the men, who had hoped to gain a rich prize.

Fred Dawson, the Queenslander, the Canadian, and Mr. Fish always messed together, and they made Corporal Potts their orderly. The latter ransacked the premises, and managed to scrape together some coffee, mealies, and eggs, which, when tasted, had the flavour of antiquity about them.

They sat down at a table in the old-fashioned kitchen, and were glad to get what the corporal had provided for them.

It was now seven o'clock, and the sun was shining brightly after the rain-storm of the previous night.

Nothing had been seen or heard of Harkaway and Andy.

Jack's prolonged absence caused the scouts much uneasiness.

The dead and wounded had been brought in, and the doctor had attended to the latter.

Neither Jack nor Andy were in the list of casualties, and were reported missing.

The corporal sat down with the others, and the five men ate their breakfast in silence, occasionally glancing at the door of the kitchen, which opened on to the yard, as if they expected every moment that Jack would enter with his usual elastic step, and greet them in his hearty tone, the sound of which always made their pulses beat quicker.

It was a quaint apartment, this old Dutch kitchen, with its high ceiling and its spacious grate, its long dresser, and time-worn pots and pans hanging on the walls.

But the most striking object of all was a large-sized plain wooden coffin, the lid of which formed a shelf in a corner, while the coffin itself hung suspended from the ceiling by a couple of ropes, and came down within about six feet from the floor.

This is a general custom among the Boers, who like to have a coffin in the house, should any member of the family die suddenly.

It is used as a receptacle for dried herbs; in fact, all sorts of odds and ends are put into it.

Corporal Potts was not a nervous man, but he did not like the look of this coffin, which was hanging right in front of him, as he sat at the table eating a musty egg with the seasoned appetite of an old trooper.

It was certainly weird, and to him appeared ominous when he thought of his missing chief, Captain Harkaway.

"What's the matter with you, corporal?" asked Kanuck. "You look as if you had seen a ghost."

The corporal pointed to the coffin, and his countenance lengthened.

"That thing up there is enough to scare even an old soldier like myself. It is like a death's head at a banquet. If it's a Boer custom I don't think much of it. Positively I don't consider it decent. I wonder what they keep in it?"

"It is a kind of store cupboard, I believe," said Cornstalk. "Come to think of it, wouldn't it make a splendid hiding-place for a spy. No one would think of looking for him there; but I'm no scout if I don't have a peep, just for satisfaction."

At that moment the coffin appeared to move slowly, like the pendulum of a clock.

It might have been through the draught, for the wind was blowing freshly outside.

The motion ceased immediately, and those who had noticed it imagined they had been mistaken, for it did not stir again.

"Hold on a minute," exclaimed Fish, as the Queenslander rose and was about to get on his chair to pry into the coffin. "Before you unearth your supposed spy I want to make a sketch. You may not know that I am a bit of an artist, and if I send a rough outline to my paper, our staff man licks it into shape. Here is the idea. A Colonial in Harkaway's Scouts looking for Boer spies in a coffin. Smart men, these Colonials. Nothing escapes them, not even a fly on a blade of grass, or a beetle on the top of an ant-heap."

The Queenslander smiled and stood still, while Fish's pencil was busy on a piece of paper.

All at once they were startled by the sound of a footstep, and, looking in the direction of the door, they beheld Andy the bugler, who staggered into the room, looking as pale as death.

His khaki tunic and his shirt had been torn from his back, which was covered with blood.

He was very weak; his legs bent under him as if they were not strong enough to support the weight of his body, and, coming to a chair, he sank down upon it with a hollow groan.

Dawson did not lose a moment in going towards him, exclaiming :

"What has happened, and where is the captain?"

"I'm afraid you'll never see him again," replied Andy, feebly. "Captain Harkaway and I were captured by the Boers last night. They treated him civilly, but they have got it in for me. I was cruelly beaten with sjamboks until I fainted, and I believe they thought I was dead. They were very savage at their plan failing and being beaten last night, with such heavy loss; but I heard them boast that they had sold us a pup as far as the stores are concerned, everything being removed as soon as they heard that Harkaway's Scouts were after them."

"This is bad news," exclaimed Fred. "Which way have the Boers gone? We must follow them up, and get the captain back if we can."

"They travelled south," answered Andy; "but I don't think their laager is far off. If you could only strike a blow quickly, you might do some good, and capture the stores after all, though you may bet they will be waiting for you; and I fancy, from what I heard, they expect to be reinforced."

"That is a poor look-out for us," remarked Kanuck, "for we are not over-strong, owing to recent losses."

"We must proceed cautiously. I am not going to run into danger, you may depend upon that. Still, it is our duty to get the stores if possible, and also liberate the captain, whom they are bound to treat in an honourable way. As for reinforcements, I don't think Joubert can spare a single man from the Tugela River. He has his hands quite full with Buller on one side of him and Ladysmith on the other. However, I shall not order any advance until I have felt my way."

This was Dawson's determination, and the Colonials perfectly agreed with him.

The capture of Harkaway was a great blow to all.

His loss created a gap in the corps which could not be easily filled, though Fred Dawson, who of course took the command in the absence of his leader, was known to be prudent as well as daring.

"My boy," added Fred, who was solicitous on behalf of Andy, "it will be best for you to go to the hospital-tent at once and have your back seen to by the doctor. The brutes have cut you up terribly with their whips, and you will be on the sick-list for some days to come."

"Don't say that, sir," answered little Andy, plaintively. "I want to go with you after Captain Harkaway, who has always been a good, kind friend to me since the beginning of the war. If he had taken my advice last night the Boers would not have made us prisoners as they did. I asked him to turn back. Not he. The captain is brave even to rashness, and, pressing on after the enemy, we tumbled into a regular hornets' nest of about twenty of them."

"Take a drop of this, my gallant little fellow," said Fred, pulling out his flask.

Corporal Potts was standing close by, and evidently thinking the remark was addressed to him, replied : "I don't know whether I will or I won't, but I'd rather."

"Get out, you hardened old sinner," cried Fred Dawson; "I wasn't talking to you."

The corporal saluted and stepped back.

Beckoning to a sentry who was standing outside, Fred gave Andy into his charge, requesting that the boy should be assisted to the hospital-tent, where the surgeon could attend to him.

As soon as he was gone, Cornstalk again approached the coffin, which the others had forgotten.

Not so the Queenslander.

He was fully resolved to explore the coffin, and see what it contained.

There was no particular reason for his doing so, but it is the instinct and nature of a scout to examine everything he meets with, whether it be common or rare.

"I mean to have a go in at this box," he muttered as he got up on an old wicker-bottomed chair.

Strange to say, as he spoke the coffin began to oscillate again.

CHAPTER XXXVII.

THE SPY IN THE COFFIN—WEBB REVEALED —DUNKO TO THE RESCUE—A BOER ATTACK —SHALKER'S SINGULAR DEVICE—DAWSON IS ORDERED TO THE CROCODILE RIVER.

FRED DAWSON and the others watched the movements of Cornstalk curiously, Fish holding his note-book, ready to jot down anything that occurred.

Kanuck kept his hand on his revolver, and the corporal slung his rifle over his shoulder.

They did not expect any discovery, but they wanted to be prepared for any emergency.

It certainly was singular that the coffin, which was heavy, should keep on moving at intervals.

There was something mysterious about it which puzzled them all.

"Look out for the family cat and half-a-dozen kittens," said the corporal, laughing.

Cornstalk stretched out his arm and put his hand into the coffin, withdrawing it with a loud cry, more of surprise than alarm.

"Come out, you skunk!" he exclaimed.

There was no reply.

His companions now became deeply interested in what was going on.

"What have you got there?" enquired Dawson.

"A man," replied Cornstalk; "I felt his flesh. It may be a body for all I know; that is to say, a corpse. There is no telling until I look closer. There is a chap inside, I'll swear. If he's alive, he is lying precious low. I don't want to go too close, because he might give me a piece of lead. I'll have him, though. Look out, boys!"

Drawing his Bushman's knife from his belt, he made a slash at one of the cords which sustained the coffin.

This caused it to fall and swing in the air, it being held by only one cord, and to the astonishment of all a man dropped out, tumbling on his hands and knees, in a very ungraceful manner.

He was dressed in khaki, being evidently disguised to represent an English soldier.

One glance at his black hair and thin, cadaverous face was enough for Fred Dawson.

He made one spring at the man, clutching him by the neck, and bearing him to the ground, before he could use the pistol he grasped in his right hand.

"Webb!" he cried. "By Heaven, it's Webb! We have got the arch-traitor and spy at last; and now we have him, we'll hold him. It strikes me, he won't tell Oom Paul any more stories. If Captain Harkaway were here, his life wouldn't be worth a couple of hours' purchase. He'd have a firing party out on the veldt, and Webb would be the target. If ever there was a case for martial law, this is the one. Potts, have the kindness to bring me a piece of rope."

The corporal complied with this request, exhibiting the utmost promptitude, as if it was a pleasure to him.

Webb's arms were bound behind his back; he was lifted up, and placed upon a chair, but he did not seem in the least sullen or despairing.

On the contrary, his face wore a satisfied look, and his thin lips curled with a sarcastic smile.

"No doubt you thought yourself remarkably clever," continued Fred, "but you are bowled out. I think we shall have the pleasure of hanging you, Mr. Webb. People as a rule do not sleep in coffins. You were caught in the act of spying, and you are a well-known Secret Service agent of Kruger, who pulls the wires in Pretoria."

"He pulls them in a way that you do not like," retorted Webb, insolently. "The Englishman's dream of empire is over. Your ferryman, General Buller, has been driven across the river three times, and is as far off Ladysmith as he was three months ago."

Fish, who had gone out of the room, now came running back, looking greatly excited.

"Glorious news," he cried. "A Kaffir runner has just come in from the front. Kimberley is relieved. General French with three thousand cavalry has beaten the Boers, and Lord Roberts is going to march on Bloemfontein."

Webb's face fell as if he had received a great blow.

"How about your South African Republics now?" asked Dawson. "That's a black eye for you, my man, and you've got to have a lot more yet."

"That's nothing," answered Webb, in a tone of confidence. "The town isn't worth having."

"It's a pity you took so much trouble to besiege it; but with regard to yourself, I shall wait till sunset to see if Captain Harkaway returns; if not, I shall have you executed without further delay, and take the responsibility on myself."

Webb breathed a deep sigh of relief, as if it was at least a poor consolation to know that he had a few hours to live.

Much might happen in that time.

While there is life there is always hope, especially when you are plunged in the vortex of war.

While Dawson was considering where it would be best to place the prisoner for safety, a bugle-call sounded outside, and Kanuck, who rushed away to ascertain the cause, came back exclaiming:

"The Boers are attacking us in front. I guess we shall have hot work directly."

A dropping fire was heard.

Fred called Corporal Potts to his side, and pointing to a large cupboard at one side of the room, said:

"Give me a hand; I am going to lock the spy in there while we chase these cheeky Boers back to their laager."

"All right, sir. The beggar won't hurt inside there, he will have time to say his prayers in the dark; that is to say, if the heathen knows any."

Rising at the word of command, Webb was marched to the cupboard and ignominiously pushed in.

It was no time to stand upon ceremony, the Boers were upon them, and there was fighting to be done.

"Lie there, and gnaw your heart out, you reptile," exclaimed Dawson, locking the door, with a double turn, and putting the key in his pocket.

"I am not dead yet," hissed Webb, "and I haven't done with you. The day of reckoning has come for Harkaway, and yours is not far off."

In spite of his self-assurance, and bitter tone, Webb was ill at ease.

He heard the shouts shouting to their horses, as they galloped away in a hurry, and the crack of the rifles fell upon his ears, but it did not quicken his pulse.

He was of a lethargic nature, and it took something out of the common to stir his blood.

He did not imagine for a moment that the Boers would retake the farm.

He thought their forward movement was made to draw the scouts, and ascertain their actual strength.

Suddenly his attention was arrested by a peculiar sound overhead, which seemed to him to be a compound of knocking and sawing.

What it could be he was unable to make out.

The noise continued for fully a quarter-of-an-hour, by which time Webb's curiosity was excited to the highest pitch.

It was quite dark inside the closet, and he could not see his hand before his face.

A few flakes of whitewash fell upon his head from the ceiling; these were followed by a cloud of dust, and some instrument having been withdrawn, a ray of light from above came down through a hole.

In a few minutes the aperture was enlarged, and part of the ceiling fell in a lump at his feet.

"Are you there, baas?" asked a voice, which he recognised as that of Dunko. "They think me friendly Kaffir. I watch through the window, when the coffin come down, and fire you out. What a surprise. This Kaffir had to laugh fit to kill himself. I see you shoved into the cupboard, and when the scouts had all gone after the Boers I came up here to work a hole, so as to get you out. Now's your chance, an' no time to be lost."

"Dunko, you are worth your weight in gold. A precious stone, a diamond of the best water," replied Webb, who was highly delighted at the clever stratagem of the Kaffir.

The hour of deliverance had come, when all was dark and dismal and he least hoped for it.

Dunko having sufficiently enlarged the opening, lowered himself by means of a rope into the closet below.

It did not take him long to set Webb free, and the pair of them scrambled up into a bedroom, which had been occupied by one of the Shalker family.

The farm was deserted, except by the doctor, the wounded, and the Red Cross assistants, and, looking out of the window,

Webb saw in the far distance the scouts driving the Boers before them.

Webb and Dunko walked downstairs as boldly as if the place belonged to them, and, going out of a side door, entered the garden, which a week or two before had been in a flourishing condition.

Now the fruit was all plucked from the trees, and the beautiful flowers trodden down by the iron heels of the soldiers.

The walls of the house were perforated with bullets, and the once smiling homestead presented a scene of desolation.

Emerging from the garden, the spy and the Kaffir walked quickly over the veldt, and were soon lost to sight.

"What made you come after me?" asked Webb.

"Shalker thought you might get into trouble," answered Dunko, "so he sent me to look after you, for he knows I am the most artful Kaffir in these parts. The scouts did not suspect me. All I had to do was to keep out of Dawson's way. He's always down on me like a vulture. It was a puzzle to me where you were spying. I never thought of looking inside that coffin—for cunning, that takes the mealie. For being artful, there is only one that can beat you, and that's the debble."

"Tell me something I don't know," said Webb, with a smile. "Where have the Boers taken Captain Harkaway?"

"He is still at the Lodge with Shalker, Vilbois, and the rest. I heard Baas Shalker say that he was a distinguished prisoner."

"Yes," remarked Webb, thoughtfully. "He is so well known in the English service that it would not do to play tricks with him. After a slight detention, he will have to be sent on to Pretoria as a prisoner of war, unless I can get my knife into him at some convenient opportunity. Ah! well, that will cut his military career short."

"Mrs. Steiner has come to the Lodge on a visit to Gretchen."

"Confound that woman!" cried Webb, sharply. "I heard she was coming, and I dreaded it. She hates me like poison, simply because I am Harkaway's foe, he being a young man she cares for, and, in addition, I did her the honour to tell her I loved her, which sentiment she repelled with scorn."

"You did more than that, baas," replied Dunko, with a broad grin. "If I remember right, you tried to cut her lilywhite throat, an' another time you shoot her in the back. That not the way we make love to Zulu girl, baas."

Webb gave vent to an exclamation of impatience.

"That feeling, as far as I am concerned, is all over," he observed, biting his lip.

"It wouldn't be no use if it wasn't—yah! yah!" laughed the Kaffir.

"Hold your tongue," shouted Webb, angrily. "Keep that mealie trap of yours shut when I am talking. Mrs. Steiner is rich and powerful. She will be a prize for any man who gets her. Now her disreputable husband, Hartz, is dead, she will try to baffle me in my plots against Harkaway. I wish the pair of them were cleared out of my path. They are two individuals in this world I have no possible use for."

"WHEN YOU HEAR THE FIRST SHOT FIRED BY THE REDNECKS, START THE HORSE!" EXCLAIMED LAUBERG."

No. 9.

"Shalker and Villebois got a big thing on for the scouts, baas."

"What's that? I have heard of nothing."

"There is a young Boer coming from Pretoria who has been brought up in London and Paris. He is the same age, an' just as like Captain Harkaway as two peas."

"What's the idea?" asked Webb, eagerly. "What do you know?"

"Shalker say, send this fellow whose name is Pretorious to the scouts. They will take him for Harkaway. He will play his part like a man acting in a play, an' he will lead the scouts into an ambush prepared for them by the Boers. A mine will be laid near the Lodge, and when the scouts get there it will explode, and blow them all sky-high. Not one scout to be left alive, Shalker say. Then this young Pretorious, who is the double of Harkaway, will be sent to the Modder River, and lead some of Methuen's men to destruction."

"It will take a clever man with an iron nerve to carry out that programme," replied Webb, "though I admit the plan is a good one. Experienced spy as I am, I frankly confess I would not like to take the job on for a pension. However, it does not interest me. Shalker and Villebois can carry on what intrigues they please. All I want is to settle Belle Steiner and Jack Harkaway."

"Both of them, baas?"

"Most decidedly. I couple them together, and I will never rest until my thirst for vengeance is quenched."

"Look out, baas!" Dunko exclaimed, all at once. "Scouts comin' back this way. They have driven off the Boers. Dodge behind one of these rocks. They have had you once to-day, an' I reckon you don't want to be taken a second time; I'm sure this Kaffir doesn't want any scouts fooling round him."

Webb, who was entirely of Dunko's opinion, lost no time in crouching down behind a boulder.

He and the Kaffir laid so low that their bodies were only perceptible at a close inspection.

Ten minutes afterwards the scouts passed within a couple of hundred yards of the spot, on their return to the farm, yet they did not notice the two men they would have been so glad to get hold of.

Fred Dawson and Cornstalk were riding together.

"I could have sworn I saw two persons standing in this locality," said Fred; "yet I must have been deceived, unless the ground has opened and swallowed them up."

"You cannot help optical delusions when the sun shines on the veldt," replied Cornstalk. "One day I fancied I beheld a troop of horse, but when I came near there was nothing. Another day I saw a vlei, as they call a pool. Being thirsty, I ran to it; imagine my disgust when I couldn't find any water."

"That is so," answered Fred, adding: "I can't make out what induced the Boers to attack us just now. They fled like a lot of sheep, and had no more fight in them than hens. I have come to the conclusion that they are no good unless they are entrenched."

"They wished to draw us into an ambush."

"That is what I thought, and for that reason I ordered a retreat, instead of pursuing them to their new hiding-place, where they have piled up their stores."

"We must do a bit of scouting, and make sure of our ground before we attempt to rush them."

"I wish Harkaway was here," said Fred. "I feel lost without him. His capture has taken all the go out of me. It's a pity he will be so headstrong. The only consolation I have rests in knowing that I shall have the satisfaction in a short time of shooting that unmitigated scoundrel, Webb."

"If all you have told me about him is true, he deserves a thousand deaths."

"I know he has done us a lot of harm as a spy, and he is a thief as well," Dawson went on. "He robbed one of his own generals, Villebois, of a box of diamonds, and he tried to steal the plan of a mine in Rhodesia, supposed to be worth millions, which belongs to Harkaway and myself. I got it back from that thundering rogue Dunko, the Kaffir, and thank goodness! it is in my possession now."

"Do you think you will ever be able to realise on it?"

"If we are alive when the war is over, we intend to do our level best."

"I wish you jolly good luck," exclaimed Cornstalk, "and if you want a third partner, my friend, who isn't afraid of work, you can count on me. I know something about mining, for I had two years of it in the Coolgardie district."

By this time they had reached the farm.

Dismounting, they handed their horses to a Kaffir, and walked into the house.

Corporal Potts was seated at the kitchen table with a long-necked bottle in front of him.

He had drawn the cork, and was smelling the contents, with a puzzled look on his face.

"What have you got there, corporal?" asked Fred.

"I'll be shot if I know, sir," replied Potts. "When a youngster I was apprenticed to the bottling trade, and I bottled every sort of fermented liquor—never touching a drop, you know, sir, always on the strict teetotal; whereby I gained the respect of my employers, and had my salary raised regular every month—but this stuff is a teaser. I found it on a shelf in the scullery, and thinking it might do some poor wounded trooper good, I brought it in here to sample the contents."

"Why don't you do so?"

"Because I'm afraid of it. It is labelled 'Peach,' but it smells like prussic acid. Fools rush in where angels fear to tread. You have a go at it, sir."

"Thank you," said Fred, "that is paying me a poor compliment. I'd rather you were poisoned than me. Sample it yourself."

"I don't know whether I will or I won't, but I'd rather," answered the corporal, raising the bottle to his lips.

He took a sip.

His eyes sparkled, and he seemed to like it.

He indulged in another, which partook of the nature of a long drink.

"Very good," he muttered, in a tone of approval. "It's peach brandy. I will put it away, to be used on a future occasion."

"I thought you were going to take it to the hospital-tent?"

"It's too strong for the wounded, far too strong. I wouldn't be guilty of such an atrocity. Why, sir, it would take the roof off any sick soldier's head. That wouldn't do at all. I should have thought you would have known better, with all your experience."

The corporal carefully replaced the bottle on the shelf from which he had taken it.

Fred Dawson went to the cupboard where he had left Webb, and unlocked the door.

"I'll have this rascal shot at once," he exclaimed.

Flinging back the door, with a violent jerk, he could not conceal his vexation at finding the place empty.

A glance at the hole in the ceiling, through which the daylight glimmered, showed him how the exit had been contrived.

"The prisoner has escaped during our absence!" he cried. "I have never been so sold in my life before."

"He must have had an accomplice," said Cornstalk. "A man with his arms bound couldn't have made that hole; besides, there is a rope hanging, which has been lowered from the top."

"Hang the luck. It is a real misfortune that such a fellow should have got away. He is the king of spies. I don't care where you go, you will not find another to equal him. In our service he would have been worth his weight in gold. He is fertile in artifices, and his disguises are unique."

"The execution is postponed owing to circumstances over which we have no control. The money will be returned at the doors," remarked the corporal sarcastically.

"It is nothing to make fun of," replied Dawson. "Webb would just as soon shoot you as he would me."

Mr. Fish now made his appearance, holding a large official envelope in his hand.

"The mail has just come in," he exclaimed, "and with it is something for you, endorsed by our general commanding on the Modder."

He handed the paper to Dawson, who hastily tore open the envelope and scanned the contents.

"What is this?" he cried excitedly. "Lord Methuen desires me, acting under instructions from 'Bobs,' to quit the Scouts for a time and ride across the veldt to Rhodesia with despatches of a secret and important nature, to Colonel Plumer, who is trying to cross the Crocodile River and relieve Colonel Baden-Powell in Mafeking."

"That is sudden news," observed Cornstalk.

"What shall we do without Captain Harkaway and you?" asked Kanuck, who had come in. "The command of the Scouts will fall upon our friend Cornstalk and myself."

"Two better leaders could not be found," answered Fred. "I am sorry to leave you, boys, but duty calls me."

"I call it a bit of luck," exclaimed Cornstalk. "You will have a chance of seeing where your mine is. Now is your golden opportunity."

"There is something in that; but I hate to leave you fellows, and it isn't an easy duty either, for the veldt all around Mafeking swarms with armed Boers."

Without any warning, Corporal Potts fired his revolver through the open window.

"Don't be alarmed," he shouted. "That Kaffir Dunko was looking in, listening to all we had to say. I missed him, worse luck."

"That makes it bad for me," replied Dawson. "He is Webb's Kaffir, and we have been spied upon again. I shall have a few foes in the rear, as well as in front."

Before the sun sank upon Shalker's farm Fred Dawson, having taken leave of his companions, was riding slowly over the veldt, on his perilous mission to the Crocodile River.

CHAPTER XXXVIII.

CAPTAIN HARKAWAY'S DOUBLE—MRS. STEINER ARRIVES AND IS DECEIVED BY PRETORIOUS — HER INTERVIEW WITH JACK—GRETCHEN'S RING—JEALOUSY AND REVENGE.

THE LODGE, which was the name Shalker had given his dairy farm, was a spacious, one-storeyed building of the bungalow description: but what it lacked in height it made up for in underground chambers, where he could store any quantity of cheeses and other goods.

Here he had placed the ammunition and provisions that Harkaway's War Scouts had failed to capture.

The Lodge was defended by two skilfully concealed masked batteries of quick-firing guns and a double row of rifle pits.

Shalker, Constrad, and Vilbois felt perfectly certain that they could hold their own, if attacked by ten times their number.

At the same time they did not dare to move the hidden supplies towards Joubert's base of operations, for fear that the scouts would intercept them.

It was therefore necessary that they should destroy Harkaway's force before they could move ahead.

There was no time to be lost either, for Mrs. Steiner, who was one of the leading Boer agents, had arrived at the Lodge with an imperative message to the effect that the Boers around Ladysmith were in want of shell, cartridges, and food.

Captain Harkaway, who had been taken prisoner by Shalker's Boers, after a desperate resistance, was placed in solitary confinement in a shed which had been used for cattle.

Two sentries kept watch over him night and day.

He was supplied with good food, and given books to pass away the time before he could be sent on to Pretoria.

It was a satisfaction to him to know that his life was safe, though he chafed and fretted at being separated from his men.

Strict orders were given by Shalker that he was to be seen by no one; but Gretchen, whom he had befriended, induced his guards to give him delicacies, such as wine, chickens and fruit.

He longed to hear news from the outside world, for he felt that the campaign was about to take a new turn.

Yet none came to him, for if he spoke to the sentry the Boer turned a deaf ear.

Shortly before the arrival of Mrs. Steiner at the Lodge, Constrad, who had been away at headquarters, came in with a young Boer named Pretorious, who was the person spoken of by Dunko to Webb.

Directly Constrad saw his marvellous resemblance in every respect to Harkaway, he suggested a scheme to Joubert, which was highly approved of.

This was that he should take Pretorious back with him to the Lodge and send him to the scouts, pretending that he had escaped.

Pretorious would then lead them against the masked batteries and rifle pits, which would insure their destruction.

It was a dangerous task for the young Boer to undertake, but he was of a daring nature, and did not shrink from the ordeal.

Constrad, Villebois (who carried his arm in a sling, and spent half his time in lamenting the loss of his ear, devoted the other half to cursing Harkaway for being the author of the mischief), and Pretorious were chatting together in a front room, overlooking a pretty garden, when Shalker entered.

"Our friend, Mrs. Steiner, has come," he exclaimed. "She knows Captain Harkaway, and I want to put Pretorious to the test."

"I understand," answered Constrad. "If he deceives her, he will be a sure card to play on the scouts."

"What is her mission to us?" asked Villebois.

"The general is getting impatient. She brings orders that if we cannot convoy the stores to the front in three days, we are to destroy them and fall back on the main body," said Shalker.

"It would be a pity."

"Call it a misfortune. We must avoid it by every means in our power."

"I'll do it!" exclaimed Pretorious. "These fighting fiends, as you call Harkaway's Scouts, shall be led by me into a death-trap."

The young Boer, who was very proud of his personal appearance, had attired himself in khaki uniform and a slouch hat taken from the English.

Anyone would have supposed him to be British, and there was no trace of the Dutch accent about his speech.

Suddenly the door opened, and Mrs. Steiner entered.

She bowed to the three Boer leaders, but started back in utter astonishment when she beheld Pretorious.

"You did not tell me Captain Harkaway was here," she cried.

"The fact escaped my memory," replied Shalker, carelessly. "He is a prisoner on parole, and you see we are treating him in a friendly manner."

"I'm glad of that," she said, while a smile came over her face. "We are old friends, though on different sides in this war. The last time we met was near the Modder River. You remember what happened on that occasion. Tell these officers what I did for you then."

This remark was addressed to the young Boer, and somewhat confused him, as he knew nothing about it.

"Really," he said, simpering, as he stroked his moustache, "I should not like to let them know too much. We are on different sides you know, as you justly observed."

"That does not matter," she exclaimed disdainfully. "I am only responsible to President Kruger for my actions."

"That is true," stammered Pretorious. "You are behind the scenes, yet you are very powerful."

"Be not afraid. Speak out. I owed you a debt of gratitude. How did I repay it?"

"No, no, do not press me."

"I insist upon it. What is there to be ashamed of? Before that, what happened in Pretoria, when that double-dyed scoundrel, Webb, brought you in shut up in a wooden cage?"

"I—I—got out, didn't I?" said Pretorious, looking perfectly idiotic.

"What made Mr. Kruger give you a pass?" Mrs. Steiner continued. "Who stole it, and who gave it back to you? Answer me! Quick! I'm not to be trifled with. Your fate is in my hands now."

"For certain reasons my lips are sealed," answered Pretorious, walking to the door as if he wanted to get away.

She extended her arm, and barred his progress.

"There is some fraud here," she said, giving him a penetrating look.

"Ha, ha!" laughed Shalker. "Our young friend, Pretorious, has stood the test very well. Allow me to introduce to you Captain Harkaway's double."

"His double?" repeated Mrs. Steiner. "It is an extraordinary similarity indeed. Where is the real man? What does it all mean?"

Shalker explained the plan devised by Constrad and himself to deceive and ruin the scouts.

"If we can clear these bloodhounds off our track," he added, "there will be no difficulty in taking up the convoy. I hope you will pardon us for playing a game with you? Surely, if you were taken in the scouts will be also."

"Say no more!" she exclaimed. "It is an excellent trick, and does not concern me. My stay here will be short, as Cronje's recent defeat has complicated matters for us, and I must go to Kimberley. Can I see Captain Harkaway before I depart?"

"I am sorry I cannot gratify your wish. Your sympathy with the captain renders it inadvisable that you should meet."

She looked annoyed, and bit her lip.

"Suppose I insist?" she asked.

"I should still consider it my duty to refuse you," replied Shalker, firmly. "I wish you a pleasant time in Kimberley. Now it is relieved it will be quite gay from Jones Street to the Gardens. The Club, the Diamond Market, the Central, the Queen's, the Grand Hotels will be full of life; while up at Kenilworth, the long avenues of gum-trees will glisten with Chinese lanterns, and the Masonic Hall will be gay with bunting; while Mr. Cecil Rhodes——"

She interrupted him with an impatient gesture.

"You may change the subject as much as you please," she exclaimed, "but I tell you to your face, Shalker, that I will see Captain Harkaway, whether you like it or not."

"It must be in our presence then," rejoined the Boer.

"Do you suppose that I should conspire with him against the Republic?" she enquired.

"Such a contingency has occurred to me."

"You are insolent. I did not expect such treatment from you, after knowing your family so long, and being a friend of your wife and daughter Gretchen."

"Forgive me if I appear harsh. Harkaway is an important prisoner, and must not be tampered with. What you have done for him in the past, you may try to repeat in the future. I know the nature of a woman. However, I will order him to be brought in here."

"Thank you," she ejaculated coldly.

"Pretorious, be good enough to retire for a time. I do not wish you and the captain to meet," continued Shalker.

"Do you think we should frighten one another?" asked the young Boer. "For my part, I should like to have a look at this man who has the imprudence to resemble me so closely."

"Captain Harkaway cannot help the misfortune," observed Mrs. Steiner, sarcastically. It is not nice for a gentleman to be caricatured by a monkey."

At this shot Pretorious changed colour, and quitted the apartment in a hurry, fearing that the lady might launch some more of her caustic wit at him.

Constrad was despatched to the prisoner, with whom he returned in a few minutes.

Jack was pale and careworn, but his manner remained unchanged.

He was, as usual, upright and dignified.

When he saw Mrs. Steiner, his countenance lighted up.

Her presence was a good sign, and a promise of hope for him.

He advanced quickly, extending his hand.

Her lips parted with a smile, her wondrous eyes beamed upon him.

She was about to take it, when she stopped short and her face darkened.

On one of his fingers she saw the ring which Miss Shalker had given him when he protected her from Villebois.

The name "Gretchen" engraved on the stone was distinctly visible, and a shudder ran through her as she came to the natural conclusion that he cared for the girl, or he would not wear her ring.

"I meet you again under unhappy circumstances," Jack exclaimed. "For me, war has its ups and downs. I thank you for your kindness in wishing to see me."

"I only wished to ask you if you are well treated," Mrs. Steiner replied, drawing herself up haughtily, and looking as frigid as an icicle, while the corners of her mouth twitched.

"Oh, yes; I have nothing to complain of."

"That is all. You can go back to your prison now. I have nothing more to say to you."

"Have I done anything to offend you?" he asked in surprise.

Making no answer, Mrs. Steiner turned her back on him, and entered into conversation with Shalker as to the probable course the war would take, now that Cronje had been forced to retire from the trenches of Magersfontein.

Constrad motioned to Jack to march out of the room, which he did, surprised and pained at the chilling result of his interview with Mrs. Steiner.

As he passed Villebois the Frenchman hissed at him:

"Ha! Sacré! English brute!" he cried, eyeing him vindictively. "Give me back my ear you crop off."

"When I meet you again," replied Jack, "I will cut off the other, so as to make your head level. A French donkey without ears would be a novelty in the Boer army."

"You add insult to injury!" roared Villebois, foaming at the mouth. "I will strike you the coward's blow!"

He carried a stick in the hand of the uninjured arm, and raised it to deal Harkaway a blow, but before the weapon could descend, Mrs. Steiner, who had been watching them with the eyes of an eagle, ran forward, and, snatching the stick from Villebois, hit him on the head with such effect that he fell on his knees.

"Mercy," cried the Frenchman. "The woman will kill me. She is a tigress."

"You are a disgrace to the name of officer," Mrs. Steiner exclaimed. "If this is the way you treat a prisoner, you ought to be turned out of the service. For shame! You are not a man, but a cur."

The Frenchman slunk into a corner, sat on a chair, and rubbed his head.

Jack bowed his acknowledgments and followed Constrad.

Mrs. Steiner bent her eyes upon him, but he did not turn.

She again joined Shalker, and continued talking as if nothing had happened, until, a minute or two later, Webb arrived with Dunko, after his escape from the farm.

Mrs. Steiner looked disdainfully at the spy, but did not condescend to speak.

She then brushed rudely past him, and walked from the room.

"I'll bring your pride down, my lady, some of these fine days," muttered Webb, savagely.

"Did you glean any news down at the old place?" asked Shalker.

"Nothing much," replied Webb. "The scouts detected me, and I should have been shot if Dunko hadn't come to my rescue. The scouts were afraid to attack. Their second in command, Dawson, has started on a journey to Rhodesia, with a despatch for Colonel Plumer."

"We must have that," cried Shalker.

"Just what I thought," responded Webb.

"Has he taken any men with him?"

"No. He is quite alone; but then he knows the veldt as well as you or I do. If you can spare three of your Boers, Dunko and I will go after Dawson; and it will be hard if we don't overtake him before he has gone two days' journey."

"Right. You shall have them. It will be a good thing to stop his merry career. The scouts won't be much good without their captain and lieutenant."

"A couple of Colonials are at their head now, but I hear you are going to give them a new leader, in the person of the young Boer Pretorious. I met him as I came in. He is the shadow of Harkaway. Smash them up, I say. When I've had a bit of grub and some rest, I'll be after Dawson, and lay him out as dead as mutton."

"I don't like the advance of Roberts and Kitchener into the Free State," observed Shalker.

"I'm not going to talk war," said Webb, impatiently. "We have risked everything in our bold defiance of the British. If we lose, we must make the best of it."

Saying this, with a careless air, Webb left Shalker alone.

The Boer leader was plunged in deep thought, and his brow was wrinkled with care. He had staked all upon the issue of the conflict.

If the armies of Cronje and Joubert were beaten, and the British flag floated over Pretoria, he would lose his farm, and become a beggar.

As for Webb, he was a clever adventurer, who, if he did not get shot as a spy, had money to fall back upon, could put his hand to anything, and could get on anywhere.

As the latter left the house in search of Dunko, who he wished to instruct about the pursuit of Fred Dawson, he saw Mrs. Steiner standing on the stoep.

Her beautiful face wore an angry expression.

"She's in a sweet temper about something," he muttered. "I'll keep out of her reach. I know she doesn't like me."

He was right.

Mrs. Steiner's mind was convulsed by one of the worst passions which afflict human nature, namely, jealousy, and Gretchen Shalker was the object of her aversion.

Ever since she had seen the ring on Harkaway's finger, she had been imagining all sorts of things.

Gretchen and Jack must have met, or how could the ring have come into his possession; and he must have some regard for the young Boer maiden, or he would not have kept and displayed it so openly.

Revenge on both was her paramount wish at that moment.

CHAPTER XXXIX.

GRETCHEN GIVES AN EXPLANATION—A SCENE IN THE SHED—JACK IS MADDENED —HE NEARLY KILLS WEBB—SHALKER APPEARS—BOER JUSTICE.

UNTIL that moment Belle Steiner had not realised to what an extent Harkaway had entered into her existence.

She was a free woman, and the ambition of her life was to win his affection.

There would be no inequality between them when the war was over, her presumption being that Briton and Boer would shake hands, living under a wise and liberal government.

She had actually come to Shalker's farm because she was told that Harkaway and his scouts were in the vicinity, and she wanted to watch over him.

In fact, Belle Steiner would have laid down her life for Jack if it had been necessary, and when she thought that Gretchen had crossed her path, she hated her as if she were a serpent.

Scarcely had Webb disappeared from view than Gretchen came tripping up to Belle with a dainty grace peculiar to her.

She was simply dressed, but never had she looked more charming.

"This is the doll-baby he loves," said Mrs. Steiner to herself, with a scowl of dark malignity.

"I am so glad, dear, you have left the Council Chamber, as I call it!" exclaimed Gretchen. "This horrid war is a dreadful strain upon the nerves, and I am sure you must be as heartily sick of it as I am."

"On the contrary, I like it," snapped Mrs. Steiner. "You are a namby-pamby girl; I'm a woman, and have got the soul of a man in me."

"But think, dear, of the poor fellows who are being shot down on both sides."

"That is nothing. I have only just come out of hospital. I was shot near the Modder River. In war you get used to that sort of thing. What's the difference between a man and a woman on the battlefield?"

"How disagreeable you are to-day," protested Gretchen. "Whatever is the matter with you?"

"Does that concern you?" asked Mrs. Steiner, with a sneer.

"Really, I cannot answer your question."

Mrs. Steiner seized her by the arm, gripping her so tightly that the girl winced, while the woman's hot breath fanned her cheek, as she hissed in her ear:

"Perhaps you can tell me how your ring came to be on Captain Harkaway's finger?"

"My ring," echoed Gretchen, stammering. "The captain's finger! How was it?"

"Yes, I said that. Speak, confess, unless you want me to rend you."

Making an effort, the girl wrenched herself free, and recovering from her astonishment, looked at Mrs. Steiner, half smiling, half crying.

"Oh, I begin to understand," she exclaimed. "Until this moment I had no suspicion that you and the captain were friends. Why, my dear, he and I have only met once, and then he gallantly saved me, at the risk of his own life, from the insults of General Vilbois. As a token of recognition of his services, I gave him my ring, to which I do not believe he attaches the least importance, save as a keepsake from a farmer's daughter he never expected to see again. Let me assure you, Belle, that I have no design on the captain's heart. It is no secret to anybody that I am engaged to young Berger, who is fighting under father now. You know him. Ask him if it is not true."

"If I thought otherwise I could kill you," replied Mrs. Steiner, from whose face the clouds vanished as speedily as they had arisen.

She advanced once more towards her, and imprinted a kiss upon her rosy cheek.

"We are friends now, dear," she said, mildly. "Forgive me if I have been rude, and promise that you will keep my secret."

"Oh, yes, it is safe with me."

"It may be," added Mrs. Steiner, drawing a deep sigh, "that I cherish a hopeless passion, for the brave young Englishman has not the least idea of the affection—I mean the deep interest I take in him. Time alone will show, but——" here her eyes flashed again. "I will allow no woman to come between us. If love for me should dawn upon him, I shall be happy. If not, welcome the bullets of the Rednecks, or any sudden death that fate chooses to send to a heart-broken woman."

She pressed Gretchen's hand with an intense, nervous fervour, and hurried away to the rear of the Lodge, where the shed was situated in which Jack was imprisoned, and in front of which the young Boer soldier Berger, of whom Gretchen had just spoken, was standing as sentry.

Having met her on previous occasions, Berger saluted respectfully, and when she came up, shook hands.

"I hope you have brought us some news, madam, which will enable us to get the best of these War Scouts, who deserve hanging, in my opinion," he exclaimed.

"What do you object to in them?" Mrs. Steiner enquired.

"They are not the English Tommies at all," replied Berger. "People call them Colonials, and we've had no quarrel with them. Why should they fight in the battles of the British? It is wrong for the Scotch and the Irish to come against us, but these Colonials—*Ach Gott!*—I hate them."

"These men come from countries which belong to the British Empire, many, many thousand miles away."

"Is England, then, so very big?" asked the poor, ignorant Boer youth, who knew of nothing outside the Transvaal, opening his large grey eyes in surprise. "I thought England was a little island."

"Ah!" said Mrs. Steiner, "I have no time to explain to you, but England, through her colonies and possessions, is the richest, mightiest, and grandest Empire the world has ever seen. The sun never sets on her dominions, and if she absorbs the Dutch Republics her flag will float from Cape Town to the Great Lakes, from the Soudan to Cairo, and she will indeed be Queen of the Earth."

The youth opened his mouth, and gaped with amazement.

"Is this a fairy tale, ma'am?" he asked. "I know you are acquainted with Oom Paul and Tanta Kruger, so that you must be well informed. If you are right, which I do not doubt, what is the use of me fighting here?"

"Hush!" she whispered in his ear; "not a word to the others. We hoped for help from other nations, but we have made a mistake. Soon all power here will be in British hands. It is sad; we have played for high stakes, but are losing the game."

The young Boer was an enthusiastic patriot.

To him the Transvaal was the world, and the Outlanders were foreign devils who had no business there.

After his Creator the President came next.

He was deeply affected at what he heard, and a tear dimmed the brightness of his eye.

"Cheer up," said Mrs. Steiner, patting him on the shoulder encouragingly; "you are young and slim. The British will improve your position. All enmity will be forgotten in a few months, and as I always liked you, little Berger, you may count upon me as a friend."

"Thank you, ma'am, a thousand times."

"Gretchen has told me all about your engagement, and when you are married, you know, I shall give you each a thousand pounds for a start in farming."

"Oh, madam, this is too much!" said the youth. "What have I done to deserve it?"

"Gretchen has been my pet since she was a child not so high as an ant-hill, and I mean to see you both as happy as the day is long. Now I want you to do me a little favour. Just a wee, tiny favour, you know, Berger."

"What is that, ma'am?" inquired the sentinel.

"I want to see the prisoner you are guarding."

"*Hein!*" cried the youth. "Do you mean the Captain of the War Scouts, the famous Jack Harkaway? That is strictly against orders. Shalker said he would shoot me if I allowed anyone to see him."

"Nonsense! I thought you were my friend. Gretchen will be cross if she hears of this. I don't believe she will ever speak to you again, and I'm sure I shan't—much as I liked you."

"If you put it that way, come on; I'll take chances."

The young Boer looked round.

The heat of the sun was intense. There was no one about, as everybody was trying to find shelter from the scorching solar rays. He wiped the perspiration from his forehead.

Taking a key from his pocket, he unlocked the door and beckoned to Mrs. Steiner, who glided into the shed, the door being closed behind her.

Then the young Boer resumed his sentry-go with a guilty look on his boyish, ingenuous face.

He passed the matter off with a light laugh, not thinking that any harm would come of his indiscretion.

He would not have been so careless and confident, however, had he seen the dark, scowling visage of Webb, who was glaring at him from behind the trunk of a gum tree.

The wretched spy, who was always on the alert, had been watching Mrs. Steiner's movements, and saw her enter the shed.

This was enough for him, because he knew it to be contrary to the rules and regulations.

He did not want to disturb her at once, but, lying low, waited his opportunity with all the cunning of a designing villain.

Meanwhile, Mrs. Steiner had come upon Jack like a flash of lightning.

He was seated at a rough deal table, with a book spread open before him.

A large sliding panel had been pushed back in the roof, to admit light and give ventilation.

She advanced, pale and trembling, her eyes downcast, and sank on her knees before him, extending her hands.

"Pardon me, Captain Harkaway," she exclaimed in a tremulous voice, "I was rude to you, just now, because I saw on your hand a ring that Gretchen had given you. She has explained all, and I come here at great personal risk to plead for your forgiveness. If I lose your friendship, I part with the only thing that makes life dear to me. I have much to tell you, and may be able to save you from your foes, placing you once more at the head of your War Scouts, whose name is already a terror to the Boers."

"It was my hope to intensify that feeling," replied Harkaway. "But, hang the luck! I am laid by the heels in this den, and don't see my way out of it. Rise, Mrs. Steiner. Many thanks for your explanation. I am sorry this bauble should have caused you uneasiness, and I can't understand why it has done so. Away with it! What is the thing to me?"

He threw the ring with all his force through the opening in the roof, and it vanished in the dazzling sunlight.

He assisted her to her feet, and they stood side by side, the woman looking up in the young man's face.

"You must think me a very eccentric person," she said, in her sweetest and most winning tone.

"No, no; not at all. I think you are a very nice lady, and a most agreeable companion, while you are wonderfully brave, clever, and energetic."

"Ah, you flatter me. I can see that you are vexed. My nature is impulsive; I am considered erratic, and never would be bound by conventionalities. I am a child of the veldt, and you must take me as you find me. After you saved my life in the first place, I had a dream, a happy dream."

She paused abruptly, and cast her eyes upon the ground.

"May I venture to inquire what it was?" replied Jack.

"I am afraid to tell you, because you will laugh at me, and call me a foolish woman, who twists ropes with sand and builds castles in the air. Yet much depends on you."

"On me?" Jack ejaculated.

She looked at him very wistfully, and with tear-bedimmed eyes.

"It all depends on you," she exclaimed, earnestly.

"On me?" he asked again.

"Yes, Captain Harkaway, for you are the arbiter of my fate. I am alone in the world. I want a protector, and was vain enough to fancy that when the English have won the war you would be my friend and guide. That is all."

"Mrs. Steiner," said Jack, "colouring slightly, "I understand you; or, at least, think I do so. It has only just dawned upon me; but while this fierce conflict rages my mind is entirely centred on the army. When it is settled we shall meet on more equal terms, and, with your permission, we will not mention the subject again until that time arrives. During the interval I shall always regard you as a true and devoted friend, and deem myself lucky at having gained your good will."

He knew now that this impetuous woman loved him, and had as good as told him so;

but he wanted time to consider whether he could return the proffered affection of this strange but impressive and fascinating daughter of South Africa.

She smiled with the glee of a child when he did not repel her advances, and then her features became rigid, her eyes flashed, and she was all business again.

"I am scout as well as a secret agent," she said. "At least, I am always listening and watching. While on the stoep I heard Webb talking to Shalker."

"Is that rascal here?" queried Jack.

"He dogs your steps fairly well," she rejoined. "The Boers have offered five hundred pounds for you, dead or alive."

"I look upon that as being highly complimentary; in fact, I did not know that such an insignificant individual as myself was worth so much."

"You under-estimate your own value. Webb has designs upon your friend Fred Dawson as well as you."

"He can't hurt him much."

"Don't make so sure of that. Dawson has been sent to the Crocodile River with a dispatch for Colonel Plumer. Webb and Dunko the Kaffir are going after him, intending to kill him on the veldt; but that is not all."

"What is the next item in your budget of news? Is any sinister plot being hatched against me?"

"It is not directed so much at you as at your War Scouts, who are to be led into a trap, where everyone of them will be killed."

"Don't tell me that unless you want to madden me," cried Harkaway, excitedly.

"It is true," answered Mrs. Steiner. "They are to be lured to a spot near this encampment, where a mine will be exploded under their feet. Scouts and horses will all be blown up together, not one man escaping to tell the tale."

"It will have to be a smart trick," remarked Harkaway, shaking his head. "Two Colonials—Cornstalk and Kanuck, as we call them — will be in command during the absence of myself and Dawson. I do not reckon the Boers will get over them, for they are up to every move on the board."

"You have not heard the scheme yet. By telling you I am betraying my people and risking my life; but there is no length I would not go to for your sake. Pay attention."

"I am listening," answered Jack, bending his head.

"Shalker and Constrad have found a young Boer who is exactly like you. When I saw him just now, I could not tell the difference. If you two were placed side by side, nobody would know which was Harkaway and which was Pretorious, as your double is named. His voice resembles yours, and he speaks English well, for he has been in London. This person is to be sent to the Scouts. He will say that he has escaped, and of course they will all take him for you; so that he can do as he likes, and lead them anywhere. Unless they are warned, their doom is marked out for them."

"By Heaven! this shall not be," cried Harkaway, angrily, while his blood coursed wildly, and the veins on his forehead were swollen almost to bursting. "I will make a dash for liberty, if I die in the attempt."

"Calm yourself," said Mrs. Steiner, trying to restrain his eagerness. "That would be sheer insanity. You are surrounded by Boers."

"Out of my way!" shouted Jack. "My brain will burst. I cannot remain shut up here when I know that my brave fellows are going to be slaughtered like sheep. What shall I have to live for when all under my command are gone?"

She looked at him reproachfully, but his aspect terrified her.

The expression of his face had completely changed in a moment.

He had the fierce look of an angry lion preparing to spring upon its prey.

He moved towards the door.

She clung to his arm.

Forgetting that she was a woman, he grasped her by the waist, and, lifting her off her feet, threw her roughly on a heap of straw close by, where she remained, cowering with fear, looking at him, cat-like, from under her long eyelashes.

Scarcely knowing what he did, Harkaway was about to hurl his shoulder against the door and break it down, when it opened, and Webb was seen on the threshold.

"What! Is it you?" exclaimed Harkaway. "You have just come at the right time. I want to pay off some old scores, and shall never rest while I am in your debt."

Webb saw his danger and drew a revolver.

With a quick movement Jack jerked it up, making it go off in the air.

The next moment his arms twined round the spy's body with the hug of a grizzly bear.

"Help! Help!" gasped Webb, who felt as if his ribs were cracking.

"I've got you now," muttered Jack in a guttural tone. "Down you go! down, I say! I'll have your life! You have tried for mine; but it's my turn now. Down!"

He forced his enemy upon his back, and, kneeling on his chest, began to grip his throat.

"Die, beast, monster! Die! I've got you now, and all the fiends you serve cannot save you."

It was going hard with Webb, and it would have gone harder had not Shalker, Constrad, and Villebois, roused by the pistol-shot, rushed in to his assistance, and dragged Harkaway from his victim, just as his breath was failing him and his eyes closing.

Several Boers followed and secured Jack with ropes.

He was stretched on the ground helpless, and could only glare at his enemy.

Mrs. Steiner was too faint to stir; Webb could only murmur a request for water.

Shalker was puzzled.

He could not understand the affair.

Harkaway was a prisoner, and he had given strict orders that no one should be permitted to see him, yet both Mrs. Steiner and Webb were in the shed.

With a sullen, cold-blooded look, the Boer went outside, where young Berger, bewildered and alarmed, was standing, rifle in hand.

Shalker knew that the youth was the sweetheart of his daughter Gretchen.

He had been acquainted with his family for many years, and they had attended the same place of worship, but this made no difference to the Puritanical Boer.

"You were on guard over the war scout, Captain Harkaway. Your orders were to admit no one," he said, in a gruff voice; "but I find a man and a woman inside. Did you pass them in contrary to my command?"

The young Boer inclined his head in token of assent, being too nervous to speak.

"Your punishment is death, which is always the penalty for disobedience in time of war."

Uttering these words, Shalker drew a pistol from his belt and deliberately shot the sentry through the head.

Then, as if nothing out of the common had happened, he returned to the shed.

CHAPTER XL.

SUDDEN APPEARANCE OF THE HUNCHBACK—A STRANGE WARNING—FISH'S MADNESS—THE STORM—A VANISHING VLEI—TEUFEL-SKINT IS ENGULFED.

SHALKER'S farm offered a very good camping spot for the scouts, who took possession of it after they had routed the Boers, removing their small amount of stores from their former resting-place at the base of the Drakensberg Mountains.

Guided by the engineering skill of Villebois, who was an excellent sapper, the Boers had thrown up trenches and earthworks, which formed excellent defences for the scouts, who had no occasion to use the spade at all.

Sheltered behind these, they could repel any attack made upon them, and here Kanuck and Cornstalk determined to remain for a time until they could either hear news of Captain Harkaway, or drive the Boers from the Lodge, where they had taken refuge.

This was not to be easily done, however.

Cornstalk had gone on an exploring expedition by himself, and at the risk of his life had discovered that the house called the Lodge formed the centre of an extensive laager.

Waggons containing all sorts of stores and ammunition were placed in a circle around it. Beyond these the Boers had been busy with pick and shovel, erecting earthworks which made it a formidable fortress, which could not be successfully assaulted with less than five thousand men having artillery with them.

The Lodge could only be captured by some sort of artifice, which had yet to be devised by Harkaway's scouts, who were sadly hampered and disorganised by the absence of their two leaders—the captain and Fred Dawson.

All they could do was to keep a sharp lookout for Shalker's men, and see that they did not get away with any of the waggons required by Joubert.

Maori, the New Zealander, was still on the sick-list, able to sit up and walk about with a crutch, but not yet strong enough to fight. Andy, the bugler, was also weak, yet both hoped to take the field again soon.

The advance post of the scouts was the wooded spot near the small lake where Harkaway had encountered Villebois, and wounded him in defending Gretchen Shalker.

Here Corporal Potts had erected a tent, and with a couple of scouts, who were relieved at intervals, maintained a daily and nightly watch.

His constant companion was Mr. Fish, who spent his time in writing a history of the Boer invasion of Natal for the benefit of the readers of the *Capetown Slasher*.

They were sitting under the trees one morning, with a sentinel standing in front of them, lazily smoking his pipe, with a bottle of wine between them, called Hermitage, made from farm grapes—harsh and sour to an English palate—when the man on guard shouted, "Who goes there?"

"Friend!" was the reply, in a deep bass voice.

The corporal and Fish sprang to their feet.

"I don't like the look of you, anyway," replied the sentry; adding, "Hi! corporal here's a comical-looking chap. Will you come and take a squint at him? At first I thought he was a wild animal, and should have put a shot into it if the thing had not spoken."

Rising above the long grass was the head and shoulders of Teufelskint, who opened his capacious mouth and grinned a greeting at the corporal.

"Hallo!" cried the latter, "here is my friend, the hunchback of the veldt, and the dwarf of the mountains, Devilskin, or whatever his name is."

"Welcome!" said Fish. "Join us, and impart the news, you incarnation of monstrosity."

The hunchback scowled at him, and placed his hand upon the hilt of a knife which protruded from his belt.

"That was only a joke," said Fish, hastily correcting himself. "I mean you peach without a stone, you cluster of apple-blossom."

The hunchback, not at all mollified by this sort of apology, gave Fish a rude, angry push, which caused him to stagger against the trunk of a tree.

He then approached Potts, handing him a small flask of spirit as a token of friendship, which the corporal did not scruple to accept.

"I don't know whether I will or I won't, but I'd rather," said he, raising it to his mouth. "This Cape wine is poor stuff. Have you seen anything of our captain or Lieutenant Dawson?"

"Harkaway is in the hands of the Boers, but his life is safe. Dawson is in great danger, for the two-headed snake is after him," answered Teufelskint.

"Who on earth is that?" enquired the corporal, looking puzzled. "I don't know anyone who answers that description, unless it is Webb."

Teufelskint nodded his head vigorously.

"You have rightly named the serpent, who is arranging a fatal surprise for all of you."

"What is that? I don't think the Boers can do us much harm; we are more likely to injure them if they break up their laager and try to get off with the convoy. We have scouts out now watching them."

"I have not been able to gain full particulars," continued the hunchback. "The Boers have been suspicious of me lately, and would riddle me with their Mauser bullets if they dared; but they know it would bring them bad luck. Ha, ha! A wonderful being is the hunchback of the hills! I am like poison to them. It is fear, not love, that makes them tolerate me. Ho, ho! They think my spirit would haunt them! Poor fools! They want good fortune just now!"

"Has anything happened?" asked the corporal, nervously.

He could scarcely restrain his excitement at the hope of hearing that the Boers had suffered some heavy loss.

Undismayed by his rebuff, Fish drew near, note-book and pencil in hand.

"An hour ago I met a Kaffir runner on the veldt, who had come from the Free State," said Teufelskint. "He told me that Cronje, retreating, had been caught in a trap on the banks of the Modder River, and after a week's hard fighting had surrendered to Lord Roberts with four thousand men and all his guns and waggons. He also declared that General Buller had relieved Ladysmith."

"Hurrah!" vociferated the corporal, throwing his hat in the air. "Majuba is avenged, and the stain wiped from the British flag. Long live Victoria! Give her Pretoria! I say, Jumbo, this is great news. What will you have? Take a drop of something."

In his confusion he handed Teufelskint the flask he had given him, but the latter refused to take it.

"No," he said, quietly; "I have work to do, as I hinted just now. A great danger threatens you and Dawson. There is a plot to destroy the scouts, and it is hoped that not one will escape. I wish to protect you, and Dawson also, which is difficult, as I cannot be in two places at once. I will first try to find out the nature of the scheme hatched against the scouts, and then hurry over the veldt after Dawson, who, I know, is to be followed by Webb and Dunko. He has a paper which Webb will wade through blood to get. Another time I will drink with you, and we will revel in the drunkard's paradise."

"That is a thing I never do," replied the corporal. "I have to set an example to the men, you know, and never had a mark against me for taking a drop too much, like the other absent-minded Tommies; but seeing that it's you, Teufel, I don't mind taking a night off to celebrate this glorious victory on my own, if you'll bring the stuff with you. Hullo! where's that flask gone to?" He looked round.

Fish had taken it from him during his preoccupation, and, emptying it at one long draught, was sitting on the grass with the bottle in his hand, staring at vacancy, with lack-lustre eyes, like a dying duck in a thunderstorm, for the powerful liquor had taken hold of him.

"Overproofsh," he muttered, in an imbecile tone, chuckling to himself. "Devilskin knows what's good—hic—hic—but it's too strongsh for me—hic—worse than a Boer pom-pom gun. He must know a distillery in the infernal regions."

Then his mood changed.

The fiery spirit mounted to his head; he was maddened, and felt as if he had the strength of a giant.

He looked cross and vexed, scowling darkly.

He rose to his feet with a defiant air.

"He insulted me," roared Fish, striding towards the dwarf. "His hand dared to touch *me*, the world-famed war correspondent of the *Cape Town Slasher*. My blood boils. My heart throbs for vengeance, which I would not forego if Rhodes offered me all the wealth of De Beers. Mis-shapen dwarf, your hour has come."

At this moment a terrific flash of lightning darted from the sky, which was followed by an appalling clap of thunder.

A low wind hissed through the branches of the trees.

The ground trembled with a slight shock of earthquake; while the waters of the vlei boiled and bubbled, now rising until they over-lapped their banks, and anon falling several inches.

Undeterred by this phenomenon of nature, which was simply a tropical storm of frequent occurrence in those parts, Fish sprang like a tiger upon Teufelskint, and twining his arms round his ungainly waist, dragged him, in spite of his resistance, to the brink of the pool, and hurled him headlong into the water.

Lightning flashed incessantly with blinding vividness.

The thunder was deafening.

A pall-like cloud obscured the sun, and the darkness of night prevailed.

Exhausted by his effort, Fish fell to the ground in a fainting condition, talking savagely to himself, and cursing the hump of the hunchback, who he thought had insulted him.

Corporal Potts stood aghast.

He was distressed at what had happened, for he regarded the dwarf as a friend, and feared he would be drowned.

A lurid flash, more prolonged than those which had preceded it, illuminated the surroundings, and by its aid he beheld a sight which made his blood turn cold.

Struggling in the centre of the vlei was the Hunchback of the Hills.

He was paddling the water with his hands in the endeavour to save himself from drowning, for he could not swim.

His face was convulsed with anguish, and his eyes were filled with a terror born of despair.

The vlei was not more than six feet deep in any part, and Potts was about to plunge in, when to his utter amazement the water disappeared into the earth with a sudden rush, dragging Teufelskint down with it.

This the glare of the lightning enabled him to perceive.

All was black as night for a minute, when the cloud burst in a deluge of rain, through which the sun was visible once more.

The corporal rubbed his eyes, for the vlei had vanished.

Not a drop of water remained in the hollow basin.

It had sunk through a chasm in the earth as if by magic, and the unfortunate dwarf was not to be seen.

The sentry, a Canadian, named Moore, who had been standing by, was as much surprised as the corporal.

He took off his hat and bowed his head.

"What are you doing?" asked Potts.

"Saluting the dead," answered the Canadian. "It is a token of respect I would pay to my worst enemy; and whatever the hunchback may have been, we shall never see him again on this earth."

"I would not like to bet on it. I believe that imp of darkness knows as much about the lower regions as he does about the upper world."

"It's a queer thing the bottom of the pond gave out the way it did. I guess there must have been something of an earthquake. That tanglefoot whiskey drove the inkslinger mad. Look at him lying there on his back, snoring like a hog. He don't know what he did."

"That shows the evil that drink does," said the corporal, sententiously, as he picked up the bottle, adding, with a wry face: "Blame his old carcase, it's empty!"

"I've got a drop of squareface, if you are not too proud to accept it," replied Moore. "It ain't old rye, nor yet Bourbon, and it ain't Canada Club, but I'll warrant it to kill at a thousand yards."

"I don't know whether I will or I won't, but I'd rather. Hand it over. A man can only die once," answered the corporal, accepting the gift. "But I say, mate, who's going down the hole after the dwarf with the hunch?"

"Not me, for certain," said Moore, shaking his head. "I'll take a back seat on that deal, if it's all the same to you. I reckon the freak is as dead as a door-nail by this time."

"He must be," rejoined the corporal, heaving a deep sigh. "It was a pity he was taken off so quickly. The tale he told us was a queer one. According to him, some great danger is hanging over the scouts, but the nature of it he was unable to explain. The story was like one of Fish's letters—to be continued in our next."

"I should go and report to Lieutenants Dunstan and Fearless."

He alluded to the Queenslander and the Canadian, who were familiarly called Cornstalk and Kanuck.

In the unavoidable absence of Captain Harkaway and his second in command, Fred Dawson, these two controlled the regiment.

Potts found them in the house, anxiously discussing the situation.

When they heard what had happened, they became seriously alarmed, because they knew that Teufelskint must have come with a purpose.

What new trick were the Boers preparing for them?

All they knew was that danger environed them, and it was their duty to exercise the utmost caution.

It was a very awkward position at the best.

How to get out of such a dilemma was a question not easily answered.

But they would do their best.

They doubled the outposts, and ardently

prayed for the return of their leader, Harkaway.

CHAPTER XLI.

THE HUNCHBACK'S AWAKENING—A TERRIBLE
JOURNEY UNDERGROUND—THE TRAP-DOOR
IN THE TUNNEL—SHALKER'S PLANS—
TEUFELSKINT'S COLLAPSE.

THE immediate cause of the breaking up of
the bottom of the pool was the slight shock
of earthquake to which we have alluded ;
but artificial means had aided the forces of
nature.

Shalker and his Boers, who were always as
busy as ants, had dug a long tunnel under
the ground lying between the farm and the
vlei, under which it stopped.

This they mined in various places with
dynamite, intending to blow up the enemy if
they were so rash as to come near enough.

Teufelskint was carried down in the
vortex of water into the head of the tunnel,
where his body was deposited on a large
barrel filled with explosive material.

Half drowned and with his system shocked,
he remained in a semi-conscious condition
for fully the space of an hour, by which time
the water, carried along the whole length of
the tunnel, became absorbed in the earth,
which was dry and parched, and when the
hunchback came to himself, descended from
his elevated position and looked around, he
found himself on dry ground.

A glimmer of light descended from the
hole above him through which he had been
sucked and drawn down ; but it was far
beyond his reach, and unavailable as a means
of exit.

His escape from death had been almost
miraculous, but it seemed as if he was
doomed to die of starvation in this subterranean digging.

In vain he shouted and screamed in tones
of frantic despair until he was hoarse ; only
sepulchral echoes answered him.

Collecting his senses, he began to reflect,
and came to the conclusion that if he groped
his way along the tunnel he must come to an
outlet, through which the miners had come
down and gone up when it was in process of
construction.

It was fortunate for the hunchback in this
emergency that he always carried a small
dark lantern firmly fixed in his belt.

It was wrapped in a leather case, and had
not been injured by the water.

Inside his buckskin jacket he had his pipe,
tobacco, and matches, which, owing to the
waterproof nature of the material, had kept
dry ; consequently, he had no difficulty in
obtaining a light.

A few whiffs from his pipe revived him
and steadied his nerves, and he started boldly
to explore the tunnel and find a way out of
his difficulty.

It was not easy travelling for him.

In places the ground was uneven ; in others
the tide of water had piled up heaps of
stone and sand, over which he had to scramble
the best way he could.

He trudged along persistently for a long
distance, which he computed to be more than
a mile, and yet no ray of sunshine or daylight cheered his aching eyes.

He felt jaded and weary, but resolution
was a main part of his composition.

He was used to wandering for days and
nights over the veldt and on the sides of the
kopjes.

It was his boast that he could find his way
in the dark, and he kept on tramping through
piles of dust, until his sight was dim and his
throat parched.

At length his strength gave way, and he
sank down in a sitting position, dazed, and
feeling as if his last hour was approaching.

Suddenly he heard the sound of voices
above him.

Casting his gaze upwards, some gleams of
light were perceptible, coming through inter-
stices between boards laid down as a flooring.

Not far from him was a wooden ladder,
which led up to these boards.

He also perceived two large iron hinges,
indicating the existence of a trap-door.

His heart gave a great thump, for he knew
that he was saved, just as he was giving way
to the worst kind of despair.

Though he had not come to the precise
extremity of the mining tunnel, he had
arrived at a spot where the Boers had been in
the habit of going up and down.

Owing to the distance he had travelled, he
was confident that he had long ago passed
under Shalker's farm, and the idea he formed
was, that he must be in the proximity of the
Lodge.

Summoning all his courage to his aid, he
lost no time in climbing up the ladder, and,
lowering his head, was about to push up the
trap-door with his hump, when he heard the
sound of a voice which he instantly recognised to be that of Shalker.

He was followed by another speaker, whose
tone sounded like that of Constrad ; and,
before he went any further, the hunchback
determined to listen to what was going on
overhead.

"I have been in doubt how to act with
Mrs. Steiner and Captain Harkaway," exclaimed Shalker.

"Why not shoot the pair of them ?" replied
Constrad, who was always for drastic mea-
sures. "Webb swears that the captain is a
spy, and circumstances are certainly suspicious against Belle Steiner, who was driven
out of Cronje's camp for being too friendly
with the English."

"A certain section of Pretoria Boers support her, and we cannot afford to defy Kruger
or the English, who would make reprisals
for the death of Harkaway. No, my friend ;
after the scene which occurred in the shed,
I had both of them separately confined and
guarded. When we have disposed of the
scouts, and have a clear field before us, I will
send the captain prisoner to the front, and
the woman can go where she pleases."

"You are master here, and I will allow you
to be the best judge, though Webb and Villebois are of my way of thinking. Death is
their panacea for a case of this sort."

"The Frenchman has to obey me," said
Shalker, arrogantly. "Webb is riding over
the veldt with Dunko at the present moment
to destroy Lieutenant Dawson, and Pretorious

has started for the farm to show himself as Harkaway."

"It is a hazardous undertaking. Do you think he will be successful?" asked Constrad.

"I have no doubt whatever about the issue of the affair," replied Shalker. "He is so exactly like the captain that the scouts, who are a mixed lot, will be sure to take him for their leader. I am having one of the ammunition waggons unloaded now, and in less than a couple of hours a ton of dynamite will be placed in the tunnel under our feet, about half a mile from the Lodge. To this spot Pretorious will lead the scouts. I shall touch the electric wire, and the whole of them will be blown into the *Ewigheit*. It is all arranged."

"What then?"

"We shall evacuate the Lodge and convoy the waggons to Joubert's army."

By listening to this conversation, Teufelskint had gathered much that was of an interesting nature, a good deal of which was entirely new to him. He knew where Belle Steiner and the captain were, and what it was intended to do with them.

Webb and Dunko had started after Dawson. The tunnel was to be mined immediately. A death-trap was laid for the scouts, and what was more startling than all, consisted in the fact that Pretorious was to palm himself off upon Cornstalk and the others as the famous commander of the War Scouts.

When prowling about among the Boers on the hills between Ladysmith and the Tugela River, the hunchback, who was a privileged person and allowed to go anywhere, had come in contact with this remarkable young Boer, and had been forcibly impressed by the striking likeness between him and Harkaway.

Yes, it was very startling indeed.

"Ho! ho!" laughed the dwarf, softly. "The wily old fox, Shalker, is up to a new trick; but I will liberate Harkaway and steer him somehow through the Boer outposts, so that he can join his men and expose this fraud who is taking his place."

The task before him was not an easy one; to accomplish his purpose he must gain the confidence of Shalker.

But there was no time for hesitation.

Trusting to his innate cleverness and cunning, he gave the trap-door a prodigious heave, causing it to rise in the air.

He stood on the top step of the ladder, dirt-begrimed and hideous, resembling a gnome who had come up out of the bowels of the earth for some unholy purpose.

His sudden movement had been followed by a crash, owing to the circumstance that Constrad had been sitting on a three-legged stool placed right over the trap-door, and the unexpected jerk had toppled him over on his back against a table covered with plates and dishes containing the remains of a recent lunch.

Springing to his feet, Shalker looked with wide-open eyes at the apparition, and it was some seconds before he could realise that Teufelskint stood before him.

"Imp of darkness!" he cried. "Where have you come from? And what is your business here?"

"Ha! ha! ha!" cried the hunchback. "Is it a sin and a crime to come and see old friends? I'm as much at home under ground as I am above. Have not the Boers christened me the Dwarf of the Veldt and the Crook-back of the Hills. I was driven forth a wanderer on the face of the earth, and have no abiding place. For me there is no rest."

"We have heard all that before. Tell us something we do not know," said Shalker impatiently. "How did you get into our tunnel, the existence of which I thought was a secret to all but a chosen few?"

"I fell through a hole," replied Teufelskint. "Having been among the scouts I can tell you that they do not know what to do, and are simply acting on the defensive. The English are beating us at all points. Cronje is a prisoner, and Joubert in retreat."

"Bad business," growled Shalker, shaking his head. "Affairs do not march well, but we shall conquer in the end. Hand me that jar of squareface. I must drink to drown sorrow. I believe you are not averse to the bottle; join me while I smoke my pipe and put on my thinking cap."

Teufelskint did as he was requested.

Constrad, who had recovered his footing, received some orders respecting the explosive, which he left the room to execute.

Never had the dwarf been so strongly tempted to drink as then.

He was tired and weary.

His great desire was to become intoxicated, and go to sleep on the floor in a corner.

He resisted the impulse for awhile, contenting himself with sipping the strong spirit in his glass.

He wanted to keep sober to help Harkaway; but at length he gave way to his favourite vice, became reckless, and soon threw prudence to the winds, making himself rapidly intoxicated.

He did not notice the Boers coming in with cases of dynamite, with which they descended into the tunnel.

He heard nothing.

He saw nothing but the jar of Dutch gin before him, and at length he rolled off his chair, lying on his back on the floor like a pig, whereupon Shalker shook the ashes out of his pipe and kicked the deformed drunkard under the table.

Captain Harkaway's chance of release was gone.

The blackness of night had once more closed in upon his chequered career, and Boer trickery appeared likely to triumph over his gallant scouts, who could not be blamed if they were deceived by the audacious impostor Pretorious.

CHAPTER XLII.

THE FALSE HARKAWAY APPEARS—CORPORAL POTTS AND THE SCOUTS ARE TAKEN IN—A NIGHT MARCH—COLONIALS IN FRONT—DANGER AHEAD.

THE sun was setting in glorious splendour over the veldt, bathing Shalker's farm in a flood of golden light.

The little dikkop and other birds were seeking shelter for the night.

Here and there could be heard the shrill cry of the paauw, and the korhaan flew by on tired wings.

The vigilance of the scouts always increased when the shades of night fell.

Corporal Potts, who had been appointed orderly officer for the ensuing twenty-four hours, was making his rounds.

He had arrived at the extremity of the outposts, facing the direction of the Lodge, when he saw a hare running through the grass.

Some of the Kaffir helps were lying lazily around, but they took no notice of the animal, keen as they generally are after any species of game.

As a matter of fact, the natives hold the hare in reverence, thinking that each one is the home of a departed spirit, and for that reason they will not harm these creatures.

Potts, however, was very partial to hare, and seeing the prospect of a tasty supper before him, fired his pistol at it, breaking one of the hind legs; but this did not stop the progress of the creature, so he started after it at a run to have another shot.

He was baffled by its darting into a shelter formed of high grass, mimosas, and stunted willows, round which he walked, but it did not emerge from its place of concealment.

About to return disappointed, he was startled by perceiving a man approaching him from the north.

He noticed that this person's arm was borne in a sling, and a linen bandage stained with blood was bound round his head.

Potts looked again through the gradually declining light, and uttered a cry as he distinguished the features and well-known form of his old friend and commander, Captain Harkaway.

One of the scouts named Williams, who had joined the regiment with a record from, firstly, the Natal Police, and secondly the Natal Carabineers, had walked up from the lines behind Potts.

He was a quiet, reticent man with a sly face.

The War Scouts were a composite regiment, and of course the characters of men could not be enquired into, but if ever there was a man who looked like a spy, it was Williams.

In reality the fellow was one of the worst kind.

He was in the pay of the War Office at Pretoria, and that very day in the early morning he had volunteered to go out and bring all the intelligence he could respecting the Boers in laager at the Lodge.

Taking advantage of the opportunity, he had given a pre-arranged password to the sentries, and, being admitted, had been sent by Shalker to Pretorious, with whom he remained in private for a couple of hours.

During this interview with the pretender, Williams afforded him all the information he possibly could about the scouts, fully describing the officers, especially Cornstalk and Kanuck, and Harkaway's friends, Corporal Potts, Mr. Fish, and others, so that Pretorious received what are called points, calculated to be of the utmost use to him when he entered the camp.

The impostor had put his arm in a sling and bandaged his head to make the men believe that he had been engaged in a terrible struggle while escaping from the Boers, and at the same time he wanted them to think that his sword-arm was injured and his head badly hurt, which would prevent him leading the men into action.

This was a wise precaution on his part, because he was going to send them to their death when he ordered the night attack on the Lodge.

"Welcome!" exclaimed the corporal. "To have you amongst us again is like greeting one back from the grave. How did you escape?"

"By the skin of my teeth, if I may use the expression," replied Pretorious. "My sentry brought me a jug of water. I flew upon him in a way you know I can do."

"Yes, yes. You are all there when you're wanted."

"I left him for dead on the floor; but in the fight I got a deuce of a blow on the head. I dodged the Boers somehow, but as I was getting off safely, as I thought, a fellow sniped me, and I was wounded in the arm. Making a circuit, I reached a small farm, where the women gave me linen for bandages, and some refreshment. After a rest, I came on here, and am very glad to see you. What's your name? I know, don't-cher-know, but I've forgotten for the moment. That blow on the head was a fair knock-out."

"Why, I'm the old corporal. The old Reliable, you used to call me," exclaimed Potts, in astonishment.

"By jove, so you are. Shake hands, corporal. Bless your old heart. Where are Cornstalk and Kanuck, our trusty Queenslander and Canadian? Splendid fellows, my Colonials. I know every man in the regiment; but I'm a little bit off colour, owing to what I have gone through."

"Glad to see you back, sir," said the spy, stepping forward.

"Ah, Williams, is that you?" cried Pretorious. "Did you think I was lost?"

"No, sir," was the reply. "I thought you'd turn up. It would take a very slim Boer to keep you."

"Go and tell the boys about my return," continued Pretorious. "Let them get ready for some sharp work to-night. I have got the inside track of the Boer position, and intend to send the scouts to victory. As I cannot sit a horse, the brave Queenslander and the equally gallant Canadian shall lead them. The grass shall not grow under my feet. To-night the Boers have a feast in honour of Commander Shalker's birthday, and while they are revelling, we will swoop down upon them and paint their camp red. I must see Cornstalk and Kanuck at once. Where are they?"

The corporal informed him that the Colonials were in the house.

As he was on duty he could not leave to accompany him, so he beckoned to Williams, who walked in front.

This was necessary, because Pretorious had not been to Shalker's farm before, and did not know his way.

Williams spoke to two or three men who were carrying water for the horses, informing them that the captain had fought his way through the Boers, and was with them once more, adding that a night attack would take place in a short time.

The news spread like wildfire, and the utmost excitement prevailed.

The scouts rushed to the rear of the farm, and collecting together ranged themselves, in two rows, through which the pretended captain had to pass.

His apparently wounded condition excited the greatest sympathy and admiration, whilst enthusiasm rose to fever heat.

Cheer after cheer rang out, and Pretorious returned the salutes of the men with a smiling countenance.

Corporal Potts, however, was not satisfied.

"The captain has changed a bit since I saw him last, and that was only a short time ago," he muttered. "His manner is altered, and he don't talk like himself. There is something wrong about him, but what it is I can't make out. It may be through his wounds. A blow on the head is calculated to upset anybody.

"I was half out of my mind for days three years ago, when I was knobsticked in Bloemfontein by a Boer who had got Majuba and the Raid on the brain. The sight of an Outlander drove him crazy, and he couldn't stand a Britisher at any price. It's the captain right enough—anyone can tell that with half an eye; but he's an altered man, or I'm a child again, and don't know anything."

The corporal stopped and lighted his pipe.

"Of course, if a man's wounded, he can't fight," he added; "that stands to reason. But it isn't like Harkaway to send his men to a frontal attack while he stays behind. I'm jiggered if it is."

While the corporal was talking to himself, Pretorious had been conducted into the farmhouse, where the Colonials were seated together smoking, and wondering what all the noise was about.

"Say, cap, is it you, or your ghost?" cried Kanuck, springing up as Pretorious entered. "I was never so surprised in the whole of my natural. Do tell where you have been. I want to know."

Pretorious related the same story that he had told the corporal, and he took a chair facing the two officers, who heartily congratulated him on his fortunate escape.

He thanked them, and unfolded his plan for a night attack, which he declared could not fail to be successful.

Their expedition, he urged, had been a long time in operation, and their services were wanted elsewhere.

They were considered a smart regiment, and it was not to their credit that they had allowed Shalker to baffle them.

"The blow must be struck before midnight. You two brave fellows shall lead the War Scouts to victory. They have confidence in you as well as in me, and would follow you to death's door if need be. But first of all, before you make a start, let a couple of scouts ride up to the Boer camp, as close as is consistent with his safety, and ascertain if the festivities are in progress, as I have been led to expect."

"I'll guess I'll do that on my own, captain," said Kanuck, "so as there will be no mistake."

"Do so," answered Pretorious. "While you are gone I will arrange the plan of attack with Cornstalk, and the men shall have orders to get under arms. If I cannot be at the head of you, owing to my wounded arm, I shall not be far in the rear, for in the hour of danger I would rather die than let my beloved scouts out of my sight. You know me, boys."

Cornstalk nodded, and Kanuck was off like a shot.

The time during his absence passed quickly.

Pretorious had the scouts drawn up in line, inspected and made a speech to them, explaining what had to be done that night.

On his return, Kanuck reported that the outposts at the Boer camp had been withdrawn.

He had penetrated near enough to hear the sound of musical instruments and merry songs, while by the light of lanterns he could see men dancing and drinking.

This was enough to satisfy every man in the regiment.

All were eager for the attack, thinking the Boers would be an easy prey.

"Forward!" shouted Pretorious, who bestrode a small grey pony, holding the reins in his left hand as well as he was able. "War Scouts, right wheel."

There was no sound of drum or bugle.

The march began in perfect silence, and Harkaway's advanced in the starlight to meet what Shalker and Pretorious intended to be their certain doom.

CHAPTER XLIII.

DAWSON MEETS ONE OF "CAREY'S CHICKENS," AND AN ALLIANCE IS MADE BETWEEN THEM—NEWS OF WEBB—A HALT, AND A SURPRISE.

THE horse that Fred Dawson had selected for his journey was rather a weedy, raw-boned specimen; but still, a very useful animal.

He could go a long way without tiring, and like a camel, he could travel without water for a considerable distance.

When his rider allowed him to walk, he cropped the grass, which was rich, green, and juicy from recent rains.

A horse accustomed to the veldt is always eating between meals; in fact, he never takes a regular meal, as a stable-fed horse does.

He has frequent tasters, like a cook in a kitchen, and thrives on it.

Fred had determined to travel by night, so as to have the advantage of the cool air, and and the protection from enemies which the obscurity provided.

In the day-time he could seek the shelter of a boulder, and his well-trained, faithful horse would sleep by his side.

After leaving camp he travelled all night, guiding his course by the help of the stars and his pocket compass.

Just as the dawn was breaking, and yellowish gleams of sunshine were streaking the sky, he espied a vlei, the water in which

"'THAT HAND SHALL STRIKE NO MORE, FOR I MEAN TO CUT IT FROM YOUR WRIST!' HARTZ EXCLAIMED."

No. 10.

was so cool and pellucid that he was tempted to strip and bathe, to get some of the all-pervading dust off his skin.

He took a header, and splashed about like a porpoise.

His horse followed his example, wading in up to his belly, drinking the while, as if he had turned on a constant supply tap.

A run in the sun soon dried him, and Fred, feeling like a giant refreshed, speedily got into his clothes, and selecting the base of a small kopje for his resting-place, unpacked his knapsack, and made preparations for breakfast.

In his saddle-bag he had a small spirit lamp, which boiled enough water to make a cup of coffee; a large biscuit and a tin of bully beef completed his repast.

Suddenly he heard a cry which was familiar to him, because some of the Colonials in camp were in the habit of using it to one another :

"Coo-ee ! Coo-ee !"

It was evidently the cry of a bushman from New South Wales, who, for some purpose or another, had been sent after him, so he answered back in the Australian vernacular "Coo-ee."

In less than a minute, a short, wiry little man with bandy legs, the knees screwed into the horse's flanks, leaning over the neck like a jockey, came tearing up at a gallop.

He had just time to round the kopje and gain shelter, when half-a-dozen shots rattled against the rock.

"Boers, by Jingo !" cried Fred, raising his rifle to his shoulder, and looking out on to the veldt, where he saw a small party of Boers, who had evidently been chasing the new-comer.

It was clear that the horse had been ridden at speed, for its coat was covered with foam.

"Give them pepper, mate," said the stranger, "and I'll be your friend, as sure as my name is Pardoe."

They stood side by side, and both fired with remarkable accuracy, Dawson being astonished at the efficiency displayed by Pardoe, who was a very rapid firer and a dead shot.

Seven or eight Boers tumbled out of their saddles in quick succession, their riderless horses scampering over the plain, panic-stricken.

The remainder took to flight, and were soon mere specks in the distance.

"That danger is over," remarked Pardoe ; "but I think you'll have to shift your quarters if you want to be safe. What do you belong to? I'm one of Carey's Chickens, as they call us. That's because Carey raised the Bushmen's Contingent. We all come from 'out-back,' a good many of us from the Darling River."

Dawson explained that he was an officer in Harkaway's War Scouts, on his way to the Crocodile river, which was many miles off.

He had heard of Carey's Chickens, who had lately arrived.

They were tough, hard-bitten men, made of leather, as you may say, who can live on a cup of tea and a bit of damper.

Pardoe had read about Harkaway and his scouts, so he and Fred became friendly at once. The latter complimented him on his shooting.

"Good shot, you call me," exclaimed Pardoe. "Well, I can break the hind legs of a running kangaroo at five hundred yards. More than that. What I am going to tell you is on the level. I can hit a bee on a thistle-blossom at three hundred ; and as for riding, I believe I was born in the saddle. I'm part of a horse, and don't know how to fall off. See that nag of mine? He can turn on a six-pence, and do eighty miles a day for a week together, and, like his master, live on next to nothing."

Fred offered him some of his limited supply of provisions, but the bushman refused to take any.

He was satisfied with a drink of water and a strip of biltong he had taken from a Boer whom he had shot on the previous day.

When on a scout, Pardoe was always on the look out for Boers, and potted them as he would rabbits in his own country.

In a short time, he and Fred became quite confidential.

It appeared that he was attached to General Brabant's force, then operating near Colesberg.

His mission was to travel as rapidly as he could, and report upon the state of the railway between Bloemfontein and Mafeking, as it was important to relieve the latter town, now that Kimberley and Ladysmith were free.

That being the line of country that Fred was about to take, though he was going a bit further than Mafeking, they agreed to travel together, which was a very useful arrangement, as the Boers were being rapidly driven out of Natal and Cape Colony, which would make the district they had to traverse extremely unsafe.

They moved on for another twenty-five miles without encountering any obstruction, and selected a comfortable place to rest.

"Here's for a dossdown," said Pardoe, after they had tethered their horses. "There is no sign of Boer, so I hope we'll rest easy. It's a lonely line of country, and reminds me very much of the bush. It isn't often you meet anyone as I did you, though last night I came across a white man and a Kaffir north of the Drakensberg Mountains. They stopped, and we exchanged a few words, though they didn't seem particularly inclined to talk ; in fact, I didn't like the look of the white man. He was a bit out of the common, being dandified and off-handed. I gave him a screw of 'bacca, and had a drink of some sort of kill-me-quick out of his flask. Now I come to think of it, he asked me a singular question."

"What was that?" inquired Fred.

" 'Peared to me that this chap was hunting for a trail. The Kaffir kept poking his nose into the grass as if he was looking for spoor, and I wondered what the idea was. Of course, the hoofs of a horse leave marks, which don't wear out all at once. I dodged Morgan, the bushranger, once. You've heard of the iron-clad demon ?"

"Yes," replied Fred, impatiently. "He wore armour, and a bullet couldn't hurt him."

"Right ! That's the man. Tell you what I did," continued Pardoe, who was very fond of diverging from the point and going into anecdote. "Morgan was after me because I spoilt one of his raids. Coming to a station, I went to the forge and had the smith turn my horse's shoes backside front, which threw him off the scent, for while I was going forward he thought I was riding back."

"That isn't what I want to hear about. What of the white man you met last night?"

"Him as was with the Kaffir?"

"Certainly. You have raised my curiosity."

"I was coming to him; but we bushmen always beat round in a circuit. It's impossible for us chaps to strike a bee-line, or go as the crow flies."

"Either tell your story, or let me go to sleep," said Fred, with a prodigious yawn, which showed how tired he was; and no wonder, as he had not had any sleep for twenty-four hours.

"I reckon you are the most impatient cuss I ever came across," answered Pardoe. "I'd let a fellow talk from early cock-crow until midnight, if he felt like it, and not interrupt him; though he told lies enough to raise the hair on your head.

"You look like it," replied Fred, sarcastically. "Give us a rest."

"I was going to tell you a lot of things, but I won't now. I ain't got no sleep in me. I'll sit in the sun on the top of this rock, and wave my hat to attract a stray Boer or two. I want to keep my hand in at shooting."

Dawson looked at the strange being before him, dressed in moleskins, Crimean shirt, and slouch hat; for he had taken off his khaki, preferring to ride in bush attire.

There was no officer to supervise him, and Pardoe was entirely on his own—a veritable son of the antipodean wilds.

"If you see the white man again, you can call me," exclaimed Fred, who began to despair of getting anything out of the bushman.

"You won't give me time," protested Pardoe, with an injured air. "I could drive a bevy of lizards into the neck of an ink bottle; I'm a rouseabout, and can herd stray cattle quicker than lightning, but I can't corner you."

"Come to the white man, or give up. You are the biggest talker I ever came across."

"Look here; that's rubbing it in. I'll swear that when I've been up country I haven't spoken a word to a living soul for three months, and nothing better to rap out at than a dingo."

"That is simply because you hadn't the chance."

"There is something in that remark of yours. A man's conversational powers are not excited by an old cow or a gum tree; still, it is a fact that my mates all call me the Silent Man, and I deserve the title, for I have never made an after-dinner speech, sung a song, or pronounced a funeral oration. 'Least said, soonest mended,' is my motto."

"You haven't got any cotton-wool about you, have you?" asked Fred.

"Good lauds! What do you want that for?"

"Just to stuff my ears up with. You can keep the white man until I wake up."

"Oh!" ejaculated Pardoe; "I forgot all about him, owing to your interruptions. I can see you don't like my style, but we shall get better acquainted in time. You are an eloquent speaker, and I could listen to you for hours at a sitting, but as you're a bit tired I don't mind breaking my rule of silence, and amusing you a little. Let me tell you a kangaroo story."

"For heaven's sake, don't!" said Fred, pressing his hands to his head.

"Have a rabbiter, or the adventures of a Boundary Rider?"

"No, no, no! Unless you want to drive me mad."

"Matey," exclaimed Pardoe, looking at Dawson with compassion, "you are darned hard to please, so help me two men and a boy, but I've been trying all along to tell you about this white man."

Fred groaned, and closed his eyes, thinking he would go off at a tangent again.

"This white man was of medium height, neither stout nor thin; his hair was black, and so were his eyes. His voice was harsh; when he spoke the sound affected me as if I was eating sour apples. His manner was aggressive, and he looked all the while as if he wanted to make a frontal attack on my laager, and I had a sensation as if a slab of ice had gone down my back. So much for him.

"The Kaffir was tall, with cunning eyes, that never rested long on one object. His lithe, sinewy form was as mobile as a black snake. I should call him a bad black anyway, and he ought to weigh in well for the Spy Stakes. The white man asked me if I'd seen a traveller going north, answering your description, which he gave me, hitting you off down to the ground, and now I come to remember, he called the Kaffir Dunko. But I say, mate, what makes you start and turn pale like that?"

"It is fortunate that you have told me this, for I shall be on my guard," replied Fred, "for now I know that my most bitter enemy is pursuing me."

"What have you done to him?"

"Lots of things in his opinion. He has an old grudge against me, dating back to the early days of the siege of Mafeking. Besides that, I have about me a document which he is crazy to possess."

Perceiving that Pardoe was anxious to learn more, Fred Dawson told him at length the history of the Jorkin mine in Rhodesia, the plan of which Harkaway had obtained from the old Jew, Malachi, stating his intention of paying a visit to the spot, after his interview with Colonel Plumer.

"It is worth trying," observed Pardoe. "Of course, it sounds shadowy, but the Jews are hard-headed people, and I bet Malachi knew what he was about. There is more in it than you think for. This country isn't half opened up yet, though it was known to the ancients, and I shouldn't wonder if you found the workings of the old mine intact. You and your friend Harkaway have got a fortune within your grasp. I wish you luck with all my heart; and when you are carting away your diamonds by waggon-loads, don't forget your new friend, Will Pardoe."

"You've only to give me a hail, and you shall have the best the land can produce," answered Dawson. "In fact, I'll give you a hatful."

"That creates a new tie between us," said the bushman. "I'll never lose sight of you. By Jake, I'll watch over you as if you were my own son, and get myself transferred from Carey's Chickens into Harkaway's War Scouts, so that I can have you under my eye. You are a promising young chap, and I should not like to have anything happen to you."

Fred could scarcely suppress a smile at this sudden outburst of solicitude and affection.

"Sleep away," continued Pardoe. "I'll sit up and watch, in case the white man and the Kaffir should steal a march on you. Perhaps they will collect some Boers on their way, which might make it awkward for us, as they are hot foot on our track. I always keep a look-out. Listen to this yarn. I was in charge of some cattle on the Darling, where the grass was rich, and a party of blacks came bullock-stealing. I shot a dozen and drove them off. But I knew thundering well they'd come back when night fell, so——"

He looked at Fred and broke off abruptly, for that promising but fatigued young officer had sunk into a profound slumber, and was snoring loudly.

"Blame my sister's cat!" cried Pardoe, "if I don't call that ingratitude. The sleepy mutton-head isn't listening to a word. He won't get me to spin him a yarn again in a hurry. I'll be as dumb as an oyster."

Placing his back against the rock, he put his rifle between his knees to be handy for use, and lighting his pipe, gazed over the veldt.

A herd of boek, travelling from one spot to another, was frolicking along, grazing as they went; but the bushman was too lazy to go out from his shelter to stalk them, as the sun was now high in the heavens, and his long ride had rendered him listless.

Some hours elapsed, and though Pardoe's eyes closed for a time, his ears were ever on the alert.

All was silent as the tomb.

The two horses were lying down in the grass.

The solitude would have been oppressive to anyone not accustomed to bush-life.

The sun had passed its meridian and was declining towards the west.

Worn out, Pardoe's pipe dropped from his mouth, and the man forgot his surroundings.

How long he slept he knew not; but he was roused by the sound of voices.

Looking in front of him, he beheld Webb, Dunko, and a couple of mounted Boers, who had drawn rein within three hundred yards of the kopje, and were looking inquiringly around them, as if in search of something.

"Here's a go," muttered Pardoe, between his teeth. "The white man and his nigger, by thunder! We shall be in queer street if we don't watch it."

He stretched out his hand and touched Fred lightly on the shoulder.

"The enemy are upon us," he whispered.

Dawson was too old and experienced a scout to betray the slightest agitation or the least excitement at any occurrence.

He sat up, nodded his head, and grasped his rifle firmly.

CHAPTER XLIV.

A DOG AND MAN FIGHT—THE HUNCHBACK IS ROUSED—HARKAWAY FREE—HE JOINS THE SCOUTS—THE EXPLOSION—FATE OF PRETORIOUS—THE BATTLE—JACK'S DANGER.

TIME crept on, and Teufelskint did not move from the place where he had fallen when the potent liquor overtook him.

He remained flat on his back, his eyes open, gazing on vacancy.

It was a peculiar thing about the hunchback that when he intoxicated himself he did not lose his senses.

It required a considerable shock of some kind to rouse him.

He could see the stars of the cloudless night through the open window.

He could hear the Boers bustling about outside, talking to one another, as if they were preparing for some great adventure; and he also distinguished the barking of a dog in the stock-yard.

This was a Pomeranian of a savage breed, who had taken an instinctive dislike to the mis-shapen dwarf of the veldt.

The animal got over his injury, but had never forgiven it.

Teufelskint saw the shadowy forms of Shalker and Constrad upon the stoep, and heard them conversing together in an animated tone.

From what they said, he gathered that Pretorious had, some time ago, departed for the farm to represent himself as Captain Harkaway, take command of the War Scouts and lead them to the deadly spot where the mine would be sprung under their feet and hurl them to destruction.

Of course, there was the probability of a portion escaping this doom; and he further gleaned that, to make the slaughter wholesale and certain, Shalker, Constrad, and Villebois were to lead all the Boers under their command by a circuit to the rear of the War Scouts, so as to cut the fugitives to pieces, and make a clean sweep of the regiment.

Only one man was to be left at the Lodge, and that was the sentry keeping watch and ward over Captain Harkaway and Mrs. Steiner.

A frantic desire to save his friend Jack raged in the mind of the hunchback, but, though he tried to throw off the lethargy which held him in a vice-like grip, he was powerless to do so.

He heard the tramp of horses, the field cornets and other officers giving words of command, and then there was a hush, as of death, around the house.

The silence was interrupted by the dog we have mentioned jumping through the window into the room.

Its name was Paul.

The hurried movements of the Boers, and being left alone, had so excited the animal that he had broken his chain, a piece of which was hanging to his collar and clanked dismally on the floor as the creature, nose to the ground, sniffed its way towards the recumbent form of the hated hunchback, who saw a venomous gleam in its large, vengeful eyes.

The mouth was open, and the gums, filled with sharp, glistening teeth, were bared.

Uttering a series of deep growls, followed by a loud yelp, the dog sprang upon the intruder—for such he regarded the dwarf to be—and made his fangs meet in the flesh of his left thigh.

The pain inflicted happened to be just what was required to galvanise Teufelskint into action.

His nervous system was revived, his vigour restored to him, and, elevating himself slightly he stretched out his sinewy arms, twining his bony fingers round Paul's throat.

A fearful struggle ensued between dog and man, which was sickening to behold.

The dog bit and tore wherever he could get a chance, and Teufelskint used his teeth for the same purpose.

It was a fight for life or death between the two, in which the dwarf had the advantage, for he was slowly, but surely, strangling the dog, whose strength waned and his efforts relaxed, until he rolled over dead, his body quivering at spasmodic intervals.

To make sure of his foe, Teufelskint plunged his knife up to the hilt in the carcase, and rose to his feet, covered with blood and staggering.

Yet he did not forget that the safety of Captain Harkaway's Scouts depended on him.

Time was precious. Not a moment was to be lost.

The crescent moon was just rising on the verge of the horizon, and, strange to say, it had a circle of a blood-red hue.

Was this ominous of the dire calamity which was impending?

Recovering himself by a mighty effort, Teufelskint hastened through the house and made his way out at the back door.

The shed in which Harkaway was confined stood before him, and, as chance would have it, the sentry had his back turned.

Gliding forward like a serpent, noiseless but rapid, with a sob and a cry, Teufelskint hurled himself upon the Boer, and, bearing him to the ground, stabbed him to the heart.

To break open with a large stone the door of Jack's temporary prison, was the work of a moment.

The captain was lying, pale and haggard, upon a truss of coarse hay, and, jumping up, regarded Teufelskint with unfeigned astonishment.

At no time was the hunchback of the hills a pleasant object to look upon, but lacerated and covered with blood he was actually repulsive.

"Rouse yourself!" shouted Teufelskint. "Up and away if you would save your brave scouts, who are being led into a devilish trap concocted by the Boers."

"What do you mean?" asked Jack, trembling all over. "I have been warned that something was going to happen."

"A man similar to you is about to lead the scouts over ground which has been mined," said the dwarf. "I saw a horse standing in the yard. Mount; gallop like the wind. Turn your men back; shoot the impostor who is representing you. This place is deserted. The Boers have gone to the rear of the scouts to cut them off. Lead the charge, and slay your foes; you'll never have such a chance again. Act bravely, and all the rich stores in this laager will be yours."

Jack had been pining for an opportunity to escape.

After his struggle with Webb, the latter had been taken away by Shalker, not much the worse for the encounter; but he was afraid that his enemy might come a second time to do him an injury. And, above all, he panted to be at the head of his beloved scouts once more, and save them from Shalker's device; therefore Teufelskint's visit was indeed welcome.

He wondered how the dwarf had met with his injuries, but there was no time to ask questions; yet in that moment of haste he thought of Mrs. Steiner.

"There is a lady in the adjoining shed, I believe," he said. "Liberate her, and mention that I told you to do so; then come on to my camp, and our doctor shall attend to you."

The hunchback nodded, and Jack bounded across the yard, the blood in his veins flowing like liquid fire.

He was free, and only an escaped prisoner knows the full meaning of that God-given word; for freedom is to man what the air is to the bird, or the vast forest to the lion.

The horse indicated by Teufelskint was already saddled and bridled, hitched to a hook in the wall.

Lying on the ground Jack saw a cavalry sword, which belonged to General Villebois, who had discarded it for a Mauser rifle, thinking the latter would be more serviceable when the time came to exterminate the War Scouts, as the Boers fondly hoped they would do that night.

Seizing the sword, and springing on the animal's back, Harkaway gathered up the reins, and trotting out of the yard, galloped over the veldt.

He was perfectly well aware of the terrible risk he ran, for in order to reach the on-coming scouts he would have to pass over the hidden mine, which might be sprung by the Boers, who were waiting in the tunnel below.

Onward he dashed at the top of his horse's speed, the night wind whistling past him, seeming to speak words to him in a strange, weird, unknown tongue.

As we have said, the stars were shining, and a pale shade of moonlight fell upon the scene.

All at once he saw the War Scouts approaching in martial array.

The horses were at the trot, and their colours were flying.

Cornstalk and Kanuck were a few yards in front.

Seeing a solitary horseman coming towards them, bare-headed, and waving a sword, they knew not what to think, and the Queenslander promptly ordered a halt.

"Back for your lives!" shouted Captain Harkaway. "Not a yard further. Not a foot. Not a step!"

The next moment Harkaway confronted the two Colonials.

"Do you not know me?" he demanded.

"You look like our captain," replied Cornstalk; "but it is a curious thing there should be two Harkaways in the field. Which is which? That's what I want to know."

"The man who has represented himself to be me, and assumed the command of my War Scouts, is a rank impostor, and a Boer in disguise."

"I thought there was something queer about him; but he would deceive the mother who bore you."

"He shall not live many hours to prolong the fraud. Where is he?" enquired Jack.

"Pretending to be wounded, as I imagine now, he is in the rear. The fellow made us believe that his head and arm were injured in getting away from Shalker's Boers, so he put us in the front, and took a back seat, but I guess I will go and corral him before he can make a bolt," said Kanuck.

Harkaway was satisfied with this proposal, and did not trouble himself any more about Pretorious, who he knew would not easily get out of the clutches of the Canadian.

Riding close up to the scouts, who, drawn up in two lines, had been regarding him with wonder, curiosity, and amazement, he stopped short, and, sword in hand, addressed them—

"Boys," he exclaimed, at the top of his voice, which was clear and sonorous, "I am back again, and with you once more. A Boer who resembles me has taken my place for a few hours. I shall deal with him later on. He was leading you into a death-trap. As far as I know, you may be even now on the verge of a mine, and the cunning Boers are massed in your rear, waiting to cut off those among you who may escape from the explosion."

The scouts were convinced that the genuine Harkaway was before them.

They knew his voice and manner, his dash and go, so they gave him a hearty ringing cheer, which rolled like the blast of a trumpet over the veldt.

Several of them broke from the ranks, and, riding up with outstretched arms, wanted to shake hands with him.

"Not now, my lads," said Jack. "Wait till the fun is over. Right wheel; forward."

He cantered round the force and placed himself at the head of the regiment.

A glance sufficed to show him that Kanuck had not been idle.

Pretorious had been dragged from his horse before he could offer any resistence.

The bandages were torn from his sham wounds, and with the bridle-reins of his horse the stalwart Canadian bound him hand and foot, saying, "Lie there, you false hound. I shall know where to find you when I want you."

Pretorious presented a pitiable spectacle. He knew that something had happened, but could not divine what it was. At any rate, he was discovered.

The project of the Boers might succeed, though that was problematical. He considered himself betrayed.

His only chance lay in the speedy explosion of the mine and the pressing on of the scouts towards the Lodge.

He was not exactly sure where the Boers had placed the enormous quantity of dynamite which was intended to destroy the War Scouts, but Shalker had arranged that he should be given a signal.

A Boer stationed at some distance on the right flank was to discharge a rocket of blue-and-red stars, on seeing which Pretorious was to turn round, set spurs to his horse, and join his comrades in the rear as rapidly as possible.

Led by Captain Harkaway in his usual gallant style, the War Scouts galloped back in the direction of their quarters at Shalker's farm.

All of a sudden, as preconcerted between Shalker and Pretorious, the rocket darted up into the dark sky, shedding its colours, the red ones looking like falling stars.

This was the signal for Pretorious to make his ignominious and shameful flight; but owing to the precautions of the Canadian, the unfortunate wretch was unable to stir.

Much against his will, he was obliged to lie on the ground trembling like a leaf, his morbid mind inducing him to fancy that the aasvogels were already picking the flesh from his bones.

Without being aware of the fact, the young Boer, who had been the dandy of Bloemfontein and Johannesburg, was lying on the confines of the carefully concealed mine, which sealed his fate.

The earth gaped in several places.

This yawning was followed by a terrific uprising which covered a large space of ground.

Amidst a mass of fire and smoke, earth and stones belched up, as if from some Tartarean gulf, Pretorious was shot towards the clouds, his body being blown into fragments.

The fate mapped out for the War Scouts had, contrary to his expectations and those of his friends, become his own.

Meanwhile, the scouts had covered the ground at their best pace, and soon came within sight of Shalker and his Boers, who were waiting, as they imagined, for the arrival of a few panic-stricken stragglers.

They had heard the awful sound of the explosion which had rent the ground with Titanic might, and they had seen the sky reddened with a lurid glare, which even nature in her maddest moments could not excel.

When the War Scouts swept down upon them in a solid phalanx, with bayonets fixed, and faces filled with grim determination, they were astounded.

There were no kopjes to shelter them.

They had no trenches or earthworks to hide behind and skulk in; and in a half-hearted manner they discharged their rifles, only to receive a withering fire in return, which mowed them down like so much grass.

Sending Cornstalk with a full company to catch the Boers in the rear, should they attempt to fly, Harkaway waved his sword and charged the enemy.

All the scouts were mounted, and they rode at a speed which precluded them from firing. They were anxious to get at close quarters.

The Boers remained stationary, awaiting the onslaught, and several of the scouts were killed or wounded by their fire.

Constrad and Villebois were close together, shouting encouraging words to their men, who did not respond heartily to their battle-cries, for they had been surprised, and were anxious to make what the mobile Boers call a strategic movement, this in reality meaning flight.

Without waiting for orders, some of them turned their horses' heads, and were about to gallop over the veldt, in spite of Shalker's efforts to stop them, when the detachment of War Scouts under Cornstalk attacked them, first with a volley and then at the point of the bayonet.

As if one was not enough to fight at a time, Harkaway dashed at Constrad and Villebois, slashing right and left.

They defended themselves as well as they could, but were no match for such a brilliant swordsman as Harkaway.

With a magnificent down stroke he nearly severed Villebois' arm from his body, and knocked him out of the saddle.

Warding off a blow from Constrad, he delivered a splendid thrust, running the Boer leader through the body, causing him to drop with a hollow groan upon the ensanguined ground.

He recovered his sword quickly, and was looking out for a fresh victim, when Shalker, who was bleeding from a gash in the neck, given him by a bayonet, galloped up, and with a sudden movement jerked the captain's sword out of his hand.

The following moment he presented a revolver at Harkaway's head.

It was a crisis of intense peril, but Jack looked defiantly at him.

CHAPTER XLV.

HARKAWAY'S EXTRAORDINARY ESCAPE ON THE BATTLEFIELD—DEATH OF ANDY THE BUGLER—AN ORDER COMES FROM HEAD-QUARTERS—HARKAWAY ON THE BRIDGE —SHOT AND SHELL.

IT would have gone hard with Harkaway at this extremely critical moment, had not a sudden intervention of a most unexpected nature taken place in his favour.

Several horses which had been rendered riderless by the bullets of the scouts became frantic with terror, and stampeding, as it is called, made a wild rush to get out of the conflict; and carrying everyone before them, jostling and knocking other horses, they came direct to the spot where Harkaway and Shalker were.

Jack received a kick on the head which stunned him, and Shalker was driven some distance off, without being able to discharge his weapon.

The Boers, thoroughly beaten and dis-organised, were flying northwards, as if they intended to take refuge with a commando under General Vandyke, who was entrenched on a spur of the Drakensburg Mountains near the River Klip, which flows by Lady-smith.

Shalker was furious at the failure of his scheme, and heartbroken to see that only a handful of his Boers had escaped slaughter by the scouts.

They were thorough-bred Boers, who had been through some hard fighting, in resisting Buller's repeated attacks, and were certainly some of the best in Kruger's Army.

When Harkaway recovered conscious-ness, he found himself lying on a pallet which had been provided for him in one of the rooms of the farmhouse, which had been turned into a hospital.

He had been carried off the field with other wounded men.

The doctor had bound up his head.

The night had passed, and daylight was streaming in through the windows.

Getting up, he walked across the room.

Beyond a dull, aching pain, and a feeling of dizziness, he was none the worse for his injury; and he was confident that after a good breakfast he could fight again all day.

Naturally, he felt very anxious to know the result of the battle, and was about to go forth to make enquiries, when the door opened and he was confronted by Cornstalk.

The sturdy Colonial had his arm in a sling, and one side of his face was bandaged, which showed that he had received rough treatment during the fighting.

"What cheer, cap?" he cried heartily. "You are up and about, I see, which none of us expected. You must be made of iron."

"I am one of the tough brigade," replied Jack, smiling. "I need not ask if we have won the battle; your presence here is a guarantee for that."

"We are not prisoners on our way to Pretoria yet. Kruger must have a cheek on him. He provided hundreds of trucks to carry away White's garrison, when he took Ladysmith, and built a street of iron houses in the capital to receive them."

"Yes," answered Jack; "and now Buller is in Ladysmith, and Roberts in Bloem-fontein."

"We shall soon drive the Boers over the border. By George! what a dressing we gave them last night. The scouts took thirty prisoners. There are one-hundred-and-twenty dead on the field, and seventy wounded have been conveyed to the Lodge."

"How many escaped?"

"That I can't tell you. Only a handful, I should guess; but I am sorry to say the arch-rebel, Shalker, is not to be found, so I presume he has got off."

"He very nearly got the bulge on me in the encounter," remarked Jack. "I was disarmed; he had covered me with a pistol. All I can remember is a rush of horses and a kick on the head. Have we lost heavily?"

"No," replied Cornstalk. "Our casualties are small. The Boers were outflanked and surprised; but you will be sorry to hear what I am going to tell you."

"I hope nothing has happened to Kanuck; the gallant Canadian would be an irreparable loss."

"He's as right as rain, and got off without a scratch. That's his usual luck."

"Is it the corporal or Fish?"

"Neither one nor the other; but I forgot to tell you about Maori. When he heard there was going to be a fight, he crept out of the hospital tent, though he had to walk with a crutch, and shouldering his rifle, sniped off several Boers, and was under fire for half-an-hour."

"Bravo," cried Harkaway, "that shows what fine stuff the New Zealanders are made of."

"It has thrown him back a bit, and the doctor had to give him a talking to."

"I am proud of my Colonials."

"We are federating the Empire," said Cornstalk, "but I am going away from my sad intelligence. Our bugler, little Andy, is mortally wounded, and wants to see you before he dies."

"Poor chap," replied Jack. "I thought a lot of that boy."

"He was on the sick list, as you know, but martial ardour inspired him, and he went into the thick of the fight. He was twice wounded, and only gave up when he fell down from sheer exhaustion."

"Where is he? I will go to him at once."

"In the adjoining room. We made up six beds there, as the hospital tent is full."

Jack followed the Australian into the apartment indicated, and saw Andy lying in a corner near the open window.

His face was wan and pale; but it brightened when he saw his captain.

The flush, however, died away, and his countenance became colourless.

His khaki uniform was dyed with blood.

In vain he tried to extend his hand, which looked like that of a wax doll.

Extreme weakness prevented him from doing so.

"Cheer up, my little man," said Harkaway. "You will soon be well again, and able to kill some more Boers."

"Not me, captain," replied Andy, in a faint voice, which was little above a whisper, while his parched lips quivered. "I'm going home fast, and I know it."

"Never say die."

"I fell fighting for the Queen, God bless her."

"Is there anything you want to say to me?" asked Jack, who was much affected.

"I believe my mother and father are in Mafeking. If you should go there again, and meet them, give them my last love."

"I will not fail to do so."

"Tell them, please sir, that I always did my duty, and was brave, fearing no danger, and I never shirked a bullet. Father always brought me up to be plucky, and it will comfort him and mother to hear what you have to say about me. Do you mind undoing my tunic at the neck, sir?"

"Certainly not. What for?"

"I wear a cross attached to a bit of ribbon," answered Andy. "It was mother's gift years ago, and I should like to press it to my lips before I go."

Complying with his request, Jack produced a small silver cross, which the bugler kissed reverently.

"Thank you," murmured the dying boy. "Bury it with me. Good-bye, captain, my eyes are growing dim. I cannot see you; but beautiful angels seem to be beckoning to me, and sweet music, such as I never heard before, is sounding in my ears."

"Are you in pain?"

"No, sir. That has all gone. I feel very happy. Pray for me."

The scene was an affecting one.

There were five wounded soldiers in the room; not one of them stirred or uttered a word. Those in agony even suppressed a groan.

Harkaway knelt down by the side of the boy, and his lips moved for a few minutes; the example being followed by the Queenslander, on whose rough cheeks tears could be seen.

There was a convulsive spasm of the slender frame, a terrible struggle for breath, a brief rattling in the throat; and then a seraphic smile settled upon the lad's face, and his soul took its flight heavenwards.

The brave little bugler was dead.

With a solemn look, and a slow step, Harkaway quitted the room, speaking a few kind words to the wounded scouts as he passed them.

He had lost a personal friend in Andy, and felt sad.

A man has no time to indulge in grief when war is raging and he had not proceeded further than the stoep when his mind was carried to other things by Kanuck, who came up to him quickly, looking full of life and dash.

"Glad to see you on your legs again, captain, so soon; we thought the Boers had pounded the life out of you last night, when we picked you up on the battle-field, which was as full of dead Dutchmen as an old churchyard is of bones," he exclaimed.

"I am not much hurt, thank God," answered Harkaway cheerfully.

"You take a lot of killing, boss."

"I am only grieved when I see my dead and wounded men; as for myself, I don't care a rap. I am fighting for Queen and country, and taking all risks."

"You are wanted, badly wanted, captain," continued Kanuck.

"What's the matter now?"

"A messenger has just come from General Buller, and he gave me the order, as you were not about."

"Quite right. You can now give it to me; for I feel perfectly fit, and in good form for anything."

"Joubert and his Boers, after raising the siege of Ladysmith, have retreated, part entrenching on the Drakensberg, others on the Biggarsberg Mountains. As you know, we are close to the former, and about ten miles off from where we are now flows the Klip River. Over that is a waggon bridge; the one for the railway having been destroyed."

"I have seen it," replied Harkaway.

"This waggon bridge is of great importance to our general, as the river is now at flood, and he wants to pursue the Boers, who have kept us at bay for such a long time."

"What am I expected to do?"

"The Kaffirs say that General Vandyke, with a strong commando, dominates this bridge with a Long Tom and other long-distance guns. Vandyke is reported to have undermined the bridge, which he could blow up at any moment by electricity, if the wires are not cut, which can only be done under a heavy fire."

"What of the night?"

"The Boers are provided with a powerful search-light."

"That makes the enterprise all the more difficult," said Jack, thoughtfully.

"Your orders, captain, are to cut the wires without any delay, no matter what it may cost us in men. When this is accomplished our general will send five thousand men across the river to storm Vandyke's position, and capture the guns."

"I understand," exclaimed Harkaway, "and shall be ready to make the attempt in about two hours time."

"How many scouts will you require?" enquired Cornstalk. "It is a sort of forlorn hope; as soon as we are seen on the bridge, the Boer guns will begin to pound away like steam, and very few will come back alive. I will go among the men and ask for volunteers if you will only state the number. How many shall it be?"

"None at all," replied Jack.

"What in thunder do you mean, cap?" demanded the Queenslander, looking at him in amazement.

The Canadian's face also expressed astonishment.

"I am going to do this thing myself," said Jack, modestly. "If there is any extra risk to be run I intend to take the burden on my own shoulders. It is only one man's work. Not for one moment will I think of exposing my fine fellows in an unneccessary manner. I'm going to play a lone hand, I tell you."

"Good enough, cap; but you ought to consider that your life is more valuable than that of any other man in the regiment," urged Kanuck.

"I do not want anyone to teach me my duty," said Harkaway, sternly.

"When you hear the shriek of the shrapnel, and the dull crash of the cannon-ball——"

"Silence!" interrupted Jack. "I know you mean well, but I map out my own plan of campaign."

This was a rebuff which the Canadian took in good part, as he knew that his zeal for his captain's welfare had carried him a little too far.

"I have to report, sir, that we have captured the whole of the stores and ammunition at the Lodge, which were intended for General Joubert."

"Good!" said Harkaway. "What have you done with them?"

"Blown up every waggon. I thought Vandyke's commando might come after them, and so I did not give the Boers a chance."

"Quite right; I approve of what you have done, and now before I go to the waggon bridge over the river, I must have some food, if it's only a mealie and a bit of salt."

"If you look sharp, you will be just in time," replied Kanuck. "Corporal Potts and Mr. Fish have been out foraging. They are in the kitchen, and have got a rattling good spread. Roast duck, ditto fowl, and plenty of green peas; with a potful of coffee. Capital tack. You ought to be in that. The corporal knows how to play the old soldier, and he will live where others would starve. Chip in at once, or it will be all gone."

This advice was too good to be neglected, and Jack joined the individuals mentioned, in the kitchen.

He was made heartily welcome, and told them of the duty he was about to undertake.

"I must send a Kaffir runner off with a despatch for my paper," said Fish, taking out his note-book. "Gallant feat of Captain Harkaway. Alone, entirely unassisted, he boldly ventures on the waggon bridge over the Klip River, which is dominated by the Boers' long range guns. He daringly cuts the wires connected with the mine which is intended to destroy the bridge. All the time he is under a heavy fire, shells are bursting on all sides of him. The river is hissing and and bubbling like a seething cauldron; but he escapes unhurt, and rejoins his devoted scouts, after having rendered the bridge safe for the advance of Buller's artillery."

"But I haven't done it yet, man alive," said Jack.

"Never mind, I know you will. War correspondents have to anticipate sometimes, so as to get a beat on the other ink-slingers. If you get shot, you know, I can put that in afterwards. The Editor will bring out an extra, and we shall have an enormous sale for a late edition."

"Thank you," replied Jack. "You are very kind. I suppose you have my epitaph already written."

Fish touched his forehead with his finger, and thought for a moment.

Then he came out with a happy impromptu, which was a sort of inspiration:

"Harkaway—shot to day—one of the best—gone to his rest."

"I don't think you can improve on that," observed the corporal. "Fish can do it bang up when he likes."

"I am not a bad hand at extemporising," said Fish, complacently. "What is it that Kitchener hasn't got, while Roberts has a little one, Buller and all the Boers a big one? It's a conundrum I hit off just now. Give it up? I thought you would. It is rather a hard nut to crack, but I'll put you out of your misery; and you can tell your friends you made it yourself if you like. I'm generosity itself in these matters."

"What is it?" enquired Jack.

"The letter B. Don't you see? There's a little B in Roberts, and Buller and the Boers have a big B to their names. I ought to copyright it. The riddle will be all over Cape Town in an hour, when I send it to my paper. I call it A1, copper bottomed."

Jack did not contradict him for fear of hurting his vanity.

Breakfast was over.

Taking a flask from his pocket, Fish exclaimed:

"Here is success to you, my fine fellow."

He drank, and offered the bottle to Potts, adding: "Have a swig, old man?"

"I don't know whether I will or I won't, but I'd rather," replied the corporal. "Though it is contrary to the rules and regulations, and I never make a habit of it, you know."

Soon afterwards Captain Harkaway left the table, and went to the medical tent, where the surgeon removed the bandage from his head, put some plaster on the wound, and over that a woollen pad, so that he could wear his helmet. He then mounted his horse, and rode over the veldt in the direction of the river.

There were no Boers to be seen.

The battle of last night, the utter rout and wholesale slaughter which the scouts had inflicted on the enemy, had taught them to be cautious; but he had no doubt that their sentries were keeping a sharp look-out on the mountain.

Having reached a spot about two miles from the river, he dismounted, and made his horse lie down.

Through his field-glass he inspected the Boers' position; but they had masked their batteries, and the men were securely hidden in the trenches, so that he could see nothing.

The sun was shining brightly, throwing out great heat.

The ground he had to traverse was sparsely covered with stunted grass, and here and there a few bushes.

The ant-hills were numerous, but smal

In fact it was an arid plain, dotted with boulders.

He reached the bridge, the importance of which he saw at a glance, for the river was broad and deep, with a swollen tide.

The banks were high, and fringed with dwarf willows.

There was no ford or drift anywhere near.

No pontoon bridge could have been made under the enemies' fire, and if the wooden bridge was destroyed, it would have been impossible for either man or guns to cross.

He had provided himself with a sharp hatchet, which was his only weapon, save the revolver he carried in his belt.

With the hatchet he intended to cut the wires, which he saw had been carried to the centre of the bridge, the mine being placed underneath.

There were two wires, which made him imagine that there were the same number of mines.

With a palpitating heart, he stepped on to the bridge with the hatchet raised in the air to cut the wires, when, with a hurtling noise, a shell from one of the Boers' Long Toms passed within some yards of him, and exploded with terrific force on the opposite bank.

The wind raised by the shell blew Harkaway off his feet, causing him to fall on his side close to the rail of the bridge.

Unfortunately the hatchet slipped from his hand and sank with a loud splash into the river.

Boom, boom, went a Howitzer. Bang thundered a Long Tom. There was not a moment to be lost. Time was indeed precious just then.

Every instant Harkaway expected to be killed, either by fragments of shell or the blowing up of the bridge; one calamity being as awful to contemplate as the other.

His hatchet was gone beyond recovery.

What to do he knew not.

CHAPTER XLVI.

DAWSON AND THE BUSHMAN BEAT OFF THEIR ENEMIES—WEBB AND DUNKO HIDE—AN INTERVAL OF SUSPENSE—PARDOE TELLS A STORY—A CLEAR FIELD—OFF AGAIN.

WHEN Fred Dawson and Pardoe the bushman saw themselves confronted by the villain Webb, the treacherous Kaffir, and two Boers, they were completely taken by surprise, for they had very foolishly imagined that they had that part of the veldt entirely to themselves, and did not dream that their pursuers would come up with them so soon.

Half-a-dozen shots were fired at them without doing any damage.

They were well sheltered, and kept their heads low.

They returned the fire at random, not daring to expose themselves to obtain a good aim.

A loud cry caused Fred to peep over the boulder, and to his delight he saw that one Boer, shot through the body, had fallen from his horse.

The second one had turned his steed's head, and was in the act of decamping, while Webb and Dunko had vanished.

With characteristic cowardice, Webb and the Kaffir, finding that Dawsoh was on the alert, and had a companion, when they expected to discover him asleep and alone, had concealed themselves behind an adjacent kopje, which was high enough to hid themselves and their horses.

Dawson did not hesitate to give the flying Boer the benefit of a bullet, which brought his career to a speedy termination; and he looked round anxiously for Webb and the Kaffir, being puzzled to make out what had become of them; the bushman was equally at fault when he saw the state of affairs.

"Lie low, mate," said Pardoe. "We have accounted for the two Boers, but the Kaffir and your foe, Webb, cannot be far off, and will give us the lead the first chance they get. We have water and food, and can stand out as long as they. It is a question of who runs first."

"The artful beggars have got behind some rock," replied Fred. "Do you think it would be safe to try and creep round them?"

"I wouldn't risk it, so I tell you plainly. We will light our pipes and sit down back to back, so that they can't take us in front or rear, nor yet make a flank movement without being seen."

"Very well," said Fred; "I have no objection to try that game for a few hours; but we can't keep it up long, as sleep will come upon us."

"So it will on them," answered Pardoe. "They are just as much mortal as we are. When night comes we will do a crawl, and see if we can't plug their hides for them. I'll tell you a story of what happened to me once, when I was in the bush. It shan't be a long yarn, for you know I'm not a great talker. I am a man of few words."

Fred prepared himself for an interminable tale.

"Well," continued Pardoe, "this is how it was. I had been up country some months, herding sheep, and only went to the station once in six weeks, to get my wages, a supply of tea, and flour to make damper. There were bushrangers about, mean whites of no account, escaped prisoners, and criminals who had fled from justice. They belonged to Morgan's gang, and after he was shot his men went about marauding in parties of twos and threes. Did I ever tell you this story before?"

"No," answered Fred, with a wearied look as he yawned.

"That's all right!" exclaimed the bushman, with a satisfied air. "It isn't a long one, and I am a man of few words. The rascals knew that I could sport a bit of gold, if I chose to, for I had no chance of spending my money, unless I went down to Sydney on the spree, which we chaps usually do when we get tired of sheep, and gum - trees, kangaroos, dingos, and blacks. I've lived upon mutton so long that I've been ashamed to look a sheep in the face. One day a stranger rode up to my diggings, which consisted of an old army bell-shaped tent, and a couple of blankets, a few tin pans, and a tea-pot. It isn't every man who has that last luxury out there; most of the fellows brew their tea in an old jam-pot. Did I ever tell you this story before?"

"Confound it—no! Haven't I said so?"

"It won't take me long. I never waste words. I'm coming to the pith of it. Don't be impatient, you must give a chap time. I know you're anxious, but I can't help that. This yarn bears on our present situation. That's the beauty of it. It's a pity I'm cutting it short, but brevity is always my motto. It is a great fact if a man can go through life without wasting words, and other people's time.

"Some fools will talk you silly, and you can't get a word in edgeways; while you couldn't make out what it is about. Have you ever met with one of that sort?"

"I rather think I have," answered Fred drowsily, for the yarn was beginning to have a soporific effect on him.

"Great nuisance, aren't they?"

"Awful," snapped Fred.

"For my part I always try to avoid them," said the bushman. "I knew a man on the Darling, he was head stockman at Barnett's Station, and when he had no one to talk to, he let fly at the sheep, and they do say that he talked all their tails off; but that's neither here nor there. The stranger I was speaking of asked me for a pipe of tobacco, which a man in the bush, always gives to another when he's broke and stony. While I was pulling out my pouch he drew his gun on me, demanding my money or my life. Regular bushranger style; but I was equal to him. Did I ever tell you this story before? Because if I did, it's no use going on with it, and wasting words."

"I haven't known you long, my friend, but you inflicted it on me five minutes after we met," said Fred, desperately, hoping to choke him off.

"Perhaps I did," replied Pardoe, with a gay and airy indifference. "All the same, it's good enough to hear twice. Don't be vexed at my cutting it so short. I remember well the day on which this thing happened. It was St. Patrick's Day. I have a great respect for Irishmen, for the biggest hiding I ever got in my life was from Pat O'Brien, a stevedore in Adelaide, where we had a fair stand-up fight. Not having a bit of shamrock, I had picked some clover, which I stuck in my jacket, and I recollect that this bushranger hadn't got any shamrock, which, you know, is the national emblem of Ireland; and I am told this year all the British soldiers are to wear it, by order of the Queen, in honour of the Irish Brigade."

"Hang it all, are you obliged to go all the way from Australia to Ireland to tell this story?"

"Keep your hair on," said the bushman. "You are as fussy as an old maid with a houseful of cats. I pretended to take out the leather bag in which I carried my gold, but instead of doing that I forked out a pistol, and there we were, gun to gun, neither of us liking to risk firing first. There were two gum-trees. I never could tell a bush story without a gum tree; but you shall hear my fish story some-day, all about that shark, you know.

"It's a regular hair-raising, blood-curdler, but all true. That's the best of my stories, there's never a word of a lie in any of them. One gum-tree was behind me, the other gum-tree was at the back of the bushranger. We both wanted a tree. He backed, and I backed, and just about the same moment we each got behind the trunks of these trees I'm talking about.

"He didn't show a bit of himself, no more did I. It might have been sudden death to look round, and the time passed wearily, you bet. Perhaps you have known what that is, in the course of your experience."

"I feel it now, and a very great kind of feel it is too."

"I knew I should rouse your feelings. It was a terrible position for me to be placed in, and I'll own up that I was fairly scared. I fluttered a handkerchief, Bushranger made a hole in it. I held out my straw hat, Bush ranger riddled it. I showed my pipe, Bushranger knocked the bowl to eternal smash. The hours dragged on wearily. Did I ever tell you this story before?"

"No!" shouted Dawson, frantically, "and I hope to heaven you never will again."

"Hey! You're not in a wax, are you?" exclaimed Pardoe. "I am afraid this thrilling shocker of mine is too much for your young nerves. It's powerful strong, but I'll cut it short. Night fell, and I couldn't stand it any longer, so I quitted my gum-tree, and went to look for Bushranger."

He stopped short, for Dawson had vanished round the corner of the boulder.

"Say, pard, where are you off to?" exclaimed Pardoe.

There was no answer, and the bushman, rifle in hand, went to look for Fred, who preferred to chance being shot by Webb or Dunko to hearing any more of the story, which Pardoe had been such an unreasonable time in telling.

There were only two rocks in the vicinity which could afford shelter to Webb and the Kaffir.

Dawson looked behind each of these, without discovering any trace of them, and it was clear to his mind that they had silently departed.

"They have gone," he shouted. "Come here, Pardoe. While you were talking they must have taken their hook, and if they were within sound of your voice, I don't wonder at it."

Pardoe came running up at the call.

"Gone, have they?" he exclaimed. "By Jingo! That's just what my Bushranger did. When I went to his gum-tree, there was only the smell of him hanging about the air. Shake. We'll get on horseback, and travel another thirty miles before we close our optics."

Fred assented to this proposal, and the pair were soon galloping over the veldt.

CHAPTER XLVII.

HARKAWAY'S SPLENDID COURAGE—A DIVE FOR THE HATCHET—HE CUTS THE WIRES —THE BATTLE—ANOTHER VICTORY—THE DEFILE IN THE HILLS—JACK IS TRAPPED AND DRAGGED INTO A CAVE.

THE hesitation and doubt which had come over Harkaway after the loss of his hatchet, and the explosion of the shell so perilously near him, did not last long.

He knew precisely where the hatchet had fallen, and, determined not to be baffled, made up his mind to go after it.

At school he had been famous for his swimming and diving, and creeping to the side of the bridge, with the shot and shell whirling over his head, he threw himself over the low rail of the bridge, and plunged into the water.

Disappearing under the surface, he reached the bottom of the river, within a few inches of the hatchet, which he picked up, and at once rose with it, holding the handle between his teeth.

The current had carried him right under the bridge, and getting hold of one of the trestles, he raised himself out of the stream, and sitting down on a timber support, paused to recover his breath and consider what he should do next.

The firing from the kopje had now ceased, the Boers evidently thinking that he had taken a desperate leap to get out of the deadly hail, and had either been drowned or carried some distance down the stream by the force of the current.

Come what might, he was more resolved than ever to go on with his undertaking, and he looked about for some means of accomplishing it.

On the other side of the river the ground was covered with beds of willows, small hills and high mounds of sand, which afforded excellent hiding room for a large body of men.

Though he had no exact idea of the present position of the British force, he was convinced that they were not far off, and were only waiting for him to cut the wires, when they would make a forward movement, and he fancied in his mind that he already heard the thundering of the big guns and the galloping of the horses, as the artillery advanced over the bridge to take up a position on the veldt, and drive the Boers from their trenches, with lyddite shells.

With great difficulty he contrived to reach the side of the bridge from which he had sprung into the water, and hauling himself up, saw the wires over his head.

Hanging on to the woodwork with one hand, he extended the other, and with two blows with the hatchet, given in quick succession, he cut the wires, which fell into the river with a splash.

This brave act rendered them useless to the Boers, and the bridge was saved.

Harkaway now had only to make his escape, and give information to the English of what he had done.

It would not do to expose himself again on the bridge.

That would draw the Boers' fire, and endanger his life once more, so he dropped into the water a second time as quietly as he could, and by swimming and diving alternately he reached the bank a quarter-of-a-mile below the bridge, having completely outwitted the cunning Boers, who considered that the wires were still intact, and that they could blow up the bridge whenever they felt inclined to, by means of their electric wires.

They were especially proud of their mine, which had been devised and perfected by a Russian engineer of note, who had been promised high pay for his work.

Gaining the bank, he crawled through the willows without being seen by the enemy, and made his way for a short distance without encountering any obstacle more serious than a couple of black snakes, which he soon despatched with his hatchet.

The willows now came to an end.

Before him was a sand-heap.

Behind him was the river which he had just crossed, beyond which was a stretch of veldt, leading up to the Drakensberg passes.

While he was looking for an opening in the sand-hill which would save him the trouble and risk of climbing to its summit, he was challenged by a voice, which exclaimed, " Halt ! Who goes there ? "

" Friend," he replied, promptly.

An English soldier had suddenly made his appearance.

It seemed as if he had come out of the sand-hill, but in reality he had been lying down under cover of some ant-heaps.

In a few words Jack told him who he was and what he had done, also adding that he was anxious to see the British commander as soon as possible.

In return the private informed him that he was one of the Suffolk regiment.

Behind the hill, Lord Dundonald was encamped with a strong force of cavalry and several batteries of artillery.

He was supported by the Lancashire, the Devon, and the Warwickshire regiments.

Jack lost no time in seeking an interview with Dundonald.

The soldier told him which direction to take.

He had little difficulty in passing the outlying pickets, and was soon in the camp; an orderly taking him to a tent where the general was discussing the situation with some of his staff officers.

Jack heard him say, in a tone of annoyance : " We are foiled ; Captain Prettyman has been watching the bridge, and saw one of Harkaway's Scouts endeavouring to cut the electric wires. The Boers opened fire on him, and a fragment of a shell blew the poor beggar into the river ; it was a dangerous duty, but we thought the scouts would be likely to accomplish it. Harkaway and his men have the reputation of being such clever dare-devils, that they can do anything ; but this time they have failed."

Jack saluted, and looked at the general with a smile on his face.

" I beg your pardon, my lord," he exclaimed ; " the scout did do his work after all. The wires are cut, and your force can go over the bridge whenever you like ; with nothing more to fear than Vandyke and Shalker's shells."

"Who are you, sir ?" demanded the general, sharply.

"Captain Harkaway," was the reply. "My scouts were all very tired, as they had been engaged in destroying Shalker's commando during the night, so when I got the message about the bridge, I thought I would do the job myself."

"Bless my soul, I thought you were blown into the river."

"I was knocked down by the concussion of the air ; but I jumped into the stream, dived after my hatchet, which I had dropped, climbed on the trestle work, and rendered the mine useless."

"'Pon my word, you are a splendid fellow, Captain Harkaway," cried Lord Dundonald, full of excitement. "Forward the artillery. Captain Prettyman, be good enough to see that your men limber up at once. Pepper the Boers with shrapnel and lyddite. Let the Dutchmen have it hot and strong. The bridge is safe for transport, thanks to Harkaway's bravery ; and when you take position on the veldt I want you to cover the advance of the Devons and Lancashires. I will take the enemy in flank, and cut off his retreat."

The camp was quickly in motion.

The horses were attached to the batteries, the drivers mounted, the bombardiers and gunners took their seats on the carriages, and the finest artillery in the world—whose motto is *Ubique*—galloped into action.

"I hope we shall have better luck, than Colonel Long at Colenso," remarked Dundonald. "All I've been waiting for is to get across the river. I will smoke the enemy out with lyddite ; the infantry will spit them like birds, and my Hussars and Lancers will know what to do with them when they run down on to the plain."

"I wish you would give me a mount, and let me attach myself to my old regiment," said Harkaway. "If you do not, I shall swim the river again, and bring up my scouts."

"You say they have been fighting most of the night. Why, my dear fellow, you must be regular fire-eaters."

"They always come up fresh as paint after a few hours' rest," answered Jack. "The Colonials are as hard as iron. I never saw any fellows to beat them."

"Very well ; have your own way. We will find a mount for you. Excuse me for a time, as I must attend to business."

Saying this, the famous cavalry leader turned to Colonel Hilyard, who had command of the Light Brigade, and getting on their horses, the two officers rode together towards the river.

Harkaway followed them, anxious to see what was going on.

He gained an elevated position on a small kopje, and was in time to see the batteries crossing the bridge, in spite of the fire directed upon them by the Boers, who, greatly surprised at the failure of the mine, fired hastily and at random, doing little damage.

Gaining a suitable spot, Prettyman unlimbered and began to shell the Boers with telling effect, and in a short time several of their guns were silenced.

Meanwhile the infantry advanced, followed by the cavalry, and crossing the intervening piece of ground, gallantly charged up the mountain side, in spite of a hot fusilade directed against them.

Skirting the base of the hill, the cavalry went round to intercept the enemy if they attempted to escape in the rear.

The movements were so hurried that the commanding officer entirely forgot all about Harkaway, who, unable to find a horse in the almost deserted camp, ran over the bridge to the place where he had left his own and found the well-trained creature precisely as he had parted with him.

Fearing that unless he made haste he would be left out of the battle, Jack jumped into the saddle, and, through his field-glass, took a survey of the situation.

To his astonishment he perceived his scouts galloping from Shalker's farm towards the hill which the English were storming.

Cornstalk and Kanuck were leading them, and Jack came to the conclusion that, hearing the firing, they thought they would be wanted.

"Just like my fine fellows," he murmured. "They smelt powder, and they couldn't keep out of it. I will gallop round the corner after Dundonald and Hilyard. My brave boys are sure to overtake me."

He started his horse at his best pace, and rapidly neared the hill.

The artillery fire had now ceased on both sides.

A sound of distant cheering told him that the trenches had been carried by the foot regiments, and he guessed that the Boers were in full flight.

In vain he looked for the cavalry, which had disappeared.

There were two defiles through the hills, not more than a mile apart.

Which path to choose he did not know, but it was no time for hesitation, and selecting the one on his right, he cantered towards it.

Seeing nothing to deter him from entering it, he did so.

He was obliged to slacken his pace, as the ground was littered with stones of various sizes, and his horse was in danger of stumbling at every step.

In the sides of the hills between which he was travelling, were several holes and gaping fissures which gave him an idea of caves within.

The sky had become overcast, and heavy drops of rain began to fall.

He had a mind to turn back, for it was the very place where hidden foe might lurk, and he knew that the slim, mobile Boer always had places of refuge to go to when hard pressed.

It was evident that he had made a mistake by taking a short unknown cut; yet it might be as perilous to go back as it would be to continue his advance.

Blaming himself for not joining his scouts, as he ought to have done, he pushed on, hoping to be on the veldt again before long ; but after going a quarter of a mile he reined in his horse, uttering a cry of vexation, mingled with dismay.

Before him was a blank, colourless wall of rock.

The defile here came to a sudden termination, and was impassable.

He was about to turn round, when the crack of a rifle was heard.

His horse was shot under him, and fell to the ground, throwing him heavily.

Before he could recover himself, half-a-dozen Boers rushed out, and throwing themselves upon him, bound his arms behind his back.

He had been caught in a veritable trap.

His captors assisted him to his feet, and a sorry spectacle he presented.

The wound he had received on his head the night before had broken out, bleeding again through coming in contact with a stone, his face and khaki uniform being stained with blood.

The first person his eyes lighted upon was Shalker, who grinned at him like a demon.

"Away with him," cried the Boer commandant. "If the day has gone against us, we have the consolation of knowing that we have taken a prisoner of importance. Jack Harkaway is ours, and I swear by the eternal, that he shall never fight against the Boers again."

The captain of the War Scouts was unceremoniously hustled to the aperture in the rock, and dragged inside.

He did not know what his fate would be.

Shalker, however, was not at all likely to show him any mercy.

He had a crushing defeat and the death of Pretorious to avenge; and the savage instinct of the Boer could be read in his glistening snake-like eyes.

CHAPTER XLVIII.

WEBB'S JOURNEY ACROSS THE VAAL—WITH DUNKO HE SWIMS THE CROCODILE RIVER —AT A KAFFIR KRAAL HE OBTAINS NEWS OF DAWSON—THE PURSUIT RENEWED— THE MINE—DAWSON'S GREAT DANGER.

THE attempt made by Webb and Dunko on Fred Dawson's life, luckily for him, failed, as we have already related; but they congratulated themselves on having so cleverly given him and the bushman the slip, after the fall of the two Boers, whom they had persuaded to accompany them.

Though he had met with a repulse, Webb was not the sort of individual to give up the chase he had taken in hand.

As we know, he had a two-fold object in view, one being to wipe Dawson out of existence, and the other to get possession of the plan of the mine; therefore, as soon as he and Dunko had taken a rest and refreshed themselves, he continued his pursuit of Fred, knowing the direction he would take to gain the banks of the Crocodile River.

He guided himself by his compass.

It was a long, weary journey; but he was used to the heat of the sun, and privations of all kinds.

The Kaffir was equally hardened.

They had lost the trail, and were travelling in a haphazard manner, hoping to overtake their prey; yet many days and nights passed without their getting any trace of Fred Dawson or Pardoe.

The route they took was considerably to the north of Mafeking.

Occasionally they met Kaffirs, who told them all sorts of contradictory stories respecting the long besieged town.

Some declared that it had surrendered to the Boers; others again were positive that Colonel Plumer had beaten the enemy in a pitched battle, and relieved it.

It was also said that Lord Roberts was marching from Bloemfontein on Pretoria.

This conflicting news made them very careful, and they journeyed principally by night, fearing that they might be captured by English scouts.

Webb was well known in Mafeking, and he knew that, if taken, he would be treated as a spy.

At length they reached the banks of the Crocodile River.

It was evening.

The sun was setting on low, leaden-looking clouds, which indicated the approach of bad weather.

Webb and Dunko were thoroughly worn out with their wanderings, and they were mentally depressed at having so far failed in their object.

They were at a loss where to go or what to do.

Noticing a Kaffir kraal not far distant on the opposite side of the river, pleasantly situated under the shade of tall trees, they determined to shelter there for the night.

Webb had money, and he knew that a little would buy Kaffir hospitality.

He suggested the idea to Dunko, who approved of it.

Together they plunged into the water, and swam across, reaching the other side without any mishap.

"We are in Rhodesia now," said Dunko. "Fine country all round. Perhaps we know the Kaffirs who live in that kraal. Got several friends around, baas. Maybe we'll get a bit of venison, or a duck, if there's any left on the farms. Been living on tough biltong long enough."

"This war has made things scarce," replied Webb. "As the Boers are being driven back, I think I shall head for Pretoria, where I have friends and money, and get on before the line is cut to Lorenco Marquez, in Portuguese territory, in which place I can stay safely until peace is concluded, and we see what the British are going to do, for I am heartily sick and tired of this ferdomdy war, out of which I have got more kicks than ha'pence, so far."

"It's all up with baas Kruger," said Dunko, laughing. "Steyn has bolted, and Oom Paul will have to go too. Everybody will be fond of the Rednecks now."

A tall, well-made Kaffir quitted the kraal, and advanced toward them.

When he saw Dunko he began to dance about in an excited manner.

"Who is that?" asked Webb. "It looks like someone who knows you."

"Very old friend of mine, baas," answered Dunko; "his name is Hiwayo. We worked together in the diamond mines at Kimberley; and the gold mines at Johannesburg, he's my mate, and will do anything for me."

Presently the Kaffirs shook hands, and Hiwayo conducted the weary travellers to the kraal, the inmates of which made a fuss with them, giving them food, tobacco, and spirits, which they had that morning bought from a peddlar.

In fact the natives made the arrival of Webb and Dunko an occasion for rejoicing.

All the information Webb could get out of them was to the effect that the Boers had fought Colonel Plumer every mile on his way to the relief of Mafeking.

Only a week back there had been fighting a few miles off.

Plumer had four armoured trains, and the Boers could not stop his progress.

Hiwayo thought that the British must be very near, if not in Mafeking by this time.

"Two Englishmen went by this morning," continued Hiwayo, "and they said Mafeking was all right."

"What sort of fellows were they?" enquired Webb eagerly.

An idea struck him that it was quite possible Dawson might have reached Colonel Plumer and delivered his despatch.

If the Boers had been beaten, as the report went, Fred's services would not be required by the colonel; and what was more likely than that he should take advantage of the chance of searching for the mine now that he was so near it?

The map he had in his pocket would give him the exact locality, and he could see in what state the old workings were left.

It was possible that they were choked up or drifted over with sand, and that all trace of the mine had been obliterated, as far as the outside was concerned, but the interior might be in a fair state of preservation.

All this was a matter for conjecture, and no one could form an opinion unless they were actually on the spot.

Hiwayo gave a description which answered to that of Dawson, portraying his companion as a rough-bearded man, adding that they had with them a bullock-waggon containing various stores, among which were spades, shovels, and pickaxes.

With the waggon were a dozen Kaffirs, who stated that they were engaged to do some work, the nature of which was a secret to them.

"That must be Dawson and his friend, who are going to the mine to make excavations," We have found them at last," said Webb.

"Hurry up, baas, and kill them," whispered Dunko.

"No, no," answered Webb. "I am not such a fool as that. Don't you see that Dawson is the goose that is going to lay the golden eggs. I wouldn't harm him for a pension. Let him find the mine and open up the ground; we will follow and reap the benefit of his labour."

"Kill him some day," said Dunko.

"Certainly. He shall not enjoy an ounce of gold, or diamonds, whichever it might be, out of that mine. Woe to any man who stands between me and the wealth I hope to get."

Webb looked perfectly demoniacal as he uttered these words.

"You frighten me, baas, when you talk like that," said the Kaffir. "Perhaps you'll kill poor Dunko too, and he's never done you any harm."

"Let your mind be easy on that score," replied Webb. "Rest satisfied with what I intend to give you, and you will have no trouble through me."

"You very good to poor Dunko," rejoined the Kaffir, submissively, speaking in a humble tone, which was not usual with him. "Me die for you if need be. Give me enough to buy a farm, and I will go back to Zululand, where there is a girl waiting for me to marry her."

"How much have you saved up to now?" enquired Webb.

The Kaffir had only a few pounds, which he kept tied up in a corner of his loin-cloth, which he unfastened, displaying his modest accumulation of wealth.

It amounted in all to seven pounds.

"I'll bet you stole that, you rascal," said Webb.

The Kaffir grinned from ear to ear.

"True for you, baas," he replied. "The Boers pay Kaffirs nothing for working, and when I get a chance to rob a dead man, I pay myself."

"Be faithful to me, and I will put a thousand on the top of that," exclaimed Webb; "perhaps more, according to how the mine pans out. We will stay here to-night with your coloured friends, and to-morrow we will follow up the bullock-waggon."

"If you want any help, baas, I should recommend you to take Hiwayo along. He good, trusty man."

"Very well. I have no objection. Speak to him, and see if he is willing to come for a dollar a day. I can't afford to pay any more; and don't let on to him about the secret of the mine. Keep that dark."

"All right, baas," answered Dunko. "Me be as dumb as a stone. No one get a word out of this Kaffir. Me study your interests. I never worked for a finer man than you. Call you splendid fellow, baas."

With these words Dunko left his master, and joined Hiwayo, with whom he vanished into one of the huts which comprised the kraal.

Webb walked down to the river, and sat down under some trees by the waterside.

He was plunged in deep thought.

At times his face assumed a greedy expression.

At others the pale cast of fear came over it, as if he was doubtful of the future.

"My life has been one long struggle for gold," he murmured, "and at length it seems to be within my grasp; but I have my doubts about that Kaffir, who is much too civil to please me. No doubt he has an idea that after shooting Dawson I shall come into possession of some buried treasure; and I believe, to get that for themselves, he and Hiwayo would think nothing of murdering me. I must be on my guard, and watch them closely."

Webb paused, and began to laugh ironically. "Ha! ha! It is a good joke," he added. "Dawson little thinks I am on his track; but I swear once more that neither he nor Harkaway shall ever enjoy the contents of that mine, be they what they may."

The thought of the mine made him give himself up to reflection concerning it.

"'I COULD HANG YOU MYSELF,' EXCLAIMED FRED DAWSON. 'WHERE'S THAT PAPER YOU STOLE FROM ME?'"

No. 11.

It must have been disused for many centuries, the map of its site had been hidden from human view, and the way it came into the possession of the jew, Malachi, was most remarkable.

Rhodesia was as yet an unsettled country, and the ground where the mine could be bought by anyone for a mere trifle.

Webb remained by the river until darkness began to fall upon the earth, when he returned to the kraal, finding that Dunko had prepared a supper of fresh-water fish for him, and made him up a comfortable bed of blankets and grass; the latter being covered with a couple of bullock hides.

In fact the Kaffir seemed as if he could not do too much for him.

In the morning he was pleased to find that Dunko had provided a horse for him, which carried, slung over its quarters, a couple of bags of provisions.

Water, they informed him, would be met with on the road; and with the game they would be able to kill, they could not fail to be well off.

He mounted, and the Kaffirs followed him on foot.

Webb had not the slightest idea where he was going, or how long the journey would take.

All he could do was to follow the track of the bullock-waggon, which Fred Dawson and the bushman, Pardoe, had taken with them.

As it was heavily laden, the marks of the wheels could be easily seen.

Webb and the Kaffirs travelled much faster than Dawson and his party, so that shortly after mid-day they came to a spot where Fred had stopped on the previous night.

It was well watered and pleasantly wooded.

Webb made up his mind to stay there for two or three days, as he did not wish to catch up with Dawson too rapidly.

If he did so there was sure to be a fight, in which he might get the worst of it.

His intention was to let Dawson find the site of the mine, and pounce down upon him, after he had commenced operations.

At the expiration of three days he started again, remaining all night at each place where Dawson had camped; by this means keeping in touch with him, never being more than twenty miles apart from him.

It was considerably a longer journey than he had anticipated.

On the tenth day of the pursuit he discovered the dead bodies of three Kaffirs, and double that number of Boers, which plainly indicated that Fred had come across some hostile Transvaalers, and that a bloody fight had taken place, in which it was fair to presume that Dawson had proved victorious, as neither he nor the bushman were among the slain.

There was plenty of game in the shape of deer and birds, but as Webb proceeded he could see no farms, cattle, or sheep.

He now rode very cautiously, fearing that he might come suddenly upon Dawson and be discovered, which would altogether ruin his plans.

Halting for a mid-day rest, the heat of the sun being almost overpowering, he called Dunko to his side.

"My instinct tells me that we are not far from the end of our journey!" he exclaimed.

"That good news, baas," answered the Kaffir. "Me 'bout tired of this long tramp. Railroad train best for travel."

"You lazy beggar. I believe you would like to sleep half your time away, if anyone would come and put peaches and mealies into your mouth, but you won't get any rest out of me, so I tell you."

"Me wait on you, baas, till me drop," answered Dunko.

"Follow the trail of the waggon, and use the utmost care in doing so. If you find that Dawson has come to a halt, spy out all his surroundings, see what he is about, and run back to me with all the news you can gather."

"Me go like the shot out of a Boer Long Tom."

"Don't expose yourself. I can't afford to lose you. From the way we have dawdled along, I should guess Dawson is at least four or five days ahead of us, which would give him ample time to locate the mine and begin work."

"He plant the corn, baas; we come in and reap it for him."

"Exactly. You hit the nail squarely on the head that time; some men sow, others reap. Fools build houses, and wise men live in them."

"Yes," said the Kaffir, laughing. "Englishman make mine, and Boer take it from him. Yar, yar! No chance for Outlander where Boer is."

"Off you go. The worst of you is, you will waste time in chattering like a monkey."

Thus rebuked, Dunko started off on the trail, and was absent until the sun went down.

He had evidently been some distance, for he was limping and footsore, which also showed that he had been over hard, stony ground.

"Did you find the party?" asked Webb.

"Ya, baas," replied Dunko. "Me come upon their camp, about ten miles in a straight line from here, not far from the railroad which goes from Mafeking to Bulawayo. They got tents spread out, and the Kaffirs were hard at work, going down a hole and bringing up bags of sand. Dawson and another man also go down and help work."

"What kind of country is it?"

"All dry, rock and sand. No trees, no grass, no water. Me see one Kaffir go long way with two bottles. They keep him on the trot all day for water."

"Did you notice anything else?"

"The sand and dirt they bring up is lying in heaps. Some of it sparkled in the sun, as I have seen the Kimberley and De Beers dirt when I worked there."

"Man alive," cried Webb, exultantly. "What you saw was diamond dust, and no doubt some genuine sparklers amongst it. Pack up; saddle my horse. We will be off at once."

The order was executed without delay, and Webb with his two followers started for Dawson's camp.

The stars were shining brightly, and they sighted it about midnight.

All was still as the grave.

Three tents were to be seen, two of which were given to the working Kaffirs, a square one in the centre being appropriated by Dawson and Pardoe for their own use.

Dunko had counted nine Kaffirs in all at the works, and knew that they were armed with rifles.

These men would just as soon serve one leader as another, and Webb was not afraid of them, for a Kaffir after a long day's work sleeps soundly, and it takes a good deal to rouse him.

Webb took his knife from his belt and sharpened it on a large, square stone.

"What are you going to do with that, baas?" enquired Dunko.

"Cut a couple of throats to-night," replied Webb, in grim earnest. "Dawson and his mate shall not live to see to-morrow's light."

"What this Kaffir do to help you?"

"Stand outside the tents where the Kaffirs are, and if one of them dares to show a head, put a bullet in it. Come! we shall take them by surprise. The fools have not posted a sentry. Come, not a word; be as stealthy in your movements as a gliding snake."

Webb led the way, Dunko following at his heels, and they noiselessly approached the mining camp.

When they got close to the tents, Webb peered into each of them, to make sure of the one in which Dawson and the bushman were sleeping.

As he had surmised previously, it was the square one in the centre of the other two.

Kneeling down behind a small heap of sand, Dunko raised his rifle to his shoulder, and awaited events.

Webb crept into the central tent.

Dawson was lying on one side, Pardoe on the other.

The villain fixed his eyes on Fred, and with uplifted knife advanced towards him, resolved to settle him first, and deal with the bushman afterwards.

CHAPTER XLIX.

AFTER THE VICTORY—THE SCOUTS MISS THEIR CAPTAIN—CORPORAL POTTS AND FISH DISCUSS THE SITUATION—KANUCK PLAYS A TRICK—FISH IS TAKEN BY SURPRISE—A CLUE TO HARKAWAY—KANUCK AND POTTS ENTER THE DEFILE.

THE English with great bravery drove the Boers from their trenches on the kopje at the point of the bayonet, inflicting great slaughter upon them, but not without heavy loss to themselves.

With their usual slimness the enemy slipped down the side of the hill, and mounted their horses to retreat to the seclusion of another kopje, where they could make a second stand against their foes.

This endeavour however was frustrated.

On the left they were outflanked by Cornstalk and Kanuck, who were at the head of Harkaway's Scouts.

Finding themselves baffled, they turned to the right, where they were confronted and headed off by Lord Dundonald's Cavalry, which was drawing a cordon around them.

In spite of their admirable markmanship and stubborn resistance, the Boers fell like corn before the sickle of the reaper.

Some fled to the mountain fastnesses, where they concealed themselves in caves known to no one else.

One of these parties, under the leadership of Shalker, had contrived to capture Harkaway when he got lost in the defile, amid the roar of the thunder and the flash of the lightning.

The main body which comprised General Vandyke's commando hoisted the white flag, and a large number of prisoners were taken by the British.

This surrender was considered an event of importance by the English general, who had also captured fifteen guns of various calibres, some of which were marked with the broad arrow, which showed that they were made at Woolwich, and had been taken from us in the unfortunate engagement on the Tugela.

Harkaway's Scouts lost many of their number in killed and wounded, but they had rendered splendid service.

The ambulances were busy for some hours, Shalker's farm and the Lodge being converted into hospitals.

The gallant Cornstalk had received two wounds, which were pronounced to be dangerous.

At his special request he was placed in the same room by the side of his friend Maori, the New Zealander, who, through exposing himself in the fight at Shalker's farm, had suffered a relapse.

Kanuck was now in sole command of the scouts, who were warmly complimented and heartily thanked by the English general for the unexpected share they had taken in the battle, and the distinguished courage they had exhibited.

In fact they were the heroes of the day, which had been so hardly fought and so brilliantly won.

In the first place no movement could be made if Captain Harkaway had not cut the wires and saved the bridge from destruction, and secondly Vandyke's commando must have escaped if the scouts had not appeared on the Boers' left.

"I shall report the behaviour of the Colonials to the commander-in-chief," said the English general; adding, "but where is your captain? I hope no mishap has befallen him."

"He is not among the killed and wounded, sir, as we have made a careful search for him," replied Kanuck. "I have put him down in the list of casualties as missing; but when we've had a rest, of which I assure you we stand very much in need, for we were fighting very nearly all last night, I shall take out a party and have a good look round. Harkaway has nine lives, the same as a cat, and like a bad penny, he's sure to turn up, though I guess he's in a tight fix this time, and will have to pull up his boot as high as his knee if he wants to get out of it."

"I also will send out search parties," exclaimed the general. "If anything happened to Captain Harkaway, the whole army would look upon it as a calamity, which I personally should be one of the first to deplore."

The Canadian thanked him for his sympathy, and took the scouts back to the farm, which they reached in the course of the afternoon.

Then came the task of burying the dead, and attending to their jaded horses, after which they satisfied their thirst and hunger, and sat about in shady spots, discussing recent events, being cheered by some bottles of spirits sent them by Kanuck, who had taken them from stores captured from Shalker at the Lodge, for the Boer, whether Free Stater or Transvaaler, is never without brandy and whiskey.

Having seen to everything, Kanuck threw off the burden of care, and went into the old kitchen, where he had a shrewd suspicion that he should find Corporal Potts and Mr. Fish, whose conversation always amused him; nor was he mistaken in his conjecture.

They were both seated in wooden arm-chairs, smoking cigars, and drinking some French wine of a first class brand, which showed that they must have found loot; while the remains of a turkey was on a side-table.

Pausing behind the door, Kanuck stood still and listened.

"We can do it, my boy," exclaimed Fish. "I waited behind a stone until the Boers were driven from their trenches, when I had a look round the laager, where I was all on my own, in a manner of speaking. The boss tent over which the Fierfluer, or the Transvaal flag, was flying, attracted my attention. It must have belonged to General Vandyke, for it was well stocked. The turkey we have just been eating was laid out for dinner. I had my bag with me; in went the bird, also four bottles of wine (prime Burgundy), box of cigars, half a ham, and at least a hundred gold sovereigns minted at Pretoria, which were lying about."

"You didn't do so badly," replied the corporal. "I would rather have been in your place than among the hail of bullets we had to gallop through. It is a wonder to me, now the battle is over, to think how I managed to escape. I must have been born lucky. I've been shipwrecked three times, and can't swim a stroke. I took poison once by mistake."

"Perhaps you are reserved for a higher fate."

"What do you mean?" asked the corporal.

Fish put a handkerchief round his neck, and inclined his head on one side, to indicate the operation of hanging.

"That's too bad," said Potts. "We have had a case in the family. In the old days my great grandfather mistook somebody's horse for his own, and they elevated him. His last dying speech and confession is among the family archives at the present time."

"Drink his health, and pass the bottle," observed Fish, philosophically.

"I don't know whether I will or I won't, but I'd rather. It's against my rule, you know, but I feel rather down-hearted to-day."

"About what? Haven't we won two glorious victories in less than twelve hours?"

"That's right enough," answered the corporal, "all the same we've lost Captain Harkaway, and I've learnt to love him as a brother. We've roughed it together, and been comrades in arms ever since the war began. He is a man I could follow to the gates of the other world."

"Bravo," exclaimed Fish, clapping his hands. "I admire that sentiment. The Colonials are all very well in their way, but it takes a Britisher to lead them."

"Exactly," replied the corporal. "The Canadian, Kanuck, is our leader now, but if he was to come across a couple of Boers alone he'd make a polite bow, and take out his pocket-handkerchief like a shot, and let it flutter gaily on the breeze."

"That is colonial style, precisely," continued Fish, again applying himself to the bottle. "Now suppose a Boer was to come in at this open door at this very moment."

"One Boer only?"

"I didn't say a dozen, did I? Now pay attention; suppose one Boer was to walk into this room. I don't say it's at all likely, though our men are tired and have not posted any sentinels. I only say suppose."

"It's a case of supposing," remarked the corporal. "I was going to get my rifle."

"Nonsense. Don't be an idiot. It isn't at all likely, because the Boers are all captured, or in full flight; I only say, suppose a Boer walked in here what would you do?"

"Do?" repeated Potts. "Tell him to walk out again; and if he wouldn't go, I'd knock him down with my fist, and sit on him. What would your tactics be?"

"I should first fire my revolver until all the chambers were empty, and if that did not settle him, I'd give him the point of my knife; and if he was still inclined to stick it, I'd take him by the throat like this, and strangle him."

In his excitement Fish stretched out his hand and clutched the corporal by the throat.

"Here, I say. Play light on it," gasped the corporal. "You're throttling me."

"Beg pardon, old son, I thought you were a Boer for a moment," replied Fish. "It's a way I've got when I see those villains."

He relaxed his grip, and the corporal comforted himself with a glass of wine.

"Don't play Boer any more with me," he said. "I don't half like that game. In the open field it is a different sort of thing; of course I shouldn't be afraid of a hundred Boers. Bring them on; let me see an army of them."

He got up from his seat and struck out with his fist, as if engaged in combat with an imaginary foe, but the wine was too strong for him. His brain reeled, he lost his balance, and falling heavily on the table, upset it, with its contents, and rolled on the floor.

"Very funny thing—hic," he laughed. "The floor is uneven—hic. It came up and struck me on the nose. This is a jerry-built house—hic—and I shall complainsh to the parish surveyor."

Fish took out his note-book.

"Over indulgence in drink very common amongst scouts," he wrote. "Attention of Commander-in-Chief ought to be called to the fact; make some allowance for hard fighting, but fact remains the same. Harkaway's tigers regular soakers when they get the chance. At this moment of writing every man drunk or asleep. I, a simple war correspondent, being left in sole charge of farm; but though not trained to arms, shall prove equal to any task required of me.

Owing to the carnage I have lately witnessed among our brave fellows, a thirst for vengeance comes over me, and I could see Boer blood run like water without a shudder. I only wish that one of this race would dare to show himself within reach of my knife and revolver. He would not live to tell the tale, for I, Hamilton Fish, Special War Correspondent of the *Capetown Slasher*, would kill him single-handed, and cast his worthless carcase on the arid Transvaal waste, to be left to the tender mercies of the aasvogels, who are the winged scavengers of the veldt."

He paused, and wiped the perspiration from his brow.

"That's good," he muttered. "You couldn't beat it in a day's march. It will do very well for my next letter to the *Slasher*. Our readers like something spicy. In war times people don't care about being fed on milk and honey. I don't think I can improve on it, so I'll let it stand."

During the last two or three minutes Kanuck had not been idle.

He conceived a brilliant idea, which he thought would produce some fun.

In a corner of the room were some suits of clothes and hats, which had been taken from some dead Boers by scouts who were collecting curiosities to send home to their friends in the colonies.

As a rule the friends of a soldier in a foreign country always expect something from abroad, if it is only an old shoe or a faded flower.

With the rapidity of a quick-change artist, he slipped on a suit of Boer clothing, slouching the hat over his eyes to conceal his identity, and put on as savage a look as his nature would permit him.

Then he advanced to the door, rifle in hand.

"Hands up," he cried sternly.

Fish who was decidedly a coward, and had a horror of cold steel and bullets, looked in the direction from which the voice proceeded.

When he beheld the supposed Boer, he turned as pale as ashes, and trembled violently all over.

His bravado vanished in a moment.

It was all very well to ridicule and despise the Boer on paper, but when the real article appeared before him it was a different thing altogether, and he felt as if he could sink into his boots, wishing all the time that the earth would open and swallow him up.

Corporal Potts had fallen into a vinous slumber, and was blissfully unconscious of his surroundings.

If a pistol had been fired close to his ear it is doubtful if the report would have roused him.

Up went Fish's hands at the word of command.

His short hair stood on end, and his eyes started from their sockets as he stared at the horrible-looking Boer in front of him.

He could not tell whether the camp had been surprised, or this was a daring Boer who had come to spy out the land in advance of others.

At all events he was afraid that his last hour had come.

He did not dare to draw the revolver from his belt, because that would be the signal for his death, as he was covered by the rifle of the intruder.

"Kind sir," he exclaimed, in faltering tones, "I surrender at discretion, without making any conditions; but I beg that my life may be spared, as I am a non-combatant. In me you behold a representative of the press. The harmless but necessary war correspondent. A simple newspaper man."

"No lies!" growled Kanuck.

"I assure you, Mr. Boer, upon my word of honour as a gentleman, and a member of the Cape Town Press Club, to the committee of which I can refer you as to my respectability and antecedents, I have never fired a shot in this war. As a matter of dry fact, I always keep in the rear and out of range when a battle begins, and seek the seclusion which a friendly boulder affords."

"No. You are one of Captain Harkaway's War Scouts."

"Indeed I am not. Fighting is not my trade."

"Stop talking," interposed the Canadian, roughly. "We have captured Harkaway. Tell me who your commander is now, and what his plans are? Be open and candid with me, and I will do you no injury."

"Certainly, Mr. Boer, I will give you all the information that lies in my power," replied Fish with a cheerful smile, as he rubbed his hands.

"Mind you do, and no ratting."

"I will not trifle with you, sir; you will find me the soul of innocence and the incarnation of candour."

"Drop that tall talk, you are not writing to your paper now. I am General Vandyke; you are speaking to the leader of the Boer commandoes, who, though defeated, are not crushed under the iron heel of the ruthless invader. Speak, I say!"

"By all means, general," said Fish. "Just give me time to pull myself together; your highly-prized visit was so unexpected and so sudden that I have not been able to recover from the shock of pleasure that you have given me. I was never so delighted to see anyone in my life; sit down and make yourself at home. Don't be a stranger; let us take wine together, general."

"You are wily and crafty."

"What makes you say that, general? I am lamb-like by nature."

"Nonsense," cried Kanuck. "Lamb's off as far as you're concerned. You're trying to gain time, you cunning ruffian, hoping that some of the scouts may come to your aid. Answer my question, you hardened old sinner, or I'll shoot you as dead as mutton."

"Don't; for Heaven's sake forbear!"

"In the Tugela hills I shot one morning, before breakfast, half-a-dozen better newspaper men than you are."

"The captain of the scouts, now, is a Canadian called Kanuck; I don't know his other name, and don't want to," began Fish, hurriedly. "He is drunk half his time, and doesn't amount to a row of empty cartridges. He is of no more use than a bully-beef tin. He is a cross between a mummy and a sardine. All he knows is how to lie down under cover and dodge Boer bullets. When the fight began to-day, he got off his horse, and hid behind a rock for two hours. I saw him. When the bugle sounded 'Cease firing,' he came out, waved his hat, and cheered like a lunatic, as if he had done all the work."

"Is that how you size the Canadian up?"

"Exactly. He is small potatoes, and very few in the row. In short, all these Colonials are overrated. They came here with a good deal of bounce, but are not fit for work. Kanuck is one of the worst of the lot, and that's saying a great deal."

"What are his plans?"

"He hasn't got any," answered Fish. "You couldn't find an idea in his head with a searchlight. He's a bad egg; I should say he will stop here until all the brandy is gone, and then make a raid on another farm, to live on the fat of the land for a week, kill a few helpless farmers, flirt with their wives and daughters, and call it strategy. Don't you take any stock in Kanuck, Mr. Boer. I don't. He's got no more fight in him than an old hen, and runs a mile when he sees a Boer's shadow."

During this abuse of himself, Kanuck had been gradually approaching the war correspondent with a menacing look in his eyes.

Throwing off his hat, and dropping his rifle on the ground, he grasped Fish's arm with one hand and pulled his nose vigorously with the other.

The special's head bobbed backwards and forwards, tears came into his eyes, and he began to kick about like a man in a fit.

"Hi! Hi! Stop! What are you doing? This is against all law and order. Leave my nose alone. It isn't yours to pull," cried Fish.

Kanuck gave it a final tweak, and pushed him down on a chair.

"Weren't you warbling sweetly just now about me, you old fraud?" he exclaimed. "I suppose I ought to thank you on behalf of myself and the Colonials generally, but I don't. If that's the kind of stuff you put in your paper, you ought to be shot on sight."

"My dear Kanuck, can't you take a joke. I thought I was speaking to a Boer, and was giving him taffy to throw him off the scent, don't you see?" replied Fish, whose eyes were opened.

"No, I don't."

"If I had cracked you up, and spoken the truth about your bravery and skill, which are household words among the scouts, the supposed Boer would have gone away with a wrong impression. I wanted him to think that we were weak and badly officered, and indeed no good since we have lost Harkaway."

"Never mind, we are square. You called me down, and I pulled your nose. Now, I will give you a chance to show your pluck, loyalty and devotion to Captain Harkaway."

"How can I do that?"

"As easy as wiring to Cape Town," answered Kanuck. "I feel positive that Jack has fallen into the hands of the Boers, and I am going to rescue him or die."

"Hurrah! That's the style," cried Fish, recovering his spirits and slapping him on the back.

"I can't rest while I know the captain's in danger."

"Tell me all about it when you come back. I'll spread myself, and do a special on it. Rescue of Captain Harkaway. Gallant conduct of the famous Kanuck. Penetrating the Boer laager. Three hundred against one. Unheard-of heroism. Canada to the front."

"You are coming too," said Kanuck, with a dry smile.

"I—bless me, what do you mean?"

"Precisely what I say, my good fellow. You shall have an opportunity of distinguishing yourself. It's a pity such a blooming shrub as you should be kept in the background."

"But I am a non-combatant."

"That be hanged; you shall have your baptism of fire. Just now you said you wanted to kill all the Boers; get your rifle. We'll take this old warrior also."

He pointed to the recumbent Potts.

"You'll have to hire an earthquake to wake him."

"Not much."

Going into the backyard, Kanuck filled a couple of buckets with water, each of which he dashed over the corporal, who, to Fish's surprise scrambled to his feet, and respectfully stood at attention.

"I knew he couldn't stand cold water. That was the one and only thing to fetch him," remarked Kanuck, with a grin.

The corporal was an old soldier, and always ready for duty.

He was used to night alarms, and had been long enough in the service to become a military machine.

When he heard that Kanuck and Fish were going in search of Captain Harkaway, his enthusiasm knew no bounds.

Kanuck informed the pair of them that a scout named Cooper, who had been looking for fugitive Boers, had discovered Harkaway's horse dead in a defile.

There was no trace of its rider, but the sides of the Drakenberg hills were filled with holes, which it was thought led into caves.

After digesting this in his mind, Kanuck came to the conclusion that Jack had been surprised by a party of Boers, who shot his horse and dragged him into some cavern.

This, as we know, was the absolute fact.

When the scouts first took possession of the farm, they found tied up in the yard a ferocious-looking dog of the bloodhound tribe.

In his spare moments Jack had made a pet of it, and christened it Kruger, to which name it answered readily.

Kanuck unloosed the dog, and made it smell an overcoat of Harkaway's, after which the animal barked and leaped upon the Canadian, pawing his breast as if he knew what was required of him.

The leash was again put on his collar, and it was with difficulty that Kanuck held him in.

Preparations had been made in advance.

Kanuck had sent twenty mounted scouts, under the guidance of Cooper, to the spot in the defile where the dead horse had been found.

They were to watch the pass closely, and await his coming.

Gladly would he have rested, after the fatigues he had gone through, but the news brought by Cooper rendered that impossible.

Leading the dog by a thick leather strap, Kanuck made a start, followed by the corporal.

After they had gone a little way over the veldt, he came to a halt and looked round him curiously.

"Where's that newspaper man?" he asked.

"He came to the gate with us, but he's fallen out," replied Potts.

Mr. Fish had discreetly vanished, and might have been found in the barn, lying on a truss of hay, with his note-book for a pillow, a cigar in his mouth, and a bottle of wine to solace the monotony of his existence.

Kanuck could not help laughing, for he had not expected him to show fight, and they went on without troubling themselves about him.

The shades of night were falling when they reached the entrance to the defile, the position of which had been accurately given to Kanuck by Cooper.

They proceeded with the utmost caution.

At any moment they might expect to be fired at by a concealed foe.

A few yards down a scout sprang up from behind a rock.

It was Cooper.

"Nothing to report, sir," he said.

"Where are your men?" asked Kanuck.

"They have dismounted, and are well hidden at the end of the pass."

"That will do," exclaimed the Canadian. "I'll soon rout these Boer rats out of their holes; but we must be wary, for the captain's life is at stake.

Without any mishap they joined the scouts, who were waiting for them, and Kanuck paused to consider how to proceed next.

CHAPTER L.

PARDOE THE BUSHMAN SAVES FRED DAWSON—THE STORM—WEBB AND DUNKO FALL INTO THE MINE—HEAPS OF DIAMONDS—DEATH OF THE VILLAINS.

THOUGH frequently exposed to peril, Fred Dawson had never been so near sudden death as he was when the villain Webb bent over him in the glimmering starlight with the murderous knife in his hand.

It seemed as if nothing could save him.

At this critical moment in his adventurous career, when the dying lamp of life was almost at its last flicker, a small sand adder glided over Pardoe's face and woke him.

"Cuss the varmint," he cried, springing up.

He knew from experience what the reptile was, and that a bite from its fangs was greatly to be dreaded, as in many cases it proved fatal.

Webb heard the movement, and paused before he struck.

Pardoe had just set his heel upon the adder's head and crushed it.

He was a man of action, not words.

Directly he saw Webb he knew him again, though he had only had a glimpse of him, weeks ago, on the veldt.

Webb's hard, implacable face, furrowed with deep lines, dogged and sullen, once seen was never to be forgotten.

When his passions were roused, there was something satanic about him, and all the slumbering devil in his evil spirit came to the surface.

"By the living jingo," he shouted. "It's you, come at last."

Bang!

He let off his revolver; but owing to the semi-darkness which reigned in the tent, he missed his aim.

Frustrated and baffled, Webb uttered a howl like that of a demon suffering from the pangs of eternal torment.

Crack went the revolver a second time.

This time it was Fred Dawson who fired.

Again the shot was unsuccessful, and Webb made a hasty exit from the tent, and stumbled up against Dunko, who had been roused by the sound of the firing.

"Away!" he cried, "the attempt has failed."

"We're done for," replied Dunko, hopelessly.

"No, no, stick to me."

Bang! Bang! Crack! Bang!

The air was filled with quickly-flying bullets.

Fortunately for the would-be murderer and his attendant Kaffir, the sky suddenly became obscured by a black, pall-like cloud, which denoted the coming of a tropical storm.

A flash of lightning descended to the very earth, burying itself in the sand.

A deafening and horrific clap of thunder followed.

Webb and Dunko were no longer to be seen, for the stars were hidden, and darkness prevailed.

The firing continued with greater violence, all the Kaffirs having turned out and joined in the fusilade.

Then the wind arose, with a terrible whirl and swirl, driving the sand about in clouds.

Webb and Dunko struggled on through this war of the elements, not knowing in what direction they were going or whither their footsteps would lead them.

Webb was furious at having been foiled.

His prey had been within his grasp.

One little instant more, and he would have given the death-blow to Fred Dawson, but the awakening of Pardoe by the gliding snake had spoiled it all.

Still he was thankful that he had escaped being shot, for the game was not over, and he might have better luck next time.

Suddenly the ground seemed to give way beneath them.

They fell down a hole or shaft, to the distance of about twelve feet.

No limbs were broken.

They were shaken, and that was all.

Dunko was the first to recover from the shock of the fall, and assisted his master to rise.

"They can't hit us now, baas," he exclaimed; "we've tumbled down a hole, where I guess we are likely to stay. It will save the trouble, though, of digging our own graves. What do you think?"

"I haven't had time to look round yet," growled Webb, who was as savage as a bear. "Can't you tell that we have fallen down one of the shafts Dawson and his Kaffirs have been digging to find out what the old mine is made of? Perhaps they have tapped the earth in half-a-dozen places, and not come across anything satisfactory."

"I understand all about mines," answered Dunko. "I have worked in a few since I left Zululand."

"In that case you must know that where the subsoil is soft and crumbly, the shafts and galleries in which the men work have to be shored up with timber, but in what we call diamond rock this is not required. The galleries once made will last for ever; we can understand the sand-storms sweeping over and blocking up the workings so as to blot out all trace of them, but it strikes me we are on the eve of a discovery."

"What you do without a light, baas?"

"I am always prepared for a case of this sort," replied Webb, producing a dark lantern from his pocket and turning on the light.

By the aid of the lantern he found that they were in a large circular vaulted chamber.

The hole through which they had fallen had been recently dug, for pickaxes, spades, and baskets were lying about.

The ladder for ascent and descent had been pulled up to the surface for some reason.

The vault in which they were looked as if it had been cut out ages ago.

Webb knew that the ancient miners would not have hewed this vault out of the rock without some purpose, and flashing his bull's-eye, he walked round, looking for the door of a gallery which might have escaped the notice of Fred Dawson and those who were working with him, however clever they might be.

After a time his practised eye saw something which riveted his attention.

It resembled a piece of iron which was half buried in sand.

Raising his foot, he gave it a kick with all his force.

There was a clanging noise and a crash.

A thin, rusty, worn-out plate of metal fell back, and a narrow gallery was revealed.

"I have solved the secret before Dawson. He found the mine, and I will find the gems," cried Webb, in triumph.

"You've done it this time, baas," answered Dunko.

"Follow me."

Webb proceeded along the gallery with the Kaffir close behind him.

They had not gone more than twenty yards before they came to another vault, in which they were perfectly dazzled and amazed by heaps of corruscating diamonds.

There were not hundreds, but thousands of them.

This vault was the store-house of the old mine, where the priceless stones had been collected for removal, and abandoned for some unknown reason.

"Our fortune is made!" exclaimed Webb. "All we have to do now, is to dig holes in the side of the shaft, climb up in the darkness, kill Dawson and his partner, bribe the Kaffirs, and run the mine on our own."

"Not yet, my boy," cried a voice behind him."

He turned and saw that he was confronted by Dawson and Pardoe.

They were close behind when he fell down the shaft, and had pursued him.

"Die, you devil!" shouted Pardoe.

Two shots rang out, and Webb and Dunko sank to the ground to rise no more; a bullet had entered the heart of Webb, and the brain of the Kaffir was shatttered.

"I think we can afford to do a small crow over this bit of biz," said Pardoe.

Fred Dawson made no answer.

The heaps of diamonds almost took his breath away.

Shortly afterwards they regained the surface.

It was arranged that Pardoe should remain in charge of the mine, while Fred Dawson returned to duty and joined the scouts once more.

When the war was over, he would come back with Harkaway and put the mine in working order.

He felt that he could trust the bushman, Pardoe, and rode away contented.

CHAPTER LI.

THE DOG FINDS A CLUE—KANUCK AND THE CORPORAL ENTER THE CAVE—THE SECRET STAIRCASE—STRANGE APPEARANCE OF MRS. STEINER—THE BOERS' CAPTIVE—TEUFELSKINT ARRIVES—A TRAP IS LAID FOR SHALKER AND HIS MEN.

THE first thing that the Canadian did, after halting in the defile, was to slip the leash and let the bloodhound loose.

The animal had been ramping and tearing the ground with his paws, displaying great eagerness to get into the cave, near the entrance to which Kanuck and Corporal Potts were standing.

Away went the dog with a dashing, swinging movement, giving vent to low growls; and disappeared within the narrow aperture.

It was clear that he was on the track of Harkaway.

His peculiar instinct and unerring sagacity enabled him to catch the scent and keep it.

"That will be a dead dog before long," remarked the corporal.

"It does not matter to me whether he is or not," replied Kanuck carelessly. "I'm not a dog-fancier, and do not take any more stock in him than I would in a mangy dingo."

"That's pleasant for the dog."

"My object is to save life," continued Kanuck. "We now know that Harkaway has fallen into a trap, and we have a right to presume that he is in that cavern. Whether he is alive or dead, we can't tell, and how many Boers he has about him is another question."

"I am afraid he is done for by this time," said Potts, gloomily.

"Don't think that."

"The pitcher goes often to the well, but gets broken at last."

Five minutes elapsed, after which the dog emerged from the cave, and bounding up to Kanuck, began to paw him, as if he wanted to draw him into the rocks.

"Down, boy, down!" cried Kanuck, pushing the creature on one side.

"It's a blank draw," remarked the corporal, "or he would not have come out like that with his tail between his legs. I'll bet my bottom dollar there is nobody inside."

"I am of the same opinion," answered Kanuck. "What is to be done?"

Potts made no answer.

He had no doubt that Harkaway had been taken into the cave, yet plenty of time had elapsed for the Boers to remove him to some other place of safety.

They were baffled, and it was difficult to decide what the next step should be.

"If you are game, I will go inside with you," he exclaimed, "and take the chances."

"Right you are," answered Kanuck. "There is nothing mean about me. Hold on tight to your revolver, and if you see a Boer, blaze away, though I do not think we shall encounter any opposition."

"The mystery is, what has become of Captain Harkaway?"

"He may be miles off by this time. The Boers are so mobile."

"I differ with you," said Potts. "Hildyard's cavalry are scouring the country, and the beggars are more likely to stick to their holes than venture into the open ground."

"Then you think Jack is not far off?"

"I am sure of it. Come on into this mysterious cavern, as Mr. Fish would call it."

Speaking a few words to the attendant scouts, and telling them to keep a sharp lookout for Boer shooters who might pick them off one by one, or shoot them down by a volley, as there was plenty of cover on the sides of the hills, Kanuck placed himself by the side of Potts, and in Indian file, one after the other, they entered the narrow passage, the Canadian going first.

The dog showed every symptom of delight, and led the way without exhibiting fear.

A cleft in the rock, about three yards long, formed the entrance way, admitting them into a large vaulted chamber.

Kanuck was provided with a dark lantern, which he flashed around, producing beautiful prisms from strangely formed hanging stalactites.

The chamber was empty, but various articles lying about showed that it had been lately occupied.

There were empty bottles and pieces of biltong lying on the floor, as well as tin platters which had contained mealies.

The dog ran to a large, long slab of stone, lying against one of the sides of the cave, and began to bark loudly, scratching at it with his fore legs.

"What is the meaning of that performance?" asked Kanuck, musingly. "The beast knows something. It's a tarnation pity he can't talk, or else he might tell us a thing or two worth knowing."

"It appears to me that slab has been picked up, and hastily piled against a hole. There is no dust on it, same as there is everywhere else. Suppose we have it down; it only wants a pull, a strong pull, and a pull all together, as the sailors say."

"That requires consideration. We don't want to put our hands in the fire unless we know we can pull out a chestnut," replied Kanuck.

"You are too cautious by half."

"I'll allow that I am an artful 'possum, but I'd rather play a waiting game than lead off all my trumps at the first go off. You should always keep a card up your sleeve, you know."

"Harkaway's life is at stake," urged the corporal.

"So are ours. Should we do him any good by rushing on our fate?"

"Stow your jaw-tackle," cried the corporal, impatiently. "You're worse than a perishing old crow on the bough of a leafless tree in the middle of winter. I don't want any croaking ravens about me. My duty is clear, and that is to rescue the captain."

"Don't sling names at me; I'm not taking any," answered Kanuck.

For a moment it looked as if a quarrel was going to take place between them, but Potts checked the answer which was rising to his lips.

With an independent air he stepped up to the long slab we have alluded to, and stooping down, was about to endeavour to move it without assistance from his companion, when in the absence of any warning it fell upon him, knocking him prostrate on the ground.

"Help, help!" he cried. "I've got half-a-ton of rock on the top of me, and it's no joke, I can tell you."

"Serve you right, you cantankerous old fool," replied Kanuck. "Lie there until it suits me to come. Grin and bear it."

"I can't; it's squashing all the wind out of me."

Strange to say, the dog began to howl, and ran out of the cave as if frightened.

"What's the matter with the tyke?" queried the Canadian.

"Hang the dog, come and help me," growled the corporal. "You're a nice sort of backer to have. I'd be ashamed not to stand by my friend if I were you. Lift this stone, you duffer."

Kanuck thought he had kept him in his unpleasant position long enough.

Strong as he was, he only removed the stone with great difficulty; afterwards assisting the puffing, panting, exhausted corporal to rise.

He drew a deep breath, inflating his lungs once more.

"That's good," he remarked. "I never knew the real value of air before. Grub's good, so is sleep; drink's good, but air is better than all."

The Canadian handed him his pocket-flask.

"Try a drop of this, old pard," he said.

"I don't know whether I will or I won't, but I'd rather," replied the corporal.

There was the usual gurgle, accompanied by a sigh of satisfaction.

With disgust he had been eyeing the empty bottles which littered the floor, the unregenerate Boers not having left a drop in any of them.

He was about to raise the flask to his lips a second time when an event took place which had never happened to him before.

His hand shook, he trembled violently all over, and the flask dropped upon the stone.

Following his gaze, the cause of his alarm became apparent to the Canadian.

Standing upon a step cut out of the rock was a radiant female figure, clad in a loose flowing white robe, holding a lighted torch in the right hand.

The fallen stone had been cleverly placed to conceal a staircase which led to an upper chamber.

Owing to his preoccupation with the corporal, Kanuck had not hitherto looked in this direction.

To his amazement he recognised in the female form the person of Belle Steiner, whom he had seen at the Lodge with Gretchen Shalker when on a scouting expedition.

Jack had often spoken to him about this woman, so that he knew her to be a true and devoted friend of the captain.

This was the cause of the dog's sudden disappearance, for the animal took her to be something out of the ordinary run of objects with which he had come in contact.

Stepping lightly into the cavern, Mrs. Steiner placed her finger to her lips.

This was a sign that there was danger lurking in the air.

"Hush!" she exclaimed in a low tone. "Draw nearer."

The men came to her side, assuming a respectful attitude.

Extending her hand to the corporal, she continued, "I'm glad to meet you once more."

"It is always a pleasure to see you," replied Potts, gallantly.

"You have come at the right time, for your captain is in dire peril. My enemies among the Boers are dead, and I have resumed my old position, as a leader; but my influence is not sufficient to save Harkaway from the doom which threatens him."

"What is that?"

"He is to be hanged shortly, and would have been dead before now if his enemies could have found a rope. This cave is one of several in the kopje. The Boers know them well, for they have hidden here on previous occasions. The flight of steps conducts to a chamber above this, in which Shalker is now resting with a score of his most determined and devoted followers, who escaped the wholesale slaughter of this day, which has proved so fatal to them."

"I wish it had included Shalker and his lot," said Kanuck.

"Above the vault I have mentioned is a third, from which a passage leads to the side of the kop, so that anyone can enter by the defile, and if he knows his way, get out on the mountain. In the second chamber I have been living since I left the Lodge, not knowing where to go, or what to do, until the battle was over."

"How did Harkaway get into this fix?" enquired the corporal.

"Shalker saw him in the defile, shot his horse, and falling upon him, with several Boers, dragged him into this place, to which I was attracted by the barking of your dog. It seemed to me that friends were near. Harkaway is lying, bound hand and foot, awaiting his fate with that manly calmness which always distinguishes him in the hour of danger."

"I don't believe that our Jack would turn a hair or move a muscle if a thunderbolt fell at his feet," observed the corporal.

"I saw him try to catch a flash of lightning in his helmet one day, which shows the sort of dare-devil he is," said Kanuck.

"His career will soon be over, unless we can save him," added Mrs. Steiner, sadly. "A Boer has gone out to procure a rope, which will be thrown over a projecting piece of rock. They will swing him off his feet, and there he will die like a dog. When the Boers leave this mountain, the cave may never be visited again. If it should be, what will the explorer find—a ghastly, grinning skeleton, or a heap of mouldering bones. Oh! it is too awful to contemplate."

"What are the Boers doing now?" asked Kanuck.

"Lying around in a half-drunken sleep," she answered. "They are worn out with fighting and confused with brandy-drinking. Skalker alone is awake. He will not rest until he has seen the last of his victim."

"Now is our opportunity."

"You have a dangerous man to deal with," she exclaimed, warningly.

"Why did not you rise equal to the occasion, Mrs. Steiner?" asked the Canadian, with a reproachful look. "You might have played a love hand, and acted the part of Judith with Holofernes, or Jael with Sisera, or Charlotte Corday with the tyrant Marat."

"I know history, ancient and modern, as well as you do, and the examples you quote were before my eyes. But I had not the chance."

"A knife! A pistol——"

"Yes, yes, I know all that," she interrupted hastily. "I would have run every risk, but so keen is Shalker after his revenge that he even suspects me, and I was disarmed as soon as they brought the captain into the cave."

"Why should they be so down upon Harkaway?"

"All the Boers attribute their defeat to him. Had it not been for his unexampled heroism in saving the bridge, the English could not have gained the victory they did. If it was not for the intense hatred with which they regard the captain, they would have shot him three or four hours ago; but that death is too good for him. He must die ignominiously, or they will not be satisfied. Shalker keeps on talking to him; taunting him with his position, and enjoying what he supposes to be his agony."

"I understand."

"Harkaway has made himself felt in the Boer ranks. His name and fame have spread far and wide. Ever since the war broke out he has been a thorn in Mr. Kruger's side, and his honour will be as glad to get rid of him as everybody else."

"It shall not be," exclaimed Kanuck firmly.

"No, I will bet my non-com's stripes that we will save him yet."

"Are you alone?" asked Mrs. Steiner.

"Oh, no. I've brought some scouts with me," replied Kanuck. "They are waiting outside."

"How many men have you got?"

"Only a score; but they are all picked men, ready to do anything."

"The staircase leading to the upper cave is narrow," said Belle Steiner thoughtfully. "Only one can ascend at a time. The first shot would rouse the sleeping Boers. I know not what to do, or what to advise for the best."

There was an awkward pause.

It was a difficult, as well as a critical situation.

The silence was broken by the Canadian, who saw that the minutes were flying by rapidly, and that no time should be lost in taking action.

The Boer who had gone for a rope to carry out the savage vengeance of Shalker might return at any moment, or he might be delayed for hours.

For what he wanted, he would have to go to the deserted laager on the summit of the kop, which, though abandoned by the Boers, would probably be held by a small force of English.

If this was the case, he would run the risk of capture.

Harkaway had always given the Boers trouble, and now, by the irony of fate, they had a difficulty in hanging him because they could not find a rope.

If the position had not been so grave, it would have been supremely absurd.

"Does General Shalker know where you have gone?" enquired Kanuck.

"No; I wander where I like. He dare not exercise any control over my actions," answered Mrs. Steiner. "Besides, he would not leave his prey for an instant."

Again there was a pause, and they looked at one another in perplexity.

"An idea has just struck me," said the corporal, "and I think you will agree that it is a good one."

"You have only to name it, and we will take it into consideration," replied Kanuck.

"I don't want to set a woman to do anything that I would not do myself, but if she likes to take my knife, and give old Shalker a dig in the back, or one under the fifth rib, she is welcome to it. After he is settled, Harkaway can be liberated in a few seconds."

"That would simplify matters," Kanuck remarked.

"Of course it would. I don't see how we are going to get the scouts up into the cave, one by one, without rousing the Boers. We should present a fine target to them, and they would score a bull's-eye every time. We should go down one by one, like a row of ninepins, and all the enemy would have to do would be to lay out the corpses, and then riddle the captain with bullets, for I don't suppose they would wait any longer for the rope."

A strange light flashed in Mrs. Steiner's eyes.

Her bosom heaved and fell with emotion, for she saw that, after all, by the force of circumstances everything devolved upon her.

"It is sweet to die for the one we love," she murmured.

"What did you say, mum?" asked the corporal, bluntly.

"Nothing," she replied. "Give me the knife. It shall soon seek the heart's blood of Shalker."

Potts drew a long, sharp pointed knife from his belt, and held it up in the air.

The bright steel glittered in the torchlight and that of the lantern.

Suddenly a croaking voice, which changed spasmodically from a deep bass into a falsetto, raised weird echoes in the cavern. Everyone started visibly.

Who could it be?

"Ho! Ho! Ho! I see cold steel flashing before my eyes. Ha! Ha! Ha! Some bloody work is going to be done, and I should have a hand in it."

They looked round, and beheld Teufelskint.

The dwarf of the veldt, and hunchback of the hills, was grinning from ear to ear.

"Where did you come from?" demanded Mrs. Steiner, sternly.

"I witnessed the battle from the top of the kop, and just now came across a man looking for a rope. I told him it was what all the Boers wanted, for they ought to hang themselves if they cannot fight better than they do. Bloemfontein is captured, and Pretoria will follow."

"We have no time to listen to your predictions."

"Everything is quiet in the second vault," replied Teufelskint. "Don't hurry. If you are concerned about Captain Harkaway, it will be some time before the man gets the rope, as the English hold the laager. Shalker is wide awake. We spoke to one another, and he sent me down to look in the defile and see if anything was going on. It is a long time since I have been in these caves, but I can find my way blindfolded, and he knows that. But tell me what you are going to do with that knife?"

Kanuck explained what Corporal Potts had suggested; adding that Mrs. Steiner was going to carry it into execution.

"Ho! Ho!" laughed Teufelskint, "that is a job for me."

"Why so?" inquired the Canadian.

"I have an old score to settle with Shalker, and by my hump, I will settle it. I had a half a mind to just now, when I saw him seated on a stone, looking as proud as a peacock, because he had captured his prey; but I let the chance slip, thinking it would come again."

"It is a pity you did so. I thought you favoured Harkaway."

"So I do," said Teufelskint. "But there were the sleeping Boers; and Shalker is not to be easily got at. I dare not fire a pistol. He wears a sword, and would think nothing of slicing my hump if I missed my mark; however, I am willing to have a cut in at him, if you will make it worth my while."

"You want to be paid for it?" said Mrs. Steiner.

"Certainly," answered Teufelskint. "I am poor, and you cannot expect me to risk my life for nothing."

"What is your price?" enquired Mrs. Steiner, drawing her purse from her pocket.

"You are a rich lady, and I cannot do it under a hundred pounds."

The dwarf was cunning as well as avaricious, and knew that he was not asking more than he would receive.

She instantly counted out gold and notes for the amount, which she placed in his hand, while Corporal Potts gave him the knife.

In fact Mrs. Steiner was not at all sorry to be relieved of the disagreeable task, though she would have gone through anything for the sake of Jack.

It was abhorrent to her delicate and refined nature to shed blood, and the dreadful scenes she had witnessed during the war had thoroughly sickened her.

"I am ready," exclaimed Teufelskint, whose face assumed a fiendish expression.

"One word before you go," said Kanuck.

"A dozen if you like ; only don't delay me more than you can help. When I undertake a thing, I want to carry it through."

"I am told that leading out of the third cave there is an opening on to the side of the kop."

"That is so," replied the dwarf. "I entered by that way only just now."

"How high up is it ?" continued Kanuck.

"Not more than three or four hundred feet, if so much as that."

"Is it easily climbed ?"

"An old cow could go up it," replied Teufelskint. "It is a slope, not a precipice, with bushes to hold on by. You will find a big hole, through which four men could walk abreast. From the third vault to the second, in which Shalker and his Boers are, is a large but short shaft, in which steps have been roughly hewn, down which half-a-dozen men could pour at once. It is not like this tricky little staircase, which only admits one at a time."

"Good," ejaculated Kanuck.

"Is that all you want to know ? If so, I am off."

"Hold on ; I must detain you a few minutes," continued the Canadian.

"Very well," said the hunchback, grinning. "I'll take a drop of dop to screw my courage up ; that's Boer custom, you know. They must have a drink every time they re-fill their bandoliers."

"First a bullet, then a gargle ; very sensible," observed the corporal, approvingly.

"Will you join me, my old veteran ?" asked Teufelskint, with a patronizing air.

"Have you got any ? Don't make a fool of me ; it is a point on which I am rather sensitive. The drink question is one which I have carefully studied, and I am firmly convinced it is the root of all evil. What fills our prisons, our mad-houses, and workhouses ?"

"Oh, shut it," cried Kanuck.

"I declare that no one ought to touch drink," said the corporal, solemnly.

Teufelskint handed him a black bottle, from which he removed the cork.

"I don't know whether I will or I won't, but I'd rather," he muttered, forgetting that he had commenced a temperance crusade.

"Corporal," cried Kanuck.

Potts instantly came to attention.

"Go outside into the defile, take half the scouts up the kop, penetrate to the upper vault, and if you hear a shot fired, swoop down upon the Boers in the second cabin. Not one must escape."

The corporal saluted and instantly departed.

Kanuck allowed an interval of ten minutes to elapse before he would permit Teufelskint to carry out his design upon Shalker.

The minutes passed slowly and wearily.

Mrs. Steiner, with a beating heart, impatiently paced up and down the vault, like a caged tigress.

Teufelskint was in a state of meditation. Kanuck smoked his pipe with the stolidity of a colonial farmer.

At length he judged that the corporal had been allowed sufficient time to take his men up the kop, and occupy the upper cave.

"Time's up," he exclaimed.

Teufelskint nodded his head.

He had concealed the blade of the knife by putting it down his back under his jacket, leaving only the handle exposed, in the Spanish fashion.

This he could easily get hold of by raising his hand to the side of his hump, and drawing forth the weapon, strike the murderous blow he intended to deliver.

When he disappeared in the darkness, Mrs. Steiner clasped her hands together.

Would the hunchback succeed in accomplishing his fell purpose?

This was the all-absorbing question which agitated her mind as well as that of the Canadian.

CHAPTER LII.

SHALKER TAUNTS HARKAWAY—AN ACT OF CHIVALRY — THE SCOUTS ATTACK — VICTORY — JACK IS WOUNDED — THE HOSPITAL SHIP—WAITING.

GENERAL SHALKER was not in a hurry; he fully believed that Harkaway was absolutely in his power, and that no one on earth could rescue him from his custody.

Though Jack was in a helpless condition, and silent as a mouse, he knew that he must be thinking of his coming end, and occaisonally he glared at him as if to provoke him into saying something.

At length Jack's passive demeanour irritated him.

Throwing down his pipe, he got up from the stone on which he was sitting, and walked up to his captive, with his hand stuck in his capacious trousers pockets.

"Have you said your prayers ? If you know any, you zachenroller thief," he exclaimed.

"I don't want to come to the Boers for religion," answered Harkaway. "They spout a little too much to please me, and can turn on the tap whenever it suits them."

"Your time is growing short. I have sent for a rope to hang you with."

"How considerate. I am sorry to have put you to so much trouble. It is a pity you don't keep those things in stock."

"What do you mean ?"

"I think you alluded to something of a fibrous nature, which would be more suitable for your neck than mine. A bullet would have done just as well."

"The rope isn't made that would fit my neck," answered Shalker.

"I don't know so much about that," retorted Jack. "You will be captured, because you are in a hole you can't get out of, and our troops surround you. You think you can do a foul deed in this lonely cavern, but you will be found out. It is nothing more or less than murder. I have a right to be treated honourably."

"Bosch," cried Shalker. "You are the cause of our disaster, and we have more than that against you."

"Be good enough to hold your tongue," said Harkaway. "I am not talking to you, and have asked for no mercy. Let me pass in peace the few minutes I have to live."

"I like to irritate you. It pleases me."

"Be a man, and not a beast. If you speak to me again, I shall not answer you."

"You do not care about my pin-pricks, but I shall keep on," said Shalker.

The cave was only lighted by a single oil-lamp, which threw a dim, religious light over it.

Suddenly Jack saw Teufelskint appear at the top of the stairs, and glide up to Shalker.

When the hunchback was within a few feet of the Boer, he drew the long knife which had been given to him by Corporal Potts, and raised it as if to strike.

Harkaway was placed on the horns of a dilemma.

The hunchback was his friend, and had evidently come to help him.

Would it be right for him to allow Shalker to be stabbed from behind, without defending himself?

He loved open, fair fighting, but hated assassination.

His life hung in the balance.

If he uttered a word of warning he would save the Boer, but at the same time seal his own fate.

Yet Jack was nothing if not chivalrous.

All through his young life he had aimed to make himself, like the Chevalier Bayard, without fear and without reproach.

He determined to save his enemy Shalker, no matter what it might cost him.

"Beware!   Look behind!   You are in danger!" he shouted.

The Boer retreated a few steps, and turned round rapidly, thus avoiding the stroke aimed at him by the dwarf.

Drawing his sword, he attacked Teufelskint fiercely, and before the latter could beat a retreat, slashed him across the hump, and brought him bleeding to the ground.

"Up, Boers!" he cried.

The sleepy burghers rose to their feet, rubbing their eyes, and grasped their weapons.

Then the Boer turned with deadly enmity towards Harkaway.

"Curse you," he hissed. "You have friends, though I knew it not; but by the Heaven above us, you shall not escape."

He pointed his revolver at Jack.

"Would you shoot a helpless man bound hand and foot?" demanded Harkaway.

The only reply was a bullet, which struck him in the side.

The Boer's triumph was, however, short-lived.

Corporal Potts, at the sound of the shot, rushed down with the scouts from above, while Kanuck came up with the remainder of the force which he had called in from the defile.

Firing began on both sides.

The scouts, not to be restrained, came to close quarters, and spitted the Boers with their bayonets, as if they were so many birds.

Kanuck shot Shalker through the heart.

Corporal Potts was wounded in the leg.

Every Boer was killed, and in a short time the cave resembled a slaughter-house.

A messenger was despatched to the camp for help, and the wounded were taken away in the ambulance.

Harkaway's injury was serious, and it was feared that the corporal would lose his leg.

Mrs. Steiner nursed them until they were able to be conveyed to Cape Town, where they were placed on board a hospital ship.

Strange to say, Fred Dawson, who came back and joined Lord Roberts in time to take part in the battle of Paardersberg, joined them on the same ship, for he had been badly hit in the shoulder.

When they were becoming convalescent they had frequent talks about their property in the Jarkin Mine out of which they hoped to reap a fortune when the war was over.

Before that, however, they expected to take part in more fighting, both being anxious to go to the front again.

Mr. Fish paid them a couple of visits, each time bringing the corporal a gentle reminder in the shape of a bottle of Mountain Dew, but they saw nothing of Mrs. Steiner who was reported to be in Pretoria.

Jack often thought of her kindly, for she had been a good friend to him ; but he knew that if she dared to show her face in Cape Town, she would be arrested as a spy.

For the present we must leave Harkaway and his friends, hoping to renew our acquaintance with them when they are again able to take part in the campaign in South Africa.

We have only to add that the hunchback, Teufelskint, recovered, and often visited the camp of the Colonials, who continued to be known as Harkaway's Scouts.

Maori and Cornstalk got well of their wounds, and under the command of Kanuck, the Canadian, they performed brilliant exploits, and covered themselves with glory.

THE END.